Captain Delightable's Magical Tales of a Minchon Warrior

Val Edward Simone

A Morningside Publishing Book
Lakewood, Colorado

Captain Delightable's Magical Tales of a Minchon Warrior
A Morningside Publishing, LLC Book

Printed in the United States of America

First Edition

Library of Congress Control Number: 2012914542

ISBN 978-1-936210-16-9

Cover Design: Val Edward Simone

For more books please visit:
www.morningsidepublishing.com

With Special Thanks To:

Editors
Rita Samols
&
Judith Sansweet
Website: http://www.proofreadnz.co.nz/
Email: judith@proofreadnz.co.nz

Musical Inspiration
Ernesto Cortazar II
Ernesto Cortazar III
Kevin Kern
Secret Garden
George Winston
Clint Mansell
Karunesh

Cover Illustration Artist
Yoo Choong Yeul

Captain Delightable's Magical Tales of a Minchon Warrior

"When only hope is left, exercise it towards a suitable intent, for the possibility of all things lies at the heart of hope's willful, purposeful, and enduring determination."

~ Captain Cornelius Alexander Delightable

ARTIST'S PAGE

~ Cover Art Information ~

Title: NEWS & Map Captain 5 or Sea Captain
Artist: Yoo Choong Yeul
Year: 2006
Medium: Oil on Canvas
Size: 20x24 in / 50.5 x60.5 cm
Country: South Korea

Artist's Website:
http://fineartamerica.com/profiles/yoo-choong-yeul-art.html

Dedication:
To all the other
Minchon Warriors,
living in the peace and
harmony of good intent.

Chapter 1

On my two-hundredth birthday I shall reach my fortunate end.

I say *fortunate* because precious few men have been so lucky as to have lived the life I have lived, to have known the people I have known, enjoyed the great adventures I still enjoy, experienced all the glorious and wondrous things I, even now, continue to experience through a magnificent grace and with unparalleled astonishment — and after all these long years, to finally be the kind of man I have become.

I was told long ago there were others who have gone before me in like manner, but during my lifetime I have known of none save myself.

To those who think they know me well, I am Captain Cornelius Alexander Delightable, a well-known and well-liked retired ship's captain. To others, who know me not as well, I am just a pitiful and insane old man, a lonely wretch walking the San Francisco streets near the harbor, lost within some inconsolable and futile attempt to relive a former glory as a seafaring man, with a strong solution of saltwater flowing through his well-seasoned veins.

To others who know me not at all, I am an ancient storyteller who spins colorful and delightful make-believe yarns, fanciful stories about his former sea voyages to wondrously exciting mythical places, and tells tales of the many strange beings and creatures he encountered along the way.

Of course, to the children who still gather around me during my weekly storytelling sessions in the park, I remain a sorely needed break from the harsh realities of their everyday life — the strange old man who makes them feel like princes and princesses or heroes and heroines. To them, I am a magical raconteur who makes them think they can fly, or transport themselves great distances within the blink of an eye — a mysterious old soul who makes them believe in themselves, believe that they can become anything they set their minds to become.

Indeed, I make them believe they can do all those things and so much more: even that they have the capacity to control all that lies around them with only the strength of their will, a purposeful intent, and a gentle tone in their voice.

To those youthful spirits that live within their ever-inquisitive minds, I am a kindly old stranger who believes in them and their potential.

Some say the smell of the ocean and the sight of the ships anchored in the San Francisco harbor remind me of both the whimsical and the courageous moments of my youth; a time when I was more than just an odd curiosity for passersby or another mad storyteller on a park bench — the sad old sea captain who cannot forget the sea.

As I recall now, that may have been true once upon a time; for years, the sea *was* my life. It was the only life I ever really knew.

Growing up on the pitching decks of wave-tossed ships, I could walk those planks as easily and steadily, and with as much flawless precision, as any man walks the streets of any great city today.

I had faced the wrath of every tormented ocean upon the earth, and still I sought other adventures upon her tumultuous and unpredictable surface. I knew the sea. I have known her at her most tempestuous, and I have known her in her moments of peace and tranquility...and the men of the sea, those intrepid souls who ventured out onto unknown waters for the noble sake of exploration and commerce, I came to know them well also. I knew their courage, their spirit, their strength of self. I knew well of their kindly manners, their stalwart friendship, and their fierce loyalty. I was witness to heroes and cowards alike. I saw men arrive on the docks as strangers and depart as brothers. I have also known frightened and despicable men of the ocean and watched them commit acts of unspeakable horror. The sea contained it all. And I was a ship's captain; I held sway over many men; I held their very lives in the palms of my hands; I even controlled their fate.

Yes, the sea was my life; that is, until I became a Minchon Warrior.

What is a Minchon Warrior? Well, dear one, to describe the Minchon Warrior requires me to tell you the *whole* story.

My life as a ship's captain was interesting, to be sure, but that life is only a part of the story. How I came to be a Minchon Warrior is quite a special tale. A special tale, indeed.

* * * * *

In the spring of 1798, I embarked upon my first voyage from the friendly shores of New York as first mate of the American-registered USS *Challenger*, a three-masted, 1,200-ton merchant vessel of East Indiaman design, crewed by 150 very fine seafaring men and officers. Although she was pierced to carry fourteen twelve-pound guns, she was only fitted with eight, never having the need for more by virtue of experience, or should I say lack of experience, having never been fired upon by any hostile forces.

The good captain of the ship was Nathaniel Xavier Delightable. A stout man with perfectly trimmed hair and beard, and one who, although he was surely a strong disciplinarian, was a fair and just master and a captain of both eminent nobility and inspiring capability. To me, however, he was known as both Captain and Father.

When I was ten delicate years of age, my life had taken a horrible turn. While carrying farm goods to market, a mere one league away, both my natural parents — the good and gentle Isaiah and Marian Willoughby — were killed in a tragic cart accident, leaving me an instant and desperate orphan.

Over the years, I have often found it quite astonishing how well-dressed men of high position and low virtue, carrying fancy leather valises filled with qualified legal documents, are able to so swiftly descend upon a young and defenseless child, and remove from that child everything he had ever possessed, in such an accomplished manner. So delicate and precise were their machinations that what they did could be likened to a skilled surgeon removing a leg or an arm.

In my case it was a man named Horatio Crabtree, a local businessman of some ill repute, who held the mortgage on my parents' farm. He pounced upon me with great alacrity and took everything, leaving me helpless, frightened, and utterly and completely destitute — a homeless urchin.

I departed my former residence with nothing of note save a small golden amulet hanging about my neck. I dare say if he had known of the bauble's existence, he would have wrenched it from my neck as well.

As fate would have it, it had been given to me by Captain Delightable several years earlier. He had been captain of the vessel upon which we, my parents and I, sailed when we journeyed to this continent from Great Britain only two years prior.

Without children of his own — his wife had suffered an unspecified but debilitating illness in her youth which rendered her incapable of bearing children — he seemed to take great notice of me on the trip over. At journey's end he gave me the amulet as he bestowed upon me the honorary title of Third Helmsman: a cleverly invented title for the benefit of an overly passionate child, as I was to learn later.

But I, even at such a tender age, took a great fancy to the charts and matters of navigation. I would spend hours upon hours attempting to read and understand all the unique symbols written on those finely crafted pieces of parchment. I was even given preliminary instruction on the use of the sextant and a rudimentary initiation into celestial navigation. I took all the given information well into my being, and I believe it was then, during that fateful voyage, I came to know deep within myself that I wanted to spend my life upon the sea.

Very soon after the death of my parents, I was formally adopted by Captain Delightable and his wife. Treated as if I were their biological son, I was truly blessed by their dedication and genuine affection.

When I was twelve years old, I signed onto his ship as a simple landsman and was allowed to work my way up the ranks under his guidance and sponsorship. In time, I became a valued and respected member of the crew, growing in rank to become the ship's navigation officer — and finally its first mate, that rank awarded to me upon my twenty-eighth birthday.

Chapter 2

I recall now, thinking back upon the day of our departure from New York in 1798, how excited I was to be making my first voyage with my adopted father as his first officer. As I think on it even now, it remains a monumental moment for me.

Still, I could not have known that with that fateful departure I would never see my adopted home and family again; even had I returned to them, I would not have been the same young, naïve lad who had left all those many years before.

It started as a glorious voyage, first making ports of call in the Caribbean, then several stops along the eastern coast of South America, eventually making the always perilous trip around Cape Horn and into the waters of Otaheite, as Tahiti was known at that time. We made our wandering way through the South Pacific with stops at other minor ports in exotic islands, called at major ports such as New Zealand and Australia, and finally reached the port city of our contracted destination at Chennai, India, which was then the destination port of many ships from other countries throughout that region.

All in all, the outbound leg of the trip took us nearly two years to complete, and even after all these years I still count it among my fondest memories.

Along the way I created my own charts, navigated most of the voyage myself, and gained the further respect of the crew as a resourceful and competent officer. In verity, during that voyage, in all matters of seafaring, I successfully learned everything necessary to become a very capable captain when it came time for such a duty to fall to me.

And so it was that while resting in Chennai, in preparation for the return leg of the trip, and with the firm support and the high recommendation of my father, I was offered command of the USS *Hampshire*, when her captain suddenly succumbed to the failings of his less than stout heart.

I should have recognized the simple omen playing itself out in all of this, but I did not, and as the USS *Hampshire* was another 1,200-ton, three-masted merchant ship, also of American registry and also of East Indiaman design but older and requiring a crew of 180 men, I accepted my new position as her captain.

I was not yet thirty years of age and now captain of my own ship, wildly euphoric about the journey home, anticipating, with great delight, my return to my friends and family as master of my own vessel. I must admit, with only a modicum of humility, that it was another most prideful moment in my yet young life.

I was also looking forward to the magical adventure of sailing through waters now familiar to me. I had no idea just how magical that journey would be.

* * * * *

In mid-January of 1800, after three months of getting well acquainted with my new crew, and upon the completion of overseeing properly the stowing of all the contracted-for cargo, I ordered the sails hoisted and we set out for our homeward voyage.

We were, at that moment, a very fulsome crew, cruising elegantly out of the Chennai Harbor and past the many other tall ships that were solidly set to anchor.

I was particularly proud to sail past my father's ship as he and his crew stood smartly and saluted my passage. Even across the great distance that separated us, I could see the proud, broad smile beaming from my father's face. I nattily returned his salute with what I can only presume now was an equally glowing smile.

My main commission was to pick up a shipment of breadfruit trees and other exotic fruit plants from Tahiti and transport them back to the Caribbean Isles. However, prior to embarking upon that fateful westward portion of the journey through the volatile section of the treacherous South Pacific between Bollabolla — now known as Bora Bora — and Tahiti, I was first given higher-priority assignments which required me to sail to many other ports in the Western Pacific.

To my complete unknowing, what should have been a simple and uneventful voyage proved to be horribly otherwise.

As I have stated, we initially set sail in mid-January from Chennai. We did so in order to avoid the most precarious part of the hurricane season in the South Pacific, that being November through April, wherein storms potentially dominated the area through which we were to travel. We had hoped by early May we would be traveling safely through the area without the worry delivered upon us by such perilous and potentially damaging storms.

Alas, it was not to be.

The trade winds in the Western Pacific were unusually strong that year, so we gained substantial time and distance with their uncommon assistance. Consequently, we found ourselves in the particularly treacherous waters of the South Pacific fully two weeks ahead of schedule, and not quite at the end of the hurricane season.

For the next several days, though, I saw nary a cloud in the sky, so I came to believe the hurricane season had fully passed and that our journey would be joyously even more uneventful. In fact, our luck had been, accordingly, so unexpectedly great that we actually believed we would arrive in New York a full two months earlier than we had originally scheduled.

We were such an eager and contented crew. No worries or troubles had we; for the lot of us, we 181 salty dogs, were a merry band, to be sure.

Something very strange then befell me. I came down with a great fever and was restricted to my rack for what I eventually discovered was ten full days. Vomiting nearly hourly in the early days, I found it impossible to keep anything down; thus, without sustenance to strengthen me, I dramatically weakened even more and soon lost all ability to think clearly. The ship's physician was at a loss to explain my malady.

It was a bizarre infirmity, for soon I apparently lost consciousness and lay eight more days wasted in my bunk. I can only tell you of this because it was told to me after my recovery.

On one morning I awoke confused and displaced. "What is this?" I uttered. "Dear me! Where am I?" I arose to a sitting position and gazed about me. After a few seconds, I recognized my surroundings. I was on a ship. These were the captain's quarters. I remembered. I was the captain. Grabbing a mirror on the near table, I gazed into it to see my face. Yes, it was I. It was not a dream.

I immediately felt rejuvenated and recovered, fit as a fiddle, as it were, and zestful to resume my duties. I prepared myself in my cabin. My first mate, Randall Jenkins, a comely and competent officer, visited me.

"I've been down ten days, you say?" I asked. "Dear me. Well, thank you, Mr. Jenkins. I am feeling much better. I don't know what came over me, but it gave me such amazing dreams."

"The doctor said it was most likely food poisoning of some kind."

"Indeed? Well, it certainly gave me fits."

He also told me that during the time of my infirmity, the seas had been abnormally calm, with only gentle rolling swells. Thus, during my illness, the trip had been uneventful for the crew, and I was relieved to know I had not abandoned them to weather bad storms without my guidance or assistance. In fact, another part of me was most elated in their accomplishment to carry on so splendidly without me. They had proven themselves to be a most capable crew, and my chest puffed with boastful pride.

In short time, I came to dismiss the entire event of my illness as just happenstance and of no particular importance.

While I reposed in a final convalescence, only a short time before my arrival on the mid deck, we had sailed past the picturesque island of Bora Bora with her safe and placid lagoon and her encircling protective barrier reef. My first mate, seeing that I was well on the mend, saw no need to stop there and rest, for we were in calm seas and well ahead of schedule. Besides, most everyone on board looked forward to the white sandy beaches, the delicate and lovely brown-skinned island angels with their long, black, silken hair, and the general good times to be had by all upon our arrival at the port of Papeete on Tahiti.

We were so far ahead of schedule, in fact, I had decided to extend our stay on those beguiling Tahitian shores. It was something that pleased us all to think of and made us push forward with all the speed we could pull from our fully billowing sails.

So many sheets had we hoisted onto the spars, we nearly floated above the calmed surface, and upon reflection I noted to myself that it was as fast as I had ever seen a ship move through an ocean.

So tranquil had been the seas to that point, and so affable the winds during my recovery, the crew had lost their fear of the ocean's expanse. Considering now, in recollection, I have come to understand that, in all the gentleness of the peaceful sea and weather, they had become lulled into lenient methods and indolent conduct. Most of all, they had become negligent of the dangers presented by open waters.

They sang their cheerful songs at night and worked during the day without any sense of concern. As I have said, they were a joyful crew.

Lost in their festive delight, they had become unmindful of how rapidly the sea can rise up, sometimes without warning, and turn joy into instant and unmitigated horror.

Later that morning, I ventured out onto the mid deck. Mister Jenkins welcomed me with a shout from the aftcastle and then urged me to cast my eyes westward.

Upon doing so, I realized that being well into the South Pacific seas as we were, our joy was about to turn to worry.

"Oh dear!" I gasped.

Shortly thereafter, that worry turned to terror, and soon after that, the terror became tragedy.

As the saying goes:
Red sky in the morning, sailors take warning.
Red sky at night, sailors take delight.

The morning of that day greeted us with the reddest sky I have ever seen. It was as if God himself were bleeding out from some deep, inexorable, mortal wound, turning brilliant white sunlight into a diffused blood-red veil.

An unspoken awareness seared every heart: what was soon to befall us was going to be dreadful — exceedingly dreadful!

For hours that morning, all eyes seemed to predictably and repeatedly turn to larboard. And we all bore terrible witness to the north-northwesterly approach of a fiendish storm.

Proceeding thus, in such a frightful and unconscionable state, an additional, most curious, and alarming event occurred. The compass, upon which we depended so heavily for navigation, suddenly began to spin wildly. I could find no obvious cause for its odd behavior, and it refused to steady itself. I grabbed my trusty sextant and took some hurried measurements of the placement of the sun in the hope of remaining on course, but in a very short time all that effort became of little consequence.

Studying the approaching tempest, I could see it was driving toward us at a speed I had never before seen from any storm. It so quickly gained on us that it caused nearly every eye to stare at it with unblinking incredulity.

In the stark absence of a dependable compass, we had no idea which way to best steer the ship. The thick clouds formed over our worried heads to rapidly blot out the sun completely. I stood on the aftcastle and ordered the helmsman to keep the wheel in its present position, but I knew the strong sea currents would very soon and very surely move us well off our intended course. Without the guiding comfort of a working compass or any other visual means of navigation, I had no accurate idea of which direction we were ultimately sailing in.

The incongruent winds began swirling about the ship and effectively nullified my navigational efforts to determine our course from the prevailing wind. For all intents and purposes, I was a blind captain leading a sightless crew through mysterious waters with no concept of which direction to steer the ship or in what manner we might preserve our desired course.

In an effort to out-dash the approaching storm, I ordered every available stretch of yard unfurled and set. It was a vain effort on my part, I admit, and one which seemed, at best, dubious at the time. However, I gave it my best effort to outrun this behemoth, or at the very least delay it from overtaking us.

Within two hours, and despite our best efforts, the rapidly rising winds had come fully upon us. Acknowledging this, I set my mind to greater purpose. I ordered both the royal and top-gallant sails furled to relieve the stress on the masts in the raging wind. As it was of little use anyway, I also had the crew take in the flying jib, leaving only the upper topsails, the lower topsails, the trysail, and the course yards unfurled and squared, expecting them alone to bear the greatest brunt of the wind while propelling us steadily forward.

Sooner than expected, the storm, in even fuller fury than the winds, sat oppressively heavy upon us.

Nearing noon as it were, the windward side of the hurricane was spinning directly into the path of the ship. The winds increased tenfold within a matter of minutes. Gargantuan waves washed over our decks as if the ship were not there at all.

Playing my final hand, I ordered the topsails and trysails close-reefed to further reduce the stresses on our masts, and had the fore top-mast staysails set. Once again, it was all in vain. Within a half-hour, I could see every effort made had failed to steady the ship.

Relenting to the inevitability of it all, I ordered the large course sheets furled and stayed, wishing no further risk to the masts, leaving the smaller canvas aloft to maintain some notion of forward motion, but after another hour, I was forced to order them also furled and stayed as a last-ditch effort to protect the structural integrity of our masts. I feared that if left to support heavy canvas in the ferocity of such winds, they would very soon snap in half.

In that precarious moment, all minds aboard the fated ship clearly understood that all hope of outrunning the beast must necessarily be abandoned. If we were to live past this day, we would have to fight the devil himself for our right to exist — if that was possible.

Tense moments passing quickly. I instructed the crew to unfurl and set some smaller jib yards but to keep them tightly reefed, in the frantic hope they might aid us in our efforts to steer our way through the hellish storm. Deep in my heart, I knew such rigging efforts were only a futile attempt on my part to stave off the certainty of our fate, and that even the partially hoisted jib canvas would not last long in the path of such punishing gusts.

14

In a few short hours, the seas had gone from gently rolling swells to bludgeoning walls of punishing might; each man knew this storm was unlike any he had ever faced before.

And from the looks on every dread-filled face surrounding me, I could see that each of us was wondering the same thing: *Is today going to be my last day on earth?*

Knowing the route as I did, I knew there was no safe port ahead to steer towards. I also understood I could not turn the ship around and head for the safety of the Bora Bora lagoon. With the direction and strength of the wind and the size of the sea, I realized that such a maneuver would result in capsizing the ship in mid-turn.

Our only course of action, as I saw it, was to keep the bow pointed directly into the heart of this beast that now assaulted us, and hope…nay, *pray* we could hold on. I dare say, each man on board that forsaken ship, be he sinner or saint, discovered prayer that fateful day.

But our prayers were not to be answered.

We felt as if our ship were a toy being abused by a wicked and spiteful unknown creature of malevolent intent, one that relished the torment of defenseless souls — or perhaps it was God himself, now angered and vengeful for some unknown wrong deed committed by us against Him.

Although I knew what was happening to us was the result of normal seasonal conditions in these waters at this time of year, I recall looking deep into my own heart in search of anything I might have said or done to warrant the Creator's need to deliver the full force of His vengeance upon us. I believe each of my crew did the same at one time or another during that dreadful ordeal.

As the clarity of day moved into the obscurity of night, the storm worsened, as if that were even possible. An hour after sunset, we lost the jib yards. I stood upon the aftcastle with the helmsman, holding onto anything that might steady me. Eventually taking the wheel myself, I tried desperately for another two hours to keep the bow pointed directly into the wind. But the ship continued its uncontrollable yaw in the midst of the grueling and mighty gale.

Lifting my terrified eyes from the helm, I saw only half of a forlorn and crippled ship stretching out before me toward the forecastle, for the balance of it was lost to sight in the near blackness which surrounded us in the fuller measure of the storm and the ever darkening skies. And squinting so, I also bore dreadful witness to an even more crippled and forlorn scene: the frightened and desolate faces of my crew — or more to the truth, those faces nearest to me, which even those I could barely see for the blackness.

In those dark faces, their expressions, frozen with fear and terror, I believed I saw my own face as if in a mirror standing before me. Even if it were today, I can barely find sufficiently adequate words to describe what I saw in their black eyes; among them would be death, betrayal, and a lost sense of true and measurable hope.

As the storm worsened and grew ever stronger, I feared that either the vigorous wind or the battering sea might snatch the crew from off the deck, and so I ordered the men of the watch on deck to lash themselves to anything that would hold them. Mere moments after they had done so, a monstrous sea washed over us with such crushing force that it tore three stout men from their lashings and took them with it back into the depths of its black heart. If the full of the crew had not been so lashed down, I can only guess how many others would have suffered the same horrific fate.

Calls of "Man overboard!" were shouted out into the night, but no one could have helped them. We were all rendered impotent to remedy the situation. Just then, another evil wave bounded over us, ripping two more men off the deck. It was as if they vanished right before my eyes. They were there — and then they were not. Two men existed, and then two men disappeared in the blink of an eye as if they had never existed at all. I could feel the terror and desolation in each member of my crew, for I felt that terror most within my own heaving chest.

Within fifteen minutes, five more decimating waves struck us, tearing the planking up from the forecastle, and with it ten more men, cleaved from their lashings, disappeared into the sea, screaming out their terror-filled cursings for all to hear.

So it was that in less than a half-hour the ship's complement went from 181 good and decent men to 166, including myself.

The wind howled as if it were the wail of Satan himself summoning us to our demise. My ears soon became numb from both the chill of the wet night air and the shrieking of desperate men vainly entreating a belligerent and hesitant god to save them. I feared, however, even He was cowering somewhere, huddled in hopeless fright, terrified to expose himself to the ravages of this heinously conceived tempest.

The night had become so black I believed we had already been swallowed by some great demon and, even now, woefully existed within the belly of Hell itself. I could see my hand in front of my face only when a bolt of lightning ignited near to me, illuminating the horror-filled air.

The rain, driven by the powerful gale, felt like bird shot angrily blasting my face from a firing blunderbuss. The only blessing in all of this was that over time my face grew numb to the stinging strikes. But it would not have surprised me if I had looked into a mirror at that moment and seen my flesh torn away and only bare white bone staring back at me.

I am forever certain everyone left on board that condemned ship heard the initial crack. The twist from the last yaw brought the ship fast and hard abeam and directly against the full force of a mighty wave.

The keel snapped as if it were a twig. Seconds later, I heard the fracturing of the midship frame timbers crying out from the ripped and shredded innards of our fated vessel. It was only a matter of a few more seconds before the deck planking began to separate. But when I caught sight, as dim as it was, of the upper futtocks and bresthooks being splintered and torn, I knew the integrity of the frame was lost and it would be only a matter of minutes before the storm would completely disassemble the bow of the ship.

We were doomed.

In that hellish wind, the splintered wood hurtled through the air like wooden spears. A moment or two later, explosions of lightning briefly illuminated four impaled bodies still lashed to the deck housings.

The ship was now surely damned as it began disintegrating before me. I heard its woeful pleas for mercy in the awful cracking of wood, the mournful squeal of iron spikes being ripped from the planks, and terror-filled screams from torn canvas whipping about in the wind.

All aboard bore witness to the awful shrieks of agony coming from the decimated hull. It resonated loudly despite the intensity of the storm. It was as if the ship itself were shouting out to a fearful God who refused to hear its desperate wail for clemency — a hopeless cry to eternity in remorseful recognition of its own failure.

The fore main mast was the first to collapse. Fortunately, it fell cleanly off the ship to the larboard side, missing me by only inches. Within minutes, however, it was followed by the center main mast. Once again, the whipping ends of flailing lines cracked loudly in the thick air just before my face as it tumbled into the sea, again to the larboard side.

I felt instantly reprieved, being spared the potential thrashing of whipping ratlines, but other lines from the flagellating yards snagged two unfortunate souls and yanked them overboard.

In the lighting flashes I watched in horror their bodies being torn and shredded into small pieces as the departing canvas dragged them across the shattered and fragmented deck. I can still hear their abbreviated, anguished screams of terror and undeniable pain.

Jagged splinters of torn planking broke free from the deck and shot past me as well. Although I could not clearly see the shards coming at me, I heard the screech of their passing over my head.

I now saw no further use to try to steer the ship, so I fell to my knees, tightened my lashing, and hugged the wheel with all the strength I could muster.

It was all clear to me at that moment. I had failed my crew.

There was nothing more I could do for them, as I was as helpless in the grip of the beast as they were. Each man, from that point on, was utterly and fatefully on his own.

As I hid beside the wheel housing, I could hear the screams of forsaken and dying men mixed in with the Devil's shouts of glee. As I was forced to watch the complete disintegration of the forecastle, I screamed my own curse into the night in a spiteful rebuke of the storm that was taking so many good souls; and then, as if suddenly deaf, I heard nothing at all.

Within seconds the silence became oppressive. I suddenly felt my body lift up off the deck, and I lost all sense of gravity. I felt that I was floating in mid-air. I opened my eyes to see where I might be, but the blackness of the storm still blinded me.

I was abruptly slammed unmercifully into the ocean; the terrific jolt snatched my breath from me. Soon afterward, seawater rushed into my lungs and replaced the air therein. I gagged and sputtered, and unclear thoughts spun wildly in my head. I could not get my bearings; I had no sense of up or down. Then, in what seemed like a flash, I simply stopped thinking altogether. I felt a certain peace wash over me until there was only an engulfing serenity of pure blackness.

Chapter 3

It was only pure white light I remember seeing initially — exceedingly bright, exceedingly warm, and it caused me immense and indelicate discomfort.

The first coherent thoughts I had were that it was the white light of the afterlife I had heard so much about during the telling of whimsical tales shared nightly on the deck of our ship by some of our most ancient crewmembers. With such thoughts came the belief that I was thus, and most surely, deceased.

The second thought I had was recognizing the omen I had overlooked before all of this misadventure had begun. With the death of the former captain of the USS *Hampshire*, it was now I and not he who must try to make sense of this tragic and confusing moment.

I did not know what condition my body was in. For all I knew, I was no longer encased in a fleshly vessel at all. All I *did* know for certain in those first few and precious moments was a great hot and white light hurtfully flooded my brain, and I wondered what it was.

It was only after several seconds that I realized my eyes were still closed.

I opened them.

Left eye was blind. A blinding flash in the right!

Sharp pain!

I closed them again and remained still. I was dazed.

Finally, after several minutes as my senses slowly returned. I heard the lapping of water. I felt a wetness against my face followed by its sudden absence, and then the wetness returned once again. This action repeated itself continually. Although still stunned, I wanted to open my eyes again, but I feared the brilliant light I had seen before might blind me forever.

After several more speculative seconds, I decided I must open my eyes once more, only very slowly this time. Bit by bit, they gradually opened. Again, my left eye was blind and saw nothing but blackness. My right eye received only glaring white light preventing me from seeing anything else. It hurt, but not with the intensity I had experienced in my first attempt. Still, I hesitated to open them any further; I shut them tight once more.

It was then that I sensed my right arm under my body. If this was the afterlife, I reasoned, my body must have transformed along with my spirit. I tried to move my arm, but it was held fast beneath me. I applied more strength to the muscles and soon it moved, if only slightly. I sensed that my hand might still be attached, and I was able to feel my fingers moving, albeit for them also, only slightly. Nevertheless, and finally, it was to my great relief that I felt the entirety of my hand begin to move beneath me. Thank goodness! My arm was still fully attached to my body.

With greater applied effort, and after several attempts, I finally freed my arm from under the weight of my body and was able to bring my hand up to shade my eyes. It worked. The intolerable brightness was gone. I fully opened my eyes and realized the bright light hurting my right eye was the morning sun. I was facing directly into it. My left eye, however, remained blind.

My head was partially buried, and it was then I understood that my left eye was beneath the sand, leaving only my right eye free to explore the immediate surroundings.

With my hand shielding my eye from the brightness of the sun, I could see I was lying face down on a sandy shoreline, just beyond the full reach of the surf. The wetness I had felt earlier was that of the waves lapping upon my prostrate form. As my senses became fully restored, I first felt the coolness of the water as it surrounded my legs, then reached my waist, and finally my upper torso. Then the waves washed downward and away from me, presumably towards an ocean immediately behind me. When the next salty wave reached higher and filled my mouth, I spat it out and realized I was in the path of a rising tidal surf.

I gathered all my strength and urgently began to push myself upward off the sand. There was, at first, a strong sucking sound in my left ear, which was followed by a pop as I freed my head from the surrounding sand.

Pushing hard against the cement-like sand, I finally raised my chest into the air and then drew my knees upward until I kneeled on the beach in the calm and quiescent morning air.

It took me several more moments, but I finally realized I was truly alive and not in the afterlife. Slowly my memory returned, and I began to recall how I had found myself earlier in the morning, well before sunrise, still lashed to the helm of the ship and floating in the now glass-like ocean. I also remembered striking the sand of the shoreline with a gentle jolt. Then I recollected loosening the ties that had kept me lashed to the wheel, and with several tender pats of my hand I thanked it for having kept me afloat throughout the night and I released it into the now mild surf.

I then remembered barely having the strength to crawl higher onto the sandy shoreline before collapsing into unconsciousness, only to finally awaken here in this glorious morning — alive and apparently in a physically well state.

I looked up to see only a clear blue sky above me. All vestiges of the angry beast that raged the night before had departed. I thought to give thanks to God for delivering me safely to shore, but I also remembered how He had abandoned me and my shipmates while we valiantly struggled for survival within the clutches of that wicked storm. Where was He when the ship was being lacerated and my shipmates were being killed and mutilated? Where was His compassion for all those other good souls who had woefully called out in vain for Him to save them?

And then I silently asked two more questions: *Why me? Why was I spared?* A third question then arose within me. *Where were my mates?*

I looked around for a sign that any of them had also washed ashore, but I could see none. Apparently, I was the sole survivor.

The peak of some long-dead volcano soared high above me in the distance. Stretching out ahead, within a few hundred paces from where I stood, was a lush green jungle that spread out widely to both my left and to my right. This told me there was sweet water to be had, hopefully nearby.

I knew I had to take care of the necessary things for survival first and foremost. I had to locate a good and dependable source of clean, sweet water, find food, and prepare a sufficient shelter.

I had no idea how long I might be marooned on the island, if it were indeed an island at all, but while I was trapped there, I was determined to survive in as much comfort as possible.

I rose to my feet and waded out into the surf and dunked my head under the water to wash off all the sand. Then I awkwardly walked along the shoreline looking for any parts from the ship that might be useful. The muscles of my legs protested strongly after being still and useless for so many hours.

Given the strength of the storm, I expected there to be a substantial amount of debris — besides me — washed up onto the sand, including, regretfully, some bodies of the crew; but there was not one piece of debris or a single body to be found. The beach was spotlessly clean. I tried to reason how that could be possible. How could a storm of such inestimable magnitude and ferocity fail to toss anything besides this wretched and lone human form up onto this beach?

None of this made sense to me at first, but then a new thought filled my brain. I had perished in the storm after all. Perhaps this was heaven for sailors, I thought. Perhaps this was where we good men of the sea end up — on a beautifully clean island, under clear skies and with water lightly licking the shores. It was all beginning to make sense to me now. I had *not* survived the storm. I *was* in heaven.

From the position of the sun, I figured that east was to my right, west to my left, and north was stretched out in front of me in the form of a luscious jungle.

If this was heaven, then I believed all I had to do was walk inland and there I would find a clean and gentle spring with a plentiful supply of clean fresh water. If this was heaven, I would find, surrounding the spring, large fruit trees loaded with my favorite fruit, mango. If this was heaven, I would find a brand new hammock to lie in and sleep for the rest of the day. There would also be plenty of chopped wood for a bountiful fire this evening.

If this was heaven, I would also find, bathing in the spring, a young and lovely native woman with long, silky, black hair, unblemished light brown skin, and a face that God might have seen fit to sculpt with His own hands. Her dark eyes would stare directly at me as I approached her, her rosy lips moist and slightly parted, awaiting my kiss. All of these wonderful things — and much more — were surely lying ahead of me in the jungle...if this was heaven.

As I began my walk through the sand toward the trees, I noticed my clothing was torn to shreds and I was mostly naked. My shirt had disappeared, presumably in a manner befitting the fierceness of the storm. My shoes were also absent. I had only my britches and long stockings on and my stockings were shredded into strips around my calves. Thankfully, however, most of my britches were pretty much intact. I patted myself, specifically my bottom, just to make sure I was not unnecessarily exposed. All was well.

If this was heaven, I thought once again, the good Lord would also have provided me with a suitable change of clothing.

I concluded, during my walk toward the jungle, that if I was dead, then death was not, at least at this time, terribly uninteresting. In fact, depending upon what I was to find in the jungle, it could prove to be yet another wonderful adventure.

After two hundred yards or so, my walk penetrated the jungle foliage. I found a beaten path and that instantly alarmed me, for I was obviously not alone. Who shared this heaven with me, I wondered. The path appeared well worn, so whoever existed on this island with me often used this trail to get to the beach as well.

If my island mate was friendly, then it would be a glorious introduction, for I would not be forced to endure the terror of loneliness. If, however, my mate was of a contrary persuasion and a keenly perceived threat, then I would have to dispatch him with all due speed. I was not about to survive a brush with the Devil's hurricane only to perish on this island at the hands of yet another demon — not without an abject brawl, at least.

I searched for a sturdy branch which I could use both as a walking stick and as a fighting staff to protect myself from man or beast. I reconciled that if this was heaven, then such a weapon would be unnecessary.

It was a good thing I was a man born of gentler points of view and intents, for I found no long pole at all. I was, therefore, completely defenseless, save my bare hands and feet, and, of course, my teeth.

I followed the path for several hundred yards more and it was then I discovered I had indeed been delivered into the loving arms of heaven. I heard the falling water before I saw it. I walked into a site with my hammock, mango trees, and a new change of britches, blouse and vest, appropriate for a ship's captain, hanging from dangling tree vines. A brand new pair of shoes and long stockings lay on the ground beneath the clothing. I did not know how such clothing could exist here, but I dared not question my good fortune.

A fresh mango lay in a wooden bowl already sliced and ready to eat. I picked up a juicy piece and placed it whole into my mouth. It tasted wonderful. I also found a hollowed gourd filled with sparkling fresh spring water setting next to a carved wooden cup. I poured a cup of water and drank. It, too, tasted wonderful and refreshing.

Reaching for the britches, I heard splashing off in the direction of the falling water. I moved toward the sound to investigate, creeping slowly, following another worn path, and as I neared the sound of the falls, I spotted a large pool of water at its base. I dropped down to a squat and continued my stealthy approach until I saw what I, at the time, perceived to be absolute confirmation that I had been delivered into paradise.

She was turned away from me at first, rinsing her long, silky, jet black hair by dipping her head backward into the pool and then running her hands across her head, wringing out the excess water. I could not yet see her face, but I imagined it was, at the very least, sculpted by angels under God's directing eye. And then I thought perhaps she *was* an angel. She had to be. If this was heaven, then perhaps she was my guardian angel, sent by God himself to guide, love, and protect me.

It was all going according to the plan I had richly conceived in my head while squatted in the sand on the beach.

Funny thing about such plans. They don't always work out in the precise manner in which you conceive them.

She turned around and our eyes instantly met. We stared at each other for what was only a second or two, but to me it was an eternity filled with bliss and adoration. I lost my heart to that native maiden in that very instant.

Her reaction, however, was not what I had eagerly hoped for.

Her scream practically split my head into two halves. She yelled at me, but I could not understand the words. The tone, however, was unmistakable. I was not welcome.

Clearly, this was not working out the way I had imagined our first meeting. I immediately stood upright, raising both hands straight out with palms exposed, my lame attempt to demonstrate that I was neither armed nor a threat to her. As you will most likely have concluded by now, my gentle yet ill-conceived gesture was not at all well received.

Her continued screaming was almost ear-splitting, but I heard bushes snapping and cracking under the weight of some unknown source several yards away, off to my right.

Those sounds were fast approaching and getting louder, so I reasoned that retreating was, for now, the better part of valor. Perhaps my love and I would find another day to meet on more pleasant terms. At the moment, however, survival was preferable.

I turned from her and ran with all my strength and will back along the path leading to the shoreline. I believed within myself that I was moving with great speed and agility. But the sounds of pursuit were quickly gaining on me. I felt my heartbeat quicken as it pumped blood into my tiring muscles. My lungs tried to suck in as much air as possible. My legs churned as fast as they could, but all I could do was not enough. The pursuers were closing the distance.

I dared not look back, fearing I might lose my momentum and relative distance from my pursuers. Instead, I ran for the pure sake of saving my foolish life.

Perhaps, I thought in that terrifying and bewildering moment, this was *not* heaven after all.

The path ended, and I was now running in heavy sand. My legs, finally betraying me, felt more like anchors. I was halfway to the shoreline when they caught me.

One of the pursuers tripped me, and I went down onto my face in the dry, hot sand. The chase was clearly over for me, for I could not breathe. I coughed and sputtered as the sand filled both my nose and mouth. I wanted to shout my surrender, but the words, sealed by sand, never left my mouth.

A second later, two brown-skinned giants lifted me to my feet. I was beyond exhausted, so I did not resist further. They stared at me with such hatred and anger I was sure I would be murdered within seconds and most likely devoured later that evening, for I had heard these near islands in the South Pacific were occupied by cannibals.

"I'm sorry," I finally managed. "I was shipwrecked. I'm lost."

They looked at me as if I were a madman. I was now certain this was *not* heaven; but just where I was, was still a great mystery.

They picked me up off my feet and dangled me in mid-air. Considering the height and mass of those two giants, I was helpless to fight back.

So there I was, a once-proud ship's captain, hanging ridiculously in the air and completely at the mercy of two angry-looking behemoths who, to my tortured mind, had a ravenous look about them.

No, sir. This definitely was *not* heaven.

The two glared at me for a few more seconds, and then a miracle happened. Their glares turned to smiles and their smiles turned to white-toothed grins. They set me back down onto the sandy shore and laughed uproariously. I was in complete shock, and must have looked a fool to them with my wide-eyed, frightened expression and sand-coated face. Finally both of them wiped their huge hands across my encrusted mug, partially knocking the sand off.

"We know you were shipwrecked. We have been waiting for you, brother," one of them said.

They spoke English! And they spoke it very well. I understood what they said, but I was still in shock and could not adequately form words of response. "He does look like a shipwrecked soul, doesn't he?" the other giant said.

"He certainly does. Let's get him back to the river and wash him up. We cannot present him to the royal ones in such a state."

With those words spoken, they turned me around, each taking an arm, and tugged me forward. I began walking with them more out of seized-animal instinct than on any conscious level. I must have seemed like a complete imbecile to these glorious-looking giants. And they *were* giants to me. Although I was not yet in full command of my senses, I observed some basic facts about them.

Both of them easily towered well above me, making them at the very least seven feet in height. Their black hair was straight and shiny and flowed down to their shoulders. Their bodies were well-sculpted, cut clean, with taut muscles rippling across their upper torsos. Evidence enough for me of being superbly well conditioned. They wore no tops, but their lower torsos were wrapped in a strangely woven, colorful cloth that bore a close resemblance to cotton. On these wrappings were bizarre symbols and what must have been indigenous animals woven into the design. Colorful beads were woven into their hair. They were two handsome specimens, to be sure.

As we walked slowly back along the path, the two men spoke to each other in another language, presumably their native tongue. The language was very different from any I had ever heard before. It consisted of a series of clicks and mumbles and meshing of both guttural grunts and song-like melodic intonations. It demonstrated great intelligence and was extremely pleasant to my ears.

They laughed a lot. They seemed to be genuinely happy and friendly fellows. My fear and confusion began to wane. Soon I was walking on my own. I didn't even notice they had released their hold upon me. When I did finally notice, I had no wish to escape. Their gentle and friendly nature put me fully at ease.

We arrived at the falls, I could not help craning my neck to look for my angel. I did not have to look long. A gentle and distinctively female voice from behind both startled and pleased me all at the same time.

"Greetings, Cornelius," she said. "You have finally arrived. It is good to see you again."

I turned to see her face finally, and it was exactly as I had imagined it. The graceful lines and sharp facets were striking. Her dark eyes seemed to penetrate deep into my soul. Her full, pink lips were moist and soft, and I wanted to kiss them. Her sly smile held a deep and old mystery. She knew me. I don't mean just my name. I mean she knew *me* and all my hidden fears, hopes, and secrets. She knew me well. I was both intrigued and shocked.

In coming to this realization, I did not even attempt to try to hide anything from her. Deep inside, I knew even then, if I had tried, I would only have deceived myself. Her eyes told me she already knew everything that made me who I was. And so, relaxed, I responded freely and openly.

"Yes. I have finally arrived. I have no idea where I am, of course, but I have arrived. And what, dear angel, do I call you? And how is it that you know my name? And, may I ask, why do you say 'again'?"

She chuckled lightly. "So many questions put to me all at once. How can I answer, except thusly. I am known to you as Lelalu. Princess Lelalu. My father is king. And I say 'again' because you have been absent a long while now, Cornelius, but you are now returned to us and I am pleased at the sight of you once more. We have known each other for many years. That is how I know your name."

"Princess Lelalu," I responded and then bowed deeply as I continued, "I have no idea how that is so, but it is a profound honor to finally make your acquaintance, Your Highness."

My words now stunned *her*. "Finally?" she asked in a surprised tone. "You know who I am?"

"I have seen your face a thousand times already. It has walked before me in many dreams I have had during the last two years."

"Ahhh," she stated, "such is a common occurrence among mates on the island."

It was my turn to stare back in stunned amazement. "Mates?" I inquired.

"Yes," she answered calmly. "It is common with betrothed souls to see their mate in a vision."

"Betrothed? We are betrothed?"

"Married, actually. But then I'm sure you already knew that before you decided to come back to the island, Husband."

"Married? No longer betrothed?"

Lelalu laughed. "You have been gone for a good long while. I'm not surprised you might have forgotten some of your warrior training."

"Aye," I admitted, "I was but jesting with you, but you seem serious about this. I assure you, Princess Lelalu, I have never been to this island before. I was shipwrecked only last night. I washed up onto your shore early this morning. I could not ever have been here before today. In truth, Your Highness, until today I had never known that this island existed. Certainly, it was not on my charts."

Again the princess laughed. "Dear, dear Cornelius, I can see your training is going to take some time to refresh. I am not speaking of the past, Cornelius. I am speaking of the future. We shall be joined soon, we shall live a wonderful life for a while, the war will threaten our beloved peace, and then you will leave to live another life...until we shall again, and finally, be forever reunited."

With her words I found myself completely confounded. I wanted to speak, but no thought made sense enough to loosen my voice. I wanted to know more of a war that would to come to this paradise. I wanted to know of this alternate life of which she spoke. I wanted to ask many questions concerning these matters, but I found it impossible to form a single cohesive thought, let alone speak one. Finally, after standing in absolute silence for several moments, I looked directly into her eyes. "I have no lucid concept of what your words attempt to convey, Highness."

"Of course not, silly man. You have not yet begun your training."

"My training?" I asked, again profoundly perplexed.

"Yes," she responded in the gentlest tone.

"And what training is that?"

"Your Minchon Warrior training, of course."

"I thought it only needed to be refreshed," I smartly returned, although I had no inkling of what I meant to imply by such a response, for I knew not of this training to which she referred. Nor, at that precise moment, had I any conception of what a Minchon Warrior was.

The princess laughed once again. "Dear one, you will need refreshment in the future. You have not yet begun your training here in the present."

I must admit that my ability to reason had left me by then. I no longer knew if I was in the past, the present, or the future. I barely knew who I was at that moment, but then I thought, perhaps I am not who I think I am at all. That thought finally forced me nearly over the precipice of the cliff of sanity upon which I had once securely stood. I now clutched precariously at its sharpened edge and was deliriously close to falling from it completely.

It was all too much for me. I could only stand in front of this magnificent specimen of womanhood with a dullard's expression on my still partially sand-encrusted face.

"Clean up in the pool, Husband. Then eat, drink, and rest awhile. The celebration of your return begins at nightfall."

"You're leaving me now?" I asked dolefully.

"No, of course not. I will remain here with you. Now go clean yourself and put on your new clothing."

I turned dutifully toward the pool and began to walk away, but she called out to me once again. "Husband," she said, "it is so very good to have you home once again. I have missed you terribly."

My mind then drastically disconnected. I did not know how to respond. She sensed my confusion and smiled lovingly at me. "Go," she ordered tenderly, the back of her right hand flicking at me.

The two giants laughed aloud again, and then charged at me. Picking me up, they carried me to the edge of the pool and tossed me out into its center as if I were weightless.

I sputtered, choked, and gagged until I discovered that the pool was only waist deep. I secured my footing and stood up, grinning broadly. The two giants burst into heavy laughter. I looked at my wife — a concept which, at that moment, seemed beyond possible — and she was laughing as well.

Although this was not heaven as I understood it to be, it was a likely resemblance of what I expected it could be. I finally concluded that I was going to be just fine here, be it heaven or not.

Lelalu reached for my hand as I stepped out of the pool. She smiled warmly at me as she spoke softly...

"That will be quite enough for tonight. Time for bed now," Suzanne interrupted. "Your great-grandfather needs his rest."

"But Mother, he wasn't finished," nine-year-old Robert protested. "I want to hear about the Minchon warriors."

"Yes, Mother," Robert's eight-year-old sister, Wendy, added as she stopped writing on a tablet of paper long enough to involve herself in the conversation. "Papa was going to tell us about the great celebration honoring his return to Minchon Island, and how he became a Minchon warrior."

"That's enough fantasy for tonight. Little boys and girls need their sleep. Now, off to bed with you. Both of you, get going."

The two children dutifully arose from the floor of the home library where they'd been sitting in front of a glowing fireplace. They warmly hugged their great-grandfather, who was seated in his favorite rocking chair, and Robert asked, "Will you tell us more tomorrow, Papa?"

"Yes, indeed. Now listen to your mother and off to bed with you."

"To the Minchon Warrior!" Robert added with a smart salute.

"To the Minchon Warrior!" the old man replied, smartly returning the salute.

The two children scurried from the room. A second later Wendy returned, and she too saluted the old captain. "To the Minchon Warrior, Papa!"

"Yes, my dear. To the Minchon Warrior!" Cornelius returned her salute with equal zest.

Wendy darted away.

"Papa," Suzanne said, "you shouldn't tell the children frightening fantasies like that before bedtime. It affects their sleep."

"Suzanne, my child, they're not fantasies, as you well know, and neither do they frighten the children."

"Papa, I don't want to get into this again right now."

"You were the one who brought it up, my child."

"I know."

"Did the children appear frightened? Besides, it is well past time the children learn the story of how I became a Minchon Warrior. In fact, they're old enough to begin their own training. About the same age you were when you started your training, as I recall."

"Papa, please! How many times must we have this conversation?"

"What conversation is that, my dear?" Captain Delightable innocently asked as he purposefully stuffed his pipe with shards of aromatic tobacco from a soft leather tobacco pouch.

"...that you made up the whole thing: the warriors, the island, the princess..."

"Oh, *that* conversation. Were you ever frightened or troubled by the story?"

"Well, no, but..."

"And neither are they, my child."

"Papa, you made up a grand story long ago to put my father to sleep. Then you told *me* the story, and now my children. It's most certainly filled with wonder, adventure, and intrigue. I think it's a glorious story, I truly do, but I think it's gone to your head. It isn't real, and you shouldn't tell the story as if it were. It's not healthy for you or the children to live in such a fantasy."

"My child, you know very well that everything I ever told you about the island is true...at least so you once believed."

"Papa, you are such a dear, dear soul. Lost and deluded, perhaps, but such a dear man. I was but a child; of course I believed your stories."

"You still do believe, Suzanne. Somewhere inside you, you know that certainty sleeps. I've planted the seed of truth well within your heart. I'm confident you shall recall your training at a time when you need it most. I'm very confident in that. For tonight, however, the children will sleep soundly knowing we true warriors, at this very moment, are resolutely protecting them."

"Papa, tomorrow I want you to go see Doctor Hamilton."

"Doctor Hamilton? Why?"

"You're not well, Papa. I want you to see him."

"Not well? Why do you say that?"

"Please, Papa."

"I don't need to see a doctor, Suzanne. And in the event that I *did* need to see one, it wouldn't be that quack."

"I don't want to argue with you about this. He's a very fine doctor. You know that. I want you to see him. I insist upon it. I've made an appointment for you in the morning at eleven o'clock."

"But I don't need to see a doctor. I'm fine."

"You are *not* fine. Eleven o'clock sharp. Be there!" Suzanne ordered in mock toughness. However, a second later, a warm smile betrayed her.

"I'm in perfect health for a man of my age. In fact, child, I'm in perfect health for a man of any age, come to think of it."

"Speaking of that, will you please stop telling the children you're a hundred fifty years old? They're not stupid, Papa. Besides, you know you're eighty-one. So enough of that!"

"But I *am* one hundred fifty years old. Will you never believe me?"

"Papa, I have seen your birth record. How many times must I repeat this? You were born on March 30, 1839. That makes you eighty-one years old two weeks from tomorrow, not one hundred fifty. So, enough of that nonsense. I mean it."

"Child, I've told *you* several times already. I made that record myself in 1850. I was eighty years old when I made it, so that people would not be alarmed at how old I truly am. It was important then that I kept my true age hidden from some, although there are precious few left who know my actual age. I've outlived most of the others."

"Papa, you're not immortal."

"I didn't say I was, girl. I've told you *that* many times before as well. They did something to me while I was on the island. I age, but more slowly than normal."

"Papa, I'm not going to argue with you anymore."

"Argue? Who's arguing? I'm simply telling you the truth...for about the hundredth time." The old captain chuckled.

"Doctor Hamilton. In the morning at eleven sharp. Now goodnight, Papa. I have a very busy day tomorrow. Don't you stay up too late yourself. You need your rest...and don't you smoke that pipe in this house! In fact, you shouldn't be smoking at all, old man."

"It is one of my fondest enjoyments, child. It helps me to relax and concentrate. Besides, I would think I should be allowed at least one vice at my age."

Suzanne shook her head and kissed him on the cheek, adding, "You should find another vice less harmful." She closed the door gently as she completed her parting remarks.

Not knowing that Suzanne was listening behind the door, he muttered to himself, "I *enjoy* my pipe, and I *am* one hundred fifty years old. I should know how old I am."

She smiled lovingly and shook her head again. She went to her bedroom, carefully removed her makeup with cold cream, brushed her long shiny brown hair precisely fifty strokes, and then changed into her nightgown. Slipping it over her head, she thought a moment, smiled, and returned to the library.

She tapped lightly on the door.

There was no response.

"Papa?" she called out softly.

Still no answer.

Thinking the old man had fallen asleep, she opened the door and stuck her head into the room. "Papa? Are you awake?"

Her grandfather was not in the room. She guessed that he had probably taken her advice and retired to his bedroom.

She walked to his bedroom and knocked on the door. "Papa? Are you in there?"

Still no response.

She turned the knob slowly and opened the door, but the old captain was not in his room and his bed was untouched.

Suzanne decided that he had gone outside for one of his usual late-night walks to smoke his pipe and think, as he was so fond of doing on refreshing nights such as this. She returned to her room, closed the door, and went to bed.

Chapter 4

Seven o'clock next morning found Suzanne up, fully dressed, and preparing breakfast.

She stopped what she was doing, picked up a pencil, and struck a diagonal line through the day, Tuesday, March 16, 1920, on the wall-mounted calendar. Returning to her motherly duties, she picked up a spatula and waited for the pancakes to finish cooking.

Seated at the table, Robert and Wendy, also fully dressed, waited patiently for their breakfast as they sipped at their glasses of freshly squeezed orange juice.

The captain finally entered the kitchen, wearing his nightclothes and robe, as all eyes turned gleefully and warmly towards him.

"Good morning, Papa," both children said as one. Wendy, however, continued writing on her tablet of paper, as she was known to do almost every hour of the day that she was awake.

With a gentle smile, the captain responded to them. "Good morning, children. Did you sleep well?"

"Like a log, Papa," Robert replied

"Yes, Papa, me, too," added Wendy, still writing.

"I hope the intensity of my story last night didn't trouble your sleep."

"No, I slept great, Papa," Robert replied.

"Me, too, Papa," echoed Wendy. "I can hardly wait to hear more tonight."

A sharp disapproving look greeted the old captain as his deviously smiling eyes met with Suzanne's.

"I'm so happy to hear that." The captain grinned widely.

Suzanne delivered a plate full of pancakes to the table with an audible grunt. Captain Delightable only smiled in response.

Robert immediately dug into the flapjacks.

"Wendy," said Suzanne, "stop writing now and eat your breakfast."

"Yes, Mama." Wendy pushed her tablet off to the side.

"Did you enjoy your walk last night, Papa?" asked Suzanne.

"Walk?" asked the captain.

"Yes. Did you enjoy it? I changed into my nightgown and went to the library to say goodnight once again, but you weren't there. You weren't in your bedroom either, so I assumed you went for a walk."

"I enjoyed my evening, yes. Thank you, child, I had a delightful time. The night air is so crisp and fresh this time of year. It helps me to sleep soundly through the night."

"I have several chores to do today, Papa. I want to get an early start. Mrs. Sanford is coming over for lunch. I must get home early and prepare it. Would you like to join us?"

"No, I would not. I don't even want to be in the same room with that dried-up old..."

"That's quite enough of that, old man," scolded Suzanne. "She is a delightful woman. And I think she has a crush on you."

Suzanne's sly smile irritated the captain.

"What's a crush, Papa?" Wendy asked.

"Anything that woman sits upon," replied the captain.

"Stop that!" Suzanne rebuked.

"I'm going for a nice long walk this morning. I thought I'd go down to the wharf. There's a new skipper I've an appointment with. I heard he just came in from the South Seas."

"Papa!" Suzanne urged with concern. "No talk of Minchon Island with him. I mean it."

"An inquiry is all. I just need to ask…"

"Please, Papa. Don't do it. Detective Cyra already warned you about that, and you know that man has an ax to grind with you."

"Yes, yes, I know. He has his agenda and I have mine. I have only a mere navigational question about some surreptitious reports I've been hearing."

"Papa, please don't give Detective Cyra any more excuses. He wants to lock you away. He frightens me so, with those leering eyes and that smug smile." Suzanne suddenly shuddered. "I don't like him. I don't trust that man. I think he's evil."

"Now, now, child, that's not the warrior way. We do not speak ill of anyone. You know that."

"And what of Mrs. Sanford, then?"

The captain shifted uncomfortably in his chair and mumbled something unintelligible.

"Indeed, Papa. And that's enough of the warrior philosophy for today. Please! Stay away from the docks. Besides…eleven o'clock…"

"Yes, yes, the appointment with that old fraud. I won't forget."

"Promise me you'll go."

The old captain remained silent, pretending not to hear Suzanne.

"Papa! Promise me you'll go see Doctor Hamilton at eleven sharp."

The old captain stubbornly held his silence as his eyes danced wildly in their sockets.

"Papa!"

"Oh, all right. I'll go see that old shyster at eleven. I promise. There, are you happy?"

"A Minchon Warrior holds fast to the truth, Papa."

"Oh, I see. Now *you* invoke the warrior code."

"Papa!"

"Yes, yes. I'll go," he grumbled.

A satisfied smile formed on Suzanne's lips, for it wasn't often she achieved such a resolute victory in a contest of wills with the captain. "Fine. Now eat, you stubborn old man," she genially ordered.

The captain playfully winked at the children. They glanced at one another and chuckled.

"That's enough, you two. Eat!" Suzanne again ordered sharply, just before another smile betrayed her true intent.

* * * * *

Suzanne had nearly completed her morning chores when she strolled into the bakery to pick up a fresh loaf of bread and some dinner rolls.

As she entered, she noticed Philomena Montique, a local spinster who just happened to be her new next-door neighbor, having moved into her home a month before.

"Good morning, Philomena," Suzanne said cheerfully.

"Good morning, Suzanne."

"That's a lovely dress you're wearing. That green color really compliments your eyes."

"Why thank you, dear," Miss Montique responded, with a mixture of both pride and shyness. "That is so kind of you to say."

A bit of concern then filled Miss Montique's face as she leaned in close to Suzanne. "I know it's none of my business, dear, being new to the neighborhood and all, but you really should not allow your grandfather out on the roof. At his delicate age, he could fall and hurt himself terribly, or worse."

Only a blank stare greeted her words as Suzanne searched for a response. "On the roof?" she finally uttered. "Did you say you saw my grandfather on the roof?"

"Yes, dear. On the flat part. You didn't know?"

"A moment, please. You saw *my* grandfather on the roof of *our* house?"

"Yes, dear. Clearly. It was he."

"When was this?" asked Suzanne, now very concerned, but still confused.

"Last night," replied Miss Montique.

"You saw my grandfather on the roof of our house last night."

"Yes, as I checked my drapes for the evening, I saw him standing on the roof smoking his pipe. I'm so sorry, dear. I had no idea you were unaware of his nocturnal activities."

"What time was this?"

Mrs. Montique scratched thoughtfully at her chin. "I believe it was near ten o'clock, dear." She thought more about her answer, and then after a quick moment, she nodded. "Yes, ten o'clock, as I recall."

"You saw my grandfather smoking his pipe on the roof last night at about ten o'clock."

"Yes, dear."

"Thank you, Miss Montique. Thank you very much."

* * * * *

It was precisely eleven o'clock when the captain's shoes struck the wooden porch of Doctor Hamilton's combination home and office. He removed his captain's cap and held it in both hands at chest level. He then rapped lightly on the door and waited, returning his hand to his hat. Within seconds, Doctor Hamilton's wife, Mildred, opened the door, wearing a long black dress with long sleeves and white ruffled collar. Her gray hair was neatly bound in a bun behind her head. She was an attractive, graceful woman with a most gentle disposition.

"Why, good morning, Captain Delightable. How nice to see you once again."

"Good morning, Mrs. Hamilton. You look particularly lovely today."

"Thank you, Captain. How kind of you."

"My granddaughter made an appointment for me, I believe."

"Yes, she did make such an appointment. Please come in. I'll let Elias know you're here. Go right into the examination room. He'll join you in a moment."

The captain politely nodded and dutifully complied without a grumble or a hint of a disagreeable manner.

Within minutes, Doctor Hamilton opened the door to the examination room and greeted the captain cheerfully.

"Hello, Cornelius. How are you today?"

"Hello, Elias," the captain said with a hint of sarcasm. "I'm just fine. I don't know why my granddaughter even made the appointment."

"I see. Well, let's take a look at you and see what we can find."

"I can tell you what you'll find. Nothing. You'll find that there's nothing wrong with me. You'll find an extremely healthy man in no need of an examination. That's what you'll find."

"Ever the protester, eh, Cornelius?"

"Ever the quack, eh, Elias?"

Doctor Hamilton chuckled. "Well, I see you've successfully maintained possession of that rapier wit and that cantankerous disposition since I saw you last, Cornelius."

"And I'll still possess those traits long after you surrender them, sir," the captain shot back in his own teasing style.

Doctor Hamilton chuckled again and placed the stethoscope on the captain's chest and listened carefully. Finally, he pulled the ends from his ears. "How long have we known each other, Cornelius? About forty years?"

"Forty-one, but who's counting?"

"Forty-one years? Let me think....Yes, you're right. I met you when I was thirty. I'm seventy-one now. Forty-one years! My, my, how time flies. And you were already an old man when I first met you."

"Yes. And you were already a quack when I first met *you*."

Doctor Hamilton laughed aloud for several seconds, and then his face turned serious. "Cornelius, in all the time I've known you, I don't think I've ever heard a wayward beat of your heart. It beats like that of an eighteen-year-old. It is truly amazing!"

"I told you I didn't need to come here."

"Let's not jump to conclusions so quickly. I'll finish my examination, and we can talk about it then."

"Go ahead, but you're wasting your time."

Doctor Hamilton shook his head and smiled.

* * * * *

The captain was waiting impatiently in the exam room when Doctor Hamilton finally entered again.

"Well, it's about time. What did you do, take a nap?"

Doctor Hamilton remained serious. "I'm sorry to keep you so long, Cornelius. I wanted to double-check all my findings."

"Well, as I said, you're wasting your time, and now, sir, you're wasting mine."

"I can't explain it. I checked all of your records going back to when I first examined you, Cornelius. They are exactly the same."

"I could have told you that. In fact, I did."

"Cornelius, you don't understand. That's just not normal. No one stays exactly the same over forty years; no one."

"Forty-one, but as I said, who's counting?" The captain teased.

"I'm serious, Cornelius. All the measurements are exactly the same. Not just close, mind you. *Exactly* the same. The exact same height, weight, blood pressure, heartbeat. I don't understand it, but it's *impossible.*

"No, it isn't."

"Yes, Cornelius. It *is*."

"They're exactly the same for me, so it's *not* impossible."

"Well, now that you put it that way, you're right. But you're the first."

"Wonderful! Can I go now?"

"What?" asked the doctor, reading the file in his hand, half of his mind occupied in deep concentration, the other half trying to rationalize how such a thing was possible.

"Go? Can I go now?"

"Not...not yet, Cornelius. What day is today?"

"Tuesday."

"And the date today?"

"March 16, 1920. Anything else you need me to help you with, you old charlatan?"

The doctor did not respond immediately. Instead, he scribbled notes into the captain's medical file. He finally looked up into the captain's eyes contemplatively. "I need to study you, Cornelius. Would you mind submitting to a more thorough examination?"

"I would, sir. I'll waste no more time. I have an appointment I don't want to miss. Good day, you old quack."

The captain leapt from the table, landing with good force upon the floor, squatting slightly, his fists clenched shoulder high. "Aha! Still plenty of bounce in these old legs too, Elias!" He grinned at the perplexed doctor. "Another time, old friend," he said with a slight salute, and then rushed out the door.

* * * * *

Suzanne walked into Hotchkiss Hardware on a clearly defined and predetermined mission. She waited patiently until Mr. Hotchkiss finished serving another customer. When it was her turn, she stepped boldly up to the counter. "Good afternoon, Mr. Hotchkiss."

"Good afternoon, Mrs. Delightable. What can I do for you?"

"I'd like you to send a man to my house as quickly as possible to install a latch and lock for me."

"Certainly. Is it an interior lock you need, or an exterior one?"

"Interior. Could he come immediately? It's rather urgent."

"Certainly, Mrs. Delightable. I can have Tony there within a half hour. Will that be soon enough?"

"That would be perfect, Mr. Hotchkiss. Thank you. I'll expect him."

"Thank *you*, ma'am. He'll be there."

* * * * *

Captain Delightable sat in O'Connor's Wharfside Tavern for only one reason: it gave him direct access to all the sailors and officers of the ships coming and going; the tavern was the sacred haunt of every seaman at port.

In addition, O'Connor's brewed the best coffee in the entire city, and considering the fact that Prohibition had begun in mid-January of that year, it was the strongest drink which could be purchased legally. Of course, every now and then, as happened on that particular day, a few bottles of pure Irish whiskey were smuggled into the room and passed around on the sly, producing more than a few good cups of Irish coffee.

And, with St. Patrick's holy day being just one day away, the sailors in the tavern hoped to ring in the blessed holiday in the truest tradition of bold Irish men of the sea — being completely intoxicated, boisterous, joyous, and shouting their pride at being Irish.

In the midst of it all sat Captain Delightable. Though only a miniscule measure of his blood identified him as being of Irish descent, he consistently celebrated each year as if he were a full-blooded Irishman. However, he only marked the event with a cup of straight black coffee and avoided any spiking, except perhaps with an occasional splash of pure cream.

The good captain had given up the consumption of strong drink many years prior to the start of Prohibition, citing his warrior training as the reason.

In the past, when alcohol had flowed freely and legally, he had often defended his position of abstinence by insisting it was a warrior's responsibility to keep his or her head clear and prepared for any contingency or happenstance wherein his or her powers might be required.

Although many suspected there might be another reason he no longer drank alcohol, under the new law any further discussion regarding such possible reasoning was now muted.

As he sat facing the door, he nervously massaged a large roll of parchment in his hands that he had retrieved from his home after his visit with Doctor Hamilton. As each new patron stepped into the bar, he perked up, wondering if this would be the man he had arranged the appointment with through the landed ship's young first officer. The only thing he knew for certain was the mystery captain's name: Captain Whitmore.

For the longest time, each man entering was immediately greeted by someone else.

The bartender approached Captain Delightable to greet him: "And how are you today, my good friend?"

"I'm doing wildly well, William. And how might you be this lovely day?"

"All is well, Cornelius. So, who are you waiting for today? Another victim, I imagine."

"Ha! A victim, you say. I say another man with a piece more of the puzzle. I just hope he makes it on time."

"Still the fretting kind, I see. Will you never change?"

"You've known me far too long to ask that, William."

"Too long, indeed. And some people never change." William laughed loudly.

"Ha, I say. It is true, then. Some never change. Still hiding your teasing jests behind your blarney, I see. The same ole William I see before me."

"Well, Cornelius, at least you and me, we're consistent. You can say that for us."

"And well said it was, my old friend."

"I shall leave you to it, then. More coffee?"

"I would enjoy that so. Thank you."

"Comin' up, then."

The bartender walked away as the captain reached for his pocket watch and pulled it from his coat pocket; he flipped the cover open and noted the time. The appointment was set for precisely 2:00 p.m., and the minute hand was just about to move to the exact minute when the door was thrust open.

He glanced up and saw the entry of a thin man who appeared to be about fifty years of age, with extended gray hair tied tightly in a ponytail behind his head. His perfectly trimmed long sideburns reached the bottom of his jaw. His coat, a basic design carried over from the days of wooden ships in the early eighteenth century, was absent the original fluff. Instead, being all black, it transmitted a clear message that he was a man who held fast to a great and abiding respect for the old traditions, and yet one who believed in presenting a simple but elegant public image without any decorations. His hat, sitting perfectly straight upon his head, was immediately removed and tucked firmly under his left armpit and held fast by his left hand, his fingers gently cradling the brim.

As he stepped further into the room, Captain Delightable stood up and signaled. The other captain nodded politely and approached reaching out his hand. "Captain Delightable, I presume."

"Yes, Captain Whitmore. So kind of you meet with me, sir. Please join me. Would you care for something to drink, sir?"

"Coffee, sir. Same as you."

The two captains sat down, and Captain Delightable signaled a waiter for another cup of coffee.

Moments later, sipping their coffees, they engaged in light, trivial conversation as each man reservedly measured the other in a self-conscious attempt to avoid the start of an awkward exchange.

Finally, Captain Delightable took the initiative and boldly began.

"Captain Whitmore…"

"Wilbert, Captain Delightable. My name is Wilbert."

"Ahhh. Thank you. Please call me Cornelius."

"Cornelius. A pleasure, sir. Captain to captain, such formality is unnecessary, don't you think?"

"Quite so, sir. Wilbert it is, then. Wilbert, I have been very excited by the opportunity to meet you. Your first officer told me you sailed directly into port from Bora Bora on your steamer. Is that true?"

"No, we made several stops along the way. First in Tahiti and then several ports along the west coast of South America before docking here in San Francisco. Why do you ask?"

Captain Delightable excitedly unrolled the piece of parchment out onto the table. It was a meticulously hand-drawn navigational plotting chart of routes through the ocean near the French Polynesian islands. Captain Whitmore gazed admiringly at the chart for several seconds before speaking.

"A beautifully drawn chart, Cornelius. Excellent work, sir! Did you draw these yourself?"

"Yes, many years ago when we only had the wind to sail by, not the sleek steam-powered vessels you captain today."

"I've never seen such extraordinary craftsmanship. My compliments to you, sir."

"Thank you, Wilbert, but I'm particularly interested in a certain spot. Right here," said Captain

Delightable as his index finger touched a specific spot on the chart between Bora Bora and Tahiti. "Latitude sixteen degrees fifty-two point seven minutes south and longitude one hundred fifty degrees eleven minutes west."

"I apologize, Cornelius, but you show an island there."

"Exactly!" replied Captain Delightable excitedly. "Have you seen it?"

"I have traveled near that route many times over the last several years, Cornelius. There is no island in that spot."

"There is, Wilbert...well, there used to be, that is."

"I don't mean to be argumentative, sir, but there is no land at those coordinates."

"So you didn't see it on your last voyage?"

"I've never seen any sign of an island at that position."

"Tell me. Have you ever noticed anything strange while traveling through those waters?"

"Strange? Strange, how?"

"Odd things, unusual swells, bizarre eddies, anything out of the ordinary?"

Whitmore sat back in his chair and thought for several seconds. "No. I can't say I've witnessed anything like that, Cornelius."

"Perhaps a problem with your instruments?"

Captain Whitmore thought for only a second or two. Then his eyes opened wide. "Come to think of it now, Cornelius, nearly two years ago, as our ship was sailing through that area, our compass..."

"It spun uncontrollably, yes?"

"Why, yes. It spun wildly for about an hour. Then it stopped as quickly as it had begun, returning to its correct direction. I had forgotten about that incident until you asked. How odd."

"And you were never able to know why, correct?"

"Exactly. So it happened to you as well?"

"Yes. While the compass was spinning during a hurricane, it was impossible to navigate. The storm eventually wrecked my ship. It was quite a devastating event, but it *did* herald a very exciting and magical time for me as well."

"You were shipwrecked?" Whitmore asked, astonished.

"Yes."

"How did you survive?"

"The island. I washed up on its shore and was saved."

"And your crew?"

"Alas, my crew was lost in the tempest."

"The entire crew?"

"Save for me, yes."

"How awful for you, sir."

"It *was* quite a mournful adventure."

"And how long were you marooned on the island?"

"Ten years full, Wilbert."

"My word! Ten years full. An adventure indeed! You look well enough for having endured such a trial."

"Yes. Well enough, I suppose."

"But Cornelius, I assure you, I have never seen an island there. How long ago was this?"

"It was in the early spring of 1800."

Whitmore's eyes spun in their sockets as he calculated. "Did you say 1800?"

"Yes."

"Sir, that was over one hundred twenty years ago! You must be mistaken."

"In fact, Wilbert, I turned thirty on the very day of my fortunate arrival on the island."

"Captain, really? That would make you..." Whitmore used his fingers, but Captain Delightable interrupted.

"One hundred fifty years old, Captain."

"That's impossible, sir. What do you take me for, a fool?"

"No. Not at all. I am one hundred fifty years old. Well, I will be on March thirtieth, that is."

"That's a preposterous tale, Captain," said Whitmore, his voice demonstrating an even more irritated tone.

"I assure you, Captain, I speak the truth."

Whitmore became upset. "Seriously, sir, I do not appreciate your humor. I was being serious and forthright with you."

"And *I* am also being honest with *you*, Captain Whitmore."

"One hundred fifty years old, sir? I don't believe you. You speak rubbish."

"Believe me or not, Captain, it is the truth I am telling you. I was shipwrecked on that island and remained there almost a year before the war threatened the peace."

"War? What war?"

"The Minchon Island War, Wilbert."

"Minchon Island War?…I've never heard of such a war."

"Of course not, Wilbert. I don't expect you to know of the war. It happened long before you were born."

"Captain Delightable, I do not appreciate your thinking me an imbecile, sir. I do not appreciate it at all. Our conversation is finished. Good day to you, sir."

With that, Captain Whitmore stood, replaced his hat with perfect precision, and walked out in a posture of controlled indignity.

Captain Delightable did not appear upset in the slightest, however. In fact, he seemed, well, quite delighted with himself. He stared at his chart and smiled. "So," he said in a barely audible whisper, "you're returning, eh?" The captain chuckled lightly and excitedly rubbed his hands together as he murmured, "We shall all soon be together again."

* * * * *

Suzanne and Mrs. Henrietta Sanford enjoyed their conversation and lunch, although Mrs. Sanford was keenly disappointed that the captain was not in attendance.

Tony, the employee sent to install the latch and lock, entered the room dressed in the customary overalls of a master carpenter and tradesman. His flat cloth cap tilted to the side of his head solidly identified him as one of the typical blue-collar class of that time. He removed his hat and held it to his chest as he spoke. "Pardon the interruption, ma'am, but the latch and lock are now installed as you instructed. Would you care to inspect them?"

"No, thank you, Tony. I'm sure you installed them perfectly. What do I owe you?"

"Two dollars and fifty cents, ma'am. That includes materials and labor. Oh, here is the key to the lock." Tony stepped forward just far enough to place the key in Suzanne's open palm.

"That sounds very reasonable, Tony. I'll get my purse."

"That won't be necessary, ma'am. Mr. Hotchkiss told me to tell you that you can pay him tomorrow should you come by."

"Thank you, Tony. And please thank Mr. Hotchkiss for me. Tell him I will be by tomorrow, then."

"You're welcome, Mrs. Delightable. Will there be anything else, ma'am?"

"No, thank you. Good day."

"Good day, ma'am, and good day to you, Mrs. Sanford," responded Tony as he replaced his cap and promptly left the room.

"Do you really think it necessary to put a lock on the attic door, dear?" Mrs. Sanford asked.

"I have to do something, Henrietta, if my grandfather insists on sneaking out onto the roof to smoke his pipe at night."

"How long has he been doing that?"

"I have no idea, but I just put an end to it."

"I imagine he'll be upset about that."

"Upset or not, he's much too old to be sneaking about on a roof. He's been acting very odd lately. More so than usual, that is. I've decided I must take aggressive action to protect him from himself."

"It *is* for his own good, dear." Mrs. Sanford smiled.

"These are the times that I really miss my father and husband. They had a way with Grandfather I simply don't possess."

"That war was simply awful, my dear. It tore apart so many families. But to lose both your father and your husband within a month — I tell you, dear, I just don't know how you do it. And then to lose your mother soon afterward! My dear, you have most certainly been through some very trying times. I'm amazed at how stable you have remained through it all. I think I would have completely lost my mind by now."

"Thank you, Henrietta, but I don't think I can hold out much longer. Grandfather's behavior is becoming more and more erratic with each passing month, and I see definite signs of senile debility setting in. On top of that, he seems to be more cantankerous than ever lately. I don't know how long I can hold out before I will have to take stronger measures."

"I was forced to watch helplessly as my husband, Harold, went through a similar change himself. I believe they call it Sundowner's Syndrome," said Mrs. Sanford dolefully. "Thankfully, for his sake, his heart gave out before his mind left him entirely. It is all so sad, dear, so very sad."

"I've noticed things steadily changing in him ever since Grandmother Victoria passed away," replied Suzanne, "and that was almost ten years now."

"Ten years ago. It doesn't seem that long. My Harold has been gone a little longer than that. She was a beautiful woman, your grandmother."

"Yes, she surely was. She was an amazing woman, too. I miss her so very much, although she was secretive about her past. She kept extremely quiet, unlike my grandfather, who was the life of any party he attended."

"Perhaps she preferred to stay in the shadows, dear. My sister was like that."

"I think there was more to it than that, but I guess I'll never know the truth of it. I must admit, I have fantasies about her coming from a less than respectable background. I've always wondered if maybe my grandfather met her in some seedy sailor's bar in one of the ports he called at, and they wanted to keep it a secret. All she would ever say was what a wonderful day it was for her when she met him. That's about all I could ever get out of her. She was so kind and loving, though. She certainly adored my grandfather, and my grandfather doted on her as well. I guess it's what I remember most about her. How much she loved others and how much others loved her in return. I don't know anyone who knew her who didn't admire her."

"She was all of that, dear, and so much more. Her past wasn't important. Besides, we've all been young and not lived perfect lives. I'd never met a more genteel woman, but I guess we all have our little secrets."

"I guess so. She passed with a clear mind and a sweet smile, I can say that. As for my grandfather, well, that's another story to be discovered in time. But I believe the deleterious effects of age have been steadily quickening their pace over the last several months. I'm really worried about him. His behavior has become much more erratic lately...more agitated and obsessive...completely unpredictable. And these warrior fantasy tales, I'm afraid they're beginning to adversely affect him more and more as well. I believe he's losing his grip upon reality.

"It's frightening to watch it happen, knowing there's nothing I can do to relieve the situation. He lives in his fantasies more now than ever. I think he truly believes he was shipwrecked on that imaginary island with that princess. It's so heartbreaking to watch someone you love fade away.

"You know, he made up those stories years ago as bedtime stories for my father. I think over time, especially during the past several months, they've taken over his life. I think he really believes he's some mystical warrior endowed with special and unnatural powers. Last night he insisted vehemently that the stories were all true. I'm telling you, Henrietta, it's beginning to frighten me."

"I'm so sorry to hear that, dear," Henrietta responded compassionately. "It's true. It's so difficult to see the people we love losing their grip on this world. Very sad indeed. It was that way with my Harold.

"I'm particularly sorry for you, though, Suzanne. It just seems that tragedy is determined to remain close to you."

"It would seem so, Henrietta. Would you like more tea?"

Chapter 5

It was sometime after supper that Captain Delightable sat in the library at his great desk earnestly studying his chart when the children scrambled in through the door.

"Papa," asked Robert excitedly, "can you continue the story now?"

Wendy shot through the door and stopped dead in her tracks next to her brother, her ever-present tablet of paper at her side.

The captain looked up at the children as they bounced about in excited anticipation.

"Do you think you're ready for the continuance of such a story, Robert?"

"Yes, Papa!"

"And what about you, Wendy?"

"Oh, yes, Papa! I'm ready."

The captain leaned back in his chair and scratched at his chin whiskers as he stared thoughtfully at the children.

"Very well, then. We have some time before your bedtime. Take your places."

The children immediately dropped to a seated position directly in front of the fireplace, where they bathed in its warm glow.

The captain arose from his seat at the great table and moved to his rocking chair. After several silent moments of rocking and thinking, he stopped rocking and resumed his story.

Wherever I was at that particular moment, I was comfortable. A light breeze caressed me and cooled my skin. Chirping exotic birds sang to me. A variety of delicate scents from ripened fruits and seasonal flowers filled my nostrils. I sensed I was floating somewhere between the realms of consciousness and unconsciousness, but I was not alarmed.

All my worldly senses told me I was somehow suspended in mid-air. I felt my body swaying ever so slightly from left to right and back again. I felt truly at peace and did not want to open my eyes, but I heard a rustle of leaves to my right, and then a deep guttural groan followed by a brisk snort as if an animal were grazing nearby.

"An animal?" I asked aloud.

My eyes shot open and I turned my head toward the sound to see the strangest-looking beast I had ever seen pulling leaves from the treetops. Startled, I tried to move away and instantly found myself turning upside down and falling to the ground with a great thump. I had rolled out of my hammock and fallen to the ground.

My fall startled the great beast and it jumped backward, grunting loudly. I rose quickly and moved backwards, tripping over some plants and tumbling to the ground once again. In doing so, I entangled my foot in nearby vines and could not immediately free myself.

The beast then took strong note of me. It grunted again, louder this time, the air rushing out of its flaring nostrils in a short snort. It stared at me as I lay ensnared in a tangle of vines, vainly trying to slide my body along the ground in an attempt to move away.

It was a massive creature. More massive than I had ever imagined any beast could be. It dwarfed the largest elephant I had ever seen. Its features were strange as well, having what appeared to be the head of a camel, a neck that stretched upward at least twenty feet, the body of a large cow, and long legs that I guessed to be six feet in length. Its bright white coat covered with large brown sections like puzzle pieces looked like nothing I could ever have imagined.

In only two or three steps, its giant hooves slammed into the dirt beside my legs. Then it lowered its head toward me. I trembled in great fear and tried to get my legs under me, but the vines held me fast to the ground. I also tried to scream, but I could not force enough air into my throat to make a sound. My lungs had shut down and I couldn't breathe. I feared that this beast would easily bite my head off at any moment. I attempted to raise my arms to shield myself from its attack, but I was too late. Its giant face was before me. In one sweeping motion, its monstrous tongue lashed out and the beast licked my entire face from chin to brow, leaving a viscous trail of saliva. Then it raised up its head to the treetop and began nibbling once again on the leaves.

It was not going to eat me! I gasped, wiping my face with my hand. Perhaps the taste of my flesh was not suitable to the palate of this monster, I reasoned.

Then behind me I heard familiar laughter. It was my angel, Lelalu.

"I see you have reunited with your old friend," she said.

"Friend? I thought it would surely devour the full of my face," I responded, a definite hint of relief in my voice.

Lelalu laughed. "Devour you, Husband? No. He is an herbivore. He eats only leaves and grasses."

I calmed down, confident in knowing that I was not so soon to become a snack for this horrific-looking creature. "What is this beast?" I asked.

"You have forgotten?"

"Forgotten? I have never seen a creature such as this before."

"Of course you have. He is your friend."

"Don't tell me. He is my friend in the future."

"Exactly."

"Well, presently speaking, what is this beast called?"

"It is called a giraffe."

"A what?"

"A giraffe. It is from the plains of Africa," she answered, squatting down in front of me and staring at the tangle of vines around my ankles.

"He looks quite ferocious." I uttered.

"He's quite tame, Cornelius. A very gentle being," she offered as she began unwrapping the vines.

"He licked my face."

"A kiss."

"What?" I asked, surprised.

"He kissed you. He likes you. He really missed you, although I cannot imagine why."

I smiled. "As I wonder also," I added.

She giggled and quickly finished separating the vines from around my ankles. She then pulled me to my feet and stared at me up and down.

"A mess," she noted.

"I fell from my hammock in an effort to escape the beast…the giraffe."

"We shall have to clean you once more, I see."

My mind and my eyes were still on the giraffe. "From Africa, you say?"

"Yes," Lelalu responded matter-of-factly, slapping dust from my clothing.

"How did it get here?"

"The same as you did, Husband."

"How does a giraffe from the Dark Continent become shipwrecked in the South Seas?"

"It was apparently being shipped to a private estate in South America…Brazil, I believe."

"To Brazil? The giraffe was being shipped?"

"Yes. Along with the other animals."

"The other animals?"

"Yes."

"Dare I inquire to what other animals you are referring?"

"You may dare," she giggled.

I waited for her to continue, but then I realized that if I wanted an answer to any of my queries, I had to ask specific questions. "Aye, I understand. Well, then, what other animals are here with this…this…giraffe creature?"

She turned me around and continued slapping dust from my back. "The other giraffe, of course."

"There is another one of these brutes on the island?"

"Yes. His mate…and the lions."

"There are lions on the island?" I asked, now alarmed, my head twisting about on my neck, seeking discovery of the creatures.

"Yes."

"Running free?"

"Of course…along with the tigers, naturally."

I was aghast; my jaw dropped open in amazement, nearly striking my chest.

"And the pair of rhinoceros," she added.

"The what?"

"Relax, Husband. They remember you also. They wouldn't harm you. They wouldn't harm anyone."

Just then, both lions and tigers appeared from the underbrush. I started to run, but the princess grabbed me. "Relax," she ordered gently. "They are as gentle as kittens."

In seconds, both pairs of the lions and tigers were upon us. I was astounded, for there was no aggression in them at all. They rubbed up against me as would a small house cat. It was unlike anything I had ever heard about these magnificent creatures. I tentatively stroked the male lion's mighty mane and he did not protest, and then the tigers wanted their turn to be petted as well.

Soon I was stroking them all, as if they were longtime friends. "How is this possible?" I asked.

"I have said they remember you," Lelalu answered.

"Of course," I retorted. "But not present me, future me, correct?"

"Exactly correct, my dear."

"I cannot say with any degree of certainty that I understand what I am saying, mind you, but it seems that future me is well known in these parts."

Lelalu laughed. "Well known, Husband, very well known."

She sat down on a large flat rock and stared lovingly at me. I was intrigued that I had two sets of wild big cats calmly sitting next to me. I believe they were actually purring, if such beasts do indeed purr at all. I looked up at my angel. She was calm and relaxed.

"When I arrived earlier today, you did not greet me as your mate. You screamed, and very vociferously, I might add. Did you not recognize me?" I inquired.

"I recognized you."

"Then why did you scream?"

"You were expecting me to be an angel in your heaven. I thought it best to break the spell lest your self-deception go too far."

She was right. I had already convinced myself this place was heaven and she was an angel. I expected her to act the way I had envisioned a true angel to act. Having that concept torn asunder immediately made me realize how fragile fantasies are. It also forced me to appreciate reality all the more.

Just when I thought perhaps I was beginning to gain a grasp on the true nature of my situation, another bizarre thought struck me soundly in my dazzled brain. How did present-day Lelalu recognize future me? For that matter, how did these beasts recognize future me when I, a human being possessed of a superior intellect and power of reason, did not? A second later, I realized that without thinking about it, I had confounded myself once again. My brain tried to make sense of the nonsensical, and instantly therein I was hopelessly lost in the unknowing once more.

Lelalu patiently watched me squirm with my conscious attempts to rationalize the paradoxical consequences of conceptual time and its impact on such events as my past, present, and future. It seemed that over the last day I had teased with them all, and I did not know with any certainty which one was my current reality.

I had never believed in doing something only halfway. Therefore, in this endeavor, I was inwardly pleased that I had so completely and so thoroughly confused myself, even to the point that I doubted my own sanity. I had therefore, at the very least, accomplished something of interest, albeit completely perplexing.

Still, there was a spark of memory of this place which haunted me. It was as a vague or long-forgotten memory beginning to emerge once again, and yet it remained far off in the hazy distance, a partially recognized event of some long-ago nature — important, but not fully visualized or understood. At times I sensed it was like a mist which had formed around my brain, blocking my clear view of what lay only a near distance from where I was at the moment.

I fell into yet another stupor trying to make sense of all that had happened to me over the past twenty-four hours; but reason, for me, was as fleeting as a spectre, not easily captured nor even momentarily detained. I could not understand anything I had experienced — or, more importantly, *why* it was happening to me.

It was most odd that I had not considered this point more fully before. *Why me? What had I done to deserve all of this blessing, if it was indeed a blessing?*

As far as I knew, I was the lone survivor of a ghastly and horrific shipwreck. While one hundred eighty good and honorable souls were winging their excellent way toward an unknown afterlife, I was prevented from taking such a journey. *How was that possible?* I was on the same ship and faced the same injurious effects of the storm as they. *Why was I spared? Why was I blessed, or was I still yet cursed?*

No answers to my inquiries made themselves readily known to me, but there I stood, stroking the mane of a wild man-eating African lion that was now content to simply sit next to me without fear or any apparent malicious intent.

And there, seated upon a rock not twelve feet from me, was the most beautiful woman I had ever seen. And I was presently known to her as her future husband who she was joyful to see once again, after a long absence. Absence from what, when, and even where, I couldn't yet say, but as she appeared glad with my re-emergence, I dismissed it from my mind for the moment, not willing to plunge into that quagmire just yet.

My temples throbbed; I felt my eyes roll in my head as I teetered in place and was about to fall onto my face. My arms felt numb and would not move; they offered no way for me to brace for the impact and I could not extend them to break my fall. But just then an arm caught me around my chest. It was Lelalu. She helped me walk to my hammock.

"Sleep," I said. "I need to sleep. This is all too much for me."

Without another word, she helped me into my hammock and softly stroked my forehead with the palm of her hand until the sun, riding high in the noonday sky, began to blur, and simple blackness once again replaced complicated thoughts and images.

* * * * *

When I awoke again into the conscious world, it was a much different rising. I was alone except for the same exotic birds hidden among the leafed branches of the trees. All was quiet except for their continued melodic chirping and the sound of rushing water from the nearby falls. This was as tranquil an awakening as I could have hoped for, given my propensity toward the self-muddling of my own brain and state of awareness.

The red sky to the west told me it was very near sunset. I had slept soundly, apparently for several hours, and I felt pleasantly rejuvenated.

I rolled out of my hammock and was instantly greeted by bowls of freshly cut mango, roasted nuts, and a cup of cool water, all laid out in perfect symmetry upon a large rock. I seated myself on the large block of stone and partook of them immediately.

Catching a whiff of her sweet scent, I closed my eyes and, in my mind, saw her approach from the green thicket to my rear.

"Thank you," I said, without looking.

"You are most welcome, Husband," Lelalu answered as she came up behind me and hugged me. "Did you sleep well?"

"Yes. It was peaceful...and restful as well."

"That's good. Wash up at the spring, please. The celebration is about to begin," she said as she sat down on the rock alongside me.

"My welcoming party?"

"Yes. My father is waiting to greet you."

"Again?" I asked with a smile.

Lelalu chuckled. "Yes, once again." She reached out her delicate hand and laid it against my cheek. "My sweet, sweet Cornelius, I have so looked forward to your return."

"I'm sorry it has taken me so long to get back," I responded, this time knowing full well what I was saying, although I was still confused as to how all of this could be real and possible.

"All things happened as they needed to happen, my love."

I wanted to inquire what she meant by that, but I knew any explanation would necessarily serve only to confuse me further. I decided, therefore, to be more like her and simply go forth into each coming moment without strife or worry, to fully go forth in gladness and thankfulness.

And when I had given it thought, I found I had much to be glad and thankful for. Glad to be on that incredible island, feeling safe and protected. Thankful to be with that wonderfully gentle and loving woman, and *truly* thankful to be alive after the ravages of such a dreadful storm.

I was becoming both excited and a bit apprehensive about attending the celebration in my honor. A swirl of anxiety washed over me, but after cleaning up at the river, I felt fully revitalized and boldly eager to make my entrance.

I walked back and stood before Lelalu and stared into her eyes.

In retelling this story, I often find it difficult to describe what I saw in her eyes at that moment; it can be best described as peace and patience. True peace and true patience.

She was at peace with all that surrounded her. Even insects did not harass her. But it was the wonderful manner with which she greeted every new moment that was most apparent to me. With great gentleness and patience, she accepted each coming instant. Without worry or consternation, she moved from one second to the next, entirely expecting each coming moment to be a blessing. And it was just that peace and patience, which she so keenly possessed, that kept me most composed and assured.

I will not say I am always an easy man to be around, but I cannot say I am an overly difficult man either. Until I landed on that island, I can truthfully say, however, I was an honorable man, a truthful man, and a man of even disposition and manner. But if I *am* a truthful man, then I must also admit that I was not one given to great patience. And if the full truth be told, I must further admit that I was not one to tolerate a fool for very long, nor was I given to tolerate foolishness in those who should have known better.

I do not endure excuses put forth by those who are unwilling to accept their responsibility for the manner in which they choose to live their lives, or by those who consistently refuse to learn the necessary lessons from previous mistakes.

I have often found it all too convenient to externalize one's responsibilities to make informed choices when given the opportunity to do so.

I, myself, was taught by my father that mistakes are only unlearned lessons, which would remain blunders if the lessons went unheeded. In fact, he often reminded me, missteps would necessarily be repeated until such lessons had been efficaciously received.

So, in all of this, and having attested to being of a truthful nature, I must also admit that I did struggle, sometimes mightily so, against my impatient temperament.

Yet when I looked upon Lelalu, I witnessed someone who had learned her lessons exceedingly well, and in so doing she had mastered herself. I understood clearly that she had championed nearly all things necessary to live without strife or anguish. Perplexity, along with its cousins of mistrust, anger, and resentment, could not abide within her. They had no rightful place within her heart.

She was not a careless person, by no means, but rather, as best I am able to describe it, she flowed with her surroundings instead of resisting them.

She grew hungry, as others did; she grew fatigued and required sleep, as others did; she was warmed by the sun and chilled by the night air, as others were. She did not live absent struggles; she lived *through* them.

She did not voice her protest at her febrility when she was too hot. Instead, she cooled herself in the spring pool until she was again comfortable. When she hungered, she did not complain; she ate.

When she was tired, she rested. In all things, she did not resist. She simply took the steps necessary to relieve her discomfort, her hunger, or her fatigue. In her eyes I witnessed the true meaning of peace. In her mannerisms I saw the perfect description of tranquility.

Somehow, through either grace or study, she had learned that strife can only exist where one allows it to exist. Lelalu neither took interest in seeking strife nor tolerated its presence. Nor did she adopt it from others. She simply did not take part in it. And so, watching her over time, I bore witness to a flawless example of how I should come to live my own life.

I knew I had much to learn, and eagerly looked forward to those future lessons. As I would later discover, at that very moment I was actually being prepared to begin my training as a Minchon Warrior. Prior to my dramatic arrival on that island, I had not even known such a being existed.

Lelalu, through her keen sense of awareness, noted that I had completed my brief introspection. She rose and gently took my hand. "It is time, Husband," she said, with an exquisitely serene smile. "The celebration begins."

Suzanne poked her head into the room. "Children, it's getting late. Let your great-grandfather rest. Get ready for bed now."

Without protest, Robert and Wendy stood up and hugged their great-grandfather.

"Papa," asked Robert, "you really did marry the princess?"

"That is a story for another time," replied the captain.

"If you married her, is she then our great-grandmother?"

"Dear boy, that question is much too complicated for a simple yes-or-no response. I will answer that question for you, but it will have to be another time as well. Have patience, my child. All your questions, even those you have not yet formed in your mind, will be suitably resolved over the course of time — and in their proper sequence. Do you understand?"

Robert nodded and then promptly departed the room with his sister. Suzanne waited until the children had gone before speaking.

"Papa, after I get the children to bed, I want to ask you about your visit with Doctor Hamilton. Do you have time for me?"

The captain chuckled. "I will always have time for you, my dear. See to the needs of the children, and then we shall talk."

* * * * *

The captain sat at his table, once again engaged in a methodical study of his navigation chart, when Suzanne stepped into the room and seated herself across the table from him.

"How did your examination go today, Papa?"

The captain continued studying his map as he responded. "Just fine, dear, as I told you it would."

"He found nothing wrong with you?"

"Nothing, child. As I already knew, I'm in perfect health."

An odd expression formed on her face. "I don't understand it."

"There's nothing to understand. I'm fit as a fiddle." He chuckled lightly as he added, "I'm in perfect health and it confounds that old quack no end. Why do you ask?"

"Why?"

"Why did you feel that I needed a doctor's examination?"

"Because, Papa, something is going on with you and I don't know exactly what it is, but your behavior is getting stranger and stranger."

The captain finally stopped his review of the chart and leaned back in his chair.

"Whatever do you mean?"

Suzanne wanted to tell him about the latch and lock on the attic door, but decided not to. Instead, she looked directly into his eyes. "I'm hearing strange things about you, Papa. And you're doing odd things as well. It makes me think that you are not yourself."

"You're hearing strange things about me? What kinds of things are you hearing, my dear?"

"Odd things about your behavior while you are out for your nightly walks, for example."

"How can that be? I rarely encounter anyone during my walks."

"That's not all. Your stories about the island..." Suzanne fell silent. The captain waited patiently for her to continue, but she remained quiet. Finally the captain felt the need to spur the discussion.

"The island? What about the island?"

"It's the children, Papa. They believe you. They believe you really landed on that island."

"I *did* land on that island, child. It's an actual place. You know it is. When you were their age, you believed it too. Why are you resisting all the lessons you learned when you were young? This is the time you should be utilizing all that training, not refusing to acknowledge it."

"Papa, they were just stories. I know that now. Wonderful stories, Papa, and I enjoyed them immensely, but they're not real."

"You mean to say the lessons you learned all those years ago have no validity?"

"I'm not saying that. The lessons also were wonderful. You taught me a lot, but I fear you're believing too much in your own fanciful tales."

"I spent a good portion of my life on that island learning the secret ways of the Minchon Warrior. I learned how to use that knowledge in my everyday life. What would you have me do with all that knowledge now?"

"I don't know, Papa, but I'm worried about you. Have you heard of the medical condition known as senile debility?"

"Senile? You think I'm losing my mind?"

"Not altogether, Papa; I just think your advanced age is beginning to effect you."

The captain chuckled lightly. "You think I'm losing my mind. Is that what this is all about? Suzanne, I'm fine, my dear; I'm in perfect health. I just think it's time to teach the children the ways of the Minchon Warrior — and also others, if they will take the time to listen."

"But Papa, *you* believe them to be true. That's what troubles me most."

"My dear, I realize I should have been more actively discussing these issues with you before now. But you and the children have lived in my home for less than a year, and until just recently I had no idea you had so handily rejected all the lessons you learned as a child."

"I haven't rejected the lessons, Papa. I use them every day to teach my children. It's just that I have known for some time your stories are just stories you made up for the sake of my father, Jonathan, and me."

"I'm sorry, my dear. I had no idea you never believed my stories to be true. I have failed you."

"You have not failed me, Papa. You took the children and me into your home without hesitation. You care for us and you have been wonderful for the children. I see that they love you very much."

"Would you have me not teach the children the ways of the warrior?"

"Papa, things are very different now than when I was their age. There are many different influences today. Life is much faster now."

"Every generation says the same thing, my child. If it is so, then those lessons are even more important today. Wouldn't you agree?"

"Perhaps, Papa. I know the children love your stories, as I did, but you need to be clear about what is real and what is fantasy. I think the line separating the two is becoming blurred to you."

"I see. And now my mind is lost in that blurring?"

Suzanne did not reply.

The captain rose from his chair and picked up his pipe and tobacco pouch from the shelf. He began tamping a pinch of tobacco into his pipe.

"I assure you, Suzanne, that I'm not losing my mind. And I also assure you that I know well the line between fantasy and reality. I think it's time the children begin their lessons in earnest. I believe they have need of the knowledge we possess, and I intend to work more with them. If their father were here, this duty would fall to him. But he has not yet returned, and so *we* are left with this responsibility."

"Papa! This is what I mean. Jonathan is dead. Your grandson is dead. My husband is dead."

"He is not dead, my child. How many times must I tell you this? He is in training. He will return home soon."

"Papa, he is not off somewhere training to become a Minchon Warrior. He was shot through the head during the Great War. The Army confirmed that. He is dead. He's not coming home. This is what I've been talking about. You miss him, too; I know that, but I've accepted the fact that my husband is not ever coming home. Anthony, your son, my father, is also dead, and he's not coming home either."

"Aye, sad to say, child, my son has chosen to move on. That is the awful truth. But your husband is not dead. He will be home soon. You just have to be patient for a while longer."

"Jonathan has been dead for over three years, Papa. He's buried somewhere in Europe. You're going to have to face that cold, hard fact yourself...just as I have had to face it and get on with my life. I don't have time to wallow in self-delusion or self-pity. I have two children who need me, and Papa, I need you. I need you to face reality and help me raise the children. Can you do that?"

"Of course, my child. I'm here every day. I'm not going anywhere. And as for your Jonathan, I cannot say more than what I've already told you. He will be home soon. You'll just have to trust me on this. He will return."

The captain paused, then continued. "It's getting late. You go to bed; I'm going for a smoke. I feel extra energized this evening."

"Why?"

"Because I received some good news today."

"About what?"

"About the island."

"The island? What about the island?"

"It's making its return."

Suzanne rose from her chair and started for the door. She stopped, turned, and moved to kiss the captain on the forehead.

"I can't talk about this right now, Papa. Good night."

"Good night, my child."

"Enjoy your smoke this evening."

"Thank you. I shall."

Suzanne walked out of the room, closing the door behind her.

Chapter 6

The front door opened. A burst of chilly morning air swept in. The captain stepped inside, shut the door, removed his coat and hat, and placed them on a wall hook.

The sounds of kitchen activity immediately attracted his attention. He walked into the kitchen to a surprised Suzanne.

"Oh my, Papa! You startled me. I thought you were still sleeping."

"I've been up for hours, my child. I awoke so excited that I decided to go for a walk. The air is absolutely exhilarating this morning. Just delightful."

"What has you feeling so chipper?" Suzanne asked in joyful earnest.

"The news, child. The island news. I'm very excited about it."

"Oh, that," Suzanne replied, now more subdued.

"Yes. Yes. It's returning soon. I have confirmation of it, finally."

"And just when exactly will it make this triumphant return?"

"Very soon, child. Very soon. It should fully materialize within forty or fifty years. Very soon!" The captain slapped his hands together in glee and giggled as he passed through the kitchen. Then he began humming a happy tune.

"Forty or fifty *years*?" asked a shocked Suzanne.

"Yes, yes...very soon...very exciting! Very exciting news, indeed." The captain left the kitchen and disappeared down the hallway.

"Absolutely!" shouted Suzanne sarcastically to her now absent grandfather. "Only forty or fifty years. Why, that's just around the corner." She smirked as she said to herself, "Crazy old man."

"I heard that," replied the disembodied voice of the captain.

A knock on the front door captured her attention.

Suzanne went to the door and opened it. There stood Detective David Cyra, fedora in hand, his slim frame concealed by a heavy overcoat and his habitual perverted sneer set solidly on his face. Suzanne felt instant fear and revulsion for the man.

"Good morning, Mrs. Delightable. And how are you this glorious morning?" His words seemed simple and well-intentioned enough, but he never said a word that wasn't carefully crafted to fit some hidden agenda. To the exacting detective, every meeting was some form of investigation.

"Good morning, Detective. I am well enough. Thank you for asking," said Suzanne, disguising her true feelings behind a mask of courtesy. "Is this about my grandfather?"

"It is. May I speak with him?"

"What has he done now?"

"May I speak with him, please?"

"After you tell me what this is about."

"I'm here in an official capacity, Mrs. Delightable. That is all I can say until I speak with the captain. Please don't make this any more difficult than it already is. I need to speak with him. Now."

"Fine, wait here; I'll fetch him."

"May I wait in your foyer? It's a bit on the chilly side this morning."

"You may not, sir. You are not welcome in this house and you know that; so, if you don't have a warrant authorizing your entry, you, sir, will wait on the stoop."

"No, ma'am. I have no warrant with me...yet. But I can get one if necessary. I am here on the lowest level to speak with the captain as part of an ongoing investigation. I'm trying to be civil with you, Mrs.

Delightable, but if necessary, I can make this painfully official at the next level."

"You are a vile man, sir. And you do not intimidate me. You will wait outside on the stoop, or you will not speak with my grandfather until you have a proper warrant to do so. Is that *painfully* clear to you, sir?"

"Fine. We'll do it your way…for now. Please send your grandfather to the door."

Suzanne shut the door sharply and hastened to her grandfather's library.

As she opened the door, she witnessed her grandfather doing a little jig in the center of the room. Her entry surprised him, but he kept dancing.

"Hello, my child. Come in. Come in. I can't help dancing this morning. What a glorious day!"

"Let's see if you can still dance with this news. Detective Cyra is outside on the stoop. He wants to talk with you. What have you done now, Papa?"

The captain stopped dancing, straightened his clothing, and sat down in his chair at the great table.

"Why, nothing at all, child."

"Papa! Have you been disturbing people on the dock again?"

"I have not. Please show him in, my dear. Let's find out what he wants."

"I don't want that man in this house, Papa. He repulses me."

"Suzanne, repulsed or not, we *will* show him courtesy."

"I despise the man. I will not show him any courtesy at all. He doesn't deserve it."

The captain launched himself out of his chair and, placing both hands flat on the table top, stared sternly at her. "Child! That will be quite enough. We are civilized warrior adults. We will always extend courtesy to everyone we meet, even to those who do not deserve any courtesy at all. Now, you show the good detective to my library. Immediately, girl!"

Suzanne knew when her grandfather took that tone with her, which was extremely rare, it was wise for her not to challenge him. She knew well enough her boundaries with him, and she seldom attempted to cross them.

"Yes, Papa." She turned to leave, but hesitated. "Papa, you know he seeks to put you away, do you not? He's not to be trusted."

The captain softened his demeanor.

"I know what he seeks, Suzanne. I implore you, trust me in this. It's not as you perceive it to be. Find just a little more faith."

"Very well, Papa."

"And Suzanne. Please bring us two teas. He likes a squeeze of lemon in his."

"Yes, Papa."

* * * * *

Detective Cyra, with a false air of politeness, knocked on the door to the captain's library and then opened it. "Captain Delightable, may I speak with you?" he asked

"Detective Cyra, always a pleasure to see you, sir. Please come in and have a seat on the sofa. How can I help you?" The captain rose from his chair at the great table.

The detective seated himself. "You'll forgive me, sir, if I get straight to the point."

"Certainly. Certainly."

"I've heard you had a meeting with a Captain Whitmore yesterday. Is that true?"

"Quite so, Detective Cyra," replied the captain, now seating himself on the opposing sofa. "And a fascinating meeting it was, too. Delightful man."

"Yes. Well, he has expressed some concerns about you to us."

"Has he now?"

"Yes, he is concerned that you may represent a danger to yourself as well as to others."

"How kind of him to exhibit such concern, but I assure you, Detective Cyra, there is no need to be alarmed. I'm quite happy and contented. I cannot see how I represent a danger to anyone."

A knock on the door prevented the detective from immediately responding. It was Suzanne bearing a tray with a pot of tea and two cups and saucers.

"I hope you don't mind, Detective, but I took the liberty of arranging for some nice hot tea. I know how much you enjoy Earl Grey. Thank you, my dear; just put it on the small table. We'll manage alone."

Suzanne set the tray on the table and immediately moved toward the door. She stopped and turned toward the captain, squinting her eyes disapprovingly, but she received only a gentle smile in return. She then closed the door firmly with perhaps a bit more zest than she would have under more normal conditions.

The detective noticed. "She doesn't approve of me. I know that. Whenever I meet her, she makes it quite clear."

The captain just smiled as he poured the tea into both cups and then placed the lemon slices in front of the detective before responding. "Please forgive her, Detective. She's young and impulsive. She is also quite protective.... Please continue. You were about to say something."

"You were saying you don't feel you represent any danger to yourself or to the community, but that is precisely what someone would say in your position. I'm sorry, Captain, I have a sworn duty to keep the public safe; I can't take the chance. I'll need you to come to the station and meet with a doctor who provides certain medical services for us from time to time. If, after he speaks with you, he says there is no need to worry, then I will cease my inquiry and you can go on with your life. Will you agree to meet with him?"

"It sounds quite intriguing, Detective Cyra, but I will have to give it some thought. At present I'm quite busy. I'll have to check my schedule to see if I have the time, and then get back to you."

The two men sat in silence for several moments, with the detective sipping lightly at his tea, his eyes fixed on something unseen. It appeared to the captain that Detective Cyra was considering his next move.

Finally, the detective set his tea cup down. "Captain Delightable, forgive me, sir, but I really must insist that you submit to an examination. It's for your own good."

"I do appreciate your concern for my well-being, Detective, I truly do. And please, I beg you, don't think me ungrateful if I decline; however, I was examined by Doctor Hamilton just yesterday and he found me to be in excellent health."

"I'm not referring to your physical health, Captain. I'm referring to your mental state."

"I know *exactly* what you mean, Detective Cyra. Please don't take me for an imbecile, sir. I understand *you* completely. And I also understand your agenda."

"See here, Captain. Make no mistake about this. I'm here to *ask* you for your cooperation. If I have to force you to comply, however, I am prepared to do so."

"I'm certainly not an attorney, Detective, and I must admit I lack a full understanding of the laws that govern us all, but I do believe you would have to show *just cause* to the magistrate before you would be able to force your will upon me. Is that not true?"

"I have enough on you right now to force such a judgment, but I am here to ask politely for your cooperation. I think that speaks sufficiently to any *agenda* you think I may have."

"Listen carefully, Detective Cyra, and be very certain of my words. I understand far more than you give me credit for, sir. If you had sufficient evidence, you would be here in the company of other officers, bearing the necessary warrant to take me immediately into custody. But you don't possess such a document, do you?

"I therefore strongly urge you, my friend, to step carefully regarding this matter. For if you pursue this investigation without just cause, you may find yourself upon an extremely slippery slope. I have seen many otherwise good men follow in those footsteps. It did not end well for them. I thus, once again, urge caution and care, for I have no wish to see you experience such peril."

"That sounds very much like a threat, sir. Are you threatening me?"

"Not all, my dear man. Rather, I'm giving you sage and sound advice. I urge you to take it. A man does not get to be my age without learning a thing or two about survival."

"Thank you for bringing me to another issue. You're still telling everyone that you are a hundred fifty years old. Is that correct?"

"It is."

"I've cautioned you before about making absurd claims like that, and yet you continue to do so. It is either through direct defiance or some delusion that you persist in this regard. I choose to believe it is the result of some delusionary state you live in, for I know well enough you are not the defiant type. Therefore, Captain, to me that presents strong evidence you may not be in total possession of your faculties, and that is precisely what I mean to discover. You don't appear to be a well man, and I believe you represent a serious potential danger not only to your family but also to this community, and, not the least in this, to yourself."

"And you, sir, represent a clear danger to yourself. I am a Minchon Warrior, Detective. I cannot stand idly by and let you destroy yourself. Not without trying to divert you from your self-destructive path."

"That seems like another threat. I assure you, sir, if you resist, this will not end well for you. I, therefore, implore you to do the right thing and cooperate.

Voluntarily submit to an examination by a qualified doctor of psychology. Do so peaceably, and I give you my word that if he finds you competent, I will end my investigation and pursue you no further regarding this matter. However, if you force my hand and require me to take stronger measures, then, sir, I shall throw the entire weight of the law against you. I will give you no quarter, nor will I show you any mercy. It's your choice...but only for this moment. The offer expires once I leave your home."

"Then, Detective Cyra, as long as it is still my choice, I choose *not* to volunteer for the examination. I also think, perhaps, it is time for you to leave."

The detective promptly arose from the sofa and moved toward the door. As he took hold of the doorknob, he stopped and stood still for several seconds. The captain could see the detective was trying to think of something else he could say that might nudge him into compliance. He did not have to wait long. The detective partially opened the door and then froze again. Without looking back at the captain, he spoke.

"I urge you to reconsider, Captain. If you do force my hand, it may have a devastating effect on your family. Is that what you would wish for them?"

"My family is strong, Detective. You have no idea just how strong they are. It is *you* who should be concerned about devastating effects."

"That sounds like yet another threat, Captain."

"Not at all, Detective. I am merely expressing concern for your well-being."

The detective finally turned and stared into the captain's eyes. "Thank you for the kind thoughts, Captain, but there is no need to be concerned for me. *I* will be just fine."

"Let us hope so, Detective. Let us hope so."

The detective turned and exited the room, leaving the door open and the captain staring thoughtfully at the vacant doorway.

Moments later he heard the front door slam shut, and then Suzanne stormed into the library.

"Do you believe me now, Papa? That man is pure evil."

"Suzanne, take care not to do anything that would warrant his attention for the next week or so."

"He threatened you, then, didn't he?"

"He clearly established his intent, dear one. But in so doing, he also telegraphed his method as well. He has left himself vulnerable once again, I'm afraid."

"I knew it, Papa. What are we to do?"

"Nothing. We need not change our lives one bit because of this. His threats are just that, only threats...empty threats without any justification or support. I fear for him, my dear. I truly do."

"For him? Why? Why would you give him any consideration at all?"

"Because he walks in darkness and is desperately searching for light. It is our duty as warriors to see that he finds the light he seeks."

"Papa! How can you say such things? *Why* would you say such things? That man intends to harm our family as far as he is able to do so. Why would you want to help him?"

"I just told you, darling. It is our duty to help him. As Minchon Warriors, it is our sacred trust to help all lost souls find their peace. Make no mistake about it — he is lost, that one. He also walks in great pain and fear. Can't you see that?"

"Papa, all I see is a man who is hateful, spiteful, and evil. That's all I see. Tell me, Papa, what do you see?"

"Child, I see a soul broken and tormented. I see a soul searching to be saved. I see a soul crying out in the darkness and hoping to be found before it's too late."

"I hope you're right and I am wrong, Papa, but I can't take that chance. I *will* protect my family, no matter the cost or the inconvenience to anyone. I *will* fight if need be. He will *not* destroy this family."

"I'm not fearful of that, dear child. I'm concerned only for him. He's in such desperate need. I just hope we can help him before he falls."

"I don't understand you, Papa. I just don't understand you."

The captain stood up, pulled his pocket watch from his vest and noted the time.

"Good gracious, my dear. Where has the time gone? I'm late for my walk to the wharf. The children must be wondering what happened to the old storyteller. I must run, dear. Have a wonderful day."

He leaned over and kissed Suzanne on the forehead and left without her speaking a further word.

What would it have mattered anyway? She thought. *He surely would not have listened to any warning or soundly offered advice I might have given him.*

* * * * *

Seated on his favorite bench, in his favorite park, Captain Delightable was surrounded by a throng of listeners young and old alike, including his two great-grandchildren, who had come to hear him after school. They all enjoyed the captain's favorite pastime — telling his wonderful stories. Wendy was already writing rapidly, using her secret form of short hand she had developed entirely by herself, recording every single word spoken by anyone in attendance.

"...And as I was telling you earlier," he continued, "my grandson, Jonathan, is married to my granddaughter, Suzanne. Now, how could he be both my grandson and my grandson-in-law? People have often asked me this question over the years."

All heads nodded as one.

"It isn't complicated," the captain continued, "but perhaps I should explain for the sake of clarity."

Once again, all heads nodded in confirmation.

"Well, Jonathan's real father and mother were killed in a tragic accident on their farm near Sacramento when he was very young. My son, Anthony, was good friends with Jonathan's parents. Upon their death, Anthony took Jonathan into his family and raised him as his own, giving him the Delightable surname.

"During those years, Suzanne, my dear and lovely granddaughter, and Jonathan, not being blood-related, became very close, fell in love, and eventually married.

"You see how simple it is. And so, I was lucky enough to have both a grandson and a grandson-in-law in the body of one man."

Everyone surrounding the old captain, including his two great-grandchildren, acknowledged the resounding logic of Captain Delightable's account with a collective "Ahhh."

"It was very lucky for Jonathan to come and live with us," the captain continued, "for I was able to teach him the ways of the Minchon Warrior while he was growing up, just as I had taught his adoptive father before him.

"Suzanne, in contrast, possesses a certain stubbornness regarding this matter. Since that time, she has come to believe my stories to be merely fanciful tales having nothing to do with reality. But I assure you, every word I tell you about Minchon Island and my magical time there is true. The first year was the most daring and challenging time of my entire life. But it also was the most rewarding time."

"Is it true, sir," an unknown young woman asked from the crowd, "that you lost your grandson in the war along with his father, your son?"

"Sad to say, young lady," replied the captain, "my son did choose to move on. But my grandson, Jonathan, did not die in that horrible conflict, as the authorities would have us believe. Why, today he is in the midst of his warrior training, and, I suspect, is doing quite well."

"How do you know that?" inquired the same woman.

"If he were not doing well, I would have heard by now."

"From whom?" asked an unknown man.

"From the High Priest himself, the priest who trained me."

"That would be the High Priest of this Minchon Island that you mentioned?" asked another man.

"That would be correct," replied Captain Delightable proudly.

"I see." The man's voice was sarcastic. "Then this is just another crazy story from another crazy old man...just another make-believe story.

You should be ashamed, sir, making light of your grandson's sacrifice that way. Ashamed, sir, I say." The man stomped off along with several grumbling others, but most of his audience stayed.

"I assure you one and all, what I tell you *is* the truth. Jonathan is not dead. He'll return home very soon."

"Captain?" a man hollered from the crowd. "Could you spin a yarn for my son here? We just came into town today, and we heard about you."

Captain Delightable laughed. "I don't know what you have heard, sir, but I would be happy to tell you of an actual event that happened to me in 1850 right here on these very streets. Would you care to hear about that?"

The man's young boy nodded his head gleefully.

"Very well, then. As I said, the event of which I speak occurred here in San Francisco during the early summer of 1850. Let me start by saying this."

I was in an abnormally excited state, for some reason or another; I found it difficult to sleep. In such a state, I decided to take a late-night stroll.

Now, that particular night in June was peculiarly strange, quiet, and still. At the time no one, in any manner, could have possibly predicted with any certainty how such a serene evening could end the way it did.

In all that stillness, I had no way of knowing what dark forces were lurking in the shadowed corners of that silent, dimly lit street, or what designs they had for me.

I was already an old man at the time of this event. Having always been in good health, I have never needed the assistance of a cane. But on that particular evening, for some unexplained reason, I had felt compelled to take one with me.

As I slowly sauntered along the harbor street, gripping tightly the handle of the cane, I became aware of some strange sounds coming from somewhere in the darkness ahead of me. I continued on my nighttime stroll, untroubled by the continuing bizarre sounds, and as I neared a building, the sounds became recognizable as voices whispering loudly. I could not comprehend what they were saying, but I was not alarmed.

I stopped my walk and turned my head to listen more intently. The voices seemed to be speaking in an unknown language, which is why I could not understand the words. Still, I was not alarmed, only perplexed by the oddity of the language. It sounded familiar, but I could not place it among the other languages I had heard around the world in the hundreds of port cities I had once visited.

I began my walk again, enjoying the cool late-night air as it rushed into my lungs with each deep breath. I also enjoyed the stillness of the night, but it was then I finally noticed an uncanny fact. I was alone.

The street that was normally crowded at that time of night with people and carriages was completely devoid of any human or animal forms. I was utterly alone as the whispers grew louder. I then became concerned, as I presumed the whispers to be arising from would-be robbers of foreign origin.

I picked up my pace, but as I said, I was old and moved at a slower gait — unable to dash away as a younger man would.

The whispers became even louder and I began to panic. I, an old man, was no match for robbers — and I clearly understood that fact.

As I continued down the street, the whispers seemed to follow me. And although they seemed directly upon me, I still could not locate their source. I then became fearful.

Mind you now, to a Minchon Warrior, as to anyone else, fear is well known. But a true warrior does not allow himself to become paralyzed by such fear; this would prevent him from acting with boldness. Fear *is*, however, something to be respected, and I did respect it, to the extent that it hastened me to retreat from the area as rapidly as I could. I was not afraid, you understand, but I recognized that I was extremely vulnerable, being alone and in no physical condition to fight off multiple robbers.

I realized my only true and reasonable course of action was to get back to where the crowds of people were, for I knew there would be safety in numbers. I also knew that merely two blocks toward the east was the main thoroughfare. Surely that street would be full of pedestrians. If I could make it to that street, I would be safe.

The whispers grew louder, and by the time I could see the end of the block where I would make the turn eastward, the whispers had been joined by footsteps. I heard them both clearly behind me, presumably in pursuit.

I turned to cast an eye upon my pursuers and was shocked to see only an empty street stretching backward into the darkness. The whispers grew even louder, however. It was my intention to reach the corner with utmost haste, but it was still many horrific yards away. I wanted to run, but my old legs could barely stand the strain of walking at such an accelerated pace.

My knees felt as if they would fly apart at any moment. My hips pleaded for me to slow down, and under the stress of such a brisk walk, it felt as if they wanted to seize up altogether. My chest began to heave mightily. My aged heart was nearly exploding in my chest. My exhausted old lungs tried to suck in more of the cool night air, but found it extremely difficult to do so. My head ached as the blood pulsed forcefully through aged arteries and veins.

The footsteps were quickly closing ground, and I feared that within seconds they would be fully upon me. I did not look behind for them again. Instead, I continued with good purpose toward the corner, which, to my elderly mind, still seemed an inestimable distance away. The footsteps grew heavier and closer. I pressed my body to its full potential, and yet it seemed dreadfully inadequate to the task of effecting my escape.

By this time the babbling whispers had become strong voices, the words still alien to my ears; I could almost feel the breath of their purveyors upon the back of my neck. It felt as if the arteries of my heart would burst, but I was intent on making it to the corner before my attackers seized upon me. Once around the corner, I could shout for help, although in my soul I feared it would be to no avail. I was fully two blocks from the noisy hustle and bustle of the main street. Even if I shouted at full volume, it was doubtful that anyone would hear my cries in time to save me from the attack.

Under the most extraordinary of circumstances, a true Minchon Warrior is capable of astounding feats of self-defense, and I had been personally trained by the Great Amog, the Minchon High Priest himself, in the incredible ways of the warrior. But it had been many decades since I had last performed those tactics of self-preservation. In those dreadful moments, I was not confident that I still retained possession of those skills at the necessary level to extricate myself from this threat.

The voices drew much closer and the footsteps were almost pounding in my ears. I decided the only course of action left to me was to stop, turn, and make a stand; for a true Minchon Warrior does not cower in the face of a threat. So that is what I did. I stopped and turned to face my attackers, my cane held upward, horizontally, in a defensive posture. At that moment I understood why I had been prompted to bring my cane along.

As I turned, I thought I caught a glimpse of a dark shape moving toward me, but it seemed to vanish into thin air. The voices halted as well, and I soon came to believe it was only my foolish old mind playing games with me; the sound of the nightly breezes coming off the harbor waters had deceived my ears.

At first shocked, I relaxed my muscles as I stood and found myself once again utterly alone on the darkened street. Then, as my fright subsided, I began to chuckle lightly at the folly of it all. I, a First Order Minchon Warrior, had been frightened by nothing at all. Or, worse still, I had been startled by my own creations — inventions of my own mind, as it were. I relaxed.

Suddenly those dreadful voices began again directly behind me, and I felt the heavy press of hands upon my shoulders...

The collective gasp from the captain's audience stopped him momentarily. He cleverly took the time tamped his pipe and relit it, leaving his audience a moment with their own thoughts. After studying his audience a bit more, the cagey storyteller continued.

Yes. It would seem they had me in their grip, but they did not know, nor could they possibly have known, that as a Minchon Warrior, I was equipped with special self-defensive powers.

I shut my eyes tightly, and through the aid of my extraordinary warrior training and my great will, I instantly dematerialized and then reformed in front of my own house, safe and sound.

I was able to use a process that on the island is known as *riding the wind*. It takes years to master this mode of transportation, but when mastered, it allows one to avoid such situations as I have just described.

All mouths dropped open and all eyes blinked.

"You did *what*, Papa?" asked Robert, in an incredible tone.

"I *rode the wind* — away from my would-be attackers to my own home. That's what I did."

Most mouths remained opened in shock and disbelief, but no one challenged the captain or his story.

"Did you beat up the attackers first before you rode the wind?" asked another young boy.

"No. Of course not."

"Did you strike them with your cane?" asked Robert.

"No, Robert. I left the street and moved to the front door of my home in the blink of an eye. I didn't strike a blow on anyone. Why would I do such a thing?"

Captain Delightable heard the grumbling from his audience. He looked into their eyes and saw their disappointment; they had apparently expected a much more violent conclusion. He studied them all for several seconds, and then offered the moral of his story.

"I feel you all have lost the lesson here. You wanted me to thrash my attackers? Is that what you wanted?"

"Yes, sir. They were trying to rob you," said the young boy who had spoken before.

"First of all, young man, I have no evidence that they intended to do me any harm whatsoever. I was merely surprised by the touch. Secondly, I was alone. If there was to be a fight, I would not have fared well given my advanced age. Besides, a Minchon Warrior does not react in such ways. The best way to avoid a battle is to avoid the possibility of it altogether. Do you understand?"

"No," said the young boy.

"The best way to avoid being hurt, lad, is to not be *where* you can get hurt."

His adult audience then seemed to understand, and several of them nodded in agreement.

"Be someplace else, far away from trouble. That is how best to survive, and that is precisely how a Minchon Warrior survives. We are never present where there is trouble. Now do you understand?"

The boy's head, along with several other young heads, nodded in agreement.

"That way," Captain Delightable continued, "none are harmed and all are safe."

"But did you really just disappear like that?" asked the young boy's father.

"A warrior does not lie, sir, but let me put this to you. Does it really matter how I avoided the conflict? Or is it more important for your young son to understand that nothing good comes from violence, and it should be avoided completely if one is able to do so?"

The man then nodded and smiled — the true lesson finally received.

The story had ended, and soon the once grumbling crowd, now nodding and smiling, began to disperse. Some chatted amongst themselves as others thanked the captain for both the entertaining story and the important lesson he had given their children.

Minutes later, Captain Delightable and his great-grandchildren were seemingly left standing alone in the center of the park.

"Did you really *ride the wind*, Papa?"

"Yes, Robert."

"Can you show me how to do that?"

"In time I shall show both you and your sister how to do that, but for now I think it best to keep it to ourselves. Agreed?"

The children nodded their heads and smiled.

"Thank you, children. I'm afraid there are some people who are not ready to hear about such things."

"I understand, Papa."

"I understand too, Papa," echoed Wendy.

"Did you both understand the lesson today?"

"I think so, Papa. If I know I might get into trouble on a certain street, I should choose not to walk down that street. Is that correct?"

"Exactly, Robert, and perfectly stated, I might add. Avoid trouble by avoiding the opportunity to be in trouble. Exactly, indeed."

Suddenly they heard applause. They turned to see Detective Cyra standing behind them clapping his hands as he walked up to them.

"Bravo, Captain Delightable. Well stated, indeed."

"What do you want, Detective? Have I committed an infraction?"

The detective stopped clapping his hands and halted just short of the Delightable family. "Not unless I find a statute making telling tall tales a crime; but believe me, Captain, I *am* looking for such a statute."

"Leave my great-grandfather alone!" yelled Robert, stepping up in front of the detective.

"Yes. You leave Papa alone, you mean man," added Wendy, joining her brother blocking the detective's path toward their great-grandfather.

Detective Cyra only chuckled.

"Such brave children," he smirked, touching both on their shoulders, but then immediately wiping his hands on his coat as if the children carried some transmittable disease.

"If you are not here to arrest me, Detective, then what can I do for you?"

"Nothing, Captain Delightable. I am just keeping an eye on you, that's all. Although, I do have a question. Do you mind?"

"Not at all. Please ask."

"If you knew you could escape so easily, why all the posturing with the cane? Why all the panic?"

The captain smiled. "Zest, detective. For the sake of the zest. Everyone likes to be thrilled. A good storyteller creates intrigued, mystery and a bit of fright before offering the resolution."

"I see," said the detective. "Makes sense, I guess. Well, I just wanted you to know that I will be like your shadow from now on when you're out in public. How's that for added zest?"

"How exciting!" exclaimed the captain, clapping his hands together. "I think I shall like that, Detective Cyra. In fact, I look forward to our spending more time together. That is most delightful news, Detective. Very delightful. Thank you."

The look on the detective's face would have caused most people to drop to the ground in laughter — the dip of his lower lip, the widening of his eyes, the high rise of his forehead, as if he had just been struck by the single greatest surprise of his life.

The captain, however, seemed *truly* joyous with the news, and Detective Cyra was at a loss for additional words. He turned and walked away without any glib comment whatsoever, hands thrust deeply into his pockets.

"Detective Cyra?" the captain called out.

Cyra stopped and turned to face the captain, still stunned.

"We're walking home now; would you care to join us? We're planning a stop for ice cream along the way. You're invited, sir. It will be my treat."

Cyra could not speak. He tried to speak, but the words became stuck in his throat. He could only shake his head.

"No? Well, perhaps another time, then. Good day, Detective. I do look forward to getting to know you better." The captain touched the brim of his hat and turned away with the children.

"I think today, children," the captain said, "you have proved yourselves to be worthy candidates for warrior training."

The captain pulled a pocketwatch from his vest and noted the time. "We should just have time for a small ice cream cone if we hurry."

The captain and his great-grandchildren walked away, hands clasped tightly together.

"Papa," said Robert, "can we *ride the wind* home?"

"No, Robert. We shall walk. A warrior does not misuse his powers."

Chapter 7

As the happy three approached the house, the front door abruptly opened and Suzanne appeared in the doorway, obviously upset. "You're all late. Where have you been?"

"At the park listening to Papa's stories, Mama," replied Wendy.

"Stories? Again?"

"Absolutely," the captain responded.

The children rushed past their mother and into the house as the captain glided happily up the steps.

"Papa," pressed Suzanne, "why do you do this? They don't need to waste their time on such foolishness. They need to study, not listen to stories."

The captain passed his granddaughter on the stoop and patted her face gently.

"There should always be time for stories, my dear."

* * * * *

The captain was seated comfortably in his favorite chair in front of a blazing fire in his library, meditating, when Robert walked in. "Papa? Am I disturbing you?"

The captain opened his eyes, turned his head, and smiled at the young boy. "Not at all, lad."

"Do you have time? I need your help."

"I will always have time for you, Robert. What is it that you need help with?"

Robert stood quite still for several seconds. He finally looked up at the captain, but said nothing.

"There is something on your mind?"

"Yes, sir. I have a problem."

"I see that. And what has you so troubled, lad?"

"At school the other kids have been laughing at me."

"And how long has this been going on?"

"Several weeks now, Papa."

"Ahhh. And this troubles you?"

"Yes, sir. It vexes me, sir."

"It *vexes* you," echoed the captain with a slight chuckle. "I see. Well, tell me, why do the other children laugh at you?"

"They say that my father is dead. When I tell them he's in training to become a warrior, they laugh and call me foolish. I'm becoming very angry, Papa. I want to punch some of them in the nose."

"But you know that is not what you should do, correct?"

"Yes, sir. I know that a warrior does not engage in such behavior, but I still want to punch Tommy Watts in the kisser."

The captain chuckled. "In the kisser, eh?"

"Yes, sir."

"Come, sit down, I have a special story for you."

Robert eagerly sat himself on the floor in front of the captain's chair, his favorite position during story time.

"I want to tell you about the time I, too, was laughed at by the other children in my school."

"You went to school?" asked Robert, surprised.

"Of course I did. You don't think we had schools when I was young?"

"I didn't know."

"Of course. How could you?"

"Before you became a warrior?"

"Long before, Robert."

"Tell me, Papa."

"All right then."

The captain rested his elbows on the arms of his chair, weaved his fingers together, and brought his hands up in front of him. He leaned over and spoke softly

"I was no more than your age when I was confronted by the town bully, William McGregor. We called him 'Billy the Bully.' He didn't like that, and I was one of them who called him the name. One day he confronted me on the school grounds and said he wanted to fight me over his nickname. I asked him why he would want to do such a thing.

"'Because I don't like you calling me that,' he said.

"'But you *are* a bully, Billy,' I said. 'You are always picking on the younger children. Just because you're the oldest doesn't give you right to pick on others.'

"'My father says I have to fight you.'

"It was in that moment, even at that young age, that I understood why Billy was the way he was."

"I don't understand," Robert said.

"Billy did not want to fight, Robert, but he felt he had to, because his father had raised him in fear. It was his father who wanted to fight. Out of his own fears and self-loathing, he was the one who felt the need to fight. And so he raised his son the same way."

"What did you do?"

"I picked up a boulder."

"Did you hit him with it?" Robert asked excitedly.

"Of course not. I backed up a few paces ..."

"And then hit him with it?"

"No. I gently tossed it to him."

"Why?" asked Robert, slightly dejected.

"Because now he had the rock in his hands. That made him feel more powerful and less threatened. He held a heavy stone and yet I had none."

"I still don't understand, Papa."

"I know you don't. Listen to me closely, and I shall explain it to you. I asked him to toss it back to me. He looked at me strangely, but he did as I asked. For about an hour we just tossed the rock back and forth. When he held the rock, it was his turn to speak. When I held the rock, it was my turn to speak.

"And so, Billy the Bully and I tossed the rock back and forth as we spoke, each empowering the other by giving up the stone. Each of us was forced to listen to what the other had to say, without interrupting. Each of us eventually told the other about his life and the problems he faced."

"So you just talked?"

"Exactly. We shared with each other all of our fears, joys, happy times, and sad. By the end of the hour, we were excellent friends. I never called him Billy the Bully again, and he never bothered anyone from that day on. For many years after that day, we were the best of friends, until he finally passed away."

"He's dead now?"

"Yes."

"He's not in training?"

"No, Robert. Not all are meant to become warriors. He is dead and has been so for a long, long time."

"I understand. So, are you saying I have to make friends with Tommy Watts?"

"No, Robert. I'm not saying you have to make friends with him, but I *am* saying you need to make the attempt."

"Is that what a Minchon Warrior would do?"

"That is exactly what a Minchon Warrior would do."

Just then Suzanne walked into the room, wiping her hands with her apron. "Supper's ready. Come eat now."

She noticed the smile on Robert's face and his cheerful disposition.

"And just what have you two been up to?" she asked with a smirk. "More fanciful stories, I presume."

Robert looked up into his mother's eyes and beamed proudly. "Men things, Mother. We were discussing men things." Robert turned to his great-grandfather and smiled. "Tomorrow, Papa. I'll try tomorrow."

"I'm proud of you, lad."

Robert jumped up and flew past his mother as the captain slowly arose from his chair.

"Men things?" Suzanne smiled "My nine-year-old son was speaking of *men* things?"

"Yes, dear, he was."

"And what things was he speaking of, Papa?"

"Things that only men speak of, my child."

"He's *my* son, Papa. I should be told these things."

"It is nothing serious, my child, but if he wanted you to know, he would have said so."

"I'm his mother," said Suzanne in protest. "I'm supposed to know what's going on in his life."

"And if his father were here, dear, he would have been speaking with Robert and still not to you. The boy is growing up, Suzanne. Sometimes boys need to speak about certain things with men."

"I see. You were filling his head with more nonsense?"

"No, my child," the captain replied gleefully, his eyes bright with joy.

As he passed her in the doorway, he suddenly stopped and hugged her tightly. "He has successfully begun his training....He asked a question, and it was a wonderful, thoughtful question — a grand question. Simply wonderful."

The captain then released her from his embrace and, humming a cheerful tune, left her standing in the doorway, perplexed but smiling thoughtfully at the realization that her son was maturing.

"Men things," she said to herself as she turned toward the kitchen.

* * * * *

Later that evening, all were in the library doing what pleased each the most. Robert and Wendy lay on the floor in front of the fireplace, reading books by the firelight as

Suzanne worked diligently on her knitting. She still had not told her grandfather about the lock on the attic door. She wanted to see if he mentioned it first, and was more than a little perplexed that he had not already done so.

The captain, blissfully unaware of Suzanne's little secret, sat at the large table staring at the chart he had shared with Captain Whitmore the previous day, occasionally jotting something into a nearby notebook.

His mind was a flutter of activity, yet externally he remained quiet and calm for a long time. Finally, he looked up at Suzanne. "I think I shall take a smoke tonight, dear, after you retire. Don't wait up for me. I may be out for quite a while. I'm feeling somewhat restless tonight."

Suzanne remained composed, though inwardly she was nervously anticipating her grandfather's reaction when he found the attic door latched and locked. She almost betrayed herself with an anxious chuckle, but managed to arrest it before it burst forth. "That sounds like a good idea, Papa. The fresh air will do you good."

"Yes," the captain responded. "I believe so."

Within another hour, Suzanne and the children retired for the evening, each giving the captain a hug first.

Suzanne shut her bedroom door and placed her ear against it, listening for any movement in the hallway near the attic door. She waited several minutes, but heard nothing. After a half hour of hearing no sign of movement in the hallway, she gave up and went to bed.

* * * * *

The sunlight was only a quarter of the way through its Saturday morning arc. Suzanne was already dressed in attire more suitable for the work involved in heavy shopping than for the mere sake of social appearance. It was going to be another very busy day. First, she needed to stop by the cobbler's to pick up Robert's old shoes that were being repaired, then she needed to go to the general store and inquire whether the new dress she had ordered three weeks before had finally arrived. Then she needed to pay Mr. Hotchkiss for the lock and latch. If she was very lucky, the vegetables would be fresh and available at the corner food vendors' carts. She hoped the Romaine lettuce was available; it would be a real treat this early in the season.

If all went well, she would be home in plenty of time to prepare lunch for her family.

Attempting to tiptoe past the library, fearing another withering confrontation with her grandfather so early in the morning, she was startled when the captain came around the corner from the kitchen.

"Good morning, Suzanne," the captain announced gleefully.

Suzanne, interrupted in her attempt at stealth, stared down at the floor. "Good morning, Grandfather."

The captain noted her reluctant bearing. "Ah, I see. You were hoping to avoid me this morning. If you'll pardon me, then, I'll be studying in the library. Have a wonderful and glorious day, my child."

Suzanne realized that her demeanor had betrayed her, but she nevertheless attempted a ruse. "No, Grandfather. I simply didn't want to disturb you."

"I'm old, my child, not blind or stupid. You are wishing to avoid a confrontation. I understand that, although I have no idea of the content of this confrontation. Could this have something to do with Robert's 'men things' conversation?"

Suzanne shook her head.

The captain leaned forward and kissed Suzanne on the forehead and smiled. "I apologize for making you feel uncomfortable around me. I wish it were not so."

"*I* apologize, Papa, if I make you feel unwelcome in your own home."

The captain chuckled lightly. "It seems, my child, that even after nearly a year of sharing space under the same roof, we still have not learned to adequately communicate. For that, dear, *I* must apologize."

"It is my fault also, Papa," Suzanne said, her eyes beginning to tear up.

"Tell me what troubles you."

"I don't have time right now, Papa. I have much to do today."

"Then give me a hint, please, so I can prepare an adequate defense for later," the captain chuckled.

"It is many things, Papa. I'm concerned for many reasons. You don't seem to understand, or you choose not to see. I have to go now. I'm sorry to trouble you. It's all my fault."

She started to move away, but the captain grabbed her and hugged her tightly. "No, my child, it is not your fault at all. The fault is mine. It seems the older I get and the more studying I do, the less compassion I show. I love you very much, and I only want the very best for you. But even as a young girl, you could only accept something if it was based on the five senses. You rejected everything else. You have a very cynical approach to life. I have no idea where you got that from, but there it is."

"I don't mean to be obtuse, Papa, but you refuse to deal with any reality at all, it seems."

The captain released Suzanne from his hug and took hold of her hand as he smiled understandingly into her eyes. "I do deal with reality, Suzanne. In my own way and perhaps not as you see it, but we just have different experiences of what is real and what is not. You're so brilliant, girl, but somewhere along the way you've lost the ability to believe in things your limited five senses cannot identify and correlate. Your intelligence oftentimes blocks any chance for faith to grow. Faith is like a muscle, my dear. The more it is worked, the stronger it becomes.

"As a warrior, I should have helped you exercise it more than I did. I should have dealt with you differently when you were younger. I'm sorry if I failed you, my dear. I will try to work with you more. I promise."

"That's just it, Papa. You don't seem to understand that I'm happy this way. I accept who I am. I understand what the five senses tell me. I'm at peace with that. I'm able to exist in that world and accept it, knowing full well all its limitations and frailties. You, on the other hand, cannot seem to accept it. You live within your heart, Papa. You exist within your fantasies.

"You see, I understand you also. And I accept who you are, just the way you are. Well, most of the time that is. But sometimes I feel that you do not respect my beliefs."

"I see," the captain said. "You truly believe that, don't you?"

"Yes, I do, Papa. You're a storyteller, and storytellers always want to change what *is* because they often don't like what they see around them. On the other hand, I accept this life I live. It's not perfect, Papa, I know that; but every day I have to deal with what is real. I have two children who need me — and no husband to help me. I don't have time to deal in fantasy."

"Well, my child, I am saddened by that revelation."

"I don't want you to be saddened, Papa. I just want you to respect me and what I choose to believe."

"You're correct. Each of us can only walk in the light we possess at any given moment."

"The light I possess, Papa, is the correct amount for me. Please understand that. I have to go now."

The captain smiled broadly. "I do, my child. I do. I have enjoyed this little chat. And I see now, very clearly, what I must do. You have appropriately now set the task before me."

Suzanne's head bowed. "Grandfather, I've just wasted my breath, haven't I? You still don't understand."

"On the contrary, my child," the captain said, with a renewed sparkle in his eye. "I understand completely. You have laid a righteous challenge before me. You have renewed my quest. Thank you, girl. Thank you so very much. I feel good and suitably invigorated; it's going to be a wonderful day."

He released her hand, kissed her once again on her forehead, and joyfully walked into his library, announcing cheerfully to the empty room, "More light. She just needs more light. How exciting!"

The door closed, leaving a dejected but sad-smiling Suzanne in the hallway staring at the floor. "Papa, Papa, why do I even try?" she muttered.

From behind the closed door, she heard her grandfather respond. "Because you're now in training once again, young lady. Yes, sir! It's going to be a glorious day today."

* * * * *

Suzanne, with a small two-wheeled cart in tow behind her, fashioned specifically by the captain to ease her burden of daily shopping, walked along the street pleasantly greeting other passersby. In the full midst of the public, she was most gracious, polite, and pleasant, hiding the fullness of her sorrow and the inner pain that lingered just below the surface.

She was always the one who kept the cap tightened firmly when it came to the potential for emotional outbursts. She usually held her tongue and forbade herself to speak boldly of that which was strongly on her mind. She was always the one who remained diplomatic, even when others had already vaporized into a blazing fury.

An emotional rage roiled within her, an agitated molten core driven mostly by her fear and anger. The pressure exerted on her seemed at times to be too much to bear. She felt more often like a volcano nearing its inevitable eruption. Unless such emotions were soon quelled, it was only a matter of time before she would unleash her pent-up sorrow and frustration in one catastrophic explosion.

At times she felt so alone; it was during these moments when she most missed her husband, her best friend, that she would feel the need to close her bedroom door and cry herself dry. She wondered how long she could bear up under the pressures that smacked her about without mercy.

"Jonathan," she would murmur sometimes. "Please help me, my love. I don't know how long I can stand this emptiness inside of me." But when no answer came, she realized she was utterly alone. There would be no ghostly assistance. She would straighten her shoulders, wipe the tears away with a hardened defiance, and press on.

"Get over it," she would urge herself. "You need to be strong. Stop this nonsense and get on with your life."

Such resolve would work for a while, but she knew it was only a matter of time before she would again succumb to the pressures and fall sobbing onto her bed, calling out for assistance from a deceased husband who was unable to offer her any more comfort or support. She knew it. She was alone — and quite possibly would be forever more.

* * * * *

The captain sat at his desk scribbling on a notepad when he heard the roar of Suzanne's voice. "Papa!" she bellowed loudly.

He looked up just as the library door was thrust open and an infuriated Suzanne burst into the room with her left hand firmly grasping Robert's collar.

"Look at him, Papa. You're responsible for this."

The captain looked at Robert and noticed the large red welt under the boy's left eye.

He leaned back in his chair and smiled at Robert. "So it went well, I presume?"

"Not at first, but yes, Papa, it went very well."

"Went well?" Suzanne again bellowed. "You call that welt a good thing?"

"Yes, Mother. It went very well. Tommy and I are now good friends."

"Explain this to me, Papa," ordered Suzanne.

"Robert met a challenge, Suzanne, and apparently he did it very well."

"Do you see this mark, Papa? My son has been injured."

"I see the mark of a true warrior, my dear. Would you care to tell me more about it, Robert?"

"Papa, I did what you said I should do. I stood before Tommy with a rock. I told him we needed to talk and about the rule of listening to whoever held the stone. Then I tossed it to him, but he threw it at me and hit me in the face."

"And he felt bad about that, didn't he?"

"He sure did. Then we talked about it. We tossed the stone back and forth, and soon he said he wanted to be friends."

"I'm proud of you, Robert. You showed great courage and strength of character."

"Tommy and I are good friends, Papa. Maybe we'll be friends for life, just like you and your friend."

"Papa," Suzanne said, "you'll have to explain this to me. I don't understand."

"I shall explain it all to you. Robert, you did well. You did very well indeed."

"Thank you, Papa."

A knock on the door interrupted them.

"That's Tommy. We're going out to play."

"It's the boy who hit you?" asked Suzanne.

"Yep."

"I need to speak with him."

"No, Suzanne. You need to stay out of it," the captain said firmly.

"But he..."

"Child, you need to stay out of it."

Robert ran to the door and opened it. "Hi, Tommy," they heard him say.

"Hi, Robert. Are you ready to go?"

"Yep."

The door slammed shut.

Suzanne stood mesmerized.

"My son is now playing with the boy who hit him?"

"The welt will heal. The friendship could last forever, my dear. Your son is becoming a man. And a very good one, from what I can see. He's filled with the warrior spirit. I expect great things from him."

"I don't understand, Papa. I'm very confused."

"Have a seat, my dear. I want to tell you a story about a boy we used to call 'Billy the Bully.'"

Chapter 8

As celebrations go, at least as far as I had known them to be, it began as a spectacularly joyous affair. I clearly heard the rhythmic drums beating from a great distance away. With Lelalu on my arm, I walked the path toward the sounds of laughter and song as they echoed across the valley.

"Will I like your father?" I asked.

"Of course you do!" she replied in her usual enigmatic style.

"Of course," I echoed, still very unsure of my existence in a sane world.

The sets of proudly prancing lions and tigers led us along the path through the lusciously green foliage toward the sounds of the celebration echoing in the near distance.

A group of small monkeys in the trees above swung from branch to branch in their effort to escort us. One of the monkeys with a peculiar white stripe of fur streaking across its head and partially down its back slipped off a low branch and onto the back of one of the tigers. The tiger, the male, missed not one step and made no attempt to rid itself of the uninvited jockey. A moment later, as the tiger slowed and came alongside me, the monkey reached out and grabbed my arm. A second later it was sitting on my shoulder. Amazingly, I did not resist, nor was I frightened by the sudden presence of the small beast.

"Her name is Ma'kawa; she obviously remembers you," said Lelalu.

"Hello, Ma'kawa," I offered. "She remembers me how?"

"You will save her life one day very soon."

"Then I am her hero?" I jested.

"You are, Husband, but then you will be a hero to us all one day."

Ma'kawa stayed on my shoulder for several yards, and then she dropped back onto the tiger's back and rode there until another low branch provided a means to slip back up into the trees once again.

After the rhinoceros and giraffe blended into the entourage, it made for a festive and glorious parade. The crowd broke out into a thunderous cheer when they saw us finally enter the clearing.

I could hardly believe my eyes when I saw the throng of well-wishers lining the final steps into the village. It was almost overwhelming to this young ship's captain, for I had never before been the object of so much affection and good cheer. It was as if I were a triumphant hero returning from a faraway battlefield.

I was instantly surrounded, and warm smiles greeted me. A woman was the first to approach me. She smiled, raised her right hand, extended it, and laid it upon my right shoulder. I must have appeared totally perplexed by this action, because Lelalu stepped forward immediately, took hold of my right hand, and placed it onto the woman's right shoulder. The woman then bowed her head. Lelalu motioned for me to do the same. Then a man greeted me in the same manner.

I realized that this was the formal custom of greeting for the Minchon people. This greeting, I would learn later, was a venerated one and older than the Minchon Nation, begun in the very distant past when enemies would gather on the battlefield in an effort to make peace or to parlay.

As two warriors approached each other, they would raise their right hands to demonstrate they carried no weapon and they were approaching only to speak. Then they would each lay their hand upon the other's shoulder as a way to further demonstrate that this was a personal peace. The bowing of the head was also of great significance to the ceremony. As they bowed their heads, their eyes would fall from the face of their opponent to the ground as a way of establishing trust; for it is common knowledge that during combat, one never takes his eyes off his opponent in order to prevent a surprise thrust from a weapon. As this was a peaceful coming together, it was meant to demonstrate that each man was exhibiting trust toward the other, and that no hostility would occur.

In time, as the wars finally ended, this greeting was retained as a beautiful and elegant way of greeting one another with respect and courtesy.

And so, such a greeting of the village was extended toward me. Each and every villager greeted me in like manner. Needless to say, it took a great deal of time for the greeting ceremony to be completed. But no one seemed to mind.

"Everyone is joyful at your return, Husband. They have all missed you very much."

"So it would seem. Although I cannot understand why."

After the villagers personally greeted me, they moved to one side of the village and stood gracefully still, their hands folded in front of them, their warm and gentle smiles still on their faces.

In all, they presented themselves as a beautiful race. Their light brown coloring accentuated their elegant form. The structure of their faces was like none I had ever seen. Such striking beauty in all the people was difficult for me to comprehend. I looked into all the faces and I could not see one who would be considered unattractive. They stood straight and proud, but their pride was not derived from their outer beauty, it exuded outward from what lay hidden within. Then I put an understanding to it all. What shone without was the peace of what lay within. Like Lelalu, they, too, were a people fully at peace, filled by a fullness of joy that only a truly gentle spirit could endow them with.

I noticed that on the other side of the clearing lay a multi-tiered wooden throne where four significantly decorated figures sat very still, and yet they also retained that infectiously warm smile and outer glow of peace and tranquility.

When the last of the villagers had finished the greeting and moved over to where the other villagers stood patiently, they bowed together as one. I looked toward the throne, and even the four great ones on the throne arose and bowed. I started to bow also, but Lelalu stopped me from doing so.

"Do I not return their respect with my own?"

"No. Not this one."

"But why, Lelalu? Why do they bow to me? I am not worthy of such respect."

"They are showing their reverence to the hero you will one day become. It is to that man they now bow."

"The future me?"

"Yes, Cornelius."

She immediately recognized the now familiar blurring in my eyes that appeared when I was about to feel overwhelmed and lost. "Relax, Husband," she said, taking hold of my arm. "Relax, and just enjoy. In time, all will become clear."

I was thankful for her grip upon my arm. It served to reassure me I was not losing my mind, nor was I how lost in some wild dementia. I could feel her devoted love for me, and it strengthened me greatly.

I could also feel the warmth and admiration of the village itself. I felt safe, and certain that I had indeed been blessed and not cursed. Perhaps, in some manner, this was heaven after all.

With the entrance parade now concluded, I was directed to the foot of the throne. I noticed how simple and yet elegant its construction was. Made of logs and laced with fragrant wild island flowers, the structure consisted of three distinct levels. Two decorated wooden thrones were on each level, separated by what I can best describe as an aisle made from smoothed oyster shells, with inlaid symbols created with polished and cut precious and semi-precious stones of various colors.

The lowest level thrones were empty. I immediately assumed they were for positions yet to be filled.

The next level thrones were occupied by a seated man and woman, was beautifully adorned with flowers, extraordinarily embroidered cloth of bright animal shapes, and what appeared to me as some form of written symbols. The man and the woman were adorned in finely woven cloth robes also emblazoned with colorful symbols and letters or hieroglyphs of some nature. I surmised the couple were also a part of the royal family, but lesser in the hierarchy of power and respect.

"Remain silent, Cornelius. At mid-level is Amog, our High Priest, and his wife, Melatu."

Upon the highest part of the structure sat what I presumed were Lelalu's parents, the king and queen of the island kingdom, King Gogui and Queen Letula. Each wore a head covering made of pure gold and encrusted with rubies, emeralds, and diamonds, the likes of which I had never seen. They were magnificent-looking creatures, with robes made of even finer woven cloth and adorned with cloth symbols, each covered with fine jewels sewn meticulously onto them. The grass-thatched roof covered the entire structure, shielding all beneath it from the elements.

Lelalu looked toward the western sky. The sun was now only a glowing red ember halfway dipped into the blackness of the sea.

"It is time, my love," she said softly.

In all my confusion, I turned to Lelalu and started to speak, but she spoke first. "Just stand and say nothing until my father speaks to you. You are never allowed to speak to him first. Whenever you wish to speak to the king, you must approach him and stand still and silent until he acknowledges you. Such action demonstrates warrior humility.

Now, lower your eyes, Cornelius. Your eyes should always be directed toward the ground in his presence until the conversation begins. It is a sign of respect, trust, and loyalty."

I did as she instructed and stood still, staring at the ground. Lelalu fell silent and assumed a similar position. Within seconds, the music finally ceased and the drums slowly wound down until they beat a final thud and then remained silent as well.

I heard the rustle of cloth from somewhere above me. I assumed it was the king standing and preparing himself to speak. Seconds later, his powerful voice boomed out over the throng of celebrants. I could not understand his words, for they were similar to those spoken by the brown giants back on the beach earlier that morning. It was a wonderfully pleasing tone, and coupled with the king's rich baritone voice, it calmed me.

He spoke for a just a minute or two and a joyous laughter arose from the crowd. He spoke once again and more laughter arose. Then he spoke a third time. Lelalu, without shifting her position, offered a translation for my benefit.

"My father officially announced your return to Minchon Island and greeted you with warmth and genuine affection. He said that he was pleased with the return of his son and brother warrior." Then she chuckled. "He also told the people of how you arrived and the events of the morning when you tried to outrun his warrior guards. It was very amusing to all. He will now greet you as an honored guest and officially welcome you back home and once again into the Minchon family."

Upon her completion, I heard the heavy footsteps of enormous bare feet walking down the steps of the center aisle. Seconds later, the king stopped directly before me. I waited, nervously, having failed to prepare anything to say. Being unfamiliar with the language, I did not know what I was going to say to the king anyway. I became afraid I would somehow say the wrong thing, or even the right thing but in an unflattering manner.

I felt sweat dripping off my face. It must have been obvious to him that I was fearful, for I heard him say other words. Laughter once again arose from the crowd, confusing me.

Lelalu chuckled. "My father noticed how wet your face is. He said you must be a great and powerful warrior to possess your own personal rain cloud to cool you."

I suddenly relaxed and even choked out a small laugh.

Then that melodic baritone voice bellowed once again. "Cornelius," the king said in perfect English, "raise your head upward and face me now as a future son, brother, and fellow warrior. Once more, will you join all your warrior brothers and sisters and be as before, now once again, a hero and good fellow to all?"

I raised my head and found the king towering over me, for he also was a giant unto me. He grinned boldly, his bright white teeth almost glowing.

I trembled and he must have noticed it, for suddenly he spread his arms wide; an instant later, they engulfed me, and I was lost in a combination of huge muscular arms and bounds of royal cloth. He then laughed such a joy-filled laugh — a laugh he had given birth to deep within his belly and bubbled upward to his mouth in an eruption of mirth. Then the whole of the village joined in the laughter.

I did not know how to react, and so I stood there dumb and embraced in the king's immense arms for what seemed a long time. Finally he unfurled his arms, and within another flash, his robe was upon my shoulders. Another instant later, his golden headdress was settled down upon my head.

I was too shocked to protest or even to respond at all. Then he grabbed my arm and pulled me up the aisle and sat me down upon his throne, dazed and bewildered. My wits were absent my brain — my thoughts refusing their existence. So there sat I, a humble shipwrecked captain, wet with perspiration, confused and stunned, upon the throne reserved for the King of Minchon Island. A moment later I noticed, through the blurring mist of my thoughts and vision, Lelalu seated upon the queen's throne next to me, resplendent in her mother's adornments. She took my hand and held it firmly, offering what support she could to the docile idiot seated beside her.

Time passed, but I did not know how long it was before my brain partially engaged and began to function — and my eyes began once more to move about in their sockets. The celebration had begun once again. The music and drums were playing, but I had no memory of exactly when they had begun.

As the mist dispersed, I noticed that out in the center of the clearing, the king and queen were dancing, singing, and laughing as if they were just the ordinary villagers enjoying the frantic frolic of the event.

Lelalu, noticing my return, squeezed my hand. I slowly looked over at her. Our eyes met, mine still steeped in confusion. She sensed my great puzzlement and offered me an explanation.

"You do not understand why we occupy the seats of command, do you?"

I could only shake my head.

"It is the warrior way of humility. Tonight the king and queen are as the common people while we are held on high, observed as holding the dignity of the island. See how they dance, my mother and father. They are truly joyful at your return, my husband. They, too, have been awaiting your homecoming for a long time. Tonight, Cornelius, the island is fully restored to its material form and its hero has returned. There is much to celebrate."

I had no lucid response. I sat mesmerized, by what unfolded below me. I dumbly watched as another brown-skinned giant walked up the aisle to deliver two gourds, each decorated with a flower sitting on top. He handed one to Lelalu and one to me. I blankly took it from his hand. He bowed deeply and then turned and walked back down the aisle.

Lelalu lifted the flower from my gourd.

I began to raise it my lips to drink, but she stretched out her hand and stopped me.

"No. You must first stand and speak to the village."

I gazed at her as a complete imbecile. I did not know what I was supposed to say or in what manner I was to speak.

"Stand," Lelalu instructed. "Stand and say something."

Finally, my voice loosened, but my brain had not yet fully engaged. "Wh…what do I say?"

"Anything, my love. Thank them for bringing you back home. Tell them how much you have missed them all. It doesn't really matter what you say. Just rise and say something. The words are not important. It is the gesture they seek. It is the anointing of the celebration they desire."

I tried to get my brain to work. My head was suddenly full of luminary images of gratitude, praise, and inspiration. My head was full, but my mouth had trouble translating the images into intelligible words.

Finally, the drums stop beating and the pipes and flutes quieted. All eyes turned toward me in anticipation of my expected blessing. In my head, I arranged some exquisite thoughts, but when I stood and prepared to open my mouth to speak, they disappeared in another haze of confusion and trepidation.

I stood in dumb stillness for what seemed to me to be the longest time, but the village stood in absolute patience and silence, breathlessly awaiting my royal words.

It seems so foolish today as I recall that glorious moment. There I was, standing upon the throne before the gathering of the whole village, numbered in the hundreds, as they awaited words of wisdom and grace delivered in eloquence and dignity from their honored guest. What they got, however, was a simple and shaken man standing before them as a blockhead, not knowing what to say at all.

Finally, fighting back my instinct to say nothing for fear of saying something wrong or inappropriate, I raised my gourd high into the air. I could hear their breathing cease. All was quiet. Not even the insects made a sound, nor the leaves of the surrounding trees. Even the nightly breeze ceased. I opened my mouth and said, "I'm home." I then fell back into silence and drank from the gourd.

The village erupted in cheers and laughter. The celebration then continued as if I were not there at all. I could not believe I had uttered only two simple and uninspiring words. I felt an incompetent fool; but below me, the celebrants reacted as if I had delivered a speech of inspiring significance. I then realized the truth of what Lelalu had told me. It was not my words but the gesture that was important. I had anointed the celebration, and that was all that was expected of me. Once again, I had allowed myself to be paralyzed with fear and idiotic thoughts of grandeur.

Then it struck me with full force. I was not anyone important yet. I had not accomplished all the things they knew I would accomplish. I was simply an honored guest. A one-night king of a celebration.

I smiled broadly, realizing they were going to allow me to grow in my own time and in my own way.

I sat down and looked to Lelalu.

"Just enjoy the celebration, correct?" I asked now in an assured manner.

"Yes," she smiled.

I understood what she meant. Tonight was for celebrating. It happened to be for welcoming me back to the island, but it could have been for any reason at all. Tonight I was to rest, relax, and enjoy. There was no pressure placed upon me by anyone save what I chose to heap upon myself. There was no expectation save only to be joyful for my return.

I looked out over the village and noted the hundreds of small and simple grass huts. They looked fresh and recently built. I wondered how long they had been there. Then I recalled what Lelalu had said to me only moments before.

"Wife," I boldly asked, "I recall you saying something about the island being now fully restored to its material form."

"Yes."

"Then all of this is newly formed?"

"Yes."

"How is that possible?"

"If I tell you while you are in your present state, your head will spin again. Might we discuss this another day?"

I knew she spoke the truth, and if she had to put it to me in those terms, then I was certain it was a discussion for another time. I wanted to enjoy my celebration without the dizziness of all that would be learned on a different day. So I smiled warmly at her. "Another time, then, my love. Tonight I will just enjoy myself."

"Shall we dance?"

"Are we allowed to do that?"

"Of course, silly. It is *your* celebration."

And so we danced.

After a great while, I noticed Amog standing with his back to the crowd, engaged in a discourse with his wife.

"I must speak with Amog," I told Lelalu.

"That would not be wise, Husband."

"Tonight I am king, am I not?"

"Tonight, Husband, you are king."

"Then the king will speak to the High Priest. I wish to set a time to begin my warrior training and he is the one who selects the trainees, is he not?"

"Yes. He is."

"Very well. Then I shall have words with him."

Lelalu laughed and shook her head. "As you wish, great one, but I would not speak to him as king, but as a man — a humble man, my dear."

I thought about what Lelalu had said and realized her suggestion toward caution should be exercised, for I did not know then just who Amog was, nor his place in the structure of Minchon Island, save as the High Priest, and I also did not yet have an understanding of the significance of that position. Still, I thought, if I was respected for my achievements thus far, I should not approach a fellow warrior with trepidation or uncertainty. A bit of boldness displayed during a first meeting was often a sign of surety and strength of character in my former world. I expected, then, it might be the same for any other world. Therefore, I strode boldly, but respectfully, up behind Amog.

"Amog, great one. I wish to introduce myself. I am …"

"Who is this who speaks to me with such impudence?" he bellowed.

"I am…Cornelius, great one." I replied, my knees suddenly beginning to tremble as bile rose from my stomach into my throat. *Had I begun this conversation all wrong?* I asked myself. *Was not my boldness appreciated and respected here in this new land?*

He did not turn around, but stood with his back to me as he continued. "Silence!" he bellowed once again. "Who are you that you feel worthy to speak to me? You are but a child in the ways of the warrior. You, who are not yet a warrior, are therefore not yet fit to speak. You, who are barely able to hear the words of a true warrior. Speak to me no more, you undisciplined wild child, lest you find your ears buried headlong in the sand below your feet."

He abruptly walked away without having looked at me at all.

"So, my husband, you have found favor in the mind of Amog," said Lelalu, walking up behind me and hugging me.

"That was a *favorable* response?"

"Indeed. It would appear that Amog is fond of you, Husband."

"He is fond of me?" I said, stunned and embarrassed. "How did you deduce that from his boorish behavior? He did not even have the courtesy to turn and face me while he dealt me such a sharp blow."

Lelalu laughed. "My precious, precious man. You do yet not understand our ways. He is greatly fond of you. You have found his favor with your boldness and your respect towards him. Raising him up as you unwittingly did, he sees you as my father does, a man of bold character and yet a man who is respectful and knows his place. I am very pleased with you, Husband. Exceedingly so."

Chapter 9

I awoke into complete darkness. I stretched out my hands and felt around for anything recognizable, but I felt nothing at all. I then realized I was lying on something firm. I felt around my body and tried to move, only to tip over and fall a foot or so onto a sand floor from a now obvious hammock. Continuing my tactile search in the darkness from this sandy level, I finally discovered I was alone inside one of the grass huts I had noticed the night before.

I remembered dancing for hours, until I felt exhausted. They must have put me in this hut and I had fallen asleep. It appeared to my mind as something as simple as that. I crawled around in the blackness until I found what felt like a door latch.

I stood up and lifted the latch. A horribly bright light shot directly into my eyes. I closed them immediately, pushed open the door, and stepped forward. I instantly felt the heat of the new day's sun upon me, but held my eyes tightly closed. I placed my right hand over my eyes and decided to open them slowly until they had adjusted to the bright morning sunlight.

Within seconds I heard voices of people gathering around me. I assumed it was more well-wishers greeting their hero once again. I was eager to greet them as well, but the blinding light made for a slow adjustment.

Finally, staring down into the sand, I opened my eyes. When I thought they might be adjusted enough, I raised my head and removed my hand from my eyes, expecting to see my worshippers standing before me. But as I raised my head, I noticed only two new brown giants grinning at me. They were holding something between them and they thrust it at me.

As I was struck full body with a splash of cool water. The coolness of the water shocked me completely awake as I was startled by my instant bath. I heard laughter coming from all around me then. I opened my eyes, which had shut involuntarily from the water, once again and saw the village people laughing uproariously all about me.

"Good morning, Your Highness," one of the giants said with a bright white grin and in perfect English. "Your presence is required on the shore, Great One. Follow us."

They dropped the large tub made from twigs and leaves and turned away. They jogged a short distance and then stopped and looked back, beckoning to me with their large arms.

I gathered my wits and jogged after them, but as I neared them they both shot away. I tried my best to follow them, but the sand was more like small traps slowing me.

We ran for several minutes until we broke through the brush and out onto the shoreline. There I saw several dugout canoes, each with its own outriggers for stability in the ocean waters, lined up along the shoreline; every boat was surrounded by many young men.

I followed my giants to one particular boat, where they both took their places alongside it. There was one empty place. One of the giants pointed it out to me. "You there," he said.

I took my place obediently. He made several indistinguishable sounds, and then they all bent and lifted the boat up and walked it to the water. I grabbed it also and walked with them.

Moments later, the canoes were out on the ocean, each man pulling on an oar and chanting in some unintelligible tones. We rowed for what seemed like fifteen to twenty minutes. Loud grunts from others I perceived to be the leaders, were meant as some kind of directions to the crew. I perceived these men to be the coxswains of the boats as I understood the position.

All oars ceased rowing. All canoes stopped and bobbed about in the surf.

On our canoe, as on the other boats, the coxswain's hands slapped together and then the oars were brought in toward the center of the canoe. Then he stood up in the boat and grabbed a coil of rope secured to a roll of netting lying in the center of the canoe. Seconds later, and after several swirls of the net over his head, like a lariat, the net was cast far out into the water, where it sank beneath the surface. After another gesture from the coxswain, everyone grabbed a place on the long rope which was woven into one of the rungs of net and began pulling it in toward the boat. Moments later I saw a bountiful catch of a wide variety of fish.

Once the fish were aboard, a quick sorting process was immediately undertaken by all. They tossed away those fish that were considered less desirable for a variety of reasons.

I stopped my sorting long enough to look around at my mates. They were muttering in their unique language, smiling, and seemed to be generally very pleasant fellows.

One of them noticed my stare. He looked up at me and grinned. I nodded to him. He grabbed a fish and tossed it into my face and laughed. Then they all laughed, and so did I. I felt instantly accepted. I picked up a fish and tossed it into his face and chuckled, thinking it an appropriate response to my comical initiation.

As with Lelalu at the pool earlier, what I had expected to be taken as my own comedic response did not carry off at all as I intended it to. His instant reaction sent my heart to flutter. His smile instantly disappeared, and his grin turned to a clenched and angry scowl. The others on the boat stopped what they were doing as well and looked harshly at me as if I had committed some unpardonable sin.

I realized at once I must have done something wrong. Panic set in. I wondered what I should do next. I felt I was about to be assaulted, and tried to think quickly as to how to defend myself. I was no match for their strength, but I was trained in the ways of close-order combat aboard my father's ship. To be clear, though, they were many against me. I determined I would use their strength, size, and numbers against them.

I prepared myself both mentally and physically for the expected assault and was prepared to strike back as a serpent. The giant whose face had received the fish leaned toward me and continued his scowl. My muscles tightened. I was ready for anything.

Then suddenly his eyes grew wide, the grin returned, and he burst out in hearty laughter. It was once again a ruse. I felt dim-witted, but I began laughing as well. Soon everyone on the boat was laughing rowdily. An instant later, two giants, one on each side of me, lifted me out of the boat as if I weighed nothing at all and tossed me into the ocean.

As my head broke the surface, I saw they were still howling. Now, certainly understanding I was the butt of all the gaiety and mischief, I laughed harder. I nodded, thus indicating my now more humble acceptance of my initiation.

Seconds later, several hands grabbed me and lifted me back into the boat and patted my shoulder. I was now officially one of the Brothers of the Boat, and until that moment I had not even known such a brotherhood existed.

The sorting process continued, and then the net was cast again and the process repeated until after a little less than an hour, we seemingly had enough fish. It certainly seemed so to me, for the small boat was nearly overflowing with fish. All of us sat, completely surrounded waist high, with the catch of the day.

As we paddled back towards shore, we sang and chanted some other strange tune. I surmised that it was intended for both entertainment and to give rhythm to the paddling.

Nearing the shore, one of my new brothers in another boat blew a shell horn. I assumed it was announcing our arrival, for like an explosion, the flailing and running bodies of many of young women and children burst out of the underbrush. They ran to greet the returning boats.

I immediately understood all that was happening. This was a daily ritual. The young men went fishing every morning to catch the fish — the true sustenance for the village, and the young women and children greeted them upon their return with gratitude and celebration for another day of good tidings.

I saw Lelalu running with the rest of the women. She was royalty — a princess — and yet, in this crowd of women, she was just another individual who joyously ran to greet the returning boats as the ritual required.

She ran directly to me and smiled, but she did not touch me. I reached out my hand toward her, but she shook her head to say *no*. I understood. The greeting was not intended for any particular individual but for the boats as a whole.

All present, then, worked together with extraordinarily efficient teamwork. As soon as the boats struck the sand, the men began to clean the fish, emptied the fish innards back into the ocean, and then handed the cleaned fish to the women and children, who immediately ran them onto a rope. When the rope was full, they tossed them over their shoulders and carried them back to the village for further processing. It was an extremely well-organized process, and one, as a ship's captain, I appreciated and respected.

I watched Lelalu work with the other women as if she was just another villager with no special privileges whatsoever. She did glance at me from time to time and smile that infectious smile of hers, but then she returned to her duties.

After the fish were suitably processed, the men carefully rinsed off their boats in the ocean and then lifted them up out of the water, returning them once again to the safety of the still sparkling clean and tidy shoreline. Their work was completed.

I observed all that happened around me and joy filled my heart. It felt good to contribute to such wonderful people. As with Lelalu, I was expected to do my job as any other young man assigned to the boats.

When we finished our work, we all walked back to the village. I noted that the crew of each boat did not mingle with the crew of another boat during the work process. Each crew took care of its own, but after the work was done, we all intermingled again. Once again, I, being a ship's captain, completely understood how each crew worked together in harmony and in their own way.

Each boat had a leader and each crewmember knew their job well. I noted, with keen interest, the precision of each crewman towards his given task. There was no need for words. The leader did not have to bark out orders. Each crewmember knew what his job was and did it. The entire process, from start to end, was a treatise on how to organize and conduct a boat operation for maximum efficiency and productivity. By any standard it was an impressive display of leadership in managing boat crews. Their training and discipline were superb.

I learned later that the position of a crewman in the boat was as precisely assigned as any task. The leader, or once again, the coxswain, as was the term that I used for this position, was the first position. He was also the caster of the net. He decided where and when the net would be tossed. If he was wrong about his decision, then the net, drawn back in empty, was met with horror by the crew. The leader was held responsible for failing his boat and the village in general. A full net was expected on each toss.

To be a boat leader was an important position in the village, as I would soon learn. A leader was responsible for providing food for the entire village. It was a position earned, not assigned. The crew would pick their leader, and he would hold that position at the crew's discretion or until he reached a certain age and was removed from the boats altogether — to be assigned a different task within the village or to begin his official warrior training.

There were twelve positions assigned to each boat. The positions further aft of the bow were positions of lesser import. The net caster and the nearer positions were of greater import to the hierarchy of the boat, and were assigned positions one through six. Typically, the leader was eventually chosen and advanced in rank from the four furthest forward positions.

I was placed in what I would soon learn was position number six, which led the aft six positions. It was still considered the 'learner's' position, but because of my seamanship experience, I was given the highest position of this aft duty. Upon learning more of my position, I took it much more seriously. I was determined to become a part of the forward four as soon as possible, and leader of the boat soonest thereafter as might be achievable. I was a brash and bold lad back then, and full to the brim with sand.

Upon reaching the village, there was what could best be called a welcoming celebration. The young boat crews were paraded through the village in recognition of their daily achievement to bring home the food.

We gathered in one end of the village and were ceremoniously served a wonderful breakfast consisting of cooked flour that could be best compared to pancakes, along with cooked eggs, fresh fruit, and fruit nectar.

The breakfast meal was provided by those responsible for tending to the fowl raised for eggs and the milk-producing animals, goats as it were, and for gathering the fruit for the morning meal. The boat crews provided the fish for the midday and evening meals. Each of them, like us, was carefully chosen for their respective tasks. I learned that red animal meat was not eaten within the Minchon Nation. I never saw any swine at all.

Each man was served by his family in honor of his successful achievement. Among the village population, the 'providers,' as they were called, were highly respected and greatly honored.

Lelalu served my breakfast to me. As she knelt in front of me to present my food and drink, she smiled lovingly and then placed her right hand against my left cheek. "I have great affection for you, Cornelius. I give thanks to you for your hard work this morning."

I was warmed by her loving remarks, and then heard similar statements from the families around me concerning other boat crewmen and providers. I realized then this greeting and expression of gratitude was also a part of traditional ritual.

Then Lelalu picked up the first piece of mango, knowing well enough that it was my favorite, and placed it into my mouth. I later learned that the etiquette of the ritual required that the family give the first bites of food to the 'providers' in recognition and gratitude for their skillful efforts. I found it to be a wonderful ritual, and one which I earnestly came to respect and take very seriously thereafter. It was a lesson in humility, unselfishness, gratitude, and respect. It was a beautiful thing to watch how the ceremonies were conducted. They encouraged a loving and reverential atmosphere, and as I watched it all, I knew I did not wish to be anywhere else on the earth at that time. I felt instantly and gloriously happy and content.

As we ate our breakfast together, Lelalu explained that to work on the boat or as another provider each day was an honor and a privilege, not an entitlement. Through ritualistic voting, the village selected each young man who worked as a provider. Not every young man was so privileged, and the position was not considered permanent, but subject to change at any time. If any provider was found negligent or lacking in his or her true purpose or spirit, then he or she could be removed from the providing crew by a simple vote of the village.

She explained that although it was far less common than one would think, people would be voted off the crews; this was done often enough to impart a clear message and a stern warning to the other young men and women to work hard and take their responsibilities with great seriousness. She also hinted that a young person could be removed from the provider crews for disciplinary reasons, to keep the young people's attention toward duty and warrior growth in line with the expectations of both his or her family and the village as a whole.

She stressed that it was a great honor to be so quickly assigned to a boat. "The assignment to a boat usually takes years," she explained. "And although I admit I am perplexed as to why the king would risk so much so quickly with you, he is the king."

"What do you mean?" I asked, perplexed myself.

"Last night as you slept, the king himself nominated you to be added to the boat crew. There was a great discussion regarding your character and worthiness. My father spoke very highly of you and said he perceived your character to be great and worthy of the villagers' trust. He also stated that your skill as a seaman and your experience as a ship's captain warranted such trust. Several others spoke up in support of your position on the boat crew. Even Amog himself stood in your support. In the end, the village agreed and a vote was taken on your behalf.

You were assigned to a boat and your position on that boat was also voted on by the crew itself."

I was stunned to hear of such a discussion and vote, for I had heard nothing during the night. I had slept soundly.

"I am honored that both your father and Amog feel so much trust for me."

"They are both very wise and astute about the character of all the men in this village," she stated firmly. "So if they found you worthy, then you must be so. And apparently, the village agreed."

"Where I'm from originally, the king's word was law. But it is not the case here? I'm not on the boat because he had decreed it?"

"His words carry much weight, but it is a matter for the whole village to decide, not for the king to decide alone."

"I have never heard of a king to be…so…democratic."

"You will find, Cornelius, that in matters which affect the whole village, my father requires all to speak and be heard. In fact, it is required as part of a warrior's responsibility training."

"It sounds wonderful. Where I'm from, it is easy to withhold your thoughts and shirk from your civic responsibilities, but then it is most often those who choose not to participate in civic affairs who grumble and complain the loudest when the rules don't suit them."

"I understand, my husband, but you will not find that behavior much tolerated here. Here it is the duty of everyone to participate in the affairs which affect us all."

"Then I shall make my voice heard when it is important to be heard. I accept my responsibility with respect and humility. I only hope the village, your father, and Amog continue to find me worthy."

She did not say so, but I saw in Lelalu's eyes that she was very proud for me for such a consideration.

A question then arose in my mind. "Lelalu, I'm confused. Why was there a question raised at all? Am I not a returning hero? Should not my history of dependence and worth already have been established?"

"That is the future you, my love. You have not yet grown into that position."

My head began to ache from the questions arising out of the paradox concerning past, present, and future understandings again. I must admit that it was a perplexing concept at that time.

Lelalu cautioned me not to become full of myself, for the vote taken the previous night had ousted another young man who was found to be lacking in his responsibilities of duties and training. He was not happy about the vote and had stormed off into the night. "We have not heard from him since," Lelalu said.

"What is his name?"

"His name is Mata'pang, and you would do well to avoid him for the next several days, if he should return."

"Would he attempt to do me harm?"

"He is undisciplined and lacks humility. He might challenge you if you press him."

"I can also fight, Lelalu. He would do well to avoid me if—"

Her index finger pressed my lips closed. "Do not speak of violence here, Cornelius. Such words and attitudes are not tolerated. I did not mean that he would seek to engage physically with you. His challenge would be more mental, emotional, and spiritual. For that contest, my love, you are currently defenseless against Mata'pang. Seek, therefore, avoidance if you are able. That is your only defense against such a challenge for the time being."

"He must be very young, then. I learned discipline at a very early age."

"He is near to your age, but he lacks maturity. He is possessed of youthful exuberance and immature sensibilities. It is why my father rejected him as my husband.

"Husband?" I asked in shock. "You and he were once betrothed?"

"It was long ago, my love. We have known each other since we were children. We were matched as youngsters, but both my father and his learned of his immaturity and his propensity for stirring up trouble. Our marriage was thus called off."

"Shall he not grow from his immaturity with training and time?"

"One's growth is taken extremely seriously here, Cornelius. During what we call the 'child' years, one's brashness and ignorance are tolerated, but when one reaches one's eighth year, that tolerance is cast aside and replaced with certain expectations. It is another ritual wherein the child is spiritually transformed into the 'youth' years. It is during these years that one begins to learn responsibilities and duty, both to themselves and to the village. Not much is expected of them. Only that they put forth the effort to learn of the ceremonies and rituals and their importance to all, and, of course, to partake in them.

"At fifteen, another ritual is performed, the 'youth' giving way to the 'young adulthood' years. It is during this period that specific duties are assigned. They learn what it takes to maintain the houses, the animals, the village. They are expected to know the rituals and ceremonies. They are also taught how to care for the elderly among us — a very important task for us all, for we take care of the old as they have taken care of us when we were young."

"But I have not seen anyone of extreme age. Where are they kept?"

"The elderly are not yet with us, my husband. It will be many, many years before they will exist here, but the lessons are taught now in anticipation of the time when they will be required."

"But there is always a previous generation. How can there be no elderly now?"

"As we have been recently reborn, time has not existed long enough for those here now to have aged that far."

I then realized I was about to dip into another area I would soon regret. "I will understand later, I assume?"

Lelalu laughed again. "Your wisdom grows quickly, my love. Already I see wonderful signs of it. Yes. You will learn of these things in the future."

"Then in the matter of Mata'pang, knowing it is but youth that now binds him, you still suggest I avoid him if I am able to do so?"

"He will come to you, Cornelius, but it will be at a time of his choosing, not yours. I can only say this. When he does come, he will be in an agitated state. You simply must remain observant until he makes his presence manifest. And know this, my love: he shall not come as a friend, but in that ill-advised youthful exuberance, seeking to provoke and challenge you. It would be best not to surrender to such impetuousness. If you must engage him, try to do so with the knowledge that it is you who will have to control the moment of potential contention. Be gentle, my love. He is at a point of great weakness. In that moment he will, no doubt, be defensive."

* * * * *

Over the next several months, I sought out more knowledge of precisely how the village taught their young, and I learned which practices were left behind as the child grew. Over time and incrementally, the child was given different tasks and responsibilities intended to bring that child into eventual adulthood.

In a very short time, I grew to love these people and felt an exceeding fondness toward their customs and traditions. In that love did I come to understand myself better. Lelalu proved to be most patient with me. I had much to learn, and much of what I needed to learn was patience, as I have stated before.

I was not a patient person by my very nature, and the lessons were difficult for me to master given my proclivity toward impulse and my weakness of mental endurance. In my younger years I was not taught about such things, and the learning thus was more difficult for me than for the children born into the village. In this endeavor, then, I studied harder in an effort to learn more quickly, but alas, it was this very attitude that created in me an even greater struggle to learn patience.

As I recall now, it amuses me to think that when one wishes to learn patience, one is not given calm moments to teach the workings of patience, but rather, one is given every nerve-racking and tumultuous experience instead.

In preparation for my expected meeting with Mata'pang, I therefore attempted to study the nature of anger, not realizing that I would not be given gentle times and kind experiences to learn from. Rather, I was prodded, pestered, agitated, and sorely provoked constantly by my instructors as they attempted to press me into an angry response to test my knowledge and understanding of anger and, through that, its true nature.

At first I often surrendered to such provocation. I was given to fits of wild rage and cursing, but over time, as I learned about the character of anger, I soon found myself able to resist the tendencies toward such uncontrollable outbursts. Eventually I learned how to harness such tendencies and avoid giving in to the temptation to respond to anger with anger. I must admit now, however, that the growth required a substantial amount of time to master. Years, in fact.

It proved a most difficult lesson for me to come to the crucial understanding that often anger is the simple result of our own inward inability to resolve an external issue — an outward expression of our internal disappointment with ourselves. And anger is often used as a mask to prevent others from seeing our weaknesses and lack of experience. In fact, anger is often met with anger because of our own perceived weaknesses in coping with certain stimuli. Mastering the artful avoidance of these uncomfortable issues, it seems, was particularly difficult for me.

Learning about loving and caring were not as tumultuous, but learning to love and care for another is not an easy task either. Lelalu did her best to instruct me, but I was apparently a slow student in this area of study as well.

It seems to me that loving and caring employ many other disciplines I was neither aware of nor had mastered. Certainly, thinking on it now, to exist in perfect love requires a mastery of patience, anger, and arrogance as well as many other contrary disciplines. In short, I found love to be one of the most difficult challenges to overcome, and the most intriguing discipline of all to master.

Lelalu, however, seemed to have mastered it all. Her grace and elegance and, dare I say, her patience with me were, to say the least, phenomenal. In time, I would come to learn, we were indeed matched on some higher level that only with additional time I would come to understand. For now, for me, it was enough to know we had been paired correctly by powers far greater than I would ever know.

At this time I felt I was living through splendid days. I must tell you this because the days to come would soon require of me the full utilization of every good and honorable discipline I had ever learned — simply to survive the great tragedies that were soon to follow.

Chapter 10

Over the next two months, my life on the island settled into a wonderfully predictable and uncomplicated routine. Although she would go off somewhere secretly during the morning hours, Lelalu and I had begun to take our simple midday meals away from the village at a spot near the spring where I had first met her.

I wanted to inquire as to where she went, but it felt inappropriate. If she wanted me to know, she would have told me. I believed, however, that it involved some royal duty she was required to perform each day.

With the constant menagerie of assorted animals lounging about in placid repose at any given time, we found it peaceful and serene by the spring. And there, together, we would eat and then we would lie in the hammock together and talk about almost everything under the sun. I often drifted off into a short nap with the soothing sounds of my animal friends about me.

On one particular day I found myself awaking from just such a nap to find her and all the animals gone. I remembered falling asleep with her rubbing my forehead as she usually did, while I watched the giraffes nibbling on leaves high in the canopy.

Although she was absent, she had prepared a small snack of fresh fruit, nuts, and cool fresh water for me.

I searched the village and surrounding area, but she was nowhere to be found. I even walked down the path toward the shoreline and our favorite tree where we would spend our late afternoons talking and gazing out over the ocean until it was time to prepare the evening meal. On this day, however, I saw no sign of her. Questioning the villagers concerning her whereabouts produced no satisfactory results either.

I finally ascertained that she must have ventured into the deeper portion of the jungle in some personal pursuit, and so I returned to our place near the spring and ate the fruit and drank of the water she'd left for me.

It was then I heard the crackling of brush and twigs accompanied by other sounds signaling the approach of some creature. I expected either Lelalu or some of my new animal friends to step out of the thicket, but was surprised to see a young man near to my age appear. He approached me directly, and as he did so, I noticed the purposeful stare of his dark eyes, his furrowed and troubled brow, and his long, black, shoulder-length hair flowing in the breeze created by his quick pace. His muscles rippled in the daylight, and perspiration made his brown skin glisten.

He marched straight up to me and stopped just a few feet short. He shouted something at me, but in his native language, which I, at that point in time, still had no sufficient understanding of. He then made several gestures with his hand and fingers, the meaning of which I also could not comprehend.

Still muddled in my own traditions, I extended my hand in an offer to shake his, but he only stared at it as if he had never seen such a gesture made before. I smiled at him and nodded my head in greeting, seeking to put him more at ease, but that also was to no avail. He simply glared at me and then snorted.

"My name is Cornelius, Cornelius Delightable. What is your name, friend?"

He spoke again in his native tongue, in an unfriendly manner, but since I could not understand him, I did not suffer any offense. In my short time on the island, I had already learned that just because someone spoke in an aggressive manner did not mean they intended such a meaning. Still, with my hand remaining extended in offered friendship, he seemed to want no part of any friendly interaction. Then it dawned on me who this lad might be.

"Mata'pang?" I asked." Are you Mata'pang?"

He stopped his unintelligible ranting and stared deeply into my eyes. I smiled once again. "Mata'pang? Is that your name?"

I was now certain that it was he, but he neither confirmed it nor denied it. Instead, he held his angry glare.

"It is a pleasure to meet you, Mata'pang. I regret that my presence here has caused you inconvenience. I regret very much your losing your place in the boat to me. I assure you, it was not my intent to cause you any displacement or discomfort."

He snorted again, but still held his irritated stare.

"Please accept my apology for causing such disruption in your life. Would you care to join me for a short meal?"

He finally took one more step toward me and pointed his index finger at my face. "Leave this place and do not return," he warned in perfect English.

"I would, Mata'pang. I would leave immediately if I were able to do so, but I am marooned here. I have no means by which to leave. My ship sank in a fierce and terrible storm."

"You find a way to leave."

"But I have found peace here. I wish to stay and I wish us to be friends."

"If you choose to stay, it will prove to be your undoing. We shall not be friends, and you will find no peace here, for I will destroy all that gives you peace. This I promise."

"It is not my fault that I am here."

"You are not wanted here. You were not meant to be here. Leave now."

"Perhaps, my friend, I *was* meant to come here. How are you so certain of the contrary?"

"No! You leave and soon."

With those words spoken, he spun away from me and dashed back into the thicket. I would have given chase if only for the opportunity to correct his misconception of me, but I thought it better to heed the words of Lelalu and avoid any matter of confrontation with Mata'pang at this time. Perhaps another day, after his anger had subsided, we would sit down together as civilized men and engage in a meaningful discussion to clear the air. Perhaps we would become fast friends. It was perhaps naïve of me to think this a real possibility, but it made me feel much better. Hope does spring eternal within an innocent heart!

For the time being, however, I had to let the incident go without response. As a ship's captain I had learned that it was often necessary to allow a crewman to finish venting and settle down before dispensing any meaningful dissertation which he might have found unfavorable to his cause or to his liking. Calm had often proved to be a better conduit toward any purposeful, constructive, and effective communication, especially in the presence of such strong emotions.

Another crackling turned my head in the opposite direction. Lelalu emerged from the brush and smiled tenderly at me as she approached.

"Well, done, Husband. I am very proud of your achievement."

I chuckled at her praise, for I had no idea what she spoke of. "And what have I done to deserve such praise?"

"You handled your confrontation with Mata'pang eloquently."

"You observed us?"

"Yes, and you did splendidly."

"I did not know it was he until well into the conversation. He does not seem as ill-mannered as I was led to believe."

"We were all shocked by his delay in confronting you. We were expecting such a confrontation within only days, but he seems to be growing. He obviously waited until his irritability had calmed."

"Ahhh, so I was fortunate, then, in avoiding his *genuine* wrath."

"That would appear to be the case."

"Still, he left me with a stern warning. Am I in danger if I remain here?"

"No," she responded confidently. "It was only a remnant of his zestful youth that announced such a warning — a dying ember of his impetuous nature. In fact, I think your excellent reaction put him off balance."

"Then he did come looking to provoke me to anger?"

"I believe he did, but your response was magnificent. You were able to still the rage that yet seethes within his heart. He was not prepared for such a magnanimous gesture."

"I assure you, Lelalu, I was not attempting to employ any special tactic. I was just seeking to have an understanding with him, but I apparently failed, for it appears he would not have it so."

"On the contrary, dear one. I think you have secured a strong foundation upon which to build. It will take more time, but I think you will not have to worry over such future confrontations."

"Then perhaps he will become a friend?"

"It is much too early to say, but it is wonderful that you would seek such a potential relationship. My father and Amog will be pleased to hear of this."

"Amog will hear of this?" I asked in earnest excitement.

"He will certainly hear of this. He has been keeping a close eye upon your scholarly advances lately."

I was shocked to hear of his interest in me, for I had been wondering if I would have the chance to speak with him again concerning my training, but was cautioned by Lelalu against such action. An audience with Amog was not typically initiated by the seeker, but rather initiated only through *his* desire. And to date, it appeared that he had no desire to grant me such an interview.

In my earlier life, as undisciplined as I was, that understanding would not have sat well with me, and in the brashness of my unbridled youth I would have pressed him to grant me such an audience. Of course, in that event, I would have been suitably educated in an unceremonious manner. The lesson itself would have been very brief, and undoubtedly harsh, and it would have included an understanding that an unrestrained expression of boldness was not always to one's benefit.

But I was, through both grace and fortune, past those more volatile days. I had grown toward a superior direction. Aided by my Lelalu and with the loving support of the village, I had ceased activity in those ways that could only be explained as inexperienced and youthful practices. I was a future hero of the village, and I was slowly and steadily being prepared for that role.

That evening I was approached by an eloquent couple.

"Captain Delightable, my name is Ge'no and this is my wife, Tela. Our son is Mata'pang."

"It is an honor to make your acquaintance," I responded.

"We have come to apologize for the actions of our son today. He has shamed our family."

"I will not hear this," I said. "You owe no debt for the actions of your son. He is young and undisciplined. That is the thrust of it. You are most gracious people. Let there be only gladness between us that we share this village together, and let our friendship grow."

"You are the gracious one. We thank you."

As they walked away, I saw and felt their sadness, as it is often those left behind in a tragedy who must endure it. I felt great compassion for them grip my heart.

It was during this time that my training seemed most challenging to me; often the difficulties appeared to be insurmountable. What saw me through this period was the gift of *grace*. This is a benefit that cannot be earned or commanded. By its very definition, it is a dispensation granted by those who wish to give it. It is something given without merit and for no reason other than it be the desire of those who can bestow it to do so.

And so it was with the attitude of the village toward me. It was simple grace, the wish of the village that I be given opportunity, goodwill, and favor. To be granted the opportunity to learn all that I needed to know, to become the man I would need to become so that I could, in the end, be the great hero warrior I was intended to be.

Still, I yearned to be selected for the formal Minchon Warrior training, but I learned that such a selection was by vote of the village itself. It was a selection earned by each applicant through both deed and word, and over a great time, and after much good growth and understanding of what such a selection embraces.

I knew that even I, the future hero of Minchon Island, had not yet earned my place among the applicants — let alone the student warriors. Thus, I studied harder than anyone else to learn everything that was being taught, and I excelled beyond anyone's expectations. Indeed, I was always the first to my boat in the morning. I was first to assist anyone regarding any need they had. I was always first to offer my assistance to the younger lads with their tasks. I was always the first one to accept the most difficult tasks. I was always the one who accepted the greatest responsibilities.

In all of this, I had no thought or understanding that all I was doing was rendering myself an unacceptable candidate for warrior training. Why would all my good deeds be found unacceptable, you might ask? For one very simple reason. I did all of it not to better myself but to be accepted. I was not interested in gaining wisdom, but gaining position. For all the wrong reasons, therefore, I performed all the correct deeds.

I was young and in great haste. I was so innocent, so naïve. I had so very much to learn and did not realize it then. As I think on it now, I appreciate how far I was from where I needed to be. It is still amazing to me that I ever reached my goal at all.

Still, throughout all of this, there was one goal that would not give me peace until it was fully realized. That was to secure the hand of Lelalu in marriage. For me, that was both a task and a reward measured far above any other. To accomplish this goal, I would need the blessing not only of Lelalu's parents but also of mighty Amog himself. To secure such blessing, I had to petition both the parents and Amog for an audience.

I felt that asking the parents was something I might be able to achieve without too much trouble, but an audience with Amog was yet another matter entirely. One simply did not petition for an audience with the great Amog. To petition Amog required great skill, tact, and an enormous degree of patience, traits at that time which I lacked in certitude. Still, I did possess an abundance of boldness and confidence. And, as I have said, I was young and without much fear; although I also lacked experience and wisdom — an indelicate and unfortunate combination for one so full of youthful enthusiasm. I would soon learn that I needed the skill of all the attributes together, and in great profusion, before I would be recognized by either party. Sometimes, the rush of youth can be so wasteful.

While it is true that Lelalu's parents held me in exceeding affection, they were still bound by the conventions and traditions of Minchon life. There were rules, customs, protocols, methods, and appropriate avenues of presentation which had to be observed, accepted, and practiced.

Being king and queen did not grant them any special consideration or dispensation. Nor did their position allow them to circumvent the highly held principles of the Minchon ways. In fact, as leaders, it was expected that they meet every intent and letter of the law to an exceptionally high degree and without the slightest variance.

It was a code of honor and ethics which guided Lelalu's parents, and being of astonishingly high moral character, there was never even the slightest hint of impropriety in the manner in which they governed. Thus, gaining an audience with them was to present itself as a greater challenge than I had at first imagined.

As for Amog, tradition and protocol guided his every action, along with strong spiritual and character attributes. His morals and ethics were above reproach. His conduct at all times was of the highest caliber. It was inconceivable to anyone that he could ever be coerced or bribed toward any action other than one dictated by all that was sacred to the Minchon way of life and his own inestimable conscience. He was trusted by all inhabitants of Minchon Island, and there was nothing more that could be said about him or his character.

I knew he was fond of me but he would show me no exclusive consideration. Any respect I received from him would have to be earned. But as I understood his nature, I knew that if I held true and fast to my own beliefs and character, which were considerably similar to Amog's, I would get my audience with him in a timely manner. First, though, I had to adequately demonstrate to him that I was worthy of his affection for me.

Seven weeks after my encounter with Mata'pang, while sitting in the village waiting for Lelalu to finish her chores, I spotted a fellow out of the corner of my eye, a curious man off in the distance, staring intently at me.

When I turned my eyes purposefully toward him, he did not flinch from his stare. We each sat for a good while just staring at one another. Truly, I say, it was a strange experience. I finally motioned to him to come to me, but he made no attempt at any movement in my direction. I must admit it fully to you, I was now held fast by my own curiosity. *Who was this man?*

Although he was differently attired, I finally recognized him. I had seen him on other days seated at the table of the great council. At those times he wore a large headdress which identified him as one of the elders on the council. From my recollection of his dress and manner, I now perceived him to be one of the senior members of the council. I had seen him speaking to Amog on several occasions over the past weeks. *Why is he so interested in me?* I wondered.

I then spotted Lelalu approaching from off to my left. I turned to greet her. Her usual bright smile warmed my heart greatly. Her sparkling eyes gave me the impression that she was carrying some favorable news to me. I became excited in anticipation of it.

"Good morning, my love," she cooed and kissed me on my forehead.

"Good morning to you, goddess of my life," I answered.

She giggled and then sat down next to me.

"Why the smile, Lelalu? Do you have some exciting news?"

"Nothing. I am just happy to see you."

"Your smile made me think you had something special for me."

"I do." She leaned over and kissed me once more on the forehead. "Is that special enough?"

"It is," I smiled. "My love, can you tell me about the man over there?" I asked, pointing to where the curious elder had been seated only seconds before.

"Of whom do you speak, my darling?"

I turned my head and was shocked to see that he had disappeared.

"Why...why...he's gone. He was right there only a moment ago. He has been staring at me for the longest time."

"Who, my darling?"

"One of the elders."

"One of the council elders has been staring at you?"

"Yes. For nearly a quarter hour we have been sitting here, our eyes locked onto one another. I tried to offer a chance at dialogue by motioning him over to me, but he refused. He refused by not responding to my gesture at all. It was most curious."

"Ahhh," she responded. as if she completely understood my puzzlement "That would probably be Wigiwig."

"You think the man staring at me was this Wigiwig?"

"I believe so."

"But why?"

"It is common for Wigiwig to keenly observe those who have caught the interest of Amog."

Perhaps, I then reasoned silently, I *was* being considered for some important post or function. "I see," I said. "Then am I to assume he will be shadowing me for some time?"

"I would say so, and you would do well to be on your best behavior during such an interview."

"Is that what this is, an interview?"

"Perhaps."

"Then I *am* being considered for something important?"

"Perhaps, my love."

I then grew more excited. "Do you know what I'm being considered for? Is it some great position on the council, or could it be that I will be asked to perform an important function for the village? What do you think, Lelalu? Do you think it could be an interview toward being accepted into warrior training?"

"I do not know, Cornelius. Wigiwig could be observing you for any number of reasons. I saw him once 'shadow,' as you say, another individual in this same way."

"To what end?"

"In that case he was deciding whether that person would be allowed to remain on the island."

"And what became of that individual?"

"He was banished from the island and never seen again."

A cold dread filled my brain. "So, I could be dealt a similar fate?"

"I have no idea, but if I were you, I would be very careful about which words you choose to speak and which activities you choose to participate in over the next few days."

Such words pierced me to my core. I would even say they wounded me deeply. The thought that I was being considered for possible banishment had not been even remotely conceivable to me.

Only seconds before, I'd thought I was being considered for something bold, dashing, and important. Now my expected life among these people was thrown into jeopardy. Lelalu noted my dejected expression and reached out to me and caressed my face with her hand.

"Fear not, my beloved. Have faith in yourself."

"But why am *I* being considered for banishment? Have I not exceeded all expectations during my study hours? Have I not been extremely active in the affairs of the village? Have I not always been the first to volunteer for all the difficult tasks?"

"Yes, my love. You have been all those things and much more."

"Then I do not understand why my life here is in such peril."

"Perhaps it is not, Cornelius. Perhaps you are being tested."

"For what purpose?"

"That would be a purpose known only to Wigiwig."

"Who is he that I should be concerned about what he thinks of me?"

"Wigiwig is the high elder of the council, second only to Amog in the spiritual hierarchy of Minchon culture. You would do well to show great respect toward him."

"What would interest Wigiwig about my spiritual nature?"

"Once again, Cornelius, that would be something you would have to address with Wigiwig."

"Then I shall do so. I shall ask him directly."

"Do you really think that wise? One does not challenge the elders so, Cornelius."

"If I am to be banished, then I should have a right to know the charges against me, to meet my accusers, and then be allowed to put forth a suitable defense. I will not cower away and be afraid to stand in my own defense. No! I shall stand straight and challenge the charges for my right to live here. After all, it was not my doing that I was cast here from the sea in a storm, but I am here, and I have tried to comply with all the requirements demanded of me. Why should I not be granted the opportunity to remain?

"I challenge the injustice of it all. First, I was forced to deal with the impetuous nature of Mata'pang, unaided. Now I must justify my existence to an elder who shows me no courtesy to introduce himself, to engage me directly, to present his charges against me to my face. I will not stand for this, Lelalu. I will not stand by and do nothing. If I must defend myself to all, then I shall do just that, but I will not live to cower before anyone. That is not who I am. That is not the nature of my being."

"If that is what you believe," she said with a compassionate expression, "then you should defend yourself, and you should do so vigorously and vociferously, my love. Stand tall and brave and speak your mind. Speak the truth, as you know it to be. Speak of the honesty that dwells in your heart. Let all know that Cornelius Alexander Delightable is no coward and does not shrink away in the face of adversity or challenge."

Coming from Lelalu, those strong and supportive words seemed completely out of place, for as I have stated earlier, she was one who flowed with her circumstances and surroundings. She was not one who struggled against anything. For her to suggest that I stand resolutely and argue against any charges with bold resolve was contrary to all I had seen from her until now.

Still, her words were true. If I felt an injustice was served up against me, then it was not only my right but also my obligation to challenge such an inequity.

Upon further reflection, I concluded that if I would not be willing to defend myself, then what good would I ever be — not only to myself, but to the people and village that, in the future, would come to depend upon my courage and strength of character? Without strength of conviction, without the courage to stand up for correct and moral standing, how could I ever hope to become the future hero of the Minchon Island nation?

I felt encouraged when I remembered that I was to be the future hero of these people. I deduced that I must have stood up against the charges being formulated by Wigiwig and prevailed or I would not be here when the time came for the hero within me to emerge.

I therefore determined to meet his challenge head on, but only after further consideration regarding the manner in which I would respond, for to stumble into an altercation without forbearance was the act of youthful inexperience and a true sign of immaturity.

"Then again, my love," she started, "perhaps Wigiwig is observing you for a great and wondrous task, as you first considered."

I was instantly thrust once more into a confusing consciousness. Was I overreacting, or overanalyzing? Was I, in my inexperience, making something complicated out of something simple? Perhaps it was as I had first considered. Perhaps I *was* being considered for a great task and he was observing me to decide if I had the character for such a task. If I were to challenge him indecorously, ranting on about my rights and obligations, perhaps he would think me too wild and unpredictable for any important chore.

I had done it once again. I had confused myself thoroughly and to the point where I questioned everything. I had bewildered myself into certain paralysis, and in so doing, I lost all direction. Then a fresh thought seared into my brain.

"I will think on it tonight, Lelalu. Before I take any action at all, I shall give it great consideration. I do not wish to act in haste or in a misdirected manner. I shall consider the possibilities for his presence carefully."

"That is a wonderful idea, Cornelius."

"But," I stated emphatically, "If there is to be a challenge tomorrow, I intend to stand with boldness and confront Wigiwig with a challenge of my own."

"Take great care, beloved. Wigiwig is not one to challenge lightly. Certainly you must approach him with boldness of surety and faith, yet you must also observe all issues of courtesy and respect. He is an elder of great standing in our community. Choose, therefore, your first words with great care, for they will be used to judge both you and your petition. Spoken poorly, both may be summarily rejected."

"I understand. That is why I shall study upon my case throughout tonight."

"Cornelius, I must further add this. You are assuming there is a challenge that needs to be met. What if you approach Wigiwig and confront him with an issue that is non-existent? What then?"

"There will be no challenge yet, my love. I shall simply inquire as to my status. To remain silent and appear weak, however, would do me more harm than good. And I will not appear weak to anyone. To do such would only serve to invite further harassment in the future. It is not my nature to allow that."

"Then tread forward, beloved, and make yourself known to him. Do so with boldness and certainty. To ease you on your way, I offer these words. It is widely known that Wigiwig is Amog's man. It is also generally acknowledged that they were once bitter rivals but now they work in unison as trusted partners.

"I would suggest, therefore, that you go forth with the knowledge you have already found favor in the eyes of Amog. Nevertheless, dear one, go lightly, for you do not know the true reason for Wigiwig's observation of you. Avoid rushing headlong into a confrontation without good reason."

I was immediately comforted by Lelalu's gentle words of encouragement and advice. And given her status and experience here on the island, both of which were considerable, I took her words as sound counsel. I would do nothing about Wigiwig's presence this day unless it was pressed upon me. I would sleep on such a decision and settle on what action, if any, to take on the morrow, during my fishing duties.

Chapter 11

Excusing herself to pursue some official duty, Lelalu left me alone with my observer, who returned immediately after Lelalu left the vicinity.

Upon seeing him again, I decided it would probably be best if I simply tried to ignore his haunting of me — as if that were possible, for he constantly shadowed me without any attempt to mask his intent or presence.

Even though I could see no constructive purpose in his behavior, it was most perplexing and, I dare say, a bit unnerving at times. Still, I resolved to take no overt action toward him until I had slept on the matter.

In any event, Lelalu's words continued to echo in my mind. I was not certain of his true purpose, and I felt a certain hesitancy to confront him over such a seemingly harmless act. I felt no immediate outward threat nor any apparent malice in his attendance, or in his actions. Perhaps there was no sinister intent at all. Perhaps it was as I had first suspected, an innocent observation, an assessment, as it were, for some honorable and greater purpose.

Perhaps he was simply an unusually curious fellow, who found it easier to surrender to such curiosity than to struggle against the addiction.

I finally resolved the matter in my head once and for all. That is to say, I determined that unless he took some openly hostile action toward me or Lelalu, I would ignore his presence to the best of my ability and dutifully go about my own daily doings until I could think on it more clearly that evening.

And so it was throughout the day, no matter where I went or what I was doing, I felt his persistent presence. Whenever curiosity got the better of me and I looked up from my task, he was easy to find, always there at a discreet distance, openly observing me with seemingly great interest.

Now, I must admit to you that ignoring him was much more difficult than I could ever have imagined; I felt his stare as if it were an insect crawling across my skin. Finally, after several more hours, his ulterior motive became clear to me. He wished to annoy me.

Perhaps the annoyance was a test unto itself, I then reasoned. Perhaps it was a simple test of nerve. He wanted to learn how I might react to such intimidation. If I responded in haste or in any way inappropriately, I felt, I would fail in such an outward assessment of my character. That was decidedly not a good thing for me, or so I believed.

Then another thought wandered into my brain: perhaps this was more of a test of courage, a test to see if I was brave enough to confront him. But what if I was wrong?

There it was once again. In only moments, I had successfully confounded myself yet another time. I truly did not know how I should respond to this matter, and I had so thoroughly confused myself by putting forth so many potential scenarios that I could not decide which one might be correct — or which one would prove me to be an unworthy fool.

This had been a problem for me since my youth. I often considered so many varying resolutions to any great question I came upon that, in short order, it became not a question of making a right or a wrong decision, but whether any decision could be made at all. It was a great disability that would plague me most of my young life.

There are, of course, worse plagues to endure in one's existence, but at the time it was more of a hindrance than was necessary. Nevertheless, it reflected an aspect of my true nature, and it was one I had to confront on a daily basis until I mastered it.

That, dear ones, is a story unto itself, however, and one which would burst your sides in laughter, to be sure. But I digress.

I resolved that if I chose to confront him about the matter, it would not be in a state of anger or angst, but rather through mere curiosity. I was more interested to know why he found it necessary to shadow me all day instead of simply asking me what questions he seemed to be formulating in his mind.

It confounded me how a simple man such as I could be the object of so much interest to any council member, let alone the senior council member.

A freshly formed and most curious thought arose in my mind after a time. It occurred to me, as strange then as it may sound now, that I was the only person who could see Wigiwig observing me. As he moved about, no one else seemed to notice him. As I continued observing him observing me, I could not help but believe him to be anything other than a spectre that no one but I could see.

With that thought, I wondered if I was the creator of my own illusion, or was it a delusion. Was I somehow creating this stealthy version of Wigiwig while in some mindless state of unconsciousness? But why him? And why would I create a spy with such a dreadful technique of espionage?

At that time I could not have answered any of those questions. I wasn't even sure *I* was present in my own delusion. Perhaps I was wandering through some random dream. Perhaps I was fast asleep in my hut.

At that moment I had no way of knowing what the answers were, but what was certain to me through all of this was I had many questions concerning my life on the island.

There were questions regarding Lelalu and our life together. There were others that had to do with my supposed future life. I believed that unless I was soon engaged in serious training to become a true warrior, I would not know how I was to become the hero to a people I barely knew and whom I was now only coming to understand.

Through all this reasoning, it no longer mattered whether or not this Wigiwig person was really observing me. Questions regarding my own state of existence had suddenly become of paramount importance to me. That much I did ascertain from my presumed delusion.

Either way, whether the events of this day were fabricated or not, I needed answers to my own compelling questions. The more I thought about it, the more sense it made to me that my inner mind was perhaps already aware of whom I should seek in order to gain some sorely needed answers. Perhaps it had, on some hidden level of consciousness, sought out Wigiwig as the purveyor of the answers my mind and heart were seeking. I concluded with a determination to learn more about this Wigiwig fellow.

Through all of the many days and weeks I had been on this exceptional island, it was only through Lelalu's steadfast and skillful guidance that I was able to maintain the tiniest grip upon any reality, if there was any to be had at all. Without her, I think I would have been a wretched and lost soul wandering in the desert of my own mind.

It was on the foundation of her sense of how things worked here that I based my reality, for I was certain my own unsecured reality wobbled to and fro without any basis at all.

In all of this, I began to question whether I was even on this island, or whether this action was playing in my head as I lay somewhere else in some catatonic state, in some other place far away from the sea or any magical island. Perhaps the salt air I thought I smelled was not the sea at all but some other scent not yet discernible to any of my remaining senses. I began to call into question everything I believed I was experiencing.

The sharp crack of an exploding ember in the fireplace returned the captain's mind to the cozy room where his family sat surrounding him. Even Suzanne was presently in attendance and listening intently, albeit from the comfort of the sofa to his left.

"Don't stop, Papa!" pleaded Robert. "Tell us more, please."

"Yes, Papa, please continue the story," echoed Wendy.

"I think I should stop there for tonight, children."

Suzanne caught sight of the gleam in her grandfather's eye and recognized it as moisture from a forming tear — the result perhaps of a saddening long-ago memory.

"That's enough for this evening, children. Papa needs his rest. Off to bed with you now."

The children rose immediately, and having given their customary kiss to their great-grandfather's cheek, they turned toward the door. Wendy was first through it, but Robert stopped and turned toward the captain, hesitated a few seconds, and then asked, "Papa, did you love Lelalu?"

At first it appeared that the captain did not hear Robert's words, but after several seconds, still staring into the flames of the fireplace, he responded with an air of both regret and sorrow coupled with some gentle memory of something lovingly recalled. "Oh, yes, Robert. Very much....I loved her so very much."

Robert thought about the answer. "Does that mean you did not love great-grandmother?"

"No, my child. I loved them both equally."

"I don't understand, Papa."

"Be not troubled by that, Robert. In its proper time I shall explain it to you. Sleep tonight with the thought that true love comes in many forms, child. Sleep on that and sleep well."

Robert nodded and then turned to leave the room.

"Robert," the captain added, "how is it going with your new friend, Thomas?"

"We're still good friends, but now some of the other kids are upset that we're friends. Why is life so confusing, Papa?"

"Come here, my child."

Robert obediently complied. The captain leaned forward and hugged him. "Think carefully on how you intend to confront the new issue, lad. Sometimes things are not as they first seem; at other times things are exactly as they appear. Be calm and of good intent, but be not foolish."

"I will, Papa," Robert said, then left the room

Suzanne stared intently at her grandfather as he rocked slowly back and forth and continued to gaze into the rich flames of the fire.

"You spoke all day. You must be exhausted," she said.

"Not at all, child. Not at all. In fact, I am rejuvenated. The memories....The memories."

"You miss her, don't you? Grandmother, that is."

"Very much, child. Very much and every day. All day long. But I have memories. They warm me. They restore me."

"I miss Jonathan the same way. I still think about him several times a day."

A sly smile appeared on the captain's face. Suzanne noticed it and was about to speak when the captain sat back in his rocking chair, rested his head against its back, and spoke. "One night, very much like this one, when Jonathan was very young, about the age of Robert and Wendy now, he came to me with the oddest question."

"Tell me about it, Papa."

"I remember the event as if it were only moments ago. At first, unnoticed by me, he had walked into this very room and stood in front of the fireplace warming his backside, standing very still and staring at me.

"It was long before we had electricity to help light our homes. In those days the fire, oil lamps, or candles were our only source of illumination."

"I remember those days, Papa."

"Something stirred my mind. When I looked up from my desk here and first saw Jonathan standing in front of the fire, I thought him to be an apparition, for I only saw his silhouette against the bright firelight. Then he spoke. 'Where does warrior training take place?' he asked."

"I thought it was some kind of test question, thrust upon me during some unannounced refreshment trial by the elders."

"'It takes place in the heart and in the mind of the true warrior, of course,' I earnestly replied."

"'You were sent to the island for your training. Will I be sent to Minchon Island for my training?'"

"I then recognized the voice. 'Jonathan?' I asked, relieved to know he was not a spectre sent to test me, for by then many years had passed since my return from the island. 'I cannot answer that, Jonathan.'"

"'Why, Papa?'"

"'It's difficult to explain, but it was a place which was well known to me.'"

"'But you did not know the island existed before you were marooned on it. How can you then say that it was well known to you?'"

"'I am a man of the sea, Jonathan. An island would naturally present itself to me, but you are not of the sea; therefore, what shall appear before you at the appropriate time will be that which most defines you. Fear not, my child, you will know it when the time is right, and it shall seem most natural.'"

"'But I want to know now, so that I might prepare properly.'"

"'And I want to tell you where your training will take place, but it is not for me to know the answer to your question in this matter.'"

"'When, then, shall my training begin?'"

"'I cannot answer that either, child, except to say that it will begin when you are ready.'"

"'But I'm ready now, Papa.'"

"'When you are ready is for a power greater than you to know. Trust in knowing that destiny arrives for us all in its own time, and not always in synchrony with our desire. Your initial training began some time ago, but your formal training will begin when you have shown yourself worthy, and not one second before. Be patient. Be alert to its coming, however, for soon enough it will be upon you.'"

"'But I'm anxious to begin now, Papa!'"

"'Harness your anxiety, boy. It is not one of the traits you will carry forward after your training is complete. Know it is now with you because you are young and impulsive and full of brash bravado. Know that these things will also fade as you grow and learn what it truly is to be a Minchon Warrior. Can you do that? Can you harness your impulses and still keep alert for the calling of your lessons?'"

"I remember with such fondness now, Suzanne, the smile that suddenly beamed across his face. In that instant his question was answered. In that moment he received his answer from a place far beyond that fire-lit room, by an unseen responder. I saw it in his eyes: he was given when and where his training was to begin. I believe, for him on that night, it was a momentous instant, for he never again asked such a question. And so it is for young Robert as well, I think."

"What makes you think that, Papa?"

"He asks the sorts of questions one asks just before training is to begin."

Suzanne suddenly became alarmed. She jumped to her feet. "No!" she exclaimed. "I will not lose my son as well."

"Child, calm yourself. Whatever are you talking about?"

"You have a sense of it, don't you?"

"A sense of what?"

"Something bad is going to happen to Robert."

"What makes you think that, Suzanne? Did I say anything about harm coming to him?"

"You said you think his training is about to begin."

The captain stood up and moved to his granddaughter's side and clutched her firmly by the shoulders. "Yes, but time is a relative matter. More importantly, though, what has that to do with something bad happening to him?"

"Just like his father. You knew something was going to happen to him. Tell me, Papa. What is going to happen to my Robert?"

"Nothing, child. Nothing bad is going to happen to Robert. Calm yourself, dear one."

"You knew something was going to happen to Jonathan. Now you see it happening to Robert. Tell me, Papa. Tell me."

"Nothing bad is going to happen, child. Calm yourself. You're forgetting your training. Trust in that training, my dear. All will be well, I assure you."

"Papa, I can't stand this any longer. What do you know about Robert?"

"I see only in his face that he has developed into a brilliant lad and that his mind is full of questions yearning for answers. He is growing toward his manhood. That is all I see, child."

He gently pressed Suzanne's head to his shoulder and stroked the back of her head, attempting to soothe her troubled spirit.

"Papa, I could not take losing my son as well. I've struggled through too much. I could not bear losing him, too."

"When Jonathan returns to you, you will see that all I have ever told you is true. Until then, my dear, you have to remain trusting. I know it has been difficult for you, but I have never told you anything that was not for your benefit or guidance for your highest good. Know now I am saying to you that Robert will be just fine."

He eased her away so he could look her in the eye. "I must say your training has been a challenge, though. You have been most resistant." He chuckled.

"Tell me, Papa. Tell me the truth. Do you see Robert being taken from me?"

"I see Robert growing into a fine young man, full of life, wit, humor, and wisdom. That is what I see. I see you also, child, happy and full of laughter, a future with nothing but joyous times to warm you in your autumn years. I also see young Wendy equally well and fulfilled."

"Are you telling me the truth?"

"Have I not always told you the truth as I understood it to be?"

"I suppose so, but Papa, the children are all I have to remind me of Jonathan. I would not want to live without them."

The captain pulled her head back onto his shoulder.

"And you shall not ever have to. But you will also have your Jonathan back as well. You will see. I know you believe that. Somewhere deep inside your heart you know that to be true. You may not believe it outwardly, but you know it inside that hidden and secret place, that special place whose existence you try to deny. You will see."

"Where do you find such faith, Papa? How do you do it, day in and day out? Always so uplifting and so believing. It is a wonder you allow us to be here at all."

The captain chuckled. "You are a most wonderful family, child. You could not be anyplace else at the moment. Besides, it is our duty to raise the children until Jonathan makes his triumphant return. Until then, my dear, we must be their strength and support. Jonathan would expect nothing less from us, would he not?"

"No, Papa, he would not. But you amaze me sometimes."

"Certainly, child, I'm an amazing fellow." The captain laughed heartily. He was successful in getting Suzanne to smile. "That's it, my dear. Believe and hold fast to hope."

"Hope is all I have left, Papa."

"Then hear me, girl. When only hope is left, exercise it towards a suitable intent, for the possibility of all things lies at the heart of hope's willful, purposeful, and enduring determination."

"It's a lovely thought, Papa." Suzanne pushed herself away from the captain and kissed him on the cheek. "I feel very tired tonight. I'm going to bed. What are you going to do?"

"I feel like a smoke."

"Don't stay out too late." Suzanne turned away and walked out the door. Before she closed it, she turned back toward her grandfather. "I wish I could believe, the way you do. You never have any doubts at all, do you?"

"None, my child. None whatsoever. You will get to that place on your own. I have no doubt of that either. Good night, my dear. May peaceful dreams cradle you through the night."

Suzanne smiled and closed the door.

"I just love these training sessions," the captain uttered to himself and cackled as he reached for his tobacco pouch.

Just then, Wendy, notebook in hand as usual, walked into the room.

"Papa, can I ask you a question?"

"Why, of course you can," replied the captain, setting his pipe down on the table and walking toward her. "What is your question, child?"

"Robert said he may be leaving for his warrior training soon."

"He did, did he?"

"Why do only the boys go away for training?"

"Ah, I see your greater question, little one. It's really very simple. Girls discover the truth of the training much more easily and rapidly than boys do. Generally speaking that is. Your mother seems determined to be the exception. But she'll come around soon."

"Are we smarter than boys?"

The captain chuckled. "It's not because you are any smarter, child. It is a fact that girls are more open to learning the ways of the warrior than are boys. It's in your very nature, as nurturing beings, to feel compassion and empathy. Some say it's called the 'mother instinct' within young girls that makes them more receptive to the teachings."

"Boys don't feel compassion and empathy?"

"Sure they do."

"Then why can't they learn the way we do?"

"Because boys simply react differently to the knowledge of the lessons. I want to say more, but let it suffice for you to know that both you and Robert will become great warriors in your own right. But Robert will require special training. You, on the other hand, are growing with amazing surety. You are well ahead of most others, and you already possess wonderful talents. You are very certain of who you are and what your purpose is. You are one astonishing young lady. I expect wondrous things from you, child."

Wendy smiled broadly.

* * * * *

Suzanne glanced at the clock on the kitchen wall. It read almost nine o'clock. With the children sent off to school, she wondered if her grandfather had slept in, so she went to his door and knocked. There was no answer. Turning the knob, she peeked in to see his bed made and him absent.

A confused expression swirled across her face. She closed the door.

* * * * *

Around the local police station there was a flurry of morning activity, with uniformed policemen coming and going as nightly duties ended and morning assignments were being implemented.

Detective Cyra and his partner, Buster Wagner, stepped out onto the stoop, chatting away. Cyra pulled a small cigar from the pocket of his vest, bit off the end, spat it out, and pulled a match from his other vest pocket. After striking the match head across the stone wall of the building, he lit the end of the cigar, puffing several puffs into the morning air. He chatted lightly with Buster for several more seconds until he saw Captain Delightable standing on the sidewalk smiling up at them.

"Good morning, Detective. How are you this fine morning? I hope you slept well last night."

Detective Cyra cringed as the burning match singed the tips of his fingers.

"Careful," said the captain.

Cyra turned to his partner. "I got this, Buster."

"Okay, partner. If you say so. Good morning, Delightable," he said with a nod of his head.

"Good morning to you, Detective Wagner," said the captain. "Would you mind if I borrowed your partner for a while?"

"You can have him all day long. He's not worth much today." Detective Wagner snickered and walked back into the building, leaving the two alone.

"Nice young man, David. I'll bet he's a good partner."

"What are you doing here, Delightable?"

"I thought we'd take a walk this morning. I'm heading toward the wharf and I thought you might want to join me. It would save time for you — not having to track me down."

"You're gloating, Delightable. That isn't like you. You must have found out that my request for surveillance on you was turned down by the chief...again."

"I assure you, Detective. I know of no such thing. But I've taken a fancy to you, sir. You seem to be full of questions regarding me. Walk with me and I'll try to answer as many as I can. They serve the most wonderful coffee over at O'Connor's in the mornings. Please join me."

"Fine, you crafty old geezer. I'll do it your way for now. I don't yet know what you're up to, but I'll play along for a while. I will find you out. You can count on that."

"Perhaps before you know it, you'll have all of the answers you seek."

Detective Cyra stepped lightly down the stone stairs and walked alongside the captain, certain now that he was being set up. For what, he didn't know, but he remained alert for it. So he walked with the captain, his left thumb inside his vest pocket, his right hand holding onto the small cigar.

"So tell me, Detective; be forthright with me. What is it that you are seeking from me?"

"To get you off the street and somewhere safe, for your own sake and the safety of the public."

"That's a noble endeavor, Detective. Noble indeed, if it were the truth."

"Are you calling me a liar?"

"Not at all. I believe you outwardly believe in what you're doing. I'm more interested, however, in your inward reasons. Your soul's true purpose."

"My soul's true purpose?" The detective snickered. "You're saying there's a hidden agenda?"

"One that you may not even be aware of at this time."

"And just what would that be?"

"I'm attempting to understand that at this very moment. I want to help you, Detective, I truly do, but unless you're accurate and open with me, I cannot."

"You think I'm purposefully hiding some underlying agenda?"

"Not your outward self, Detective, but your inward self apparently is. I feel you are a man who harbors a very conflicted nature."

"I see. So you think by turning this around and making it about me, you'll convince everyone you are the sane and rational one? Is that your intent?"

"Not at all, but I can see why you would think that."

"I've been a detective for almost twenty years, Delightable. I've worked all the big towns from Seattle down to Los Angeles. I've seen it all, but you have a unique twist on things. I'll give you that. You're a shrewd one, to be sure. I'm not yet certain of your intent, but I will ferret out the true nature of your deception. I never fail. You should take that to heart, sir. I always succeed in my investigations."

"I am neither attempting any deceit nor exercising any shrewd effort to trap you. I'm just trying to prove to you that your concern regarding me is unjustified."

"And just how do you expect to prove that?"

"By simply showing you who I am. I believe the more you get to know me, the more you will understand my true intent."

"And just what is your true intent?"

"To help you find your way back home."

"I'm lost, am I?" The detective snickered again.

"You are, sir, and you are most desperate to find your way back. Back to where you belong."

"This should prove to be a most interesting morning, Delightable. You're correct, I think. I want to know everything I can about you. I'll need it for my report."

"Then you shall have it, sir. You shall have it all."

"And where shall we begin?"

"Let me start by telling you about how I came to be in this wonderful country. Then we shall go forward from there."

Chapter 12

Suzanne walked into the butcher's shop and immediately noticed her neighbor, Philomena Montique, waiting in a short line.

"Good afternoon, Philomena."

"Why, good afternoon, Suzanne."

"How are you doing today?"

"I'm afraid I'm doing much better than you, obviously."

"Whatever do you mean by that?"

"I see you're still having difficulties with your grandfather."

"Explain please."

"Then you still don't know about him smoking his pipe on the roof at night? Oh dear, I'm so sorry to bring it up again."

"Oh dear is right. He must have found another way out onto the roof, then. I just don't know what I'm going to do with him. Just when I think his zaniness might only be in *my* head, he starts this sort of nonsense once again. Thank you, Philomena. I appreciate your bringing this to my attention."

* * * * *

Tucked away in one of the corners of O'Connor's Wharfside Tavern, Detective Cyra and Captain Delightable sat steeped in heavy conversation. Cyra scribbled into his notepad as the captain recited his exciting tale. Finally the captain stopped speaking and waited patiently as Cyra finished his writing.

"I'm not going too fast for you, am I, David?"

"No, no. This is magical! This is simply *magical*. I couldn't ask for more."

"Good, good. I wouldn't want you to leave out one single detail."

Cyra looked up into the captain's eyes as if he had discovered the lost treasure of the ages. He noted the gleeful smile beaming back across the table at him from the old man's aged and etched face. Considering the possible reasons for such an expression on the face of his nemesis for a quick moment, he dismissed it handily as the look of someone not in full command of his faculties. His own reasoning and purpose once again renewed, he continued, "I'm getting most every word, Cornelius. Please don't stop,"

"You still need more evidence? Haven't I yet given you enough to send me away to the asylum forever?"

"More, Cornelius. I want more."

"Very well, where was I?"

"You were just trying to reason with yourself over whether this Wigiwig fellow was in your head alone."

"Ahhh, yes. Well, it's getting very late. Please come by my home this evening, for dinner perhaps, if you are able. We shall share a meal, and then I shall continue my story. Coincidentally, it is precisely where I stopped the other night with the children. You will join us for dinner, won't you, David?"

"Certainly, Cornelius. I wouldn't miss it for the world."

"How delightful. It will be a most enjoyable evening, I should think. What would you say to an ice cream cone, David?"

* * * * *

Suzanne walked into her kitchen and dropped her grocery bag onto the counter. Without even removing her wrap, she went immediately to the library. Upon entering, she took note of the window which overlooked a portion of the roof.

The sly smile gave way to a smirk. She walked over to the window and stared out. Until now, she had never thought about the direct access it provided to the roof, although the roof here was sharply sloped. She couldn't believe that an old man could negotiate such a slope, but if Philomena was right, then the captain must have.

"So, old man, this has become a test of wills, has it?" she announced aloud.

* * * * *

Suzanne was slicing a tomato in the midst of preparing a salad as Tony, the carpenter from Hotchkiss Hardware, walked into the kitchen. With hat in hand, he cleared his throat.

"Have you finished, then, Tony?"

"Yes, ma'am. Would you care to see it?"

"No. I'm sure it's well installed."

"As you wish. Here is the key again. I made it so it uses the same key as the lock on the attic door," said Tony as he dropped it into Suzanne's opened palm.

"Thank you, Tony. I appreciate your coming out so quickly. Please tell Mr. Hotchkiss I will be by early tomorrow to settle my account with him."

"Yes, ma'am. I'll do that. Good day, Mrs. Delightable."

"Good day, Tony. Please forgive me if I don't show you out. I'm late getting supper ready."

"That's fine, ma'am. I know my way out. Goodbye, then."

"Thank you. Goodbye."

The workman departed and Suzanne continued with her supper preparations until curiosity got the better of her. She picked up a towel and dried her hands as she went to the library. Standing before the now latched and locked window, she could not help but let a devious smile form on her lips.

* * * * *

As the captain entered his home, he heard a strange clinking sound. Walking toward it, he discovered Suzanne sitting at the kitchen table, an empty tea cup in front of her, lightly tapping the side of the cup with a spoon in a rhythmical beat.

"Hello, child," the captain said with a warm smile. "And how has your day been?"

Suzanne did not return his smile. With a serious expression, she stared up at him from her seat. "You and I are going to have a very serious conversation, Papa."

"Wonderful!" he exclaimed, in his usually disarming manner. "But I have something to tell you, as well. I had a wonderful day with Detective Cyra. I think he is truly warming up to me."

"What do you mean?" Suzanne asked, jumping up from her chair.

"I met him out front of the station this morning. We walked to the wharf together. I told him everything about me that I could squeeze into such a limited time. I must say, it was most refreshing and liberating."

"Everything? Papa, you didn't do that, did you?"

"Yes, yes. It was wonderful. You should have seen his face light up with wonder and amazement."

"Papa! What is wrong with you?"

"Nothing, child. You should have seen it, my dear. I really think he's beginning to understand."

"Papa! He's trying to put you away and you gave him everything he needed to do just that."

"Not everything, darling. He's coming for dinner tonight. I promised to continue the story."

"Papa! Have you completely lost your mind?"

The captain walked over to her, placed both hands on her shoulders, leaned over, and kissed her on the forehead. "I'm truly excited, child. This is a great moment for all of us. It has been ages in the making. Tonight we begin to save a brother."

"You *have* lost your mind, Papa. I will not have that man in this house again." Suzanne was now shouting.

The captain was not shaken by her outburst. Instead, he remained joyful and exuberant. "Now, now, my child. It's all a part of what must be. Just flow with it, Suzanne. You'll see, it all will work out just fine. Have faith, my child."

He walked around her and into his library. Suzanne followed immediately, continuing to bark at him.

"I'm not cooking dinner for that man in this house, and I'm certainly not allowing him to sit here and gather more evidence against you. What were you *thinking*, Papa? This man will cheerfully destroy our family if we let him."

The captain snickered. "He certainly thinks so." The captain chuckled again. "Can you imagine how surprised he will be when he fails in that enterprise? I'm so excited! This has been such a wonderful day. I can't remember when I've been this excited....Will I need to go to the store for more food?"

"Papa! You're not listening to me. I refuse to cook dinner for that man."

The captain almost skipped around his library, but stopped and turned toward his granddaughter. "You're just going to remain a stubborn soul right up to the end, aren't you?"

"I'm not being stubborn, Papa. I'm being protective of you, but I'm afraid you have possibly done more damage than I can repair. I don't know what I can do now to protect you."

"You assume I need protecting, girl. I assure you, I don't. No harm will come of this in the end. Why do you find it so hard to trust me? When you were a child, you trusted everything I said."

"Papa, I was a child; isn't that enough of an answer?"

"Perhaps you need to return your mind to that child-like state, then."

"And perhaps yours has already made that journey."

The captain chuckled. "Perhaps. Perhaps it has. This day just keeps getting better and better. What a joy!...What a wonderful joy!"

"Papa, I'm not cooking for that evil man. I'm serious."

"Suzanne, I once heard a very short story which might illustrate my position much better for you. Sit, child, and let me tell it to you."

Reluctantly, Suzanne sat down on the sofa, shaking her head. She could not believe she was even giving her grandfather the opportunity to defend himself, let alone allowing herself to be taken in by another one of his fanciful tales.

The captain walked around the room, his right index finger scratching at his whiskered chin as he began to recall the story.

Once a near-starving man, call him Ansell, sought to steal the fishing net of another man, whose name was Zachariah. For the longest time, spying as he so enjoyed doing, Ansell licked his lips as he observed Zachariah pull in his net full of flopping fish. He watched as Zachariah would check the net for any tears, and then mend them if there were any. Ansell watched as the net was hung to dry on the wall near the opening of the small hut as Zachariah took the fish inside, presumably to prepare his meals.

Ansell figured out when would be the best time to relieve Zachariah of his net, and he waited for the most opportune moment to make his move. But just as Ansell attempted to steal the net, Zachariah came upon him.

Ansell immediately took a defensive posture in an effort to defend himself in anticipation of Zachariah's imminent attack, but there came no attack. Instead, Zachariah, offered him a fish. After a moment, and realizing it was no ruse, Ansell immediately snatched the fish from Zachariah's hand and ran away back into the forest.

The next day, Zachariah noticed the man once again on the edge of the forest, staring at him with yearning eyes. This time Zachariah offered Ansell two fishes. Once again, Ansell snatched them greedily from Zachariah's hand and dashed back into the forest to feast on his good fortune.

The very next day, Zachariah again noticed Ansell staring at him longingly. So Zachariah motioned for Ansell to come forth, and this time Zachariah gave him all of his fishes. So many, in fact, that Ansell could not easily carry them away.

On the morrow, when Zachariah had finished hauling in his net full of more fish, he did not see Ansell at all. Two more days followed hence, and gathering up his net to head to the shore to fish, he finally noticed Ansell standing on the edge of the forest. Zachariah sent a large grin over to Ansell and waved for him to come over. As Ansell approached, Zachariah signaled for him to follow.

That morning, Ansell and Zachariah worked together and pulled in the net nearly full of fish. Then the two sat next to each other and cleaned the fish as they engaged in conversation and laughter. It turned out to be a glorious day for both men, and in a short time they became close friends and remained so for many years after.

"Papa," Suzanne finally said, "Why don't you just come out and say what you mean? Why do you have to give me parables? I'm not a child."

"You don't like my stories anymore?"

"Your stories are lovely, but I can discuss things without your needing to hide them in gentle tales, Papa."

"I see," the captain answered with the slightest pout.

"Don't you dare do that, Papa. Don't you dare give me those puppy-dog eyes. That doesn't work anymore."

"Tell me, child, when did you decide to harden your heart? Can you recall precisely when you determined to do that?"

"It was when I lost Jonathan and you tried to make me believe he was in warrior training by reciting another little story about how he was whisked away to some hidden place.

"Papa, I love that you are gentle, kind, loving, and eager to replace pain with hope in those who hurt the most. I understand what you need to do, but I'm long past the need to be coddled and protected. I'm a grown woman and well able to face the realities of life now. I thank you for gently bringing me along to this place I now find myself, and I know you also wish to keep the children protected. I love that most about you, Papa. You genuinely care about others. That makes you so very special. But life is sometimes cruel and unjust, and the sooner Robert and Wendy understand that, the sooner they will be able to deal with life's harsher moments."

"I see. Then you have solved all the mysteries of life? You have all the answers to everything you need to get along in this world? There is nothing left for you to learn? Is that what you're saying to me, child?"

"Of course not; what I'm saying is I don't think it helpful to keep relying on stories to get your points across — especially to the children. I believe it best to give them the information they need without hiding it in fanciful parables."

"And of course my stories are just that: make-believe tales that could not possibly be true."

"Papa! Minchon Island? A mysterious island never seen by anyone other than you? People who are able to appear and disappear at will, use magical powers, and manipulate time itself? And you being one hundred fifty years old? Really now, Papa, how could you ever expect anyone to believe that to be true? Tell me, please."

"So it has come to that? Everything I have ever told you was just a fantasy? Is that what you truly believe?"

Suzanne moved toward her grandfather and hugged him tightly in a caring embrace.

"Your stories got me through many difficult days when I was a growing child full of wonder and questions. I well learned all the great lessons hidden in your words of fancy. They were wonderful. They were magical. Magical, mysterious, and most intriguing. All of that and much more to a child's imagination. They are all truly special. In fact, I think you should sit down and write a book about Minchon Island. I think it would make a wonderful fantasy for all to read. But the truth is, Papa, they were all just wonderful stories, nothing more. You need to understand that. You need to accept certain realities we all have to face sooner or later."

"What can I say that will restore your faith?"

"Stop deluding yourself, Papa. You're an eighty-one-year-old man who lost his wife over a decade ago. You are in remarkably good physical health, but your mind seems to be failing you."

"So I'm crazy, then? Is that what you're telling me?"

"Not crazy, Papa, just deluded, confused."

"I see. Lost in fantasy, am I, then?"

"Yes, Papa. That's all. But I'll be here to help you through it all. I promise you."

"Well, then, I guess there's nothing left for me to say to you. I think I shall go for a walk and have a smoke."

"Speaking of that, I know you've already found the attic door locked, but you'll now find I have also locked the window you use to get out onto the roof to smoke your pipe during your 'walks.'"

"Locked doors and windows?" stated the captain, genuinely surprised. He looked to the window and found it secured with a hasp and lock. He looked at Suzanne with wide-eyed amazement. "Whatever prompted you to do that, child?"

"Don't start with me about that, Papa. I know you've been sneaking out onto the roof to smoke your pipe."

"But child, I don't use ..."

"There will be no more of that. It's too dangerous for you out there, so I've locked both of your routes. If you must smoke that pipe of yours, you'll do it on solid ground from now on."

"But..."

"And that's that. I have the only key, so don't you think you'll be sneaking out there again. Now I have things to do. I can't sit here babbling with you. You find something better to do with your time. If you *have* invited that despicable man to dinner, then I'll have to go to the butcher's and get another piece of meat. I'll need time to poison it properly. I'll be back in a half hour or so. Have a good afternoon, and please think about what I've told you. I love you, Papa."

Suzanne kissed him on the forehead and left him alone in his study stunned to silence. Finally he uttered aloud but to himself, "I love you also, my child."

He looked at the locked window once again, and then sat down in his chair. A perplexed expression formed on his face. "Why would she think I would use that window? A person could get killed crawling out there."

Chapter 13

At precisely six o'clock, as Suzanne was in the midst of preparing the nightly meal, she heard a sharp knock on the front door. She grabbed a kitchen towel and wiped her hands as she moved toward the door.

Opening the door, she found Detective Cyra, appropriately dressed for dinner, standing with a bouquet of flowers in his left hand and his hat and valise in his right.

"Good evening, Mrs. Delightable. Cornelius invited me for dinner." The detective offered the flowers to Suzanne. She hesitated, but then took them from him, along with his hat, and nodded as politely as she was able to summon the will to do so.

"Good evening, Detective. Cornelius, is it?"

"Yes, ma'am. At his insistence, I might add."

"Thank you for the flowers, sir, but I warn you, Detective ..."

"David, please, Mrs. Delightable."

"No, Detective, and I will make this very clear, I'll have no threats expressed in this house tonight, veiled or otherwise. Or you shall be asked to leave. Is that clear, Detective Cyra?"

"Absolutely. I assure you, Mrs. Delightable, I'm only here to enjoy a meal with your family and to listen to a good story this evening."

"See to it that remains your only agenda, sir. I presume you know the way to the library."

"Yes, I remember."

Suzanne moved to the side to make way for the detective to step past her. "I'm sure he's expecting you. If you'll excuse me, I have some poisoned meat to prepare."

Detective Cyra chuckled, but Suzanne thought she noticed the slightest hint of uncertainty in the detective's reaction. She returned to the kitchen while Cyra moved down the hallway toward the library.

* * * * *

The captain was sitting at his large desk making notes in his notebook and continuing to study the parchment chart in front of him when he heard a delicate knock on the library door.

"Enter, please," he called out, standing up.

The door opened and Cyra walked into the room, saying, "Good evening, Cornelius."

"Good evening, David," the captain said warmly. "Drop your things on the sofa and come over to the desk. I want to show you something I hope will fascinate you."

Cyra dropped his valise on the sofa and strode to the desk. Peering down at the chart spread out in front of him, he studied it for a few seconds. Then he stretched out his arm and pointed to a spot on the chart. "I take it this is where Minchon Island is located?"

"Precisely," replied the captain. "More accurately, though, that is where it was at the time."

"I don't understand."

"I know, but you will. I haven't gotten to that part of the story yet."

Just then the children rushed into the room. "Papa, can you tell us more until —" Wendy stopped when she saw Cyra standing next to the table. "What is *he* doing here, Papa?" she asked with scorn in her young voice.

"Detective Cyra is going to join us for dinner this evening. Isn't that lovely?"

"Why?" asked Robert.

"Because he wants to hear more about my adventures on the island, just as you two do. Now, please don't be rude. Say hello to the detective."

The children hesitated.

"Is this how a warrior greets an honored guest?" asked the captain.

"Good evening, Detective Cyra," said the children as one.

"Good evening, children," replied Cyra, extra politely. "I'm very excited to hear more of the story. Are you?"

"Yes, sir," responded Wendy.

"Yes, sir," echoed Robert.

"After dinner, children. I shall continue the story after dinner. Now, please excuse Detective Cyra and me. We have some important issues to discuss. See if your mother needs any help."

Suzanne entered the room carrying a tray of hot tea, but said nothing; her eyes remained fixed on the tea tray. She set it down, poured two cups, and departed the room the way she had entered, with no eye contact. With a flick of her hand, the children followed her immediately, shutting the door behind them as they left the room.

"Now then," said Captain Delightable, "where were we?"

* * * * *

Dinner was awkward for Suzanne. Although she tried to mask her disgust for Cyra, it leaked out in bits and pieces throughout the meal in the otherwise light and well-confined conversation. Cyra kept his segments of the conversation light and gave no hint of any threatening or challenging remarks.

The children added little to the conversation, and only spoke when asked a direct question by Cyra. In her own innocent way, through her most expressive eyes, Wendy made it clear she did not like the detective, although she glanced at him often throughout the meal. As was her usual way, she spent most of the meal scribbling into her notebook as she tried to capture the entirety of the conversation between mouthfuls.

Robert, however, listened intently out of pure interest. He was a listener, a learner, a gatherer of information, but his keen mind also studied the detective, carefully considering just what and who the man truly was.

The captain was the only one at the table who seemed completely oblivious to anyone's awkwardness or underlying angst at Cyra's presence. His words and manner remained as uplifting as normal as he inquired about the health and general well-being of Cyra's family, whom he had discovered still lived in Los Angeles. He learned that the detective's mother and father were in generally good health and that, being an only child, Cyra sent a goodly portion of his pay to them for their care and comfort. Despite his other shortcomings, he was a good and dutiful son. The captain was most impressed by this fact.

It would have become clear to anyone observing the conversation that the captain's interest in the detective and his life was genuine. And his caring nature, gentle words, and affable gestures would have supported that conclusion. Cyra appeared to be completely relaxed around the captain.

As the dinner progressed, it was Suzanne who took particular note of Cyra's calmed demeanor. She began forming new thoughts and questions regarding him. *Could she have formed an improper opinion of the man? Could she have misjudged his intent? Was he really here just to listen to the captain's fanciful stories? Had he, like all the rest, succumbed to the spell cast by her captivating grandfather? Was it possible her grandfather had captured another closet believer?*

No matter how much she wanted to believe the detective's motives were sincere, she held her opinions in check. She would withhold her final judgment of the man until she was absolutely certain of his true nature and intent. Until the moment of his exact unveiling, she refused to give him her full trust.

* * * * *

As the meal concluded, everyone, including the detective, at his own insistence, helped with cleaning the dishes, pots, and pans, and the kitchen in general. When they retired to the comfort of the library, Suzanne stayed behind to prepare a tray with coffee and dessert for later.

As the others made themselves comfortable and prepared for the continuing account of his exploits on Minchon Island, the captain put fresh logs on the fire.

The orange glow filled the room and danced to some unheard rhythm, its undulating light and shadows flashing across the book spines on the shelves.

Detective Cyra sat impatiently on one end of the sofa, notebook and pen in hand in anticipation of another exciting story to record, while the children gathered at their favorite spot in front of the hearth. The captain sat himself down in his rocking chair to wait for Suzanne to make her entrance before beginning the evening's storytelling.

Although he knew she had already heard the story several times, he eagerly wanted her to hear it again. To the captain, it was particularly important that she hear every word of it tonight; it might take stronger root within her heart this time around.

After several minutes, Suzanne entered the room carrying a tray of cups, saucers, and plates filled with squares of cake. She handed out the plates and departed, to return with another tray holding a pot of coffee and glasses of milk for the children.

With everyone's dessert needs satisfied, Suzanne took her place on the couch beside Cyra, a bit uneasily.

Small talk about the quality of the dessert occupied them until the captain announced he would continue his story.

When at last I spoke, I was confused as to my true state of consciousness regarding the assumed presence of Wigiwig.

Still uncertain if he was truly following me around the village, I constantly looked about for him. I felt somewhat eased, as I stated before, that he was quick and simple to spot, for he still made no attempt to conceal his interest in observing me.

All afternoon he shadowed me about the village. But when I met with Lelalu later, under our tree on the beach, I lost sight of him.

For all I knew, he was hidden in amongst the foliage and still spying on me, but I was not able to see him then. And if the full truth of it be told, when Lelalu came to me, I instantly lost all interest in Wigiwig and devoted my full attention to her and to her alone.

As we lay next to each other and discussed the events of each other's day, I was soon lost to everything around us. Whenever I was with Lelalu, it was as if the world shrank away from us, leaving us alone in a world that that consisted only of our loving forms. She was the sole person I saw or heard during those times.

Whenever she approached me, my heart was instantly filled with both unbounded elation and hushed serenity. Her mere presence brought with it an instantaneous peace that seemed to flow effortlessly over me, calming every cell of my body.

When she was near, I worried about nothing. We often held hands while we shared those moments together. The connection made me feel a part of something much larger than the two of us. It was as if while we were together we were joined with the universe on a higher level.

I professed my undying love for her at every turn, and inquired as to how I might make my petition to her parents and Amog for her hand. She understood my desire, but she cautioned me not to act in haste. She plainly knew how much I wanted her to be my wife. There was never any lack of clarity in that matter. She wanted the union made manifest also, but she knew it was a certainty; she knew exactly what the future held for us. There was never a doubt in her mind.

I, however, was not as tuned into the nature of time and space. I wanted her to be my wife immediately. As I have already confessed to you, patience and I were uneasy partners, and not yet able to amicably and forever resolve our differences.

During my formative years, I was taught that time waited for no man. I was trained to push steadfastly toward any goal I set my mind upon. It was a determined and creative man aggressively moving toward his goal who achieved it. But here in the land of Minchon, things were different. Patience was held in higher regard than achievement.

Perhaps it was that everyone except me knew that achievement of any pursuit was a foregone conclusion, and it was the nature of the journey toward that achievement which was valued most. Another way of putting would be that it is the quality of the journey toward the end which is of paramount importance rather than the final achievement of the desired outcome.

This was difficult for me to understand; for all of my life I had tended to think of the end as justification enough for anything attempted. I was goal oriented, and this found me in stark contradiction to the values of life as it was lived on the island.

I was not a complete fool, though, for I well enough understood the importance placed on the journey, and I did not take that fact lightly. Still, it was a greater challenge, one seemingly too difficult for me to ignore: the value of achieving one's goal.

It was Lelalu who educated me well on the magnitude of the journey and its place in Minchon life. Still, perhaps because of my unbridled youthful nature in such matters, I wanted to already be at the end of the journey, not *on* the journey, as it were.

"Are you still being observed by Wigiwig, my love?" she asked.

"Until we met here, yes, but I do not see him anywhere about now. Perhaps he honors our privacy."

"I think not, Cornelius. If he had need to observe you further, he would do so. He is not a man who is easily impressed with the need for privacy when he is so set on a task of discovery."

"Well, I can only say I have not seen him about since you arrived. And I care not to think of him right now."

"Then he must have reached his considered conclusion regarding you. There can be no other reason."

"That disturbs me, Lelalu. Have I now been judged? And if so, how can he make judgment of me so quickly?"

"I cannot say, my love, but remember, you are a future hero of the people. Understanding that, I must conclude that any judgment will be in your favor and not one opposed to you."

"It gives me great comfort to hear that, for I can think of nothing I have done or said that should cast doubt upon my sincerity or worth."

It was Lelalu who spotted Wigiwig first, walking toward us. "Take care, my love. Wigiwig now approaches."

I turned my head and saw his approach through the thicket. Instant anxiety filled my stomach. I was not prepared for this confrontation.

"What do I do?" I asked, now amply disquieted.

"You are a bold man, my love, and you have just stated that there should be no lacking in your sincerity and worth. I suggest only that you greet him with the respect he is due, and hear what he has to say with an open heart and mind."

"I shall. I shall do exactly as you suggest."

Wigiwig was about halfway to us when Lelalu stood up and walked toward him boldly. He bowed to her at the moment of their meeting. Then they greeted each other with the ritual greeting and spoke a few words together. They were too distant for me to hear their conversation, but it was clear he wished an audience with me. I saw Lelalu nod to him and then walk away without looking back at me.

As Wigiwig continued his approach, I immediately moved to my feet and bowed my head, remaining still until he stopped just before me.

"You honor me with your respect, Cornelius. Please look up at me."

I did so immediately and he continued, his expression aglow as a warm and congenial smile formed across his broad, smooth face. "I wish to speak with you, if you have time for me."

"I always have time for an elder of the council, great one," I replied.

I extended my hand toward his shoulder so that I might greet him in the traditional Minchon manner, but instead, he grasped my hand as was my tradition. We shook hands.

"I am most pleased to hear that. Let us sit as brothers, then, and dispense with any further formalities."

"As you wish, sir."

We both dropped to the sand, he still smiling broadly.

"Interesting custom of yours, this grasping of hands," he said. "What is its history?"

I was at first startled by the nature of his question, but then I realized he was a man not unlike me, held fast by curiosity.

"I believe the custom began in order to assure that neither man was holding a weapon, and secondarily to insure that a weapon hand was not free to grab such. I'm sorry to say the custom was not initially based on friendship but rather on the hope that there would be no bloodshed. Of course, today it is a simple gesture of greeting, lacking any issue of mistrust or fear. Although a first meeting always has its questions and curiosities naturally built into it, does it not?"

"An excellent response to a difficult-to-answer question, Cornelius. I do find you to be an exceptionally impressive young man."

"You are most gracious, great one, but what, may I ask, was difficult about the question?"

"The correct response required diplomacy, exactness, and honesty, and yet its delivery demanded openness and a bold manner. I know of your 'handshake' history, and you are correct, the gesture was originally based on mistrust. Your direct appraisal and speedy disclosure of such a delicate history demonstrates your sincerity and forthrightness. You are also accurate when you wisely described first meetings. There are many questions and suspicions, no doubt, floating about in your head at this very moment that concern my reason for speaking with you.

"My name is Wigiwig, as you have no doubt already learned, and I beseech you not to call me 'great one.' That title is reserved for the king and queen, and also, I imagine, at present for Amog.

"Although few Minchonians actually refer to Amog as 'great one,' I do believe your initial words have elevated him in his own mind and have made him feel most illustrious and significant; I suppose, with little doubt, he is presently entirely full of himself."

Wigiwig laughed heartily.

I, on the other hand, was confused.

"Should you speak unflatteringly about the Great Amog?" I asked in earnest concern.

"He has you soundly mesmerized, I see."

"I do not understand, sir."

"Now you call me sir. Is that also a title of great respect where you are from?"

"It is."

"Did I not plainly iterate my desire to speak as brothers?"

"You did."

"Then please, just call me Wigiwig, or brother, or 'you there' if that pleases you." Wigiwig laughed loudly once again. His continued gentle manner put me finally into a relaxed state. I chuckled.

"I now fully understand why Amog wanted you observed," he confided. "You have pleased him mightily. You have found good favor in the old man's heart. I commend you, young Cornelius. It is not often I see anyone get to that cantankerous old man so swiftly."

"Pardon me, Wigiwig, but you seem to have little respect for the Great High Priest."

"Not at all, but everything in its due course. Amog and I have known each other well for what at times seems like eternity. The truth of it is, however, we have known each other since I was a young and fiery lad like yourself, in the beginning stages of my warrior training. At that time he was already a confirmed warrior of very high grade, but not yet appointed to the position of High Priest."

"Then you have a long history with each other."

"We do. And I must say, we had our tempestuous moments in the beginning."

"I heard tell that you and Amog were once bitter rivals."

I blurted it straight out in boldness and with lack of thought. I immediately cringed, thinking that perhaps I spoke inappropriately, but Wigiwig laughed uproariously, slapped his thigh, and calmed my fear.

"One could say that," he replied, still laughing.

"Forgive me, Wigiwig. I sometimes speak with an unbridled tongue."

"And you should always do so, Cornelius, for what lies truly in the heart should be spoken from the mouth. Truth should never be subdued."

"There are some who find the truth hurtful, though."

"Those who find the truth hurtful are most often giving over to something that is not the truth. The knowledge of truth does not have a place within them. It is fright, not hurt, that they feel. Truth frightens those who do not understand its cleansing nature."

"Yes," Wigiwig began again, "Amog and I began our relationship on somewhat less than amicable terms. That is the truth."

"Do you recall the event that prompted such animosity?"

Wigiwig took my new words of brash curiosity in stride and did not miss a beat.

"It was long ago, Cornelius, but we were rivals then, as you have heard. I do not say we were bitter rivals, but we did share a contest of wills.

"I do recall the moment that initiated such strife. To be truthful, it was a most injurious, rude, and indelicate outburst from me that launched the disagreement."

"You?" I inquired, surprised.

"It is true, I must admit. I was a callous and guarded lad, and my youth was strong and shouting loudly and boldly from within me during the initial phases of my training. I further admit that I was, at first, bullheaded and sorely resistant to Amog's teachings. I was uncomfortable to expose my inner conflicts to anyone, including myself. Also, I did not care to deliver into the light any weaknesses in my character and thereby make them visible and available for all to view. In short, Cornelius, I was of a keenly vindictive, stubbornly protective, and wildly irrational nature. I was also carelessly boisterous and crazily vociferous in expressing my discomfort."

"If you don't mind my bold inquiry, what words were spoken that initiated such ire?"

Wigiwig smiled knowingly.

"As for the particular verbiage of my outburst," he started, "I could well tell you, for I recall each word with crystal clarity, but they would be of no consequence to you, for you are not of like spirit and thus could not relate sufficiently to them. Instead, I would impart to you his response, for that was most noteworthy.

"We had been in the midst of disagreement for quite a while before the incident. As I said, I was resistant to his teachings of peace and serenity and how they must necessarily abound within in me if I were ever to achieve warrior status. Over the many preceding months leading up to the moment under discussion now, I stubbornly and, I must say, viciously attacked his position, thinking it a weak one. The term 'warrior' at that time had a different meaning for me. And so I pressed him continually on the issue of just what a *warrior* was supposed to embody.

"Suffice it to say, I knew with great certainty, on that particular day, that with such an inglorious outburst I would instantly encourage him toward wild anger.

"And so it did, for his eyes pierced me with a seething rage, the likes of which I had never seen. His manner was curt and direct. His huge hands immediately seized upon my shoulders. Then his right hand soundly took hold of my throat. He lifted me completely off the ground with his one arm — as if I were a feather — and brought my face fearfully close to his. His breath scorched my skin as he spoke; the complete, searing conversation is forever etched into my brain.

"'If you, wild one, you of a malicious and enraged spirit, be of sound mind and sturdy constitution, and I believe you to be so endowed, hear thus my words. Take care, exercise good reasoning and judgment, and remember it is only the present gentle persuasion of my heart and mind that retains me sympathetic and ever vigilant to the plight and circumstance of your impetuous youthfulness.

"'You would do well to keep this thought held fast within your own heart and head. For if my mind and heart falter, and in so doing they fail to continue in such a gentle and understanding manner, then you would surely and forever bear witness to the full tempestuous nature of my wrath that even now lies in disquieted slumber at a shallow depth within me — beneath this thinly veiled surface of the kindly and forgiving nature I display toward you in this moment. I mightily urge you, therefore, to speak to me nevermore of this matter — and in such a zestfully disrespectful and indecorous tone — lest you awaken one morning to find yourself brought down from the great height you so now enjoy, to further find yourself shattered upon hardened ground, your maladapted skull decisively crushed beneath my heel, never to rise up out of the dust of this land again.'

"He then dropped me unceremoniously to the sand, where I lay still in a silent rage, calculating with precision my next move — without any fear or mindful thought that he might keep true to his word to duly crush my head into the sand if I stirred even slightly without his permission."

"Incredible!" I remarked in utter awe.

"Indeed," replied Wigiwig. "Even then, not yet a high priest but still a warrior of high order, he was well known to possess great inward power, wisdom, and strength. Nevertheless, in the gloomy depths of my sorrowful foolishness, I disregarded his words and intended warning. Instead I, in my youthful exuberance, considered them a challenge. And though he was not one to suffer any kind of fool for very long, he was even less prone to suffer the brazen imprudence of such an untamed youth as I. I was but a trainee, and while I, within my own heart, knew all too well my limitations and fuming spirit, yet I ignored the knowing of it.

"I understood that an unjustified fury did surely dwell deep within me. I had never known the reason for either its birth or its continued and extensive habitation within my soul, yet I long knew of its existence. It was a fury I obviously had not learned to control.

"Although I heard his words and well understood them, I did not heed them. So in short order, it came to pass that I dearly paid the full price for my youthful misdeeds. As I have already stated, Cornelius, I was sorely possessed of a wholly unbridled adolescence, hopelessly and outrageously unwise, and lacked any definable sense of nobility or assertable reason."

Wigiwig's head dropped to his chest. He hesitated a moment, then shook his head and chuckled. I considered that he might be reliving the actual event within his silence, and I chose not to interfere. A second or two later, he raised his head. A broad smile had formed on his lips and it remained as he spoke.

"Forgive me," he finally said. "I was recalling the incident."

"I thought as much," I returned.

"My recalling of my mistake that quickly followed his dissertation of his pained constraint oftentimes causes me laughter. As I said, my mistake was to rise up boldly to the perceived challenge."

He fell silent once again, but only for a few seconds before looking directly into my eyes. "The price paid for both my injudicious action and blithering ignorance, as I would soon learn, was of a magnitude I had failed to consider before my initial regrettable outburst. When the lesson was accomplished, however, I would not ever forget it."

Wigiwig lay back upon the sand, placed both hands under his head, and stared up into the cloudless sky as if he were preparing to fall into a gentle slumber.

"So he thrashed you?" I asked innocently.

"Indeed he did, and it was a thrashing I had never known could be imparted with such interminable consequence," Wigiwig replied. "But not a physical beating, as you imply."

"Not physical, you say? He did not beat you?" I inquired with great intrigue.

"As you well know by now, Cornelius, physical assault is not the way of the Minchon Warrior. No, his chastisement was delivered unto me in the more diabolical, definitive, and resolute form of being banned from the village for six months. During that time I was forced to live as an outcast: alone and unheard. It was the most frightening time of my life, and yet it was the most awesome, inspiring, and informative time of my life as well."

"Still," I said, "It is not the reaction I would expect from one so enraged. I don't understand why you call it a thrashing. It doesn't appear to have been at all a thrashing as I understand the word."

"A thrashing does not have to include a physical battle in order to be effective, Cornelius. Psychological drama can often achieve the same results."

"Sometimes," I suggested. "But if it was not a physical beating, why, then, did he threaten you with the crushing of your skull? That does not seem to be a method well wedded to the warrior code as you have described it."

Wigiwig laughed. "He was not always a warrior, Cornelius. In *his* youth he was also of an enraged spirit and prone to fisticuffs and the like. He and I were very much similar in many ways during our youthful moments. I, in my thoughtlessness, pushed hard at him, trying to incite him to physical intercourse, but he would have none of it. We pressed each other for a very long time, he and I. He by way of the warrior's code, and I, fool that I was, tried desperately and continually to bait him into a physical confrontation. I must admit, at times he both sorely angered me and perplexed me by his refusal to meet any of my physical challenges, and I *did* press him hard with such intent.

"Over the years, and by means of much study, however, we eventually became as brothers and men of kinder manners. I, for one, am forever and mightily pleased with the relationship we now enjoy, knowing unceremoniously that it was born from such bilateral pressing. For through such struggle we came to better understand, each in our own way, of course, the nature of the rage that lives within both of us still today. Through the proclivity of our sparring natures, we finally learned the more peaceful ways we now know, and we take great pleasure both in our steadfast brotherhood and in our present mastery over such inclinations.

"Speaking for myself, they no longer reign with any potent power over me. I am no longer given to fits of anger and thoughts of physical thrashings. The warrior ways have calmed the raging and bullish instincts, though they still live within my wounded places. My life is serene now, and coming from one such as me, that is saying much."

I had not been born with an overwhelming rapacious and rage-filled spirit constantly seeking to do battle with my inner self, so I could not fully understand how he had so effectively faced his ranting, implacable, and fuming demons with such understanding, humility, and tender acceptance. Those were not my lessons to be learned.

As he closed his eyes, I could not help but note almost a glow about him. This man was truly at peace with himself and with all that surrounded him. It was the same acceptance I saw in Lelalu. In fact, I saw the same in almost everyone on the island.

I stared at him for several moments and wondered how long it would be before I would develop the ability to discover my own true nature and call into the light my own troubled emotions and inciting inclinations.

I did possess those terrible traits, you understand. However, thus far, I had not given name to them, and although I stood in enormous contrast to him in many respects, I, myself, was not of the purest of heart, and I was also not of an untroubled spirit. No, not by any stretch of the imagination.

My soul harbored its own dark and foreboding elements. They were not, perhaps, possessed of the same caustic and wild demons he owned, but they well existed and I knew they did so; and at times, they battled for possession. Although my tests of emotions and incitements were well within manageable limits, it bothered me from the start, and to no end, that I carried such personality deficiencies within me at all.

I initially wanted to expunge them quickly and completely from my being, and I fought vigorously with myself on that issue for some time, as I believed them to be great inhibiting factors in my life. I believed I could actually cast them out and continue to exist as I was without their insipid interference in my growth as a warrior. As I said, I was young, hard-bristled, and very naïve.

Through my long discussions with both Amog and Wigiwig over the many years that followed, and with the ever-delicate aid of Lelalu, I finally came to accept the fact that those supposedly debilitating deficiencies were a necessary part of my being. They purposefully helped define who I was. But I am now getting ahead of myself.

During my short time on the island up to then, there were three questions I often asked myself which helped me come to terms with my dark and hidden parts with a higher grace and more dignity:

How would I ever know who I could become if I erased who I was before?

How would I ever know the path to my future if the trail of my past was absent and unable to bear witness to the route upon which I had once traveled?

How would I come to recognize victory in my life if the failed battles of my past were obliterated, thus eliminating all necessary evidence that there had been a good fight waged?

With more time, certainly, I would come to look upon such paucities and be aware of my separation from them. I eventually came to realize one very important facet of my insufficiencies, which bears repeating here. Those sore elements would, in all likelihood, forever remain a part of me whether I accepted them or not. But they were not to be feared or loathed. They belonged to me, and they could not be taken away from me by any force, only by my willingness to surrender them. And I have since come to hold them fast unto me, because I finally came to realize they were a necessary part of me, like my arms or my legs.

Upon further reflection, I concluded that I could no more exist without those pestilent faults within me than I could live without my head attached to my body. In all their indelicacies, they were integral factors in any measure of achievement I would ever come to know and enjoy.

Even in their restrictive nature, they provided certain elements which I came to honor and to hold in great regard. For each, in its own way, supplied the necessary energy and motivation to propel me forward along my destined path to become a true warrior — to give me the courage to do battle with those other surging and unsettled elements within me which I had found to be most undesirable. To give me just the briefest moment of celebration when, as my eyes closed for the last time, I would see the battle concluded and victory achieved, my splendidly shining self standing before my eyes, my heart warmed by sweet peace and serenity and a flowing glisten of true and complete joy in my eyes.

What I refused to endure, however, was to allow the presence of those terrible things within my soul the means to cause me any more ire or grief. I intended to persist in the fight for mastery over them and their destabilizing effects. Thus, on that day of glowing insight and stalwart determination, my real training began.

Chapter 14

Wigiwig remained silent and still for several minutes. I began to think he had drifted off to sleep, for under that precious tree I had, myself, on numerous occasions, also surrendered to its peacefully shaded beckoning.

Without opening his eyes, he suddenly blurted out, "I hear you wish to join with Lelalu, Cornelius. Is this true?"

I was taken aback by the abruptness with which he voiced those words. After several seconds of stunned silence, I found the words to respond. "It is true, Wigiwig, but how did you know that? I have discussed the matter only with Lelalu. Did she speak with you about it?"

"No, she has said nothing about it, but I know of your desire to make petition to Amog and her parents regarding the matter."

"Forgive me, Wigiwig, but I am puzzled as to how you know about this."

"If I told you how I know such things, Cornelius, it would send your head spinning about on your neck. I know how such thoughts get you spiraling. Just know that I know. Have you given any thought as to how to prepare the petition?"

"I have not, but I know there must some protocol to follow. There seems to be a protocol for every aspect of life here on Minchon. Am I correct?"

"Amog, in his inestimable intelligence, perceived you as a witty lad. Don't ever tell him I said he was of a particularly strong intelligence, though; your elevation of him to greatness already has him believing he is. It has made him almost unbearable to be around."

Wigiwig opened his eyes and grinned at me. I burst out in laughter and fell backward onto the sand.

After a time I sat back up, wiped dry my eyes, and grinned at Wigiwig. "You are not at all the man I had suspected you to be."

"You mean I am not the bloated, self-absorbed pinnacle of purity you thought me to be?"

I chuckled. "Well, I shall say only that you do not appear to be what I imagined a high elder of the council to be."

"You, Cornelius, are a politician," he quipped. "You choose your words very carefully. For the most part, that is a good thing, but there will come a time, and soon, when it will become necessary to speak plainly and run the risk of offended someone for the sake of the truth. Do you think yourself capable of doing that?"

"I assure you, Wigiwig, when there is a need to be plain, I can be plain. As a ship's captain, I found that there was always such a need, and I think I did speak plainly enough to the crew to be well understood when there was reason to do so."

"I believe you, lad. Again, Amog's assessment of you appears to be perfect. He is...oh, what is the word your kind uses...ah, yes, he is a *fan* of you. And as the future knows, you will do great things here. For now, however, I have been instructed to give you counsel on how to prepare an appropriate petition for marriage."

"May I ask at whose bidding you provide me such counsel as this?"

"You may ask, Cornelius, but I cannot presently say who it is. I am under strict direction to keep silent about that."

I again chuckled. "Then it would seem to me I have a guardian angel of sorts watching over me."

"Yes, you do, lad. Now, to begin, let's discuss some of the history and protocols for preparing such a petition."

The captain's eyes glistened as if some long-ago memory had suddenly returned to the forefront of his mind. Suzanne was again the first to notice it.

"Papa, perhaps that's enough for tonight. You look tired."

"Not at all, child. I was just touched by a tender memory of my magical past."

Suzanne then noted how still and silent Detective Cyra was. His eyes were slightly misted as well, and he sat staring blankly. From the looks of his notebook, he had ceased taking notes quite some time before.

"Detective Cyra," Suzanne asked, "would you care for some more coffee?"

Cyra did not answer.

"Detective Cyra," Suzanne prodded. "Detective."

Finally he stirred. "Yes," he replied unconsciously.

"Would you like more coffee?"

"No, thank you, I'm fine."

"Are you feeling all right?" Suzanne asked.

"Yes. I want to hear more of the story," he said.

"It's getting late. My grandfather tires quickly this time of night."

"Forgive me. I didn't mean tonight," he said, still dazed. "I want to hear more, Cornelius. Could we perhaps get together tomorrow?"

"So you like the story, David?" asked the captain.

"Cornelius, I don't think I've given you your just due regarding your ability to spin a yarn," Cyra said, coming around now. "You tell the story so well and with such detail that it is as if it all truly happened, as if you experienced every instant of it. You, sir, have a gift. A glorious gift."

"It *sounds* true, David, because every word of it *is* true."

"I have little doubt that you believe it."

"For once we agree, Detective," said Suzanne.

"We believe you, Papa," Robert said.

"Yes, Papa," Wendy added. "We believe you."

"Thank you, children. That means a great deal to me."

"Have you given any thought to writing a book about your adventures?" asked Cyra.

"No, David. Writing a book would require more effort than I would be willing to make on its behalf. I have far more important issues that need my attention. In fact, there are three of them sitting right here in this room."

"Thank you, Papa," said Suzanne. "You are most important to us as well."

"That's right, Papa," said Wendy. "Besides, I'm going to write the book myself someday."

"Are you now?" asked Cyra. "So, are you the author of the house, then?"

"She is," replied Robert. "She's always writing something."

"I see. Well, I must say, Cornelius, that was more than I could have hoped for. I truly would like to hear the rest of the story."

"I'll be enjoying lunch tomorrow with the children down near the wharf. Would you care to join us then?"

"I'll be there. What time?"

"Let's say eleven thirty."

"Fine. Good night, Mrs. Delightable. I cannot thank you enough for the wonderful dinner. It was delicious, and I suspect the poison was not strong enough to do any harm."

"Then it appears I didn't use enough," was Suzanne's wry reply.

Detective Cyra chuckled. "Well, I hope you'll have another opportunity to do me in completely sometime in the near future."

"We shall see."

Cyra stood up. Suzanne stood up also. "I'll show you to the door, sir."

Cyra bid everyone a good night and departed.

Robert took the opportunity to ask the captain another question.

"Papa, about Amog and Wigiwig. Are they still alive?"

"In a sense."

"What does that mean?"

"I'm afraid I can't say more right now, Robert."

"Why?"

"It's complicated, too complicated for your young mind at present. I can say this though; they are arranging to meet with your great-grandmother to prepare the island for its formal return."

"With Great-grandmother? But she died, Papa."

"Robert, I can't give you a better answer than that at the moment. Please have patience, child. All your questions will be answered in time. I can say no more right now, but be assured, all is well. Just believe in me a while longer. That's all I ask."

"I believe in you, Papa. I can wait."

"You're a very remarkable youngster, Robert — well ahead of me when I was your age. You will undoubtedly make a wonderful warrior some day. And Wendy, my beautiful girl, you will also make a fine warrior."

"Thank you, Papa," she replied, then returned her attention to her writing tablet and continued scribbling notes into it in her special code.

Suzanne came back into the room. "Time to get ready for bed, children. Get bathed now, please."

"Yes, Mama," said the children as they rose from the floor and left the room.

Suzanne sat down on the sofa and stared at her grandfather.

"I forgot how wonderful your stories are, Papa. They're truly magical. I think even that horrible man became lost in it tonight."

"Not lost, child. It's much deeper than that."

"What?"

"His soul is crying out for the truth, Suzanne."

"Papa, what are you talking about?"

"I cannot say more right now."

"You're speaking in riddles now, Papa. Why?"

"Suzanne, why did you feel you had to lock the window and the attic door?"

"Because you have been crawling out onto the roof to smoke your pipe and it's too dangerous for you out on the roof. That's why?"

"Dear child, if I want to go up on the roof and smoke my pipe, I do not need either attic door or window to do so."

"I see, Papa. If you want to, you'll just *ride the wind* up there."

"Precisely. I don't want you to tell the children about that just yet, but yes. The locks are unnecessary. I do thank you for your concern, but I'm just fine."

"Papa, you can't dematerialize and rematerialize someplace else. Please don't start on this again."

"Why is it so hard for you to believe in anything anymore? Your heart has become so hardened, my child. I wish I could help you see what is true."

"I see everything I want to see."

"I wish, then, that you wanted to see more."

"Papa, let's put this to rest. I want you to *ride the wind* up to the roof and back. If you do that right now, I promise to believe everything you say from here on out. Deal?"

"Child, you know that I would never use my power to persuade you to believe. That belief, that faith, has to come from you willingly and without physical evidence, or it is not faith at all."

"*Ride the wind* and I'll willingly believe you."

"That's not how the power should be used, Suzanne, and you know that."

"You can't do it, can you, Papa?"

"It is not a matter of *can't*. I *won't* use my power in that way. That is not why I have it. I don't use my powers to entertain or force issues of belief on anyone."

"No, Papa, you can't do it. You can't move things with your mind; you have no special powers, except that you have a special gift in telling wonderful stories — and that should be enough for anyone. But not you. You want people to believe you have special powers because it makes you feel special to have the attention of people who *ooh* and *ahh* over such make-believe stories.

"You miss Grandmother; she used to keep you in balance. She's gone now, Papa, and you have to accept that and move on. The children need you to be whole again. *I* need you to be whole again. Without you to keep us safe and financed, I would have to get a job or find another man to marry. I need you to stick around a while longer, Papa. I need your strength. I need your wisdom. I need *you*. Try, Papa. That is all I ask of you. Try to separate reality from fiction. Tell your stories if you must, but be sure to keep it in your head that they are just make-believe stories. Can you do that for me?"

"I will be here a long time, Suzanne. As long as you need me to be here. Never, ever worry about that, or about money or protection. All will be well. You will soon be happy again, and you will understand everything that has ever happened to you. There is reason and purpose to it all. You just need to find the faith."

"I have faith, Papa. I have faith in my five senses. They tell me all I need to know."

"Then so be it, child."

"I'm tired. I'm going to bed. Please think on what I've said. I really need you back to your old self, Papa, and I need to find out what Detective Cyra is going to do with all those notes he has on you."

The captain chuckled. "They'll become dust before too long. You'll see."

"I hope you're right. Good night, Papa."

"Good night, my child."

Suzanne bent over and kissed the captain on the forehead as usual, then left the library, closing the door behind her.

The captain opened his leather pouch and began stuffing his pipe. "Come to think of it, I believe this is a perfect night to have my smoke on the roof," he murmured.

* * * * *

Detective Cyra rounded the corner and easily spotted the captain and the children seated at a large table near the wharf docks. He glanced down at his watch. It was precisely 11:30.

As he neared the trio, Captain Delightable stood up.

"Right on time, David. Suzanne made an extra sandwich. She said it was for you."

The two men shook hands and Cyra sat down.

"Good morning, children. Thank you, Captain, but I brought my own."

"My granddaughter said to tell you she put extra poison in it this morning....It's roast beef."

Cyra looked at his own sandwich and then at the one the captain held. "Well, poison or not, it's still probably better than the liverwurst sandwich I made for myself. Thank you, Cornelius. I'll take it."

"Did you catch up on your notes?"

"Yes. Yes, I did. I do enjoy your stories, but I have to do my job, you understand."

"I would expect you to do nothing less, David. Now, where did I leave off last night?"

"Wigiwig was going to help you write the petition," offered Robert because Wendy was far too busy scribbling down every word already spoken.

"Ah, yes. Thank you, my boy. Yes."

Wigiwig was kind enough to help me research all the different petition protocols. After all, I was not born on Minchon and had not been taught all the customs and traditions as I grew. I was, therefore, forced to cram several years of natural learning into a very short period. It was exhausting at times, and I often thought I might fail because of my naïveté.

Over the next few weeks, however, after I had completed all my other daily chores and duties, he helped me rehearse my presentation. It was very precise and orderly, and the manner of its deportment so old and revered that no one could accurately recall how it had ever been accomplished before in any other fashion.

In a very short time, and aided immeasurably by the circumstances of our close labor, Wigiwig and I became very good friends. After learning much from him, I soon understood why he had been elected to the high council position he held. His knowledge of the traditions and customs of the Minchon was immense and thorough. He clearly understood, with exacting precision, how and why the rituals were to be performed.

Completing my preparations, I finally sat down to write out my petition. It was a task with which he did not assist me, saying it was my responsibility to exercise all the knowledge, in precise detail, he had given to me. It was also a test of sorts to see if I had learned properly all I needed to learn.

He left me alone for the next several days while I worked on the petition, and after I had finished writing it, he looked it over and found it perfectly prepared and in complete compliance with all the rules and protocols. I must admit, in that moment I was exceedingly gladdened with my efforts, for it took every ounce of skill I possessed to write it with such precision and eloquence.

I now had only to present the marriage petition through the correct channels and in the proper form with the wish that it be accepted. This meant, of course, that I had to request an audience with the council. This was also accomplished through exacting protocols and manners. I will not impose upon you to labor with me through all the necessary and dull details of that procedure. Instead, let it suffice to say I filed my petition with the council, and within three days' time discovered, to my great joy and unbounded relief, that it had been accepted.

The council, having accepted my petition and affirming its compliance with all the traditions and customs expected, passed it on — with their approval — to Lelalu's parents.

There being nothing more for me to do in the matter, I awaited — impatiently, as you would expect — their response, knowing that if approved by them, it would then be presented to Amog for his approval. If I passed that test, I would then be allowed to officially propose to Lelalu.

Oh, dear me! That is a story sure to have you laughing to burst your sides; but I shall hold that for later and give you time to prepare yourself.

However, let me say, in the matter of preparing a proper proposal I learned that such requirements were employed to ensure that a man's intent to marry was sincere and not one made in a heated moment only to be regretted later. These ways had endured for millennia. They were proven and respected procedures, as were all of the Minchon ways.

Throughout it all, I marveled at how their society functioned so smoothly and calmly. This is the way it was, and looking back on it now, I see no need for any modifications.

With my petition accepted, I went about my days in as much a normal fashion as I could, as impatient as you, my dear friends, now know me to have been. Wigiwig and I spent much time together when Lelalu was unavailable.

Time sped by rapidly.

Three weeks slipped past with my hardly realizing it. In my former life, the time spent waiting for any word on my petition would have driven me utterly and completely mad, or to such outbursts of emotion that I would have failed miserably to gain acceptance. But here, with my daily activities so well managed by the expectations of the community, and my busy study schedule with Wigiwig, I hardly had an occasion to think about the petition at all.

Besides, married or not, I had Lelalu to comfort me. She never brought up the petition, and neither did I. Not because it wasn't an important issue; it was just that we were so very much in love and active in so many of the village activities, we simply did not think about it.

* * * * *

One day, alone on the beach wading through the cool surf, I spied a lone figure walking toward me from a great distance away. As the figure neared, I saw that it was a man. Upon a nearer view, I realized it was Mata'pang.

During all the time since our previous confrontations near the spring, I had neither seen nor heard from him, and that day was now long past. So long, in fact, I had a difficult time remembering with any degree of exactness just when it had been. I knew not why he had chosen this day to confront me once again, but he was approaching and there was no escaping it.

I had grown much since our last encounter. I neither feared nor relished this coming encounter, but I felt confident enough to hold my ground if I needed to.

As he walked toward me, I noticed the great purpose in his stride. His long black hair floated behind him. His eyes seemed to be determinedly set upon me, for the position of his head stayed straight in an unrelenting pose. I saw a definite purpose in his direct approach.

Within minutes he had stopped and was standing not four feet from me. His eyes stared defiantly and directly into mine.

"Mata'pang," I said, "it is good to see you. You look well. How have you been?"

Not yet comfortable with the Minchon welcoming gesture in that circumstance, I extended my hand to him, but he refused it yet again, remaining still, silent, and continuing his menacing stare.

I decided very quickly that I would not be intimidated, so I stared back at him with equal stead.

He remained silent. I believed that he was studying me. To what end I could not say, but his stare was bold and challenging. I dared not show any fear or wavering in my demeanor, for he surely would have taken that as a sign of weakness. I was admittedly and certainly most curious to discover why he was standing in front of me, but it seemed — for he had made it most obvious — that it would require me to begin the conversation. I decided to break the stalemate with a measured boldness.

"It is not polite to simply approach one and stare so intently. If we were not on such a peaceful island, I would think you intended to do me harm. I assure you, if it comes to that, you should be advised I am well able to defend myself. But you should not take my words as a challenge. I mean only to serve notice that I am prepared for anything."

He continued standing silently. He was trying my patience, to be sure. I had to set a boundary, if for no other reason than to establish my position.

"You are rude, sir. If you have nothing you wish to say, then I shall step around you and continue on with my delightful stroll, dismissing you from my mind. If that is your wish as well, then remain the mute beast you appear to be, but I would expect more from a true man of Minchon."

I quieted my tongue and waited for his response.

After several moments and the continued silence on his part, I adjudged my efforts a failure and wished to terminate this confrontation. "Fine, have it your way, but I tire of this childish and brutish behavior and will tolerate it no more."

I stepped to the side and immediately started walking past him.

"Why are you still here?" he finally said. "Did I not make myself clear to you before?"

I stopped in my tracks immediately beside him, staring straight ahead. "You did, but I am not a man easily swayed by an emotional outburst from an immature child acting with such poor manners."

"You anger me, Delightable. Take care that your ill-spoken words do not anger me further."

"I do not seek to anger you or anyone else. I seek to discuss our issue in a rational manner, to find some common ground upon which to repair our relationship, which I have not broken. But that requires two willing souls of mature insight and of a wishful nature to resolve the matter. Your silence makes me think you are not yet ready to sit down and have that discussion."

"You have no place here. You were not invited here. You have taken everything from me — my position in the boat, my position in the village, and now you seek to take my woman."

"I took nothing from you. You were voted off the boat by the village because of your own failures, without any input from me. I had nothing to do with that. The same can be said for your loss of Lelalu. That also was decided long before I came to the island. You, thus, place blame on me without support or reason. Still, if you wish to parlay, I will be only too happy to sit right here in the sand, at this very moment, and hear your side of the story.

But you will have to agree to hear my side of it as well, for I shall not stand falsely accused of wrong doing and remain silent. I shall speak boldly in my defense. And although the plainness of my words might offend you, I will have my say. Do we agree on those terms?"

"I will not agree with you on any terms. Leave this island. This is your last warning. Heed my words before I take from you that which you hold dear. And know this also: we should never meet again, but if we do, I shall not be so accommodating and kind."

"Have it your way, as I said already, but we shall meet again, for I have no intention of being driven off this island by you or by anyone else, failing good reason."

Mata'pang only grunted his response and then walked away. I did not turn to watch him go, but I heard the fading sound of his splashing footsteps along the water's edge.

After several minutes of standing alone, I sat down on the shore and considered what had just occurred. Questions filled my head immediately. *Did I respond correctly? Did I react appropriately and in a fashion commensurate with the ways of the warrior? What now? What will be his next move? Is violence in my future?*

If he rejected the ways of the warrior and refused to speak with me, would he also reject the warrior ways of non-violence?

Thus I sat, immeasurably frustrated, my head filled to the brim with so many unanswered questions that I began to feel overwhelmed.

As if in answer to some desperate message sent out into the universe seeking guidance and compassion, I felt Lelalu's hand upon my shoulder.

"You are troubled?" she asked, sitting down next to me.

"I am vexed, my love, lost in the midst of a black quandary, and I know not how to bring the light of resolution to the matter. The more I think on the situation, the more I feel bound by the clutch of uncertainty."

"Tell me of this quandary."

"I was just once again confronted by Mata'pang. He will not hear my words. He will not consider the fact that I had no part in the interference of his life. He only threatens. I am so tormented by all of this, so disquieted. I seek no victory, no vengeance. I seek only a resolution."

"Find the strength and the patience necessary, my love. He is not presently of the right mind to hear you. Give him more time."

"I have not confronted him. It is *he* who continues confronting me. How will the passage of more time soothe the raging beast within him?"

"It is for him to find the answer to that question, Cornelius. It is his responsibility to find his way out of the darkness he created. Your only duty is to continue walking in the light."

"Your answers seem so simple and right, but I find them so difficult to comprehend and practice at times."

"Then find also the patience and the strength necessary for you to endure. It all lies within you already. You just need to seek within yourself for them and take hold once you have found them. I cannot do that for you."

"I am trying, my love. I am trying."

Chapter 15

Once again, Cyra had stopped taking notes of the captain's story and sat with a blank expression on his face.

"Is my story entertaining enough for you, David?"

As before, Cyra did not immediately reply, while his faraway expression concentrated on some sight only he could see.

The captain stretched out his hand and lightly touched Cyra's shoulder, bringing the detective back to the present time and place.

"I say, David, is my story entertaining enough for you?"

"Y...yes, Cornelius, quite. But I wonder, can you tell me more about this Mata'pang fellow? He seems to be a most indelicate man. May I ask whom you have patterned his character after?"

"I have not created him at all. He existed."

"I find that unbelievable. His character is most curiously odd and displeasing. He must be the counter to the hero in the story. The created antagonist, as it were, to yourself as the protagonist. Do I have that correct?"

"Well," replied the captain thoughtfully, "it would coincidently seem so, though I had not considered him as such. He was just a man who lived on the island with me. I hadn't thought of him as a story character, but giving it some thought now, I would say that you must necessarily be correct. Hmm, a protagonist and an antagonist. Very interesting, David. A very interesting observation."

"Well, I only assumed...I mean you are a storyteller. I just assumed you created both characters on purpose. All stories have both characters as a necessary counterpoint to each other, to create the conflict one of them will necessarily have to resolve during the conflict-resolution stage of the story. I was just wondering who you might have used as inspiration for Mata'pang."

"You seem to know much about storytelling, David. Did you study writing in school?"

Cyra became a smidgen uneasy with the question, almost embarrassed. His eyes dropped to the table. "Well, Cornelius, to be plainly honest, I did a small bit of writing in my younger years. Not at all like young Wendy here, who has been scribbling like mad ever since you began your story, but at one time in my younger life, I did give some consideration to becoming an author. And in some small way, I guess I am a bit of a writer. After all, writing up reports does require a morsel of skill. I mean a story must be told, yes?"

"Indeed it must, David. I could not agree with you more. It does require skill to create a report. To charge someone with a crime is one thing, but to present the charge in court in an orderly and concise manner necessarily demands an ability to arrange all the facts and suppositions in a way that can be understood by all parties."

"You have an extraordinary way of putting that process into words, Cornelius. I never thought of it in that way before, but I suppose there is a bit of art involved in prosecution. It's strange, but I do feel wonderfully brightened by your words."

"No doubt your skill in preparing a report, your skill as a writer, must be partly responsible for your success as a detective."

Cyra's disposition brightened further. "By George, I think you're correct. Of course, I would not consider myself a storyteller on par with you. My stories are based on hard facts or suppositions based on the reading of clues. You, on the other hand, have the unique ability — at least in my mind — to create all the clues and facts and present them in a most delightful way. I am finding myself captivated by your stories, Cornelius. Your gift is extraordinary."

"Why thank you, David. It's most gracious of you to say so."

"It is going to be most difficult for me to press these charges against you. I must, of course, it is my duty; but I shall take no joy in it at all. I want you to know that. My first duty is to protect the public, but beyond that I do thoroughly enjoy your gift as a storyteller. Perhaps some of your gift will rub off on me and I shall someday put pen to paper myself and tell a good story. Perhaps it will be your story that I pen."

The captain chuckled. "So you think I'm still a danger to the community?"

"No doubt. I would not say so if you did not actually believe your stories are true. I understand how you might think so. You tell them with such great zest and detail, I have found myself lost in them as well on both the occasions I have listened."

"But it's not possible that they could be true. Is that what you're saying?"

"Cornelius. You're not being serious. *Riding the wind* — really? Shipwrecked nearly a year on a magical island. Lions and tigers that live peacefully with humans. Minchon warriors who have harnessed all negative emotions. Come now, Cornelius. Even you must see how none of that is possible."

"You sound so much like my granddaughter. Do you not believe in anything, David?"

"Certainly I do. I believe in the law. I believe in what my five senses tell me is real. I believe in God."

"What would you say if I told you that I was God?"

Cyra laughed raucously. "Then I would say you suffer from some illness of the mind towards arrogance. That's what I would say."

"Okay. What if I told you that you were also God? What would you say to that?"

"I'd say you suffer from an illness of the mind, period. Look at me, Cornelius. Can you not see that I am but a simple policeman?"

"Is it not possible for God to be a simple policeman?"

"Well, I guess so, but I am not God, Cornelius."

"Could God not be a farmer, a butcher, a merchant man? Could he not be a doctor, a teacher, or anyone else he chooses to be? Could God be a she?"

"Well, certainly. I suppose so."

"Then why couldn't you be God?"

"Because I'm not. That's why."

"Tell me this. How can you believe in God? Have you ever seen his or her face? Have you spoken with God?"

"Of course not."

"If you cannot see Him or talk with Him, how can you believe in Him? Certainly, an unheard and invisible being presents contrary evidence from the point of view of what your five senses can give you."

"God is a question of faith, Cornelius."

"So, you can have faith in something that cannot be seen, touched, or conversed with. But is not the existence of God a story that has been passed down for millennia by ancient storytellers?"

"Well, I suppose you're right about that."

"Yet in that story you find faith and belief. Why is my story any different? Why do you find it so hard to believe in my story?"

"Because it is so outrageously fantastic."

"Is it more fantastic than the story of Jesus the Christ raising a man from the dead, or walking on the surface of storm-tossed sea? Is it more fantastic than a God bringing rain to the earth, flooding it, and killing nearly everything on its surface?"

"No, but it's different."

"How? How are my stories any different from the stories you have put your faith into?"

Cyra remained silent, his eyes darting about as his mind searched for a reasonably constructed response to the captain's questions. Finally, after several conflicted seconds, he spoke. "I have no answer for you, Cornelius. I don't know how to answer you, except to say that *God* is God. *You* are not God."

"How do you know that?"

Cyra scoffed. "Because I just know."

"Yet I just asked you if you have ever seen or spoken with God and you said 'no.'"

"Wait! Let me ask you a question, Cornelius. Have *you* ever seen the face of God? Have *you* ever spoken to Him?"

"Every day, David. I see God's face everywhere I look; in all the faces I see Him or Her. I hear His voice loudly in every voice I hear, or Hers. I see Him, in fact, right now, sitting across from me, in your eyes."

"I am not God, Cornelius."

"Can you prove that you are not He? Or, better still, try and answer this. You are a policeman, David. You operate in facts and evidence. How can you believe in the story of God, someone whom you've just admitted you've neither seen nor talked to? Why is the existence of God so profoundly real to you, and yet you consider my stories — stories you can hear from a man you can see and touch — so outrageously fantastic to the point you have decided they must be false and believed only by a madman such as I?"

Cyra remained silent for a long time. The captain could see the detective's mind struggling to wrap itself around those thoughts and questions. He expected no answer from the detective. Instead, he sat in equal silence, pressing the matter no further, satisfied to sit and allow the policeman the time he needed to discover his own answers to his own questions — ones the captain was sure were flying about in his confused mind.

He glanced at the children, who remained silent but intrigued as to how their great-grandfather had so effectively silenced the detective.

Robert smiled up at the captain and winked; the captain was delighted to see his great-grandson's mind diligently working to understand what had just been debated. Wendy, on the other hand, continued to be keenly focused on her note writing, completely oblivious to her surroundings.

After several more minutes of silence, the captain laid his hand upon Cyra's arm. Cyra's eyes, dark and lost, turned toward him. "Think no more on the matter for now, David. Let us just enjoy our company together. You asked to know more about Mata'pang. What questions about him would you like answered?"

"I don't know," answered Cyra, still dazed and confused.

"Do you have questions about his character?"

"He seems so angry and muddled, so out of place in the world of Minchon Island. How could one exist so contrary to such a well-ordered community?"

"Then you *do* know the questions…and sir, that is an excellent question. He does seem to exist in divergent opposition to the ways of the society surrounding him, does he not?"

Cyra nodded his head.

"Well, let me jump a mite ahead in the story and perhaps the question will be answered."

On a particularly wonderful afternoon, about three weeks after my confrontation with Mata'pang on the beach, Lelalu and I went on an extended stroll which carried us toward the far eastern side of the island. While we walked, we chatted. We covered a myriad of subjects, but nothing of any great importance. It was just the casual conversation of two lovers enjoying their splendid time together.

I, myself, was lost in the trivial nature of our discussion and had dismissed the landscape in front of me. My mind was a flutter of differing images and my words were tumbling out of my mouth.

I suddenly felt Lelalu's hand stop me abruptly. My mind came around and I found myself standing before a wooden gate. It was simple in its construction, slats of wood planking attached to pole crossbars. It was not of a sound design and could have been torn apart without too much effort. But it was there, blocking our path.

To the left and right was a fence built flimsily of wood pole and vines, that disappeared off to either horizon, presumably to each coast, bisecting the island. It would have not been able to stop anyone from crossing through it. But, once again, it was present. And both the gate and the fence, only four or five feet high, were respected as a blockade.

Above the gate, mounted on poles, was a large sign, stretched between them, and covered with strange symbols I could not decipher.

During my time on the island thus far, and in my preparations for the petition, I had certainly seen the Minchon language in its written form, I had even learned to read some of it, but these symbols were completely strange to me. "What is this gate and what do the symbols mean?" I asked.

"This is the entrance to the Forbidden Land. The symbols are the ancient form of the Minchon language. They announce that the land beyond is the Forbidden Land. We must turn back now."

"The Forbidden Land? What is the Forbidden Land? Why is it called such?"

"I cannot say right now. The story itself is forbidden to be told without permission from Amog."

An expression of frustration must have formed on my face because she raised a hand and laid it against my cheek and smiled. "I know you long to hear the story. In time you shall, but it is law placed on the people for good reason, my love. In time you will understand why such a law exists and why this land has been forbidden to the people. It is a cursed land, and you shall also hear the explanation of why it is so cursed. But not today. We have walked as far as we are able for now. We should return."

I was about to speak when a voice from the other side of the gate spoke loudly.

"Why have you come?"

We both snapped our heads around and saw Mata'pang standing near the gate wearing a sneer.

"What business have you here, Princess?" he growled. "Is your side not enough for you? Do you feel the need to harass me even here?"

"I was not aware you were here at all," she replied. "Why have you disobeyed the law and crossed this gate?"

"Your outdated and corrupt laws apply to me no more, Princess. I am no longer bound by them or by any others. I am free from the tyranny of the Minchon king. I have been voted out of your society. I should give them my thanks for liberating me, but you shall hear no gratitude from these lips. You shall hear only my contempt for you all."

"Return now, Mata'pang, and no one will hear of this breech," Lelalu pleaded. "I give you my word. Return to the village with us and rejoin your people. You have been sorely missed."

"Ha!" he spat. "You are *not* my people. I have never been of your race. I know that now. All has become clear to me. I am not of the One. I am a proud son of the Other and I once more claim the Forbidden Land for my master."

"You speak in pain, Mata'pang," replied Lelalu. "I feel your pain. I understand your outrage. Please, brother. Forgive us and return to the fold. Your hurt will be healed. All shall be well again."

"You disgust me. You're pathetic. I have no need to be healed, for I suffer no pain, no hurt, no malady that needs to be healed. I am better now. I am stronger now. I am home now. Be gone from here. We have no need of you."

"We?" she asked in surprise. "Who are 'we,' Mata'pang? I know of no others living in the Forbidden Land."

"We are here. We have survived for millennia without your knowledge of us. These are my true brothers and sisters."

"How many are you?" I asked.

"Enough to utterly ravage your adopted land and destroy your adopted nation completely if we so desire."

"Why do you expose yourself now?" Lelalu asked.

"Because in a short time our race will rise up and take its rightful place once again upon the earth. We have been hidden away for too long. We once were a great power and we shall be again. You Minchonians, in all your vain piety and false righteousness, have been like a knife to our throats. No longer. No longer will you keep us hidden and out of the minds of Earth's population. We ruled this planet long ago. We are now born again, and growing stronger each and every day. Soon we shall rule once more and bring the world to its knees. Our master will be worshipped again and his rule will last forever. We have learned the ways of Man and all of his weaknesses and false beliefs. When we rise up, Man will fall on his face and beg us to rule again."

"It pains me to hear you speak thusly, my brother," said Lelalu. "We have known each other since our childhood. I cannot bear to hear such words fall from your lips. I have great affection for you, Mata'pang. Please speak no more these terrible words. It hurts my heart, brother."

"You call me 'brother' and yet you were the first to turn your back on me, even before my own father turned against me and dissolved our betrothal. You were the first to disown my affections. And now you wish for me to hearken unto your words of affection? And where were you, *sister*, when I was being voted off the boat and out of society? Did you stand in my defense? Did you speak on my behalf? No! You were too busy singing the praises of your new mate, Cornelius Alexander Delightable. The future hero of Minchon Island. The friend to Minchon Island. The savior of the Minchon race. Bah, I say. Bah, I say to you both."

"Mata'pang," I finally said. "I understand your anger toward your village. I know nothing of your history with Lelalu before my arrival, so I cannot speak to that issue at all, but why do you loathe me so? Have I not twice extended my hand in friendship to you?"

"Friendship!" he scoffed. "You do not extend your hand to make me a friend, but to snare me and take me prisoner."

"How could you find reason for that in my kindly gesture?"

"You seek not to befriend me, but to demonstrate that you are victor over me. You seek a position above me, to rob me of the woman I was promised, to steal from me my position as a warrior, to denigrate me in the eyes of the nation — to prove to all that I have never been of a worthy caliber as a man. Your presence has made me irrelevant. I would rather be dead than irrelevant."

"I understand none of your charges against me. I refute them all as well. I sought only your friendship."

"You have Wigiwig and Amog to guide you. They show favor toward you. But for me they show only disappointment and contempt. It is in their eyes."

"Perhaps you misunderstand their look. Perhaps those looks are meant only to encourage you toward greater being. I have been told you are wise, strong, and courageous. Are these not good traits to possess?"

"I am all that and more. You shall soon learn the power of my attributes. Go and tell your village to prepare themselves. Tell them to make ready for the return of the Other and his children. Be gone now! And do not come hither again, or you shall be torn asunder."

"Mata'pang, let us sit and discuss this matter further. I promise to give ear to your cause. I promise to listen with an open heart. I promise to hear all you need to say and to give good attention to all your words. There is no need to threaten. We are brothers."

"We are not brothers!"

"Surely all mankind are brothers and sisters under heaven, are we not?"

"The heaven you speak of is meant only for the sons and daughters of the One. The sons and daughters of the Other have been offered no such place. There is no kinship between us. Be gone now!"

"Mata'pang. I know nothing regarding the *One* or this *Other* of which you speak of. Please, I beg of you, let us sit and you can tell me all about this matter. I have a strong desire now to learn of these things."

"You will learn of these things before too long. You will hear only lies, however, for only lies are spoken about my master. But hearken unto this, Son of One. Soon there will be a cloak of darkness spread over your world. Then you will hear the truth of the Other, for he will be shouting loudly and clearly into your ears — and absent any lies. I say again, prepare yourself. Dig out your ears, for you shall hear the voice of my master soon enough."

Mata'pang turned away abruptly and walked off into the thicket beyond the gate.

"I feel great sorrow in my heart for him," I said.

"Feel the sorrow, my love, but do not take his words of woe into your heart. Retain there, instead, only light sentiments. Take care not to burden your shoulders with his heavy loads of anger and disappointment. Those burdens are his alone to carry."

"I need to know about the One and this Other he spoke of. Can you instruct me?"

"I cannot, but Amog will teach you when you are ready to hear."

"I wish to learn, Lelalu. I wish to understand so that I might sit down with Mata'pang and understand him. I believe he needs to be heard."

"My love, I cherish your desire to greet his darkness with the light of understanding. But I am afraid you do not comprehend the true problem. It is impossible for light to meet with darkness, for in the moment of their meeting, darkness would be instantly dispersed. You must also understand that, for light, there can be no compromise with darkness, for there is lacking any common ground upon which the illumination of reason might exist within darkness. Darkness wishes no understanding with light. It seeks only light's destruction."

"I am becoming confused again. You speak of light and darkness as if they have body. But Mata'pang and I are men. We have bodies in which both darkness and light may simultaneously dwell in the form of our contrary natures. But on the most basic level we are just simple men. We each have ears to hear. We each have minds with which to comprehend the words spoken. If we can sit down and discuss this situation as men, then I am certain a meaningful and fair resolution can be reached. Is this not the true way of the warrior?"

"You are young in the ways of the warrior, my love. On this day I wish it were not so, but it is. I can only say this without burdening you with too much. If you allow either darkness or light to dwell within you, then you have become either Darkness or Light. Contrary to your belief, only one may exist within you at any given moment. Do you understand this concept?"

"I do understand the concept, and if there is a choice to make, then I choose light to dwell within me."

"Spoken well, my Cornelius. Spoken very well, but you do not yet understand what obligation there is in living with the Light inside you. This is what you must learn before confronting Mata'pang again."

* * * * *

Immediately upon our arrival back at camp, Lelalu bid me to wait for her near her hut while she went before her father's throne to tell him of our confrontation with Mata'pang.

She was not at the throne long when she turned and motioned me to her. I trotted to the base of the throne, bowed my head, and remained still. A second later King Gogui spoke, his beautiful baritone voice calling me up the stairs to the throne. "Good Cornelius. Come and stand before the throne."

I dutifully climbed the stairs until I stood before both the king and the queen, my head bowed in humility as I remained silent.

"Cornelius," his voice boomed out, "let us dispense with formalities for the moment. Look up at me and tell me of your confrontation with Mata'pang."

"Great King Gogui, Queen Letula, I saw on the beach some weeks ago Mata'pang. He confronted me there with repeated words of warning that I was to leave the island or suffer retribution. He holds me responsible for his loss of Lelalu, his place on the boat, and his diminished status among the Minchon people.

"Then today, on our walk to the eastern side of the island, Lelalu and I were confronted. He was standing on the far side of the gate and well inside the Forbidden Land. I tried to reason with him. Lelalu made an equal effort as well, but he would have none of our well wishes. Instead, he told us there were many others. He said they were of the Other and warned us there would be a large confrontation. I took that to mean he threatened to make war against us."

King Gogui remained silent. Through his soulful eyes, I could see his mind working on what it all meant. He looked down at his lap and then up and into my eyes.

"My daughter tells me you made wonderful and graceful gestures to speak of the issue in an honest effort to resolve his pain. Cornelius, my son, my faith in you has been confirmed. I am well pleased, and so is the queen."

The queen bowed her head in agreement and smiled warmly at me. I returned her smile, then turned my eyes to the king again.

"As an experienced ship's captain," the king continued, "how would you take Mata'pang's threats? Would you take them as a serious warning or only as the rantings made by a disobedient and rude youth in full bluster and bravado?"

"Speaking from the point of view of a ship's captain, Great One, I would take his threats with exceeding seriousness. In that position of authority and responsibility, I must necessarily consider the safety of my crew and the safety of my ship and cargo first and foremost. Such a duty falls to the captain: to consider any threatening word spoken, whether it be with merit or lacking such, as an actionable threat requiring preparations to be made forthwith."

"Well stated, Cornelius. And so you suggest that I take his threats seriously and make preparations for war?"

"Yes, Great One. If I were you, I would order preliminary preparations at least until I saw sufficient evidence either to support the need or to render the need unnecessary."

"And again, as ship's captain, how would such preparations be undertaken?"

"I would give orders to my first mate to get preparations under way."

"It is the captain who gives those orders?"

"Yes, Great One."

"Then you shall be my captain, Cornelius. Wigiwig will be your first mate. Begin preparations as you see fit. Tomorrow you, Amog, Wigiwig, Lelalu, and I will travel to the cliffs overlooking the Forbidden Land and we shall investigate the matter further."

"Aye, Great One. By your command I shall make ready for war. May I now take my leave to begin this work?"

"Not yet, my son. I have one more decree."

"Yes, Great King."

"I have kept a careful eye on you since you arrived. You are an exceptional young man, and although you lack the experience in our ways and traditions, you have availed yourself of every opportunity to learn the ways of the Minchon Nation; you have also completed an excellent petition for marriage with our precious daughter. I am pleased to tell you that your petition has been found worthy."

"Great One, if you have found favor in my petition, it is only because of the assistance offered to me by Wigiwig."

"Such assistance would not have been allowed if you had not earned it. That is why my wife instructed Wigiwig to assist you."

"So it is you, Great Queen, I must thank for Wigiwig's assistance. I cannot begin to thank you enough for such a wizard."

"You have earned it all, Cornelius," the Queen said with a smile. "My daughter speaks of you very highly and often. She loves you, Cornelius, and I see your great affection for her as well. I see no reason why you two should be kept apart any longer."

I bowed deeply toward the queen. "My thanks will never be enough. I can only show you my gratitude by taking her into my life and taking care of her to the best of my ability. I hope that will suffice."

"It shall."

"Therefore, Cornelius," said the king, "I grant your petition and will forward it this day to Amog for his blessing and approval. The final judgment will now fall to him."

"Thank you, Great King. In all humility, please accept my gratitude for your trust in me as your son-in-law — and as your captain. I will strive to be worthy of both positions."

I looked at Lelalu. Tears of joy streamed down her face, and her broad, white smile beamed brightly.

The captain stopped speaking and glanced over at the detective, sitting motionless. A hint of a smile on the detective's lips, his pleasant but distant expression, and his vacant eyes confirmed what the captain had suspected. The strange policeman was disconnected from the reality of the chilly San Francisco afternoon — he was on vacation, as it were, from his duty of protecting the city's citizenry from the hauntings of this menacing, crazy old man. He was off on a faraway island somewhere in the South Pacific, bathed in warm sunlight, the scent of salt air filling his nostrils as he nestled safely within his own fantasy.

Several minutes passed without another word being spoken by anyone. Even the children noticed the distant gaze of the detective's eyes. Robert looked to his great-grandfather. The captain raised his index finger to his lips, signaling Robert not to make a sound. He wanted to allow Cyra to live a while longer within his vision.

Finally, after several more minutes, Cyra's eyes blinked. He had returned.

"Did you enjoy yourself, David?"

"What?"

"Did you enjoy yourself? On your trip?"

"Ahh," replied Cyra, now understanding. "Yes. Yes, I did. I almost felt myself actually there. A broad smile formed on his lips. "I'll say it again, Cornelius. You have a gift for telling stories."

"Thank you, David. The story is easy. The ending, however, might be difficult to hear."

"Why's that."

"The journey is not yet completed. I don't know how the story ends. I'm still waiting to see how all of this concludes."

"Still believing in your own fantasies, eh?"

"Not fantasies, David, remembrances; I'm simply recalling my life."

"You do understand how this makes you sound?"

"Like a crazed maniac, I would assume."

"Your stories are certainly vivid and real sounding. You make it easy for your listeners to immerse themselves in the world you create. At times, I almost feel I'm actually there seeing everything for myself. It is a rare gift you possess. There, however, is one major difference between you and me, Cornelius. I understand that it is a fantasy. A wonderful fantasy, to be sure, but only a fantasy. I can see in my mind's eye all the wonderful things, people, and places you describe so elegantly and completely, but I know it is only a vision placed into my mind by a master storyteller. I don't, for one moment, think it is a true story being recalled by the storyteller."

"What if *this* life is only a vision of your dreaming self in another reality?" asked the captain. "Does it mean you should enjoy it less? Does it mean it has less value?

"If that is so, it means, to me, it shouldn't be taken seriously. Soon enough I would awaken from it and I would need to get on with my real life in whatever reality is true."

"Tell me this, David. What if true reality finds you in prison with no chance of ever being free again? Is it better to live in that reality or to live in a fantasy where you are free to live life as you choose?"

"Your questions are theoretical and require speculation, Cornelius. I don't live my life in speculation, I rely on facts. To answer your question, however, I would rather deal with the reality of whatever life I am actually living, be it for well or ill. At least I would not be deluding myself and living in a false world — living an untrue life."

"Well said, David. Living honestly, I think, would most often be the best choice for me as well."

"Then you admit that your stories are just make-believe?"

"No, not at all."

"Then you admit you are living a lie?"

"For me, David, my life is the honest truth."

"Then there it is. I have not judged you; you have judged yourself."

"Then there it is."

"I guess so. I have what I need, Cornelius. I'm sorry for that. I truly wish it were not so, for your gift is immense; and for what it is, I think it would have great value to our community. But if you believe your stories are true, then I cannot allow you to be out in public unescorted. I will have to file my report with the judge. It pains me to say I will have to recommend that you be put away for the safety of yourself as well as for the safety of the public. I'm sorry, Cornelius. I truly am."

"If that is the way you see it, David, then do what your heart tells you to do. I do feel for you. You are searching so hard to find your way. I can only hope you discover the path before it's too late. I can only guide you to the path; I cannot walk it for you. I sincerely hope you find your way back home soon."

"Then again, Cornelius, your own words condemn you, for I am home. It is you who are lost. Good day, Captain. Good day, children."

With no further words, Detective Cyra closed his notebook and walked away.

"Papa," asked Robert, "is he going to make trouble for you now?"

"It would seem that he will try, lad."

"I'm frightened. What will we do if they take you away from us?"

The captain chuckled. "Have no fear of that, Robert. That will not happen."

"Papa, can you continue the story? I want to know what mean old Mata'pang did next."

"Yes, Papa," echoed Wendy. "I want to know why Lelalu was crying. Was she sad?"

"No," said the captain with a gentle smile. "She was not sad at all."

"Then why was she crying?"

"After supper, children. I will finish the story right after supper."

Chapter 16

The children joined the captain in his library after helping their mother clean up after supper. Taking their usual places in front of the fireplace, they stared up at the captain in anxious anticipation of his continued story. Instead, he rocked back and forth in silence, nibbling on the end of his unlit pipe, his eyes locked on some distant object or scene only he could see. He looked troubled by his vision.

The children remained silent but restless.

Finally, without adjusting his eyes, he spoke.

I remember not sleeping soundly long into the night; the thought of confronting Mata'pang once more was discomforting and made it impossible for peaceful repose. As we were still unmarried, Lelalu did not share my hut; this left me alone and troubled to work it out for myself.

With no one to talk to about the matter, and tossing about as I was, I decided that lying in bed would not bring me any more composure. I guessed it was at least two hours before sunrise, so I arose from my bunk, dressed, and made my way through the still-sleeping village and out to the boats on the shoreline.

I strolled up and down the empty beach thinking of what I was going to do if Mata'pang made good on his threat to attack. Being in charge of the preparations, I had ordered the making of spears and bows and arrows; I had also ordered the building of hand-held shields.

While instructing the village to build wooden defense walls, I knew well that but a single fiery arrow would very soon demolish them. Being on an open sandy plain, we had few ways of defending the village, and considering that we had neither mud nor straw enough to build the fire-resistant walls necessary to surround the village, we stood completely vulnerable to an open attack.

As frightened as I was about that possibility, I was more perplexed as to how best to defend the people of Minchon. The king had placed me in charge, but I was not an infantry commander, I was a ship's captain, a merchant vessel captain at that. I had never been engaged in any form of combat.

I delivered cargo into beautiful and safe ports. I had never even had occasion to have the cannons on board our vessel fired, thinking it a preposterous eventuality to have the need to do so.

Still, it was I who had been tasked with this inordinately mammoth responsibility, and I had to find a way to fight a battle that before two days ago I could not imagine would ever be conceivable, let alone necessary.

I thought also on just who the One might be, and who this Other character was. *Was he the never-seen-again outcast that Lelalu had mentioned a while back? Had he gone into the Forbidden Land and raised an army there? From where did he get the people to raise an army? Had other Minchon people revolted many years ago?* I had never heard tell of any defections, but that might be something not to be spoken of, and thus I would not know about it.

In short, I was beginning to see inconsistencies in the history of the Minchon Nation, or rather, I was beginning to see that the history spoken of might be incomplete. Or, even worse, some shameful event that had occurred long ago might have been purposely hidden from view, and the ruling elite did not want the world to ever hear of it.

I was a newcomer to the island. Perhaps I had not yet won the full trust of the people. Perhaps there were some awful secrets they had not yet seen fit to disclose to me.

I walked up and down the shoreline in utter confusion. I tried to reason it out in my head, but I could not discover the key to it all.

A voice startled me in the darkness. It was Wigiwig.

"Have you found it difficult to sleep?" he asked.

"I have. I'm troubled."

"About what?"

"Many issues, Wigiwig. Many issues give me pause to think that things on the island are not as they seem."

"You are thinking that some things are being withheld from you?"

"Yes. I am."

"Trouble yourself not about them, Cornelius. Nothing has been withheld from you. I sense, however, that there is another matter that is troubling you more at the moment."

"Yes. There is. Were you aware of others hiding in the Forbidden Land?"

"I had suspected, but I had never heard anything to confirm it."

"Do you think anyone knew of their existence?"

"There were once rumors, but that was so long ago — and because we never heard from them, I think everyone just forgot about them. The king was shocked to learn that such rumors might be true after all."

"How long ago was the Forbidden Land established?"

"To us Minchonians living today, it has always existed."

"And no one has ever breeched the gate to find out if the rumors were true?"

"I have never heard of anyone entering the land until now."

"What can you tell me about the Forbidden Land?"

"I know only that it is forbidden for anyone to enter. It is said the land is cursed, but I have no idea whether or not such a curse is real."

"Who is the Other?"

"That, Cornelius, can be explained only with permission from Amog. Not even the king may speak of it without the blessing of the high priest."

"It must be a wondrous story."

"I cannot say how wondrous it might be. I can only say that Amog holds the permission to speak of it. I suggest that you ask him."

"Must I make another petition?"

"No, I think not. Being the King's Captain, in your capacity as protector of the people, I would think you have the right to know about such things. But you must speak boldly concerning your need for such information, and from that point of view only. Be insistent, because he may resist."

I nodded as he turned to leave. He took only one step, then stopped and turned his head toward me. "Cornelius," he said solemnly, "what you seek to know is of a very delicate nature to the Minchon Nation. Do not treat the pursuit of such knowledge lightly. Only a few warriors in the course of our entire history have been given this learning. Give it, then, the honor it deserves."

"I shall, Wigiwig. I promise you. Thank you."

He nodded, turned, and walked away, disappearing into the darkness. Then a new thought came to me: Why is it, Wigiwig, that *you* are abroad at such an early hour?

Of course, as I spoke those words inside my head, I received no response to my inquiry. I was now alone again with all my varied thoughts as to how I was going to proceed to accomplish tasks I had never before undertaken.

* * * * *

Sunrise came finally, and after the fishing boats had been washed and secured once again and the morning meal completed, Wigiwig approached me.

"Cornelius, the king wishes to set out for the eastern side. Are you ready to go?"

"Yes, I am."

"What, then, are your orders, Captain? Shall we arm the men?"

"Yes, select ten of your best warriors, arm eight of them with bow and arrow, arm two with spears, and all will carry shields. Assemble them in the village center in ten minutes, I will inspect them there. You and I will carry spear and shield as well. Your first duty is to protect the king; I will provide protection for Amog."

"Shall Lelalu carry weapons?"

"Yes, give her a bow, arrows, and a knife."

"Excellent, Captain."

Wigiwig turned away and left me alone with my still many thoughts. Within minutes, Lelalu approached.

"Cornelius, Wigiwig orders that I be armed during our walk. I do not wish to carry arms."

"They are not intended for your use, my love. I need you to carry them as backup only."

"Then you do not expect me to partake in any violence should the need arise?"

"No, they are for me should the need arise."

"Then I still my objection."

"Thank you for not resisting further. My head already beats with strong and distasteful thoughts. I would not want your anger to be among my many concerns."

"I understand, my love. Be calmed, though, for there will be no need for weapons today."

"I believe that also. I arm the men more as a demonstration for Mata'pang's sake than for battle."

"Ahh, I see. You wish to present a strong show of force to give him pause and concern."

"We cannot appear weak and unprepared. That, I fear, would only embolden him further. If he observes us from the bushes beyond the gate, he will see a line of men prepared for any trouble. It is my wish that such a sight will make him reconsider his threats."

"My father has chosen his captain well, I think."

"Thank you. I just wish none of this were necessary."

"But as captain, you must be prepared."

"Yes, I must be prepared."

* * * * *

It took our miniature legion the better part of two hours to march all the way out to the eastern side of the island. In all, we were thirty strong. This included the king's and Amog's servants and those who carried our supply of food and water for the long journey in the hot sun.

I spied a sharp rise in the landscape I had not noticed the previous day. It was high enough that we could overlook the entrance to the Forbidden Land. I realized this must be the cliffs mentioned by the king. It would certainly give us the high-ground advantage if hostilities were to break out.

I felt, despite being a simple ship's captain, that I was making the sort of decisions a field infantry commander would wisely make.

I thus ordered the party to the higher ground. Along the way, I spoke of my reasons for making everyone climb the high hill in the heat of the day.

The king was pleased with my decision and reasoning. I even saw Amog nod his head in agreement.

Within another half hour, we all sat on the hilltop overlooking the entrance to the Forbidden Land.

The king gathered around him his four advisors: Amog, Wigiwig, Lelalu, and me.

"What do we see here?" he asked.

"We see only an unattended gate and the Forbidden Land stretched out ahead of us," Amog said, omitting the usual flowery twist to his words.

"And what sees my captain?"

I was thus and instantly put on notice. The king sought my advice, and I was woefully inexperienced in the ways of warfare — I had been but a simple seafaring man who had only delivered cargo. Now he was asking for my strategic and tactical advice concerning the possibility that a large, potentially hostile army lay hidden somewhere out there in the Forbidden Land. I swallowed hard and my knees began to wobble. "Your captain sees," I began, the words tumbling out over trembling lips, "a land void of any army at present, Great One, but he also sees the need for a stealthy agent to penetrate the Forbidden Land and discover if there is, indeed, such an army looming in the unseen distance which has the real potential to attack our nation. That is what your captain sees."

"I see, Captain. And do you have such an agent in mind?"

"Yes sir, Great One. It is I. I am such an agent, I believe."

"And do you possess the skill and experience necessary to make this incursion?"

"I have no experience at all in such matters, Great One. I was a merchant ship's captain. I simply delivered cargo to exotic ports."

"But you believe you can summon the skill necessary to stealthily infiltrate the Forbidden Land and successfully complete the search?"

"I believe so, Great One."

"You are a man of great courage, my captain."

"I have courage enough. It is experience and skill I find sorely lacking at the moment. But I believe I can penetrate the land with enough covert ability to find the answers we need."

"Amog," said the king, "What is your assessment of Cornelius's suggestion?"

"He be still a wild child and of an even wilder disposition. No doubt he possesses the nature to gallop in and make some discovery. But I believe he also possesses the skill and cunning necessary to make entry employing a slyer character, and to find the truth of the matter if he so desires."

"And you, Princess. How do you measure the plan?"

"I believe in Cornelius, Father. If he believes he can accomplish this task, then I say he must be given the opportunity to do so."

"Very well, my captain. Make the incursion when you are ready to do so. You have our permission."

"Thank you, Great One. I shall make my attempt tonight."

"Very good. We shall make camp here for the night."

"Pardon, Great One, but I believe you should return to the village immediately, along with your entire entourage."

"Why do you say this?"

"Because if they are observing us, as I think it most likely they are doing at this very moment, then we should make it appear that we have come and, seeing no threat, returned to our village none the wiser. It would be my hope they would relax and let their guard down upon seeing us depart. My entry later this evening would thus be less complicated."

"So, you are encouraging us to use deceit to accomplish your stealthy incursion?"

"I, Cornelius Alexander Delightable, would encourage no such thing. Your captain, however, the one charged with the nation's safety, would do so without hesitation. For the very definition of stealth demands the employment of overt deception, else we might just as well march boldly into the Forbidden Land immediately. I do not suggest that move, however. To protect the people, Great One, I would do what is necessary. If deception is required of me to accomplish the necessary end, then I am more than willing to use it."

"You were correct, Amog. He does possess the cunning to perform this feat. Fine, my captain. We shall depart now back to the village as a deception to cover what needs to be done. Will you remain here?"

"No, my king. I will also go with you for now, but I shall return when the sun is low on the horizon, wait for full darkness, and then press inward."

"I have chosen my captain well, I see."

"Thank you, Great King. I am honored to be of service to you and to the people of Minchon."

* * * * *

By the time night had fully fallen across the land, I had readied myself for the intrusion into the land beyond the gate. Earlier that day, Wigiwig had insisted that he accompany me into the eastern lands. As I did not seem to have any choice in the matter, I decided to put him on the hilltop with bow and arrows to act as a rear guard, which might better facilitate a potentially hasty escape from the Forbidden Land should I be pursued by hostile forces.

If the truth be told, I was glad he persisted in accompanying me, for fear had certainly taken a great hold upon me by then.

Wigiwig and I slowly made our way up the steep hillside for a better view. To get to the top of the hill unseen, we crawled on our stomachs, maintaining the lowest possible profile against the backdrop of the sun as it dipped beyond the western horizon.

From the edge of the cliff, we looked for any signs of fires, hoping the orange glow of the flames reaching upward in the darkening skies might reveal their positions. We lay on our stomachs on the hilltop until well past sunset.

About an hour after sunset, we caught the first glow of firelight. It was a substantial way into the Forbidden Land, and although it was not a particularly bright glow, I surmised it must surely be the light of an enormous fire. From the size of the glow, I suspected it was a large pit set ablaze in the center of a village. This indicated to me that Mata'pang may have been telling the truth when he announced there were others.

It now became an urgent matter for me to slip into the area and make count of just how large an army had been amassed there.

I whispered to Wigiwig that I was going to begin my attempt to breech the gate. I crawled backward until I was well out of sight of any possible sentries, and then stepped carefully down the pathway and around the base of the hill until I was crouched just before the entrance.

A high fence extended out into the darkness on both my left and right, making the gate the only logical entry point.

Creeping up to the gate, I stopped just short, hearkening carefully for any sign that sentries might be hidden in the nearby bushes.

After listening for several minutes and hearing nothing, I lifted the latch of the gate and slipped across into the Forbidden Land.

It was a slow process to move about, because I was effectively blinded by the darkness. There was no moon on that particular evening, so although the darkness aided me in infiltrating the area, it also made it difficult for me to move about. I had concern that while I was venturing in toward the fire's light, I might carelessly step on a dried twig and thus signal my intrusion to any sentries who might be near and in an already heightened state of alert.

My inexperience showed itself immediately when I ran directly into a tree, my nose mashing hard against the trunk. It hurt, and I almost yelped from both pain and surprise. Thinking back on it now, I am often set to laughter. I imagine if such a performance were to be played out upon a stage, the audience would snicker loudly at my folly.

I felt a bit of blood dripping from my nostrils, but I recovered quickly and squatted low and remained very still.

I judged, by this time, I had penetrated into the area nearly two hundred yards. My calculations were crude, of course, due to the fact that I was surrounded by pitch blackness. Nevertheless, in counting the number of steps I had taken by then and estimating the approximate length of each stride, I thought I was at least close to my guess.

This bit of perspicacious knowledge, however, was only important for me to know in the eventuality I found it necessary to make an expeditious retreat from the area. I felt better knowing the approximate distance to the relative safety of Wigiwig's position, although I doubted that his arrows would successfully find their targets in the midst of such blackness. Still, as I said, knowing about where I was gave me some small measure of comfort.

A short time later I found myself on an apparent footpath. This made it much easier to walk, but I was aware that it increased my chances to meet others as well.

Just as the thought entered my head, I heard low voices in the distance. I had no idea if they were moving or stationary. I stopped and listened carefully, trying to determine their exact position. True enough, they appeared to be moving toward me.

A slight panic swarmed over me. I moved off the path to my right several yards and found a tree to hide behind. I squatted down and remained as still and quiet as possible.

From my position I saw that the voices were guided by a torch. Within only minutes, two large men were approaching my location. I felt confident I was far enough off the path and hidden well enough by the tree that I would remain invisible to them. My alarm receded somewhat until I heard another voice behind me and off to my left. Another man carrying a torch was walking toward me as well.

Being armed with only a large knife, I pulled it from my belt and gripped it tightly, preparing myself to use it if circumstances warranted it.

The single man to my left almost walked over me, but at the last second he turned left and then after several seconds he turned right, heading directly toward the two men I originally heard approaching.

I suddenly realized that I was located at an intersection of crossing paths. The three men met and words were exchanged, and there was some laughter, but the words were strange to my ear and I did not understand them. The exchange continued for several minutes. There was more laughter, and then the single man continued on his way.

I did not recognize Mata'pang's voice as any of the three, which immediately brought me to a heightened state of awareness, for in that moment I had, at the very least, confirmed his statement that there were others. I was now more determined than ever to discover just how many more there were. If it *was* an army that occupied the Forbidden Land, as Mata'pang had suggested, the potential consequences of this revelation could prove disastrous for the Minchon Nation.

Abruptly, all sense of fear left me and I discovered new abilities I had not known I possessed. I moved over the darkened landscape with almost cat-like agility, fully aware of my surroundings, the lack of light becoming inconsequential. That is not to say I could suddenly see in the dark like an animal, but rather, I could sense obstacles ahead of me and was able now to avoid them easily.

As I moved toward the orange glow ahead of me, I began to hear the faintly distant sounds of other voices, both female and male. I surmised I was nearing a village, but it was still hidden from me in the darkness and by the topography of the landscape.

After a good while longer, the glow became more pronounced. I knew I was getting close. I was forced to stop and hide on several occasions, as what I perceived to be roaming patrols walked what I presumed was a security circuit through the area. However one would view it, they seemed prepared, but for an army, not for a lone intruder such as I.

As I neared what I thought was the village, I was obliged to stop and take cover more often. The increasing number of people walking about became somewhat alarming. I adjusted my tactic and walked a bit forward and then stopped, making sure no one standing silently was blocking my path before I continued. The last thing I wanted to do was come upon a well-armed sentry by accident. It wasn't the brawl that frightened me as much as it was the sound of the brawl. Surely others would hear us tussling and come to investigate. I might be able to subdue one sentry, but I was no match whatsoever for more than one of those giants.

Considering stealth to be wiser than battling, I kept low and slow while moving toward the village, also keeping count in my head of everyone I encountered. By that time I had slipped past twenty-four other people and was nearly a quarter mile in from the border.

My new fear, then, was that Mata'pang had not exaggerated. There was a standing army of others and a battle was being prepared.

With my pace now substantially slowed, it took me well over an hour, noted by the shifting stars above, until I finally neared the rim of some ancient caldera and was able to peer over its edge.

Down inside the caldera, which I quickly estimated to be about one hundred feet to the bottom, I was startled to see what I had been fearing. The village was immense. I saw hundreds of people roaming about on the caldera floor. The glow I had seen was not from one large fire, but the combined glow of hundreds of small individual fires.

I had unmasked Mata'pang's secret army.

An army it was, too. From what I could see from my advantaged location, there were weapons lying about everywhere, and some weapons were being made.

It appeared to me that preparations for war were very near concluded. This army looked well able to sustain a long siege against any enemy. The design of their defenses made the meager attempt I had made for the Minchon village woefully inadequate. Should our village be attacked, it would be easily overrun within the first few moments of any conflict.

Slapped hard with this staggering new knowledge, I understood that we would have to relocate our village to a place much better fortified than what we presently occupied.

I cannot say with any certainty that a war was imminent, but what I can say is Mata'pang's village was very well prepared for war.

Not being a military man with any understanding of how to make war, it nevertheless occurred to me that if such a war should become unavoidably apparent, we might do well to attack first. The position up here along the rim of the caldera might give us the decisive advantage we would need to bring any hostility to a quick end, for we would occupy the high ground. Our archers would have the distinct advantage over theirs, and it seemed to me that battling *down* a hill would be less taxing than battling up it.

As the initial shock of seeing so many people and armaments began to wear off, I began to see the 'army' differently. Children played, women gathered and mended clothing, men sat together and laughed.

I began to see their village as no different from our own. Perhaps, in my haste to judge, I had overestimated their intent. The weapons I perceived might only have been created to kill game. There were weapons strewn about all over the village, but not in such a manner as to form a common armory such as we had built. Those who possessed weapons held them nearby. In my attempt to put more meaning to it, they looked to be deployed more in a defensive strategy than in an offensive one.

Perhaps, I thought, they were living in the fear that our nation would attack them. Perhaps we represented a greater threat to them than they did to us.

I observed the goings-on in the village for a great long while. The more I watched, the more I saw a very simple people who lived their lives much the same as we did. The children seemed like ours, more interested in pursuit of play than in anything else. They seemed happy and at ease. They appeared as our village, a loving family of people just trying to get from one day to the next. I began to wonder if Mata'pang's posture was more boastful than true.

I had seen what I needed to see. The next task that lay before me was to safely extricate myself from this area and make it unseen back to the gate. The king would surely be awaiting my report, but what would that be? A vicious army preparing for war, or a passive village living peacefully but perhaps in some fear? And how was I to gauge the impact of Mata'pang on such people?

I had turned away and begun to work my way back toward the gate when I heard a rustle of bushes very near me. I ceased moving and almost ceased breathing, for a huge man began moving almost directly toward me. Had he been there all along, I wondered, and I had not seen or heard him before?

Fear returned once again. I pulled my knife from its sheath and prepared myself to take his life. He stopped only a foot or two from where I lay. I could see the silhouette of his head against the starry sky, his long mane of hair drifting about in the light breeze.

I did not wish to strike him dead, for sooner or later his body would be found and my stealthy intrusion would have failed. At the same time, I could not allow myself to be taken prisoner. The welfare of the Minchon people fully depended upon my getting back with a report.

The giant stood over me looking left, then right. My heart beat so loudly in my ears that I thought for certain he would hear it as well. I clenched the knife's handle more firmly and felt my muscles tighten in anticipation that I would have to make a forward lunge.

He stood towering over me for several minutes, apparently not sensing my presence, for he then turned around and walked away.

I felt a great and sudden pain in my chest, and realized I had stopped breathing. My lungs were starved of air, and upon seeing the giant disappear into the night, I instantly took in a huge gasp. The pain immediately ceased. *Is this what soldiers experience while in battle?* I asked myself. *How do they do it? Is one able to overcome this dread, or is it a constant companion?*

I guessed that with time and experience the dread of it might diminish, but I had no experience with combat, and this was my first time skulking around within an adversary's domain. I was terrified, and I had no desire to experience this terror again anytime soon.

Assured that the giant was gone, I slowly made my way back toward the gate. With my enhanced senses returning, I was able to keep track in my head of the distance I traveled back to the gate. As I have already stated, I calculated that the encampment was just over a quarter mile from the border.

As the King's Captain, I had to consider the possibility that they were indeed a hostile lot planning to attack our village, and not just a docile nation of simple and peaceful people. Upon that consideration, I determined a good-sized army of our own, remaining as silent as possible, would be able to infiltrate the area successfully and set up on the edge of the caldera and remain hidden until it was too late for the villagers, thus giving us the advantage of both surprise and higher ground. Our archers alone could well bring the battle to a quick end.

While I considered this tactic, I realized it was dependent upon one decisive fact — that no one here learn of my intrusion tonight. I had negated their size advantage by knowing exactly where they were. We were all now on level ground in that respect, but they still held great advantage over us in the preparations for war, given the number of weapons I saw already produced.

If there was to be an attack against us within the next few days, we would be summarily slaughtered. I fully intended to remove that advantage as well, if I was able to do so.

Having now some better idea of what lay ahead of me in the dark, it took much less time to negotiate the path back to the gate. I was, of course, slowed by a few roaming patrols, but being mindful of them, I managed to remain unseen.

Within an hour, I had slipped back through the gate and reattached its rope carefully and quietly. I made my way back to the hilltop, whispering my approach to Wigiwig.

"I was beginning to worry about you, Cornelius," he whispered.

"There is either nothing to worry about or much to worry about now, my friend," I whispered back, "I have witnessed a very large and well-prepared army, if that is what they truly are. If they choose to attack us within the next few days, they will surely be victorious. We must get back to the king as fast as possible."

"Then we shall run all the way back."

Running as we did, we made it back to the village within an hour. Upon approaching the sentries I had ordered to keep vigilant watch at the village's edge, we identified ourselves. Then, with great relief, we collapsed onto the ground in the center of the village, where we lay trying to recuperate. My lungs felt as if they were about to burst. My head throbbed with sheer exhaustion. I believe that Wigiwig felt much the same, for neither of us spoke or moved for a good while.

Before long, King Gogui and Amog approached, absent their usual adornments. I fought to get to my knees in reverence, but the king dropped to one knee, his hulking form towering over me as he pushed me back to the ground with understanding and concern. He could see how thoroughly exhausted I was.

"Rest, Cornelius, rest. Are you able to speak?"

"Yes, Great One," I replied, still panting. "There are a great number of people living in the Forbidden Land. I estimated their numbers to be in the hundreds. I cannot say they are an army preparing for war, nor can I say they are a peaceful bunch living a simple life. What I can say with certainty, however, is that they possess many times more weapons than we do. If they attack soon, victory will be a surety for them and accomplished very quickly."

The king grew silent and stared out into the darkness of the late night. "Then it is true; the Sons of the Other were not destroyed in the ancient times as I was led to believe."

"So it would seem," said Amog.

"Our brothers and sisters yet live. This is a wonderful and joyous moment for us all."

"Yes, it appears there is good cause to rejoice," Amog said with a smile.

I can only say I was stunned to silence. I lay back against the ground and could not believe my ears. I had just announced that a potential great army might be preparing to attack their people, and they both regarded my news as something to be celebrated.

To say that my mind became utterly and hopelessly confused would be an egregious understatement, and I dare say if either man had asked another question while I was in that state, I seriously doubt I would have possessed the ability to respond. So it was good that they asked nothing more of me.

In that moment, I ceased trying to understand anything at all. I lay there, still panting as a dog, perspiring profusely, and uncertain about everything I thought I had known before.

Chapter 17

The captain sat at his desk scribbling on a piece of paper when Suzanne walked in.

"Have you a moment, Papa?"

"Certainly, child," he replied, continuing his writing.

"Have you heard anything from Detective Cyra?"

"I have not. Why?"

"It's been over a week since you last saw him, right?"

"That sounds about right," answered the captain without looking up.

"After his threats, I should think we would have heard something from him by now."

"Don't trouble yourself about that, child. Nothing will come of that. I'm more wondering when the children will have time for me. I really need to continue the story, for their sake."

"They're busy with school projects this week, Papa. But I'm sure they'll be haunting you for more stories soon enough."

"I do enjoy them. They're wonderful children. You've done well raising them, Suzanne."

"Thank you, Papa. I couldn't have done it without your help, though."

"I'm delighted to help, child. Is lunch ready? I'm very hungry."

"It will be soon, Papa," Suzanne said as she sat down on the sofa. "What are we going to do about him, Papa?"

"Who is that, child?"

"Why, Detective Cyra, of course."

"I just told you, Suzanne. Do not worry yourself about him."

The captain glanced up and noticed her nose scrunch up. "What, child? What truly has you so troubled?"

"I heard something this morning while I was out and about."

"What is that?" asked the captain, setting down his pen and leaning back in his chair to give her his full attention.

"I heard he has been pressing Judge Harrison hard for a warrant for your arrest. Apparently he has prepared a rather large report on you."

"Has he now?"

"You see, Papa, this is what I've been talking about. You gave him all of it. It required no investigation on his part. You simply handed him everything he needed. Now what are we going to do?"

The captain snickered. "He is determined; I'll give him that."

"You really don't understand the nature of this, do you? He's preparing to attack you full on, Papa."

"Yes, child. Yes, he is."

"What are we going to do about it?"

"There is nothing that needs to be done. Don't agonize over this, my child. There is nothing to fear. All will be well."

"Papa, I am worried about you. I can't help it. He means to do you great harm if he is able."

"What he means to do and what he will accomplish are not the same. He will fail in his attempts, but I cannot fail in what I have to do."

"What are you talking about?"

"For the moment I cannot say, but I must not fail. Several wonderful souls depend on it."

"Papa, you're speaking in riddles. I don't understand."

"I don't mean to speak in riddles, darling. I am just not able to say what I mean at this time. You'll have to be patient a while longer."

"I wish I were more like Grandmother. She understood you perfectly. She knew what to do and what to say to you."

The captain smiled as his eyes rolled upward toward the ceiling. "Yes. She knew me well."

"How are you going to defend yourself when Detective Cyra makes his move against you? Have you given it any thought at all?"

"No, none at all, my dear. There will be no need to defend myself if I act appropriately, decisively, and in time."

"Riddles again, Papa?"

The captain chuckled lightly. "Yes, riddles once more, it seems. I'm sorry, Suzanne; exercise just a wee bit more faith. I plead with you on this. Trust in the warrior spirit that lies within you. There is no need for concern."

"Fine, Papa. I'll try."

"That is all I can ask of you."

A sudden memory lurched forward in Suzanne's mind. "Oh! I almost forgot completely. Judge Harrison stopped me and asked if you could come to his office sometime this afternoon."

"How lovely. I'll go see him during my afternoon stroll."

* * * * *

A knock on Judge Harrison's door interrupted his reading of a law book. "Yes?" he said, looking up.

The door opened and the captain walked in, smiling broadly. The judge stood up immediately, rounded his desk with his hand outstretched, and grinned broadly as well.

"Cornelius. Good to see you, old friend. Thanks for arriving so quickly."

"Hello, Edwin. You are looking well, as usual. Your message seemed urgent. What can I do for you?"

The judge's face grew solemn. "At long last it begins, Cornelius."

"Yes, my friend, I know. Finally, the journey home begins."

* * * * *

The captain walked through the door and was instantly greeted by Suzanne.

"Hello, Papa. Did you by chance get over to see Judge Harrison this afternoon?"

"I did. It was lovely to sit and chat with him. I really should do it more often, but he's a very important and busy man. I hate to disturb him."

"And?"

"And what, Suzanne?"

"Did you speak with him about Detective Cyra?"

"I did."

Suzanne waited for more from the captain, but he moved around her and walked into the kitchen. Suzanne followed closely.

"Papa, what did he say?"

"He said to say hello to you and the children."

"Don't do this, Papa. You know what I mean."

The captain stopped and took her face into his hands. He smiled at her and then kissed her on the forehead. "Stop worrying, child."

He released her and reached for a glass. He filled it from the tap and drank it down completely.

"I was so thirsty. Where are the children?"

"They're in the library. Waiting for a story, no doubt."

"Then I shall not delay." He started for the library, but stopped and turned. "Suzanne, all will be well. Have a bit more faith."

"Go tell your stories, old man," she said, a smile cracking her otherwise morose expression.

"I shall do just that."

"You are even now, after your search in the Forbidden Land, still of a wild nature, I see."

"Yes, Amog, and I still possess an untamed purpose within me as well. In this situation, I must acknowledge my wild side as protector of the people. In considering all possible attacks from Mata'pang's forces, I must yield to my feral nature so that I might prepare suitable defenses. I must keep all options open, for he will surely unleash all the unruliness that dwells within him. I must understand my own wild nature so that I might consider what options he might exercise against us while ferocious and seemingly unpredictable. I must become him if I am to defend against him."

"You are a shrewd and resourceful man, Cornelius. The king has chosen his captain wisely. It is true, you must see with the mind of your enemy if you are to protect the people. I will give you permission to speak of the things you need to know — when you most need to know them."

I wanted to know the story of the Other and the One immediately, but I refrained from pressing him further on the matter. He was a man who chose his words with exacting precision and toward good purpose. He obviously did not feel I needed to hear the story at that time.

I accepted the fact, and instead of voicing my objection, I bowed my head and spoke. "You are great, Amog. You are a wise and fair man. I look forward to someday learning from you all you wish to teach me. I am honored to be in such an honest presence. I hope I never give you cause to doubt me or my willingness to learn all I can to become a true warrior. Thank you, Great One, and good day to you, sir."

I left him quickly and without an opportunity to respond, knowing it would place him in an awkward position if he had to reply to my kindly words. He was a hard man, and displaying gentleness was not simple for him. I, therefore, left him hard and proud, not knowing if my amiable words, spoken earnestly, had touched his heart in any way. For me, it was enough that I'd had the opportunity to speak them directly.

* * * * *

A full month had passed since my incursion into the Forbidden Land. Nothing more was said to me about the matter. The preparations I had made were now nearly discarded. The armory of weapons we had so diligently prepared, we left completely unattended.

Life in the village returned to normal.

I, alone, maintained a watchful eye toward the eastern horizon. I had ordered daily runners to the east to see if trouble was brewing, but after a few weeks I was overruled by the king and the runners were stopped.

I was confused by the cavalier manner in which Mata'pang's threat was now regarded. Nevertheless, I remained the King's Captain. I thus took it upon myself twice each week to visit the eastern border. No adverse indications seemed to be coming from the Forbidden Land, but I was determined to remain steadfast and prepared.

Perhaps that is why the village had returned to normal activities; the people knew the King's Captain was mindful of the matter, and this allowed them to return to their regular lives. I had no idea if it were true or not, but that simple thought made me feel better.

Lelalu and I continued to meet every afternoon beneath our favorite tree after the daily preparation work for the village's survival was completed. The quiet of those lazy afternoons found us chatting as we gazed out over the open sea. For me, and I think for Lelalu also, it was a most restful place. I could think clearly there, and I did so often.

What thoughts I had knocking about in my skull while there under that tree varied widely from moment to moment, but most were of a simple and temperate persuasion. And yet, when it was appropriate to do so, in my mind I could form deep contemplative visions which appeared to me clearly and precisely. Never, while resting there, was I ever in great confusion. Never was there any tumultuous idea darting about in the many bottomless canyons of my brain. And, more so, never was I immobilized or stranded in some quandary about any superfluous issue of little importance. There was never a lingering doubt about what must be done to rise above myself and find my place in Minchon society.

Everything was always well ordered, well structured, the path clearly laid out before me. Needless, then, to say that I accomplished much toward good purpose while resting there in the splendidly quiet calm of that shady tree.

For some unknown reason, that spot under that particular tree was where I believe peace and serenity themselves rested also. With Lelalu by my side, the world, with all of its troubles, concerns, complications, and challenges, seemed so very far away and of such little consequence I wondered why I should ever venture away from that spot.

And so it was a fitting place, on one of those lazy and joyous days as I awaited Lelalu's arrival, from which to see the Great Amog appear out of the thicket and walk onto the sandy pathway. I noted that he approached with a solid and purposeful intent in his stride.

I fell instantly to my knees and cast my eyes downward to the sand as he finally stopped short and spoke. "I have come to discuss your petition to marry

Lelalu. Are you of suitable mind to presently speak of this?"

"Yes, Great One, I am prepared."

"Then you acknowledge the preparation of such a petition?"

"Yes, Great Amog. I acknowledge it," I responded, still kneeling and staring downward into the sand.

"Who are you that you should dare to make such a petition?"

"Tis I, Great One, Cornelius Delightable, the King's Captain and a humble and contrite soul, who makes the petition."

"You are still the wild child, I see. You remain brazen in your ways and brash in your belief in yourself, it appears."

"I am, Great One; and yes, I do hold faithfully to my boldness."

"How dare you present yourself in such a way! You have only begun to understand what commitment it takes to become a man. You have no understanding of what it is to become a provider and protector of a mate. To make this petition at this time is to speak with contempt for our customs and traditions — and with a loud and sustained insolence."

"With respect, Great One, it is not so. I make this petition in full conformity with and in full appreciation for the great ways, times, and traditions. I have prepared my petition in full compliance with the protocols required of the petitioner, as instructed."

"And who instructed thou in these ways?"

"It was my friend and mentor, Wigiwig, Great One."

"So, it was Wigiwig who instructed you in this matter and assisted you in making this petition?"

"It was he, Great One."

"And what else did he instruct you to say unto me?"

"He stated only that I should remain humble but bold. That I should hold onto the truth of what has been prepared correctly and in a just manner. He told me you would challenge me on the exactness of the preparation of this petition, and having prepared it correctly, I should stand by my petition with an unwavering sureness."

"So, you bind me to this petition and hold me fast to its form?"

"I do, Great One, but only so far as you deem me worthy of it."

"What means this?"

"It means that I have prepared the petition to the strict *letter* of the law, but it is to the *intent* of the law that I hold the deepest respect, and yield unto. I am Cornelius Alexander Delightable, sir. I am a former ship's captain who ruled over many men and held their very lives in his hands. I am presently the King's Captain and charged with the security of the Minchon Nation, but, Great One, I am still a stranger to the wonderful ways of this great community. I pledge myself to work hard to prove my worthiness to you and to the village. I only *ask* for consideration of the petition to marry Lelalu. I do not bind you to the letter of the law, Great One, or to its intent, if you find me unworthy.

"I only ask for your permission should you believe I am suitable to receive a gift in your sole estimation. I make this pleading in certain boldness, but if your answer at this time is no, then I shall accept your judgment and work harder to prove myself more worthy of such a woman as Lelalu in your eyes, in hopes you shall grant me a new petition at a future time."

"And did also Wigiwig instruct you to speak such words?"

"No, Great One. The words were born in my heart alone. They are spoken through my mouth alone also. They are spoken in humbleness and sincerity, but if they have not found a favorable place in your mind, then the consequences of your disfavor are mine alone to bear. Despite all my learning thus far, I yet remain regretfully ignorant to many of the ways of the Minchon Nation. But I beseech you, Great One, hear this clearly. My feelings for Lelalu are real and true, and they shall never waver from the truth of it regardless of your decision."

With my eyes still staring down at the sand, I heard Amog turn and began walking away. I peeked up to see his back. I thought he was done with me. Somehow, I thought I had failed.

He halted and turned back toward me. My eyes shifted back to the sand at my feet. He walked back toward me and stopped but two feet from me.

"I judge you to speak the truth," he said. "You are but a small way along the path toward understanding our traditions at present, and you are — beyond question — of a daring and brash character. Still, I find your pleading to be authentic and sincere. Your petition has been prepared and delivered in respectful compliance with the laws and traditions of this nation. Your work on the boat continues to prove valuable to the village and is of an exemplary nature. I have heard that your crew speaks well of you, and in my observance of you with them, it would appear they hold you in good stead. In consideration of the fact you have opened your mind to all possibilities and have not bound me to the letter of the law, nor to the intent of it, I shall give your petition suitable consideration."

"Thank you, Great One. I shall await your decision with humbleness, patience, and reverence."

"That remains to be seen, wild child. Patience is obviously yet a stranger to you. Humbleness is apparently hidden from you also, despite your words. Still, you are a mindful, obedient, and reverent child, and that, lacking all else, must still be credited to you."

Then the Great Amog leaned well over and near to my face. In a soft tone, completely contrary to his normal voice and speech pattern, he added, "I carry great expectations for you, Cornelius. Do not let me know regret in believing in you."

"I...I...will not let you down, sir. I give you my word."

"Then it is by your word that I shall judge you worthy or not."

With those words spoken, he resumed his stately and stout manner, turned from me, and walked away without looking back.

Moments later, finally looking up, I watched Lelalu walk toward me. If angels existed on this earth, then she would surely be counted among them. Even in the soft and shifting sand, she appeared to glide. Her open smile was as a beam of brilliant light seen from a great distance, and it only grew brighter as she drew nigh.

She must have noticed my own pleased expression as she walked up to me. "And what has you so extraordinarily exuberant this afternoon, Husband?"

We came together in a warm hug and kiss, and then we sat down in the sand under the shade of the tree. "Amog left only moments before you appeared. He has agreed to consider my petition."

"How wonderful, my love! I knew he could not resist your petition."

"I have no idea what decision he will make, but at least he is considering it. Still, I must admit, present me knows future me will be your husband, so I should not concern myself with *whether* he will approve it, only *when*. But then I would guess I should not be concerned with that either. It will happen when it is meant to happen. Is that not correct?"

"You are becoming a true warrior with each passing day, Cornelius. I'm most proud of your development."

"I am becoming so only because of you, Lelalu."

"That is not so, Cornelius. I did not suggest that you prepare the petition. And it was not I who suggested you become the King's Captain and go off into the Forbidden Land. You made those choices and many others on your own."

"Still, it was your love and faith in me that propelled me forward with such courage."

"I would love you and have faith in you no matter your choices. We are chosen for each other, Cornelius. We are fated to be together. That is all I need to trust in."

"Your words are spoken so beautifully and your knowing is so pure. How can I not believe in you and become ever more brave, brash, and successful?"

And it was all true. I felt stronger, wiser, and more able when I was around her. She was a great part of any strength, courage, or wisdom I might have possessed alone.

She filled those places within me where I lacked substance. She was becoming a part of me, a part I would soon learn was as much a part of me as my heart, my lungs, my legs, or my arms. We were beings of fate itself.

Chapter 18

Approximately three weeks later, after my morning chores, I was already stretched out in my hammock near the spring and resting comfortably when one of my boat mates, Tainini, who held the next-lower position just behind me, dashed up the path and skidded to a halt directly in front of me.

He was nearly out of breath, sweating profusely, and virtually exhausted. As he stood panting hard, he settled his hands upon his knees to brace himself.

"Friend Tainini," I implored, "what has happened that you rush to me in such a state?"

"The…tree," he replied, forcing the words out of his mouth in between labored breaths.

"What tree?"

"Your…your tree. Come quickly."

With that, he rushed away, no doubt expecting me to follow him. I rolled out of my hammock and gave chase immediately, having no idea what he meant by it all.

Minutes later I slid to a stop immediately next to him, my mouth dropped open in disbelief, my eyes locked onto what lay before me.

My tree! My peaceful tree had been felled to the sand, leaving only a short, hacked stump.

"Who would do such a thing?" I asked of no one in particular.

"It is a question only one or few can answer, Cornelius. I happened upon it only a short time ago while on my way back to the beach."

I put my left hand on Tainini's right shoulder. "Thank you, friend, for coming to tell me. I thank you twice."

"I am truly sorry for your loss, Cornelius. I have very few words for this."

"Your care is spoken enough."

Just then Lelalu approached from behind. She stopped next to me and stared solemnly at the fallen tree, but remained quiet.

"It would seem I have an adversary nearby, my love," I said softly. "And it appears I have provoked him into taking despicable action."

"So it would seem, Cornelius."

"It was a good tree. I shall miss it so."

"It was, Husband, but it is now ready to be converted into kindling. What are we to do about this?"

"I cannot say, but the message announced is clear enough. This contest of wills is lifted now to a higher plane."

"Have you any idea who would do this thing?"

"I would guess it to be an agent of Mata'pang. But who this agent is, I cannot guess. We are infiltrated. A spy does live among us. Of that I am now most positive."

"Deceit is not our way, Cornelius."

"Nevertheless, my dear, I'm afraid it is the way of our adversary, and we would do well to prepare for more of it to follow soon. The fist is clenched; the challenge put forth, the contest initiated with sedulous intent."

"You are the King's Captain, friend Cornelius," Tainini offered. "How will you prepare for what is to come?"

"I shall first alert the king and then respond to his orders with my full and most ardent effort."

"I will attend with you."

"No. I shall do this alone, Tainini. Would you inspect the weapons we have already prepared, to see if they, too, have been tampered with?"

"I shall do so immediately, Captain."

Tainini departed in as urgent a dash as he had come to me. I walked to the fallen tree, squatted, and placed my right hand on its trunk. "Fare thee well, good friend. Know we shall sing praise to you this evening as you honor us through your welcomed warmth and light."

"You honor it well, beloved," said Lelalu.

"Where now will I find my peace and serenity? Under which new tree will I find solace? Or will my very action selfishly condemn another to death?"

"It is not your action that condemns; it is the heartless action of another that destroys. Love does not condemn, dear Cornelius. Choose another tree to sit under, and in your enjoyment you will bring distinguished honor to it. Go seek now. Find another quickly. Through the grace of your discovery, another tree shall be blessed, and there, under its branches and leaves, shall you again find all that you seek."

"Anger grows within me even now, Lelalu. Not so much for the tree's sacrifice, but for the needless waste of it. If one has cause against me, why not bring action against me directly? Why take out anger on a defenseless tree?"

"To attack the tree is to attack you, Cornelius."

"Yes. This I already understand, but what is mystifying to me is that attacking the island is worse than attacking me. This coward, this loathsome wretch, does not understand the nature of his murder. The island will not accept this sacrifice with graciousness. The island will strike back. Not out of revenge for avenging's sake, not out of malice for the sake of hate, but as a natural response to an attack. This island will defend itself. I have learned that much."

"To hear you speak of this with so much compassion fills my heart to the brim with joy. I had no idea you were so in touch with the island. Your bond with it has grown quickly. Your understanding has increased greatly. Amog must be pleased with your progression."

"I doubt Amog knows of this, and I do not intend to make him any wiser regarding the matter."

Lelalu chuckled. "Dear Cornelius, Amog already knows. You are not able to hide spiritual growth from him. He is the High Priest. He knows each and every heart in Minchon. He knows them well enough to know what resides within them. You have only deceived yourself."

I was shocked to hear her words, for I had labored hard to retain my secrets regarding any knowledge gained. To hear now that my efforts were wasted was not pleasing to me. I felt no rage over the matter, mind you; I only felt inadequate. If I could not effectively protect what lay inside my own heart, how would I, as the King's Captain, protect the confidential knowledge of our strategy and tactics from any adversary? *Was I an open book to be easily read by all? Was I myself a threat to the security of the Minchon Nation through some inability to remain inscrutable?*

For the next while, I stood still and silently contemplated my questions. Lelalu must have sensed my dilemma; though she held on to my arm, she remained quiet, allowing me to digest and process.

After a time, finding no immediate and suitably adequate answers, I returned to present awareness.

"I must report to the king what has happened here."

I started to walk toward the village with Lelalu still grasping my arm. I did not speak, and she left me to the silence of my own thoughts as we walked along the path.

Upon reaching the village, I immediately presented myself to the king, employing the appropriate protocol, standing silently before him, my head bowed, my eyes staring at the sand.

"Speak, Cornelius. What have you to say?" Again, his words were plain and simple.

"Great One, I have failed you as your captain."

"How have you failed me?"

"Over the past weeks, I have grown indolent in my duties as your captain. I now believe a spy lives amongst us, and I failed to know of it."

"What makes you say this?"

"A tree was felled. I believe it to be the work of an agent working for Mata'pang, but I do not have any clue as to whom the agent might be. Forgive me, Great One."

"Trees are felled often, Cornelius. What is special about the tree you mention?"

"This tree was of particular importance to me. I believe the felling of the tree was a blatant challenge communicated directly towards me."

"If directed towards you only, then why do you feel that you have betrayed me?"

"The challenge is put to your captain. It is, therefore, a challenge also put to the Minchon Nation. I should have been more diligent in preparing for spies."

"If we have a spy, Cornelius, then understand that it is the very nature of a spy to remain hidden. Now that a spy is revealed, I am confident you shall soon successfully seek him out and identify him."

"Great One, over the last several weeks I feel my calls for preparedness have not been taken seriously by the nation. We have returned to the more languid ways."

"Then, as my captain, what would you have us do?"

"We must once again make strong preparations for a battle I feel is coming soon. Through his spy, Mata'pang has successfully penetrated our village. We must be tactful in uncovering the spy, and we must have guards each night. We must do all we can to secure the village at all times."

"This preparation will require much of your time, will it not?"

"Yes, Great One. I shall immediately adjust my schedule to make us ready."

"Then your duties on the boat must cease. You shall spend your time making all things ready for defense. Henceforth your duty will be solely as the King's Captain. You shall have no other duty or responsibility."

"I understand and will obey your command."

Just then Amog approached.

"You have lost something special to you this day. Is this not true?"

"Yes, Amog," I answered in typical reverence.

"Stand boldly, Cornelius. You shall bow no more to me. I am High Priest, but you are the King's Captain. We shall stand as equals from now on. Thus you will stand straight and proud in my presence. Henceforth, you shall command the respect of the nation as Protector Captain, the King's Captain of Honor. You have earned this honor."

"As you wish, Amog. Thank you for your support."

"Great One," Amog then said to the king, "I shall give my allegiance also to your captain. What is your wish for me in this matter?"

"Amog," responded the king, "lend whatever assistance Cornelius may require of you to seek out the spy and make the village again secure."

Amog bowed to the king and then bowed to me. I was in such great shock that I found it difficult to respond.

"Captain?" Amog then asked. "What is your command?"

"I...I have no command...of you at present," I stuttered. "But we should bring Wigiwig to a conference where we will discuss our plans."

"I shall fetch Wigiwig immediately if you wish."

"Yes," I said, now feeling the position of command sinking in. "Yes, perhaps we should do so right away."

Amog bowed once more to me and then departed. I realized at that moment he did not bow to the man, but to the position of command that I held. On the ship it was well known that the crew saluted not the man but the rank. So I understood it was to be the same here.

"Great One," I said, "may I be excused to ready myself for the conference?"

"Go now, Captain; make yourself ready."

I bowed to the king, turned, and departed, but was stopped once more by the king's voice.

"Cornelius, once again: I have chosen my captain well."

"Thank you, sir." I bowed once more, then turned and departed the presence of the king.

* * * * *

Sometime later Wigiwig, Amog, and I sat on the rock near the spring. I suggested we plan to set a trap for the spy, but I urged that we should not give any outward sign that such a plan was in progress.

"I think we should endeavor to keep our activity low and hidden from the knowledge of the village. We should give no hint to the spy that he is being pursued, although I think the spy has made his move and will be expecting some form of reprisal. It may be he has already departed the village for the Forbidden Land."

"A wise assessment, Cornelius," said Wigiwig. "I think that is highly possible."

I then spoke to Amog. "What is the nature of knowing in the village? By that I mean what does the village know of the future? If they are tuned to the same level of knowing, as it seems you, Lelalu, Wigiwig, and the royal family is, would not the spy also know of events of the future?"

"You are wise to ask such a question, Cornelius. The simple response is no, the village is not tuned to knowing the future — or the past, for that matter. It is only we few who are possessed of such knowledge, and we impart to the people only as much as we deem necessary for them to function appropriately. The spy would thus have no knowledge of what we plan here."

"I am relieved to know this. I feared that our plans were already compromised."

"What is your command, then, Captain?" asked Wigiwig.

"I ask two things: one, seek quietly and find out if someone is missing from the village who would ordinarily be present, and two, if there are specific warriors whose loyalty you trust, I need to know who they are."

"All warriors are trusted, Cornelius."

"Could the spy also be a warrior?"

Wigiwig pulled on his left ear as he prepared his response. "It is possible, but quite unlikely."

"Then all warriors cannot be trusted equally."

"Our young captain is wise," stated Amog.

"Wigiwig, do you know of special warriors who have proven their trust and loyalty?"

"Yes, Captain, I have ten such warriors I would trust with my life."

"Be certain of this, Wigiwig, for it is, in fact, your very life that you gamble with as well as the lives of every Minchon citizen."

Wigiwig smiled knowingly.

"Why the smile?" I asked.

"I smile knowing that you are clearly on your path toward your destiny, Cornelius. Your thoughts are of the quality expected of the King's Captain. I also know these warriors. They are loyal and trustworthy in all respects."

"Then we must assign them the duty of guarding the village all day and all night. But we must instruct them not to make their presence in that vein known to the village. They must continue as if they have no special part in this plan."

"I shall see to it, Captain."

"Make it so, Wigiwig. You are second in command. I charge you with this responsibility. And I know the king has selected you well for this task."

"Amog, is there any other form of defense I am not aware of?"

"Other form? Your question is a strange one."

"You are High Priest. Is there an incantation or some otherworldly knowledge you possess that would serve me in securing the village?"

"There are many things I can do as High Priest, but I cannot say at this time what they are. I am forbidden by the king's law to discuss them. I am sorry."

"No need for that. It is enough to know I have options should the need arise."

"You are a wise man, Cornelius. You shall make a glorious warrior someday."

"It is only my wish that I will have the opportunity to enter the training. To do so, however, will require that the Minchon Nation remain safe and secure."

Amog smiled. That alone brought surprise to me.

"Captain, your day will surely come. Be at peace regarding this matter. Concentrate only on what you need to do now."

"I hope one day we shall be more, Amog. I hope one day we shall become fast friends."

"We already are, Cornelius. We already are."

"Thank you. I hope you shall never have cause to regret it. Now, Wigiwig, I shall require two of your best men to accompany me back to the border of the Forbidden Land. Please have them report to me tomorrow morning two hours before sunrise. It is my intent to let Mata'pang know with certainty that we are once more on guard against him."

"Yes, Captain." Wigiwig then giggled. "I think you have become a pebble beneath his blanket, Cornelius."

"If he presses me, Wigiwig, I shall become more than a pebble. I shall become a crushing stone upon his skull."

Chapter 19

"Papa?" Wendy asked. "You have told Robert and me that violence is never the answer to any problem, but you said you would strike Mata'pang with a stone. I don't understand."

"Child, I was young and I lacked the warrior training. In truth, I said such things because I was afraid. I was the King's Captain, but I had no understanding of warfare or its terrible consequences. In all my life, I had never even been in a fistfight. I possessed no fighting skills or experience whatsoever, and yet here was I, the King's Captain, charged with preparing the defenses for the entire nation. I had never made a spear point, or a bow, or an arrow. In fact, my child, I have never used a weapon of any kind against anyone, then or since."

"Then why did the king make you his captain?" asked Robert.

"As I said, Robert, at that time I was a brash lad. I was ill tempered and quick to react to tauntings. It would be long after I was accepted into warrior training that I finally learned to overcome those tendencies.

"The king was a most clever man. By assigning me such a task, in a manner completely unknown to me he had wittingly laid the foundation for my warrior training. It was a test of sorts. It was also a way for him to gauge my progress. It was a way for him to study me from afar and learn about the kind of man I was and would become. What I did not know at the time was that Amog and the king had conspired with Wigiwig to set this 'pre-training' into motion.

"Remember, I had not been born into the Minchon Nation; I was not taught from birth how to find my rightful path; therefore, training for me was necessarily accelerated. I had much to learn. Being the King's Captain brought me under the direct tutelage of my instructors without my being the wiser.

"I thought I had been given this great opportunity because of my experience. Instead, I was given the opportunity to learn because of my *lack* of experience."

"So they tricked you?"

"No, Robert. They attempted no deceit. They tapped into my hidden strengths and exposed my weaknesses by allowing me to be what I was, by allowing me to grow in my own way and in my own time."

"I still don't understand, Papa," said Wendy.

"The best way to teach someone is to set a task for them and watch how they go about carrying it out. It is the way they set about accomplishing their task that reveals what they know and what they do not know. As I have tried to tell you before, Minchon Warrior training is very specific. The needs for each warrior vary widely, and the training is specifically calibrated for each student.

"Let me explain it this way. You take many different tests in school, correct?"

"Yes, Papa," replied Wendy.

"You take some math tests, some writing tests, some geography tests...each test is different so the teacher can learn what you know and what you lack. In this way the teacher understands in which subjects you excel and in which subjects you need more help. Does that make more sense?"

"Yes, Papa. So, if I'm good at math and not so good at geography, then my teacher would work more with me on geography?"

"Excellent, child! You got it in one pass. Each person learns differently; we are each born with certain gifts and lack others. To be well-rounded in this life, our instructors and our parents need to understand our strengths and weaknesses so that they can bring us to a greater understanding of how things work in this world. And so it was with my instructors on the island."

"So the king made you his captain to see what you knew and to gauge your strengths and weaknesses by how you went about your assignment?"

"Excellent, Robert! You understand exactly.

"But did they not truly need a captain who could prepare for war?"

"Yes, my son. The threat was real, the challenge was real. The task set before me was real and urgent. The need to prepare for an attack was authentic. But the real test was for me, to watch how I went about my task, to learn if I possessed a genuine truth within myself, to test my resolve, to test my ability to learn."

"The king seems a very wise man."

"Yes, Wendy, he was a most wise man, as were Amog and Wigiwig. I was fortunate to have these men as my instructors. And Lelalu, also. Her instruction was just as wise and as wonderful. Without her initial guidance and support, I might never have gotten far enough along the path to bring the others to me. I can only say that my success was largely due to their faith, trust, and good instruction. Together, they showed me the true path to success."

"Papa, how can *I* become successful?"

"Wendy, dear, success can be measured in many different ways. In most general terms, I would say, do what you love to do and you shall become successful. The only restriction is this: do no harm to others in pursuit of your success. Keep this true in your heart and success will find you."

"I don't understand."

"If you want to sing, *you sing* and never stop singing. If you want to dance, *you dance* and never stop dancing. If you want to love, you *love* and never stop loving. Continue on in whatever it is that makes you happy — and success by it and through it will surely follow."

"Can I continue writing?"

"By all means, my child! If it is what you love to do, then do it with constant joy in your heart. Be of good cheer and take great delight in your task, and you shall be successful. Do you understand?"

"Yes, Papa."

"What about me, Papa?"

"What about you, Robert?"

"What task is right for me?"

"What is it you want to do?"

"I want to become a Minchon Warrior like you."

"Then you will, Robert. Keep your mind focused on what you intend to accomplish, and it shall become reality. But there are many different warriors, Robert. Becoming a warrior is not an end unto itself, but rather a path to follow. There are warrior writers, such as your sister here. There are businessman warriors. There are firemen warriors. Being a warrior only helps you become better at what you enjoy. As I told your sister, find what it is that brings you happiness and satisfaction. Your warrior training will then aid you to become the very best at what you already enjoy doing. It is during the journey, not arriving at your destination, where you will discover the most joy. The arrival is merely the result of your joyous journey. So now I ask you, Robert, what is it you most enjoy doing?"

"I am not certain yet, Papa, but I like helping people."

"That's wonderful, Robert. I would consider that to be a noble endeavor. But it is too generally stated. You need to be more specific, for there are many ways to help people, and there are many vocations you can undertake to help you go about doing just that. Consider each carefully, have faith, and be of good intent. In time, the right path will present itself to you."

"Papa, can you continue the story now?" asked Wendy, pencil already in hand and prepared to take notes again.

The captain chuckled. "Certainly, child. Now, where was I...Oh, yes, I recall now.

The next morning came quickly, and we soon found ourselves standing tall on the hilltop's edge, which I had named The Ledge of the Observer, overlooking the plains of the Forbidden Land. To let our adversary know for certain that we were bold and unafraid, I ordered a large fire to be built.

Once it was completed, we struck the fire alive. The flames rose high into the early morning sky. From the height of the ledge there was no doubt the flames could be seen well inside the Forbidden Land. We had fully and brazenly announced our presence.

When daylight was fully upon us, I ordered green leaves to be cast upon the fire, thus creating a large column of smoke which rose high into the clear sky.

Having presented a bold challenge of my own to Mata'pang, I then stood my ground straight-backed and head held high well out on the edge of the ledge. I stood proudly for any to see me who cared to look.

I stood for nearly a half hour on that ledge, daring any of Mata'pang's people to show themselves in answer to my challenge, but none did so.

After several more minutes, and thinking my challenge would not be answered, I noticed a man step out from behind a rock. It was Mata'pang himself come to answer my provocation directly. Then, stepping out into the sunlight came another man, an archer.

From my lofty perch, I stared down at them both. They were such a great distance away, they presented no real threat. It was more a show than anything else. We were two adversaries, each meeting the challenge of the other without any possibility for a truly physical confrontation.

I decided to call down to him in a vocal challenge. "Mata'pang," said I, "I have tried to reason with you, but you answered by murdering an innocent tree. You, sir, are of very low character. But I will not respond with the same cowardice. Here I am, standing before you. I am here staring down at you. I do not need to destroy anything to present my challenge. I am prepared to face you directly."

"Then you are truly the fool I thought you to be," yelled Mata'pang.

The distance was so great, however, that his words reached me as barely a whisper. He then motioned to his archer, who nocked an arrow, pulled back the string, aimed it up at a great angle, and fired the arrow up at me.

I was shocked to watch the arrow coming at me, but then the strangest thing happened. As I observed the flight of the arrow, I noticed how quickly it lost its speed. The trajectory was such that the arrow shot into the sky high above where I was on the ledge. I watched it arc upward and outward and then track downward directly toward me. Its flight, however, slowed so much that I could see the arrow spinning. I realized the speed was dropping off so quickly it presented little or no threat to me. I could have waited until it got near to me and simply stepped aside. Even if the arrow were to strike me from this distance and speed, it would have only scratched my skin and bounced off. In a flash, a bold thought struck me.

As the arrow descended toward me, I held my ground. My guards urged me to step aside and let the arrow drop harmlessly to the ground, but I had another plan. I stilled the voices of my guards with a short command, and as the arrow neared me, I reached out and snagged it from the air just in front of my chest. My guards gasped loudly.

Then I held it up for Mata'pang to see.

Although, again, from such a great distance, I could not clearly see his face, I witnessed his shocked reaction to my catching the arrow in mid-flight. His body jolted noticeably in surprise, as did his archer's.

"Is this the best you can do?" I called down to him.

I then took hold of the arrow with both hands and broke it over my knee.

"I laugh at your challenge, sir. I mock you openly in your pathetic attempt. I see we can now return to the village and feel safe. The Great Mata'pang is no threat to the Minchon Nation."

He offered no comment, but turned and stomped off into the bushes and I saw him no more. His bowman quickly followed after him, and we were once again standing alone.

"Captain," said Gamomo, "that was an incredible feat. You have had no warrior training, and yet your warrior skills are already keenly present."

"No, Gamomo." said I, suddenly realizing my folly, "the arrow was slow. It required no warrior skill, just a steady hand and good eyesight. I was not threatened. Had I missed, it would not have been a harmful strike. My action proved me a failure.

"Captain," said Adagi, "surely you are overly harsh on yourself. Mata'pang ordered your tree cut down. That was an overt act of hostility. Your response was not hostile in any way. I do not compare the acts as equal."

"Hear me. You cannot equate the loss of a tree with the cruelty I have inflicted upon Mata'pang through my words, spoken in haste and with hubris. My actions were that of a brazen and infantile fool, without good merit and deliberately designed to inflict emotional harm.

"The tree, lads, although felled, may yet still be of use to stoke a fire. But I have wounded a spirit. I have crushed a man's sense of self-worth. Aye, if comparison is to be made of both actions, mine should be counted against me as much worse, for I have been charged with a higher duty than to wrestle with a young man's wounded pride and as such, to my duty, I have failed. Indeed, I lay vanquished by my own unbridled nature and I owe you both an apology for this catastrophe. I should have done more to reconcile our differences. Yet, all I have succeeded in doing, I fear, is to raise the ire of a man who must now seek vengeance if only but to save face amongst his peers

"But it is he who walked away," said Adagi.

"And yet he walked away as the victor."

"Put the fire out, lads and let us return to the village. I have suffered defeat enough over the last two days; I desire no more. This has not been a good day, nor is it a just reason to be proud and celebratory."

Once we returned to the village, I dismissed my guards and went to the spring to think, but if I be more honest about the matter, I would tell you that I went to the spring to sulk and pick fault with myself — to sit despondent with my failure.

Amog appeared through the bush and approached me.

"You sit alone brooding in the face of such triumph?"

"There was no victory today, Amog. There was only utter failure on my part."

"But you courageously stood your ground, snatched an arrow out of the air, and chased Mata'pang back into the Forbidden Land. Is that not a great victory?"

"No, it is only a capitulation to my youthful bravado."

"You have learned something of great worth today, Cornelius. Victory can be measured in many ways, and so can defeat. You feel defeated because you surrendered to your tempestuous youth."

"Yes, I had an opportunity to do something wonderful, and yet I may have only served to agitate a man who should not be agitated at all. My actions may have brought more harm to the people I was charged to protect. All in all, Amog, it was a poor showing for the King's Captain today."

"Perhaps it was a poor showing for the captain, but it was a wondrous day for Cornelius Alexander Delightable."

I chuckled knowingly. "Yes, Amog, Cornelius the captain may have suffered a defeat, but Cornelius the naïve and unbridled, storm-filled wild child did take some knowledge from the day."

"Then call it not a day of defeat, Cornelius. Call it a day of growth. Call it a day of apprenticeship training, and go forward on that basis."

"I have much to learn, Amog. You grace me with your kindness and patience. I will take today as a lesson, as you suggest, and I will move forward in that vein. Thank you, Amog."

"I have said it before; it bears repeating once more. The king has chosen his captain well."

"Thank you."

"Now mope no more, for I have brought you news of great joy."

"Tell me, Amog. I am in great need of joy at the moment, for it has been a stranger to me thus far in the new day."

"More because you are open to learning than for your deeds, I grant you your petition."

So much elation suddenly overwhelmed me that I nearly fell off the rock. I caught myself before tumbling over its edge and grinned up at Amog.

"Thank you, Amog! Thank you, Great Amog."

Then, as I had been instructed by Wigiwig in the protocol of approval, I knelt to one knee and bowed my head reverently. "Amog, I accept with great joy and full elation your approving response and I shall further strive to prove your decision a wise one."

"Then rise, Cornelius. Your petition is completed, and this matter is now well concluded."

I stood up and extended my hand toward Amog. He stared at it for a moment, then extended his. We shook hands.

"A curious gesture, this clasping of hands. Is there significant history to this?"

I laughed, remembering the similar question put to me by Wigiwig.

"There is, Amog. Please sit and have some mango and water and I shall tell you the story of it."

* * * * *

It was much later in the afternoon before I completed my critical assessment of my early morning failure and accepted the lesson of it. Curiously, Lelalu had remained absent from my presence. It might have been that she was allowing me the time necessary to complete my learning, or it might have been her royal duties that kept her occupied, but nevertheless, I had not seen her that day.

When the joy of my granted petition took control of me from the whipping I had given myself the last several hours, I dashed to Wigiwig and told him the great news. He was very happy, of course, but when I asked for parchment and quill to prepare my proposal, I remember him laughing out loud. "Can you not just speak from your heart, Cornelius?"

"I am a poor speaker in these matters, Wigiwig. I think I should write it down first and see that it is perfect before opening my lame mouth and have the words come forth, dribbling ineffectively as they surely would without such preparation."

"Ahh. The word 'perfect' is what I was looking for. Hear me, wild child. A woman need not hear perfection. She need only hear words spoken in truth and sincerity. Do not sacrifice these for accuracy."

He then laughed loudly and slapped a hand down onto my shoulder. "But then, if you have no words at all, writing them down first may prove to be helpful. Take what you need and give it your best. I expect nothing less from the King's Captain, the man who snatches arrows out of the air." He laughed again.

"So my guards cannot control themselves, it seems."

"It is all over the village now. Take joy in this."

"I am trying to forget it."

"Best wishes on accomplishing that today. Children are speaking of how they, too, want to snatch arrows out of the sky. It seems the hero you are destined to become is emerging even now. Thus it begins, Cornelius. You must now confront your fame in kind."

"Nay. On the rest of this day, I shall only confront the manner in which a proper proposal should be made. Are there protocols for this as well?"

"Yes, but only those between a man and his wife-to-be. I cannot help you on this one, my boy. You are, as they say, 'dangling from the yardarms' alone in this."

"Then I can only hope I shall not dangle unto my death."

Wigiwig laughed again. "That, my boy, remains to be seen."

* * * * *

After making inquiries as to the whereabouts of my Lelalu and learning that she had indeed gone off to accomplish some royal duty deeper into the jungle, I set myself to the task of writing my wedding proposal while awaiting her return.

Having never before undertaken such an arduous and frightening task, I really did not know where to begin.

I had successfully written her name, and then, as I sat nibbling from a plate of sliced mango, my mind went completely blank. I wanted the proposal to come from my heart, as Wigiwig had wisely suggested, and I intended to do just that.

My quill stood poised and ready to write. The ink well awaited the dip of my quill, but alas there came no words to my head worthy of being written.

I became perplexed and there was now no special tree under which I could crawl and set my mind free to invent wonderful words and phrases.

I could use the lack of a peaceful place to write as an excuse, but it would not lend itself to accomplishing the task set before me in so much earnest determination. I closed my eyes and leaned back against the rock on which I sat and tried to free the jam in my brain, but it was to no avail. The words were hidden from me, locked somewhere deep inside my heart with no sign of an open doorway to gain exit.

It was then I heard the loud snap of a tree branch and the crash of its falling through to the bushes below. Then I heard the screech of an animal. It was horrible to hear; the wail sounded like a holler of approaching death.

I ran to the part of the jungle where the scream came from and found a young monkey trapped under a large portion of tree trunk which had apparently broken free and fallen to the ground carrying the young monkey with it. I realized had I not been seated on my rock near the spring, I might never have heard the cries of terror, and the monkey might have died alone and frightened, unable to move the log off.

I approached the little monkey and recognized its white streak. I instantly recalled it was the monkey that escorted me to my welcoming party. I then recalled Lelalu telling me that it was I who would save its life.

I bent low over the monkey and whispered words to calm it. It worked, for as soon as the monkey saw my face and heard my voice, it calmed and awaited my rescue.

The log was much too heavy for the monkey to push off its body, but it was a simple task for me to lift it and set the monkey free.

I suddenly recalled her name. "Be calm, Ma'kawa, for it is I, Cornelius, come to rescue you as you knew I would." Then I braced myself against the weight of the log and lifted it carefully off the monkey's body, freeing it immediately. I tossed the log to one side and gingerly picked up Ma'kawa in my arms; cradling her gently, I carried her back to my rock and laid her down delicately. She neither resisted nor tried to get away. Instead, as I tenderly handled her legs and arms, searching for breaks, she lay calmly immobile and appeared to be smiling up at me; although in reality, it most likely was normal for monkeys to bare their teeth in that manner, I suspect.

"I feel no breaks, Ma'kawa. I think it is just shock that keeps you still. You took quite a tumble, no doubt. I think you'll be just fine. Would you like a piece of mango?"

I lifted a piece from my plate and handed it to her. She immediately sat up and began eating the mango. After she'd finished it, she crawled up onto my shoulder and hugged my neck, perhaps in some form of monkey gratitude.

"There, there, little one. I was there for you. All is well. I know it was not the best way to your heart, but you are safe and we are friends. And that must necessarily be enough."

Suddenly the words to my wedding proposal burst forth from that hidden place within me and in full measure. With Ma'kawa still clinging to my neck, I picked up my quill and parchment page, dipped my quill point into the rich black ink, and began writing freely and with ease.

Chapter 20

After a preparatory war conference with Wigiwig and Amog, I walked along the path leading from the village toward "my" rock near the spring. Guards had been appropriately camouflaged and deployed in selected places around the village. I had only to await Lelalu's arrival, which was expected soon.

Ma'kawa, still clinging to my neck as I walked, abruptly grabbed a low-slung branch and lifted herself off my shoulders and up into the trees above. I took that as an immediate sign she was again her normal self and had sufficiently recovered from her ordeal.

Coming to my rock, I lay down upon its flat surface, closed my eyes, and let my mind drift to where it pleased. Where it pleased to go, however, was back to the ledge overlooking the Forbidden Land, and recall of my harsh and provoking words spoken to Mata'pang.

Somehow that incident had not been successfully driven from my unconscious mind as I thought it had, but instead lingered in the back of my brain, still pressing me to a measure of anger and frustration. Now it came consciously to front and center once more, propelling me to a higher level of consternation.

What was it about Mata'pang that troubled me so? He was no physical threat; he was two hours away from me. He was not a spiritual threat; I knew my own soul's content well enough to be sure of that.

He was instead both a mental and an emotional threat as yet inadequately defined; but somehow, since our last confrontation, he had held me captive in an uncomfortable state, wondering now if a more

overt attack against me was imminent. My tree, where
I had found relief from all stress and anxiety, was
destroyed. I believe it was his intention to demolish
my safe haven, as it were. And while it did serve as a
blow to my sanctity, I found myself more concerned
with thinking on a more serious matter — the spy and
who it might be.

Questions replaced serious thoughts. *Did this
spy still walk among us by day, studying our defenses,
noting our plans and preparations? Did he or she
then, by night, report back to Mata'pang those
findings?* If so, I wondered in what manner I might
draw this spy out and capture this watcher, ending the
espionage.

Then it came to me clearly. *Were these
attempts at subterfuge being applied toward
discovering the weaknesses of the village, or were
they being directed at me personally — attempting to
discover my own weaknesses?* Toward yet a greater
simplicity, *was the spy studying the village or was the
spy studying me?*

I saw then what troubled me most, and this
became the defining moment: I recognized what
vexed me emotionally and mentally. The spy was
probing *me*, seeking out *my* faults, trying to discover
the chink in *my* armor.

This was *personal.*

I believed then that the spy cared nothing about
the village or the people. This was a blatant attack
upon me. I realized Mata'pang was keeping a promise
he had made to me several months before, when he
vowed to destroy all that gave me peace here. The
tree was the first to go, but what would be next, I
wondered. A chill shot up my spine at the thought of
it.

I began to consider all that had given me peace
here in an attempt to discover what his next targets
might be. Then I recalled this very spot, this place
where I first met Lelalu. Since the tree's destruction, I
had secondarily adopted this location as the place

where I found peace. This is where Lelalu and I normally took our midday meal. My hammock was here. The great flat rock was where I rested and thought wonderful thoughts. *Was this area the next to be destroyed? And how would this spy go about it? How* **could** *he or she do it? Would I return here someday soon and find my hammock torn to pieces? Would this spy see to it that every tree was cut down?* I had no clue as to how this menace might accomplish the destruction of this place, but I feared my nemesis would spare no effort to make it awful and personal.

Then a horrible thought sent additional shivers like bolts of searing lightning up my spine. *Could there be plans to attack Lelalu directly?* I could not bear this thought. It frightened me too much.

Even as King's Captain, I could not protect individuals from harm. Besides that, Lelalu would never allow me to hover over her filled with such dreadful worry. She would only laugh and tell me I fretted too much over such things. She would take no measures to protect herself either, for she would never allow a disparaging consideration to enter her head and make a home within her.

I trembled at the notion of losing Lelalu; my stomach turned to jelly, and I became nauseous at the thought of such a thing happening. *Could Mata'pang harm Lelalu?* Or, perhaps, it would be his intent to first harm the innocent animals on the island, realizing they also bring me peace? I had no idea to what lengths Mata'pang would go in achieving his atrocious goal.

Inwardly, I was a proactive sort of fellow. It was not my nature to wait and react to things I thought important or dangerous. As a ship's captain, it was my duty to be well prepared for all contingencies. My crew's safety, comfort, and security depended on my anticipating what lay before us at all times.

So it was now, as the King's Captain, that my honored duty was to guard against any threat

Mata'pang might initiate against the people of Minchon. To be clear, his actions against me were also actions against the Minchon Nation. Therefore, my first task was to determine where or who he might strike against next.

The problem of accomplishing this task, however, was that I did not know Mata'pang at all. I was not raised here. I had not observed his growth from childhood within the structure of the Minchon Nation. I had no knowledge of his previous reactions to events he disliked. I lacked this knowledge, but I knew that Wigiwig understood Mata'pang very well, so I decided to consult him on this matter.

After further thought, I came to the decision that I would not wait for his next attack. I would take this fight directly to Mata'pang. I would take the field against him and try my best to defeat him soundly before his people. If I were victorious in this coming battle, then the others of his clan would know that I, the King's Captain, was not one to trifle with. The threat would be extinguished. Perhaps then, I would prove myself worthy to be selected for formal warrior training.

I felt much better then. I was once more in full command of both my mind and my emotions. No more would Mata'pang's threats and actions infect me with fear and worry.

Just then, I felt a warmth sweep over me as a glow from behind brightened the already sun-filled air in front of me. I turned immediately and watched as Lelalu, almost glowing, walked toward me, her usual smile dazzling me even more.

"Lelalu," I said warmly, "you are like the approach of a second sun."

She giggled as she walked up and hugged me tightly, the flowery aroma of her hair firing my senses. "If that is so, then you must be the jewel that sparkles in the glow of my light. I have missed you so much."

"Your royal duties have no doubt kept you from me this morning."

"As your captain's duties have also kept you from me."

"Ah, yes. My captain's duties. I am afraid I have much to learn in that regard."

"You are troubled? The man who snatches arrows out of the air is troubled?" She smiled. I laughed.

"No, my love. I have no troubles at all when you are near me."

"Come, Cornelius. Let us eat and drink and rest. I wish to simply lie next to you and let this joy of seeing you again wash over me.

And so we ate succulent fruit and drank cool, sparkling spring water until we were full. And then we lay in the hammock as we held each other and chatted about simple things until we drifted off into a restful sleep.

* * * * *

I sat on my rock, giddy with anticipation. Lelalu finally stirred and awoke, surprised that I was already awake and smiling at her from my rock.

"And what has you smiling so brightly?" she asked, her own illuminating smile shining back at me.

"I have written something for you and I have tried to put it to memory, but alas, I fear I lack the capacity to do so. I am not gifted in such a manner, it seems."

"Then read the words to me from off the parchment," she said, rising from the hammock and coming to sit beside me on that great flat rock. "It excites me to know you have taken the time to set down your thoughts for me in the first place, and I tremble now in wild anticipation."

My stomach quivered once again, but I gathered my strength of resolve. I took her left hand in my right hand, reached for the parchment with my left, and boldly began.

"Lelalu, though this may not be the truest way to your heart, I feel certain it is near enough to the path to allow me to take this risk. I have found with you it is always the simplest effort that pleases you most.

"When I washed ashore as a shipwrecked wretch, you took pity upon me and welcomed me. Since then, when I have stumbled, you have caught me. When I walked straight and true, requiring no assistance, you were there nevertheless, on the path simply and patiently awaiting my approach.

"You have always been there for me, and I believe with all my heart that you always will be — with an ever-broadening smile and a delightful disposition.

"But no matter in what form or manner I may have arrived, you have always greeted me with love and graciousness. When I fret, you comfort me. If I should ever cry, I know you will dry my tears; when I speak, you listen with great care and patience.

"Hear me then once more, cherished one, as I cry out loud — even out into the distant depths of the universe with all honest sincerity — I intend to love you forever. But if forever proves to be too long, know that even so and despite all my frailties, my lack of good character, and the weakness of my spirit, I shall hold you dearly in my heart and adore you at least until the end of time, but longer if I am able to do so by will or consciousness. I shall be there for you until I am taken away by a power greater than I. But in my taking, know that I shall protest with a great and loud voice, and know also that I shall resist the taking with all my strength and resolve.

"Until then, dear one, accept me in joy as your husband and know that I make this request of my own free will and desire. I implore you, sweet love, take me with you on your journey through this life and through your lives to follow.

"Never doubt my intent, for I shall never doubt yours. In this I make declaration to whomsoever will hear. I am and will always be your husband. In all things and manner, I shall remain by your side through my death, and beyond if I am able to do so. I shall comfort you and care for you. I shall be an uplifting spirit when you need to be uplifted. I shall be a calming spirit when you have need to be calmed. I shall try to be all things to you when you wish me to be, and I shall remain silent and absent when you have need of that.

"By all that we hold dear in this life, I proclaim my deep and abiding love for you now and ask you to be my wife."

Lelalu, having sat motionless staring at me with both patience and intrigue, remained now very still. I believed, through her inaction, that my words had not touched her heart as I had hoped they would, and I began to feel sad and unworthy, believing my proposal had not carried my true feelings to her heart. Despondency began to creep in, but I remained still and silent, not wishing to further overwhelm her with my inadequacy. I studied her eyes for any sign, but she just stared at me vacantly. Her expression had not changed since I began speaking. I waited for any sign at all, but after a time the shame of my horrible attempt overwhelmed me. I tried to release her hand, but she tightened her grip on it and held it fast.

Then, as if by some miracle, her eyes moistened, filled, flooded, and tears began streaming down her cheeks. A small smile formed on her sweet lips. The manner of smile I knew not. Was it a smile of pity for such a diminished attempt, or was it a smile of politeness? I was not certain.

"I know, my love," I finally said. "It was a pitiful attempt. You need not respond. Release me and I shall go away to find better words and phrases if I am able to do so. I regret that I am no poet, but a humble ship's captain, and given more to barking orders to a cowering crew than to speaking loving words to such a beautiful and deserving woman."

Her lips moved, but no words spilled over them. They only quivered.

I felt less than a man. Of all the women I had ever known in my life, this woman was more deserving than any. I knew my ability to speak loving words to be sorely lacking, but after I had so carefully written them, and worse still, had failed to set them into memory, it seemed all the worse.

Would I have invented a better proposal if I had taken more time? It was too late for that, I feared. Why would she want to marry a man who could not find a way to memorize sufficient words necessary for a proper proposal? I was a deplorable excuse for a suitor.

I dare say that Mata'pang would have most likely found more perfect words to speak, and could have recalled them from memory, for his heart was more adequately full of passion and his spirit more correctly seasoned for such a task.

I tried to pull my hand free once more, but just as I tugged on it, she released my hands and wrapped her arms tightly around my neck and whispered in my ear.

"Yes."

That is the only word she uttered and the only word I needed to hear.

"Yes?" I asked.

"Yes," she repeated. Then she pushed me away, clasped her hands upon my face, and smiled at me as tears streamed down her cheeks.

"You need not take pity on me, Lelalu."

"What pity?" she whispered. "I never expected such wonderful words. My ears have never heard such pleasing words and phrases."

"It was a sorry proposal. You deserve so much more."

"Be still, Cornelius. The words were perfect. Spoken with honesty and so much love, you stunned me to silence. Yes, Cornelius, with all my heart, I answer yes. I would be honored and so fortunate to be your wife. I will love you and care for you as well. Until the end of all things, my love, I will forevermore be your loving and devoted wife."

I tell you now that it was I who was then sent into silence for a time. I shuddered. I heard her words, but they were not what I had anticipated after such a poorly presented proposal. Still, I did recall hearing the word 'yes' spoken clearly enough. Lelalu had accepted my proposal.

Elated as I was beyond words, I was as joyous beyond understanding, blithe beyond conscious or caring.

I was *betrothed*.

Tragic thoughts of retribution and revenge against Mata'pang had no place in either my heart or my head. No heinous wish to attack anyone was given entry to my being. Darkness found no access to my lighted soul. There was no intrusion of doubt.

I was, instead, fully infused to overflowing with hope and good will. Only illuminating visions filled my head, accompanied by the possibility of all things of the highest caliber becoming manifest in my life. I felt only the touch of the universe's highest wishes for my highest good.

* * * * *

While Lelalu went alone to tell her parents the good news, I went, instead, and boasted to Wigiwig.

"See, my friend. See how my neck remains unbruised. See also how I am still to be counted among the living."

"Ahhh," he said, his face filled with a smile. "Then you either made no proposal or it was accepted."

I laughed. "I had not considered the first part, but I *have* received an acceptance."

"Then that explains the sorrow I see on your brow."

"Sorrow?" I asked, confused. Then I saw the rise of his eyebrows and knew it then to be a jest. "Yes, the sorrow, it glows, does it?"

Wigiwig chuckled. "Yes, and such a dreadful sorrow it is. I hope such an expression never leaves your face."

"Aye, if this be sorrow, then it shall be my new expression forever," I chortled.

I seated myself on the bench next to him. "Tell me, Wigiwig. When shall I set the day to marry?"

"That is not for you to determine. That would be a choice made by Lelalu."

"I see. Then I should remain silent on the matter? Is that what you are saying?"

"Quite so. Your immediate task is completed. Go about your daily life and consider it no more. It is Lelalu who now carries the task."

"Then I shall bask in the glory of my achievement."

"You shall put your mind back on track as to our defenses."

"I do not wish to carry such morbid thoughts within my happy heart at the moment."

Wigiwig did not respond. His face grew solemn and his eyes stared back at me as black pits. After several seconds of wondering, it finally came to me why.

"Yes, Wigiwig, as usual, you're correct. I must return to my task as it lies before me. This has been a brief interlude, a wonderful respite, however, and I did enjoy it."

"I know, but it is a luxury that is not yours to possess for too long. A challenge has been set before you. How you respond will determine the course for the rest of your life."

"Why should this simple challenge, made by a man too immature to see the folly in it, be of such a magnitude as to define my whole life? Mata'pang pouts. He tantrums as a child who does not get his way. I have decided to meet him on the field of battle and thrash him if I am able to do so. In that way the threat will be removed. I am to be married. I have no time for his childish rantings and petty threats."

"It is deeper than that, Cornelius, much deeper. The seed of his anger was planted long ago, back in a time when there was a great division in the Minchon Nation, and the threat of a great war was on the horizon — a time when the very future of humanity was on the precipice and facing total annihilation."

"But his actions are directed at me alone. He does not come before the village and threaten. He seeks me out and finds me alone and drops these challenges at *my* feet. This is personal. I have come to see that clearly. He calls *me* out."

"His actions serve but a small, selfish need on his part. The growing threat, however, is much greater than even he understands."

"I do not understand any of this."

"Cornelius, he is only the voice to the thoughts of the people beyond the border. His stirrings and anger are from their words. He does not understand he is as a puppet — the strings binding him to his actions are being manipulated by someone much greater than he from behind the scene."

"When I infiltrated their camp, I saw no such master puppeteer. I saw only people like us, living in a manner very similar to how we live here. I observed no outward sign of threat. I saw a large number of people who, if stirred to anger, would represent a large and formidable army. But again considering all I observed, I saw no evidence that an army was being prepared for battle."

"Disregard for the moment what your eyes saw, and see with your heart. Would the others hide away in the Forbidden Land if they were of like mind and spirit with the Minchon people?"

"I see your point. My guess would be no. If they were actually like us, then there would be no need to exist separately."

"Precisely, Cornelius."

"But the people I saw *seemed* like us. Small children played, men and women talked. Nothing seemed any different."

"They are very similar to us. We have all descended from the same original source."

"So why are they not living among us?"

"Because they are not exactly the same. There are differences — great and profound differences."

"And what would they be?"

"Forgive me, Captain, but I am not permitted to say at this time. It has to do with a belief that goes a long way back, to the darker days when the Other's power extended far out into the world as it was then."

"Then all of this turmoil is based on differences in faith?"

"Something like that."

"All of this because of simple dogma? That seems silly to me."

"It is far beyond dogma, Cornelius."

"I'm trying to understand the context for what you tell me, Wigiwig, but alas, I am not able to put it all together yet. There is certainly a great secret being held from me. It stifles my task to make things ready for an attack."

"I know it is difficult for you, young Captain, but you will have to be patient a bit longer. This is the way it must be."

"Then I shall try to do so, and continue making the necessary preparations within the context of what I do understand. Still, that this information is hidden from me vexes me greatly."

"Prepare for the battle you are expecting, Cornelius. All the rest will be revealed to you in good time."

Chapter 21

I heard it said once that there can be no student without a teacher, and there can be no teacher without a student. I do not recall where I heard it exactly, but it made sense to me then. It makes more sense to me now.

I studied on my own a good long while over the next several weeks, but the more knowledge I gained, the greater the need I saw for a teacher. I was in desperate want for knowledge, especially regarding the history of the Minchon people.

Over a three-day period, I bombarded Wigiwig with so many questions I thought he would never answer another one the rest of my life.

In his nearly exhausted state, he finally raised both hands up above his head in mock surrender and rolled his eyes. "Enough, my friend, enough. I can answer no more questions today. My throat is parched and near to cracking wide open." He laughed loudly and stood up, dusting the sand from his bottom.

"I'm sorry, Wigiwig, but my head is bursting with questions. I need to know so much more about the Minchon history. I need information so I can understand the collective mind of the nation. I know I exhaust you to silence, but how else can I learn such things?"

"Your warrior training will give you all you need and much, much more."

"But I have not yet been selected as a candidate for such consideration."

"Speak with Amog about it."

"I cannot."

"You are the King's Captain. You have need of the information. Approach him on that basis. He will assist you."

"I seek no special consideration."

"You have been given a special assignment, Cornelius. To perform your assignment well, you have need to learn of these things. Amog only awaits your bold approach."

"He has said this?"

"No. He does not have to say this. It is obvious. Approach him as the King's Captain. He will open the library to you, or he will use his position to assign you a place in the training."

"Library? There is a library?"

"Yes. It is deeper in the jungle, where the students go to learn the warrior ways."

"No one has told me about a library, but now I understand where Lelalu goes from time to time."

"Yes. She is one of the exalted instructors."

I laughed. "She has never told me this."

"Have you asked?"

"No, I have not asked; I did not feel it was my place to ask where she goes."

"Then you should, but first go and see Amog."

I thanked Wigiwig for all his help and answers, and then went directly to Amog's hut and knocked on his door.

"Who is it that bangs like a charging bull upon my door?" he yelled with ire.

"It is I, Amog, the King's Captain. I have urgent need to speak with you."

The door opened. Amog's wife, Melatu, smiled broadly.

"The King's Captain, you say? Well, then, we should not delay you another second. Please enter, Captain."

"Thank you, Melatu, and greetings to you."

"And to you, Cornelius. He awaits you in the next room."

I went straight away to Amog and entered his meditation chamber.

"Amog, thank you for seeing me without prior notice."

"Of course, Captain. Please sit. What can I do for you?"

"Amog, over the past several weeks I have tried to study all I can to learn about the history of the Minchon people. I do this so I can better understand the mind of the people as a whole in order to prepare our forces for the defense of the village."

"That seems a wise thing to do."

"Thank you. However, the more I try to learn on my own, the more need I see for a teacher. Much of what I have learned serves only to confuse me further. It seems a great deal of the history has been hidden in strange and anecdotal formats. I have read all that Wigiwig has given me, and I have given it much thought and consideration, but I remain lost and baffled. Over the last three days I have nearly exhausted him with questions, and he has been most kind to offer answers the best he could. Today, though, he resigned himself from answering any more."

"I see. So, he is now spent?"

"I think so, but he suggested I speak to you regarding a teacher, and he also mentioned a library in the jungle. Would you have advice for me in this matter?"

Amog chuckled. This surprised me, for it was not his character to express humor when acting as High Priest. He noticed my shock. "What? Can I not express my delight?"

"Certainly, but I have never heard you laugh before."

"I take great glee in finally seeing someone who can bring Wigiwig to silence. He is usually like a raven, squawking day and night."

I realized he was speaking lovingly about his former rival. It was then I truly realized how much history they had shared; they were indeed brothers in every sense of the word.

I snickered. "I'm afraid I have done just that."

"Captain, you have brought to me the need to make a great decision. Access to the library is strictly forbidden to all who are not initiate warriors or students. Captain or not, I cannot grant you access, but give me time to consider the matter and I will come to you when such a judgment is decided."

"Thank you, Amog. If no access is granted, I accept it as so, but I still have great need of one to teach me what I need to know in my capacity as the King's Captain. Please consider that need also. I thank you for this audience, and I shall take my leave now so you can consider all that has been said here. Good day, Amog."

"Good day, Captain. Cornelius, I understand you have been given a great and burdensome task to perform. Do not think me ungrateful for your willingness to undertake so boldly the challenges meant for broader, more trained shoulders. I know the duties of a ship's captain are not the same as an infantry commander, but you carry the burden well."

"Thank you. I shall do my best. I just pray that my best is good enough."

"All answers shall come in their own time."

I bowed my head reverently to the High Priest and left him to reflect on the issue in his own time and in his own way.

* * * * *

The next morning I went to greet the fishing boats as they came ashore and to chat with my former mates. As they finished stringing the fish and cleaning out the boats, I jested with my friends until I heard one of them gasp sharply. I looked at him to see him staring at something of great interest over my right shoulder.

I turned to see Amog standing tall and fierce-looking in the sand about seventy paces away. His usual throng of servants surrounded him. His shade servant, as was customary, held the grass umbrella perfectly positioned so it shaded him completely. He was stately in his manner. This was an official visit by the High Priest and could only indicate that something extraordinary was about to occur.

Soon, every young man and woman stopped their work, turned, and stared at the High Priest. In the midst of all my study and work, I had not forgotten that today was the day three men and three women would be chosen from among the youth of the nation to begin their warrior training, but I had not thought that Amog would announce such a decision here on the beach. If it were so, I believed it would be a first.

From the looks on the faces surrounding me, no one else believed it either. I was stunned.

One of his runners approached the boats, but came straight at me and stopped just short.

"Amog wishes to speak with you, Captain."

All eyes were instantly upon me and whispers began all around.

"Certainly," I responded. "I shall come immediately."

The runner turned and ran back toward Amog as I walked to him. I wanted to run. I wanted desperately to break out into a gallop, but I remained in proper form. The King's Captain does not show excitement or exhibit childlike exuberance in front of his potential field soldiers. Instead, I held my head high, my shoulders back, and walked smartly to him, or as smartly as I was able to in the shifting sands of the beach.

"Tell me, wild child," he said as I stopped before him, "do you possess the will and courage sufficient to begin your warrior training?"

Finally, in front of all the boatsmen and the villagers who had gathered around us, my fate was being decided. I did not feel much like the King's Captain at the moment. He had addressed me as 'wild child' once again, so I knew his decision was not based on my standing as Captain, but as a young candidate.

My 'wild and tempestuous nature,' as he coined it, was beginning to ooze from my pores. Without timidity, I wanted to scream my answer loudly for all to hear, to remove any lingering doubt that any of them might hold for me; however, during my time with the Minchon people, I had somewhat matured, so I held my exuberance well in check.

I needed to be daring, though, for he had set a clean challenge before me in front of the entire village. I noticed Lelalu standing in the back of the crowd. She stared at me, but I refused to acknowledge her presence. This was a challenge, but for me alone to answer. I must admit, however, it was comforting to know she was there. I felt her remote support surge through me.

I looked directly into Amog's almond-shaped eyes and perfect face. I stood tall and straight, my shoulders arching backward in true officer's military stance, and replied with boldness, simplicity, and certainty. "I do, Amog."

His gaze was hard upon me, but he appeared fair in his appraisal of my capabilities.

"The training is difficult and the expectations are great for you."

"I have need to learn so I may serve the people as their protector. That knowing alone will be sufficient to carry me through whatever may come."

"Well stated, Cornelius. I have judged that you have great need to begin the studies. I hereby grant you a special dispensation and approve your candidacy petition and declare you a 'student warrior.' Tomorrow, after the morning meal, you will be shown to the library to begin your study. Considering your need to be urgent, your study will be accelerated. I and Wigiwig will be your instructors."

The gasp of the crowd was as one. I was stunned nearly to silence myself. To be personally instructed by the High Priest was an honor above honor. To my limited knowledge, no student had ever been taught directly by the High Priest — until now. Once again, I followed no precedent; I created it.

"I would be honored to become your student, Amog. I look forward to all you are willing to teach me. I am humbled before you, for I expected no special consideration or assistance."

"And for Cornelius Alexander Delightable, none would be granted by me. But for the King's Captain, whose task it is to protect the nation, such will be given. This is a burden too great for anyone to undertake without knowledge. Know also this, Captain: your studies will be intense and the path toward your enlightenment a difficult one. The pressure upon you to succeed will be greater than upon any other student. You will be tested at every turn and your every limit of endurance shall be mightily put to the test as well. Expectations for you will be demanding and most severe. But as I have seen you in action, and I have heard of your exploits into the Forbidden Land, I say only this. Strive with the same courage, determination, and willingness to succeed, and you shall stand well enough against the challenge. That is all I have to say for now."

Without another word, he turned and walked away. The moment he disappeared through the bushes, the hands of several of the workers were upon my shoulders and head. Others slapped me across the back in warm congratulations.

It was, however, the smile I received from Lelalu that thrilled me most. As she approached, all others separated and bowed their heads, leaving her a well-defined pathway directly to me. She laid her left hand against the right side of my face as she continued to smile warmly. "My betrothed, it pleases me greatly that you should begin your warrior training so soon. It is a great honor to be chosen so quickly, but see how everyone agrees with Amog's decision. You are found worthy by the people. You have shown your love for the people and your respect for the ways of the Minchon Nation. I have no doubt that you will make a great warrior."

She then hugged me tightly as smiles and gentle supportive looks from all present confirmed her words.

"I shall endeavor to work hard and retain your support for me," I said, speaking to include as many as I could get my eyes focused upon. "I will not let you down."

* * * * *

After the morning meal, delayed somewhat by the ceremony and the subsequent revelry now finished, Amog returned to select the next six warrior students. Two of the men chosen were Adagi and Gamomo, the two guards who had accompanied me to the borderland. We embraced each other and swore an allegiance to one another to continue together as fellow soldiers. I, as the King's Captain, promoted them both to the position of my First Lieutenants.

Afterwards, Lelalu and I decided to walk along the beach and talk. As we walked, I could no longer resist my temptation and began to ask her questions.

"Lelalu, I have discovered that you are an instructor at the school."

"I am, Cornelius."

"I have often wondered where you went when you went into the jungle. You never told me, and I felt it wrong to ask you about it."

"My love, it was never a secret. I didn't tell you because I thought it of no interest to you."

"Everything you do is of interest to me."

"Husband, you thrill me so with your caring words. Tomorrow we shall walk hand in hand along the path to the great library. You shall see where the sum total of human understanding is stored, preserved, and protected. You will be amazed at what knowledge lies on the shelves waiting to be devoured and understood. It is the greatest and most complete library in the world."

"Greater than the Library at Alexandria?"

"Yes, many times larger and more complete than that sacred library."

"Larger than the mysterious library I heard spoke of in the great mountains of Tibet?"

"Much larger than that even."

"What is it that you teach?"

"I teach the Oneness classes."

"The Oneness?"

"Yes, I instruct the students about the One. The Singular Consciousness, the Oneness that is All, the Source, the Light."

"I see," I answered, obviously overwhelmed and not understanding her words or meaning.

She giggled. "No, my love, you do not see at all — but you will. All of the knowledge will become a part of you in time. Do not struggle with it now. Both Amog and Wigiwig are supreme instructors. With those two, you could not ask to have better teachers. Your learning will be quick and full. You have only one obligation."

"And what is that?"

"To ask questions."

"Ask questions?"

"Yes. If you do not understand anything being taught, stop the instructor and ask for a deeper explanation. Question everything, Cornelius; take no statement as the truth unless it matches your inner understanding. Allow your inner self, the true student, to raise questions and challenges."

"My inner self?"

"Yes."

"Is it not I, the King's Captain, who is being taught?"

"It is much to accept right now, but you will discover that it is your inner self, the inner consciousness, that is the primary recipient of the knowledge you will receive."

"Not I? I am not the one who must learn? It is my inner self that needs to be taught?"

"*Re*taught, to be precise. It is your inner consciousness that is actually trying to reconnect with the Singular Consciousness. It possessed the knowledge to do this before, when it was truly connected to the One. It has forgotten much of what it knew then because of the separate consciousness it developed when it became encased in the physical plane. Now, to reconnect, it must relearn the knowledge, for it can survive only when it is once more connected to the Singular Consciousness."

"The Singular Consciousness."

"Yes, or if you'd rather, the God Consciousness."

"The God Consciousness? Oh, that makes it much clearer. I *completely* understand now," I said sarcastically, with a bewildered and devious grin.

She laughed again. "You will, my husband. You will. You must understand that everything you see, everything you touch, is all part of the whole. Everything is all. All is everything. We are all one."

"I do understand what you're saying; but if we are all one and not separate from each other, why is there strife in the world? Why does Mata'pang despise me so? If we are all connected and we are all one, then does he not despise himself?"

"Exactly, Cornelius — excellent, Husband! He does. He does not know this yet, but yes, it is his part of the whole that he despises most. It really has nothing to do with you. He sees his own reflection when he stares at you. It is the reflection of his own separate self that tortures him."

"His separate self? But if he is separate, then how…?"

"Enough for now, Cornelius. Any more will cause you to wobble again."

"Yes," I said grinning, knowing she was correct.

"Let us just walk and enjoy each other."

"Speaking of that. Now that I am emboldened, what is the date you have selected for our marriage?"

"That is for me to know. You must be patient."

"I understand. Forgive my inquiry; I just wanted to know how much time I have left to enjoy my freedom."

"Freedom?" She stopped dead in her tracks.

"Yes, I wanted to know how long I have before I must surrender my freedom."

"You feel that marrying me will destroy your freedom?" she asked, hurt filling her eyes.

"Well…of course, and I'm in terrible dread of this, for I so enjoy my freedom." I tried not to give evidence of my jest. But alas, my teasing nature gave way to a meek smile which fully betrayed me and I finally burst out into a hearty laugh.

The truth now revealed, she laughed as well and playfully punched me in the arm.

"I am not one given to violent reactions, my dear, but you deserve this." Then she laughed again and sent a punch to my stomach. I doubled over from the surprise of it rather than the force, for the punch was absent any force at all. And I knew well enough that she would never intentionally harm me in any manner.

Chapter 22

After several months of intense self-training, I had learned much about the Minchon ways, her people, and the history of such a fine race. Still, I lacked so much of the knowledge necessary for my intended growth.

To finally have access to all I would need to complete that growth was extremely exciting. I looked forward to seeing, with my own eyes, the great library that purportedly dwarfed all others.

The next day came quickly, and after the morning meal celebration Lelalu and I strolled along the path deep into the jungle toward the library. I must admit that as I grew nearer, I felt a wild anticipation surge through my body in an almost uncontrollable quiver.

I attempted to mask my feral exhilaration, but Lelalu once again saw through me. Her hand grasped my arm tightly in support.

"Calm yourself, Husband, and know that everyone reacts to the library in the same manner upon first seeing it."

"I was trying to."

She chuckled. "I know."

Of course she did. I was foolish for attempting to hide my true emotions from one who was so well connected to all things on this island. My childlike wonder was in full bloom, however, and so I released my grip upon it and let it run wild with as much giddy anticipation as a child opening a gift.

"Knowing that it contains the total sum knowledge of humanity, its size must be immense," I suddenly blurted out.

Lelalu smiled. "You will be shocked, my love. Give pause and reflect upon it as you must, but still it will not be sufficient until you see with your own eyes."

"As you say. Still, the knowledge of mankind seems so immense, I cannot fathom how it could be contained under just one roof."

As we rounded a bend in the path, the answer became clear to me. The library was simply enormous. Lelalu told me it measured fully three square hectares. As I understood such terms, that could also be expressed as almost seven and a half square acres.

Finally, standing next to the entrance, I estimated the walls to be almost twenty feet high. Quite simply, then, it was the largest building under one roof that I had ever seen.

Once inside, I quickly experienced the shock she had warned me about. I was nearly dumbstruck, for I plainly saw that only about one quarter of the shelves were full; the rest of them were bare. I assumed they were available for additional books in the future.

But in all its glory, there it was. The sum total of human knowledge to date occupied but a quarter of the available space. Everything man had ever known was not even close to filling the available shelves. I felt humble, to say the least. Humble in that I knew nothing, and yet the totality of man's knowledge was only enough to barely cover 1.8 acres, twenty feet high. It was a staggering revelation to me.

"This is it?" I said sadly. "Everything that man now knows or has ever known before barely fills a quarter of the library?"

"Yes, Cornelius, this is all of it as far as we know. This is it in its entirety."

"What that means is that with all I know, barely one shelf would be filled — if even that."

"There is knowledge here enough to fill several lifetimes, my love. Do not be troubled with that. Each of us need learn only that which we need to learn. We could not possibly know it all while trapped in this mortal shell. Take comfort in this, however. Once we shed this physical vessel, our mind will have instant access to all of this and much, much more."

"There is more?"

"There are the Akashic Records."

"Akashic Records? Dare I ask what those are?"

"Records that contain not only the accounts of all human existence but also the accounts of the history of the cosmos. Once we are reconnected to the Singular Consciousness, all of it will be at our fingertips, so to speak."

I must have staggered a bit, because I felt her hand grasp my arm. A second later, I regained my own consciousness. "Dear Lord," I squeaked. "The sheer power of the knowledge on these shelves alone would be enough to change the world, if we all had access to it now."

"This world and many others, Cornelius."

"Others? Others, did you say?"

"Do not think on that now. Amog has arrived. I will leave you in his care. My class forms even as we speak. I must make myself ready. Enjoy this day, my love. You have earned it."

She let go of me, kissed my cheek, and walked away just as Amog approached. In passing, they bowed to each other and continued on their respective paths.

"Let us immediately dispense with all formality, Cornelius," Amog said abruptly. "We have much to cover this day alone. We shall begin. Wigiwig will join us later."

"Where do we begin?"

"At the beginning, of course."

"And where does the beginning begin?"

"At the —"

"The beginning, of course," I interrupted, knowing already what words he was about to speak.

He chuckled. "of course."

"What *is* the beginning, Amog? I mean where does one begin to understand the beginning? The beginning of what?"

"I think it is best if we start at the beginning of all things. Let us start with the universe itself."

"Wonderful!" said I in mock astonishment. "This should be easy to understand."

"It may or may not, but it will be easier if you open your heart and open your mind to all possibility."

"It's open, Amog. It's an empty and barren cavern, to be sure, but it is open. As open as it can be, but I feel already overwhelmed by the sheer size of it all. The library, I mean."

"For the sake of your freshness, Cornelius, I will keep my answers very simple and straightforward until your mind has suitably expanded."

"Tell me this, Amog. How can all this be?"

"An excellent question from the start, lad. It is very simple. Let us begin with the word 'all.' Everything in the universe is all there is. All is everything. We are all. We are everything that ever was or ever shall be. Before the universe, there was nothing but us and we were one. There was only I. But then there was the great tragedy. We fell out of the Singular Consciousness — the One. And ever since then, we have existed separate from the One with only one task in our hearts — to get back to the One — to be reconnected with the Singular Consciousness."

"Back to God?" I asked innocently.

"Cornelius. *We* are God. Everything is God, and God is everything. We are individually parts of the whole. We can never separate ourselves entirely from the whole. We are forever One."

"Believe me or not, Amog, I understand everything you've just told me."

"That's good. We shall use this bit of knowledge as our foundation, then."

"A question, though. Why are we called warriors?"

"Because we are constantly at war with the darkness within ourselves. As warriors, then, we are compelled to do battle with the darkness that wants to reside within us and keep us separate from the light of One."

"Then that is the purpose of darkness?"

"Exactly. Its only purpose."

"The only goal of darkness, then, is to destroy light?" I asked.

"That's correct. It has no other purpose; it simply cannot exist where there is any light. Therefore, to exist at all, it must eradicate any light whatsoever; for the smallest bit of light dispels darkness completely."

"Then we might be called Warriors of the Light?"

"In fact, Cornelius, we are called Children of the One."

"I've heard that term before. Which brings another question to mind. Who are the Sons of the Other?"

"An astute question, but for the moment let the question live within, without an answer."

"I have many other questions, Amog. May I ask them?"

"You may ask any question you wish to ask. The answers, however, may each take some time, and you may not yet possess the inner knowing to understand them."

So I asked my questions, but I received no more straight answers to any question I asked. Not that he meant to hide them from me, but he was correct: my mind was not yet prepared to understand them in their exactness and completeness. After a while, I stopped asking questions altogether.

He then called me 'master' and suggested that he be called 'student.' When I asked why, he explained that titles were unnecessary. They were just words. It was the belief behind them that gave them meaning. With certain words came certain expectations; some fair, some unfair, some deserved, and some undeserved.

"You are here, my boy," he said, "to gain your way back to the Singular Consciousness that was misplaced so very long ago. We are on the path back toward that understanding, but please be patient. There is much to learn. It cannot happen in one instant. You must learn, above all else, to live in harmony with the Singular Principles; this is what sustains us."

"Are Mata'pang and his people then living in *dis*harmony with the Singular Principles? Are they frustrated by the fact that they are separated from the Oneness of the One? Is this why he despises me so?"

"You present so many questions at one time, Cornelius, it is hard for me to answer."

"Wigiwig said the same thing," I said with a chuckle. "I am possessed by a hungry mind. I apologize."

"Your hunger is admirable. You demonstrate an innate desire to learn. That cannot be taught."

"Then it is a good thing that I seek knowledge?"

"Within reason, but possessing knowledge is not enough."

"Please explain."

"Having knowledge of water does not prevent thirst. Having the water in your hand does not prevent thirst. Only drinking the water can prevent thirst from coming on us. It is the same with the One or the Singular Consciousness. It is the same with light and darkness. Do you understand?"

"I believe so. Having knowledge of a lighted path does not lead one out of the darkness. You must actually take the first step along that path in the light. Belief is also not enough. There must be action taken in belief."

"Well done, Cornelius. Exactly. In fact, it could be said that your beliefs control your destiny. Beliefs, however, in and of themselves are merely conceptual; they possess no substance. But *acting* on your beliefs does have consequential effects. It is the good or ill of such actions that gives value to those beliefs. A kindly action taken towards me requires no particular translation or explanation. The kindly act in and of itself could be defined as a good belief, could it not?"

I nodded in agreement.

"Conversely, then," he continued, "if you take an unkind action against me by way of your beliefs, then such a belief can rightfully be judged by me to be not a good thing. Do you understand?"

"Yes. So, when someone says something about the problems of the world — be it from greed, or money, or war, or lust, or vanity, or carelessness, or whatever — what do you say?"

Amog thought for several seconds before answering. "That these things are only branches of a much larger tree, and the roots, which are all problems, all evil, all suffering, are merely manifestations of selfishness…and that selfishness is the result of separation from the Singular Consciousness."

"How does one regain the Singular Consciousness?"

"There is only one way, Cornelius. Through unselfish love, self-sacrifice, caring, giving, and identifying the illusions of self-consciousness that we carry within our minds, and then casting them away from us, refusing them a place in our soul, declining them residence within our heart."

"I understand, but I find myself presently struggling with the thought of loving Mata'pang. He has shown no love towards me."

"That is your separate self-consciousness talking. You must overcome that thinking and feel compassion for him instead. Think of his struggle. Imagine how he feels at this moment. He believes he is unloved here within the Minchon Nation. He does not understand that he is both greatly loved and greatly missed."

"Despite all his aggressive actions thus far, you say the village would take him back?"

"In an instant, Cornelius. He is one with us. We feel his pain because it is ours also. We feel his separation from us and the agony of his absence because these are ours as well. When you are of the Singular Consciousness, we are all one, as I have said before."

"Yes. Now I understand even better. Although he has separated himself from us, we are still connected to him. Thus, his pain is our pain."

"Exactly."

"What about the spy? Is he or she also connected with us?"

"The spy is one of us, but the spy is not *of* us. Therein lies the difficulty."

"Then I am fallen into a paradox once more. If the spy is one of us, would not the Singular Consciousness be able to detect the deceit in the spy's heart, mind, or spirit?"

"If the spy lives outside the Singular Consciousness, then it is possible we would not detect his or her presence as a spy."

"But living amongst us, would not someone discern the separation? How could one separated from the One not be detected? There seems a contradiction existing in all of this. If one is a part of the whole, then would not the whole know of the separation of one of its own?"

Suddenly my mind went blank, and my mental state must have displayed itself through my eyes because Amog waved his hand in front of my face and smiled compassionately.

"And now you know why I must proceed slowly with you, Cornelius."

"I have sorely confused myself once again and I have lost all way through the confusion. I know nothing. That's all that is clear to me at present. I fear I am woefully inadequate for the task of learning any of this."

Amog placed his hand upon my shoulder. "You are at a great disadvantage, Cornelius. Children growing up here with us are taught from a very young age, and over many years, all that you must now discover and know quickly. The task before you is a daunting one, to be sure, but take heart. You are very intelligent, and you are spurred on by good intention. It will soon all become clear to you."

His words soothed me, but they were not enough. I had to gain knowledge very quickly and I had to learn it well enough to successfully prepare myself for the task of protecting the people. I had to learn principles so strangely new to me, principles so deeply profound and important, that I could not perceive how such learning would be accomplished in the time necessary.

"It must be the darkness dwelling inside me that prevents me from understanding."

"It is not darkness that dwells within you, Cornelius. You are just incomplete within."

"I feel that I am beset with evil within, and I think it is also true that the whole of the world is in the same condition as I. The world appears so confused. Priorities, it seems, are dreadfully misplaced. A question, Amog. Are all things evil upon Earth? And if so, am I then born of evil also?"

"No. Both you and Earth are just incomprehensibly incomplete in your present state. But be sure to understand this: no problems will ever be solved unless people themselves make a change within. No form of humanity will ever really work, or last, while separate consciousness exists. So it is also for Earth itself. Why is this, you might ask? Because there is a separate consciousness existing within all things of man — and within the universe itself — at present. When you stop and think about these things, it is easier to understand why the Children of the One teach that only when all people once again possess the Singular Consciousness, and everyone is primarily governed from within by the Singular Spirit, will there ever be peace, harmony, goodwill, and freedom from evil. Remember also this. Earth is us. We are Earth. The universe is us and we are it also."

"All is one and one is all. Yes, I at least understand that, but not much else. Are we to fear darkness?" I asked, almost regretting the question for the veiled answer to come.

"No. We must only reject it."

"Must we seek to destroy it?"

"You can never destroy darkness. Darkness is what exists without the presence of light. Without light, there must necessarily be darkness. The universe must maintain balance in all things and at all times. As such, evil or darkness must remain — to balance out goodness and light."

"If they must remain to keep the battle going, then why should we struggle against them? If they are a part of the whole, then they are a part of us as well. They must be kindred with the whole, no?"

"No. Darkness and evil exist only when there is separation from the One. Remember, in the beginning there was only *I*. There was no darkness or evil then. Such things were created only when we chose to separate from the Singular Consciousness. Darkness and evil were then created."

"Yes, I forgot that. Thank you. Tell me, though, why must it be the task of darkness to destroy light?"

"Because darkness cannot understand light. It must destroy light so that it may exist — and perhaps feel safe."

"Then for Mata'pang and his people, it must be the same. They follow the dictates of the Other. And as such, they need to destroy what they cannot understand of the One so they will feel safe and protected once more. Am I correct?"

"No, Cornelius. They are not of the Other. They do not seek to destroy. They wish to return to the light, but are gone astray now in the darkness and cannot find the path leading them out of it. They are thus lost and desperate. That is all."

"Thank you, Amog. I have learned much, but I fear it is only a single drop into a very large tub. Nevertheless, I grow fatigued from the weight of it."

"That's true. Let us lighten the task a bit, then, and learn something more fun, exciting, and very simple."

"That would be a welcomed change. What do you have in mind?" I asked.

Amog scratched momentarily at the end of his nose. He then raised his eyes to meet mine and smiled. "Have you ever heard of *riding the wind*?"

Chapter 23

Detective Cyra had been inwardly seething over the past two weeks and felt hopelessly cursed. His every attempt to get Judge Harrison to sign an arrest warrant had been thwarted.

He knew well enough that the judge and Captain Delightable were close friends. He also knew that the judge was adept in the matters of jurisprudence. So it was of little surprise how quickly the judge was able to find some obscure and enigmatic edict to support his reason for not issuing such a warrant.

Cyra, a mere policeman attempting to outthink Judge Harrison, a very learned man who worked in the law every day in a wide variety of ways and manners, soon had to accept the fact that he had little chance of succeeding against the mount of such a resistive personality armed with such formidable knowledge and skill. Still, in the face of it all, he continued, spurred onward by his own formidable tenacity, determined to keep chipping away at the mountain of nepotism that blocked the path to his end purpose.

He suspected the judge was protecting the captain in some fashion, but he was at an utter loss as to why. The thought had occurred to him that perhaps the captain knew of some mysterious and foreboding secret concerning the judge, something dark and terrible involving his past which could keep the judge pliant and in wicked service to the needs of the captain.

Certainly some reason existed, but exactly what it was lay darkly shrouded and just beyond his sight. Determined to learn what it was that kept the judge in service to the wants and desires of the enigmatic captain, he pressed forward. To his mind, it was just a matter of time before he discovered the awful truth. Of that he remained most confident despite these recent disappointing failures.

In all his years as a detective, he had never felt more sure about some kind of connection between a suspect and a judge. He certainly had looked into this judge's past, but it was positively glowing. From his birth, to college, to his exquisite work in the courts of Los Angeles, to San Francisco, his record was simply impeccable. There wasn't a hint of any wrongdoing or a speck of shady behavior anywhere in his public history. His record was one of exemplary honor, towering achievement, and unmitigated respect.

Still, in spite of this superlative history, he suspected something was amiss. The judge was simply too perfect. Added to that, every policeman's instinct racing through his body told him there was some odd connection to the captain, and he was determined to find that connection no matter what. When he did, he vowed he'd not hesitate a moment to expose it all — to devastating ends and in support of his own purpose.

For now, however, he would continue whittling away at the mystery as best he could, taking delight in knowing he represented a nagging thorn in the judge's side, an irritating pebble in the captain's shoe, and a heckling and persistent voice in both their ears. He would never cease in his pursuit of the truth, and he would do his best to keep them clearly and forever mindful of his intentions.

In that vein, then, the reason was clear as to why on that particularly chilly night he found himself standing across the street from the captain's home, hidden within the darkened space that fell between the gas lamps, and considering deeply what his options were.

It was grossly late, nearing ten thirty. He should be home resting, he thought, but here he was, wrapped up tightly in his overcoat and shivering away while surveilling a man who was most likely tucked warmly in his bed, fast asleep and probably enjoying some peaceful dream.

The more Cyra thought about it, the more it bore into his soul. The house was dark. Not a flicker of light could be seen anywhere. *What the hell was he doing here at this time of night? Why was he standing here nearly freezing to death? What had prompted him to even come here tonight?* Certainly no answers presented themselves, only more idiotic questions.

After a while, he pulled his pocket watch from his vest and squinted at the dial. As it was much too dark where he stood to see the time, he stretched out his hand to the edge of the light cast by the closest gas lamp. Ten fifty-seven. It was ridiculously late now. Withdrawing his hand back into the blackness, he waited a couple of minutes more and then decided to return to his home to thaw out. This had been a complete waste of his time, he thought.

Just then he caught a glimpse of a flicker of light on top of the captain's roof. A sudden spark and then a small flame burned. There he was, the captain, standing alone on the flat part of his roof, lighting his pipe.

Cyra surmised that Suzanne must have relented and unlocked the attic door, the one he'd heard she'd padlocked. Tony, the handyman at Hotchkiss's Hardware store, had revealed that fact during one of his surreptitious investigations of the captain.

There he was, smoking his pipe and probably inwardly laughing at him, having heard, no doubt, about his failed attempts to secure a warrant from the judge. Yes, there he was standing on his roof, smugly enjoying another day of freedom while he, Cyra, felt incarcerated, ensnared by his need to bring the captain into custody.

Life was certainly not fair, and the captain was his constant reminder of that fact.

Suddenly the bitter cold no longer bothered him. The furnace of his anger ignited and warmed him. The nova exploding within him grew brighter and hotter. There, above him, stood an old man with every comfort and grace available to him. The people loved him. He was welcomed everywhere he went. Everyone enjoyed his company. He'd never had to endure any unkind remarks about himself, remarks often spoken in surety and loud enough to be overheard.

Anger raged on in a deeper place inside Cyra's being as he realized, by contrast, that he was scorned everywhere he went. Despite being an honorable and incorruptible policeman who tried to do good for the community, he was despised by nearly everyone he met. Nobody wanted to speak with him. Everyone avoided making eye contact with him, afraid he might somehow be in the midst of some haunting investigation of them.

He had seen people cross the street to avoid passing him on the sidewalk. Nobody, it seemed, ever greeted him warmly, with friendly eyes and a welcoming smile. No one, that is, except Captain Delightable, who always offered a kind word and a friendly and caring disposition.

But it was a false disposition, he believed, intended to put him off his game. Cyra would like to know what the captain really thought of him. It was most likely the same as the rest of San Francisco thought. It was an old story. He was a cop, and everyone hates a cop until they need one.

As he stared up at the captain quietly smoking his pipe on the rooftop, he wondered what was going through his mind.

The moon, previously hidden by an overcast sky, suddenly burst forth, throwing a bright yellowish glow down upon the captain. He observed the old man's reaction. The captain looked up at the moon and rendered a salute to the glowing orb above him.

Then he watched as the captain emptied his pipe and rapped it with his hand, knocking out the last bits of burnt tobacco. He placed the pipe into one of his coat pockets and remained gazing up at the moon for a few more minutes with what Cyra could only identify as a reverent stare.

Then the captain nodded his head toward the gentleman in the moon and disappeared in the blink of an eye.

That was it. The captain was there and then he was not. Cyra continued staring disbelievingly up at where the captain had stood only seconds before, attempting to confirm that he was no longer standing in the center of his roof.

What had just happened? Cyra rubbed his eyes and trained them again on the roof. It was confirmed; the captain was now gone. He had vanished into thin air right before his eyes.

Cyra refused to believe what he had just seen. *Did, in fact, the captain vanish or did he just move out of the light of the moon and exit the roof through the attic doorway?* No. He was certain of what he had seen. He had witnessed no forward movement. Being a highly trained observer, his eyes efficiently noted the small details that normal people would not even be aware of. The captain made no move toward anything. He was there and then he was not. It was just that simple, but Cyra's eyes could not explain it to his brain. What he had witnessed was simply impossible.

Although he remembered the captain mentioning something about the wind, he couldn't quite remember exactly what the phrase was. His mind searched for memory of the captain's exact words. He found them. *Ride the wind.* Yes. He had heard the captain say that he *rode the wind* home following his attack on the darkened streets near the docks. *Is that what he had witnessed? Had the captain been telling the truth after all? Did he possess the ability to transport himself through the air to another place?*

"Crazy thoughts, you idiot!" he whispered to himself. "Nobody can dematerialize and rematerialize someplace else. That just isn't possible."

Then he thought: *The man was standing there, and then he was not. What the hell just happened?*

He walked home in total and abject confusion. Suddenly his supposedly logical policeman's mind failed him. He could not understand what he had just seen. *Or had he really seen what he thought he saw? Was his mind just playing tricks on him? Had he been so caught up in his investigation that his mind pretended to see some justification of all he had learned about Captain Delightable? Had he, like so many others before him, also now fallen victim to the captain's wild tales?*

He was not able to sleep that night. His deliberately keen and restless mind kept him wide awake as it replayed over and over what he had seen — or thought he had seen — without discovering any satisfactory bits of logical explanation.

* * * * *

"Good morning, Papa," Suzanne said as she stuck her head into the captain's library. "I'm going shopping. Do you need me to pick anything up for you?"

"Thank you, my child," replied the captain, looking up from his charts on the table. "I need nothing at all, but thank you for asking."

Then Suzanne walked fully into the room. "What do you have planned for today?"

"My days are fairly repetitious now, my dear. Pretty much what I did yesterday, and the day before that, and the day before that — and, I suspect, pretty much what I'll do tomorrow as well. Just walk about and visit with people, stop at the park to tell a few tales, and then come home."

"Well, I've been feeling strangely over the last few days. I can't yet describe it, but keep a close eye out for Detective Cyra. I'm certain he'll be skulking about."

"Oh, I do hope so. I miss chatting with him."

"Leave well enough alone, Papa. That's my advice to you."

"And wonderful advice it is, Suzanne. Enjoy your day, my child."

Suzanne nodded and stepped out of the library, gently closing the door as she did.

* * * * *

The captain ambled about town in the sun-warmed morning air. The clouds had parted wide, leaving a bright blue sky directly above the city. Perhaps it would last through the day, perhaps it would not, he thought, but while it was with him, he was determined to enjoy it. He whistled lightly as he walked along the bustling city sidewalks.

Everywhere he looked, he saw smiling faces. Apparently, many others were enjoying the freak day of warmer weather, but then, to the captain, every day just being alive was a good enough reason to smile.

He finally stopped, pulled his pocket watch from his vest pocket, and noted that it was nearly lunchtime. Today he would take lunch at O'Connor's Wharfside Tavern, but he did not relish the thought of eating alone.

A sudden feeling of being watched slipped into his mind. "David?" he uttered in a low voice.

Feeling a bit mischievous, he led his observer towards O'Connor's. As he walked, he felt the constant presence of the detective lurking somewhere behind him. His eyes twinkled with glee. This was going to be fun, he concluded. He hadn't had this much fun in years.

* * * * *

Detective Cyra was withering fast. His sleepless night was quickly catching up with him. The five cups of coffee he drank earlier only aided him minimally.

He had trailed the captain seemingly all over town for the last hour, and it didn't appear that the captain would make this easy for him anytime soon.

Creeping behind the old man on the sidewalk, he maintained a discreet distance between them, which over the last half hour he had stretched out to nearly a full block. *Where is the captain heading now? he wondered as the old man turned the next corner.*

In observing the consistently charming manner with which the captain greeted everyone, Detective Cyra almost regretted his own dogged actions. Almost. The captain did have a way about him, though. Smiling faces greeted him at every turn. He would often stop his walk and have several words with each person. It was obvious that all enjoyed their meeting with the captain. Whatever else the captain might be, he appeared to be a most delightful fellow to meet on the street.

The need for sleep, however, attacked Cyra's brain, dulled his senses, and drooped his eyelids. He had picked the wrong day to follow this particular prey. That much was becoming painfully obvious. He had tracked him nearly every mile on the west side and it seemed this old codger was going to surely lead him all over the city before he was through.

Growing only more weary, he picked up his pace to narrow the distance between the captain and him. Perhaps he should end this. He could end it very simply by just stopping, but it felt a waste. Besides, all of a sudden and for no apparent reason, he felt compelled to speak with the man.

He had closed to within yards when the captain approached an intersection and turned left around the corner. He was now gone from sight again. And although this had been a normal event until then, it suddenly troubled the detective. So he picked up the pace.

As he turned the corner, he was shocked to see that the captain had disappeared from the sidewalk. "Impossible!" he mumbled.

It made no sense to him. The captain was walking slowly; he had only turned the corner seconds before; he'd had no time to get anywhere but perhaps a half-dozen steps around the corner. So where was he?

Suddenly, a voice behind him startled him to near paralysis. His heart jumped in his chest with an immediate charge of adrenaline.

"Good morning, David. How very nice to see you again."

It was Captain Delightable.

"Jesus, Mary, and Joseph. You scared me!" yelped the detective.

"I do apologize for that, David. Please forgive me."

As the immediate reaction subsided, a new realization struck hard upon him.

"How...how did you do that?" he asked, bewildered.

"How did I do what, David?" responded the captain, innocently.

"I was...you were...did I ..."

"Calm down, dear man. What has you so discomposed?"

"I was behind you. I followed you around the corner. How did you then get behind me?"

"I don't know what you're talking about, David. I rounded the corner and here you were before me. Are you all right?"

"No, that's not how it happened."

"How what happened? My dear man, you look a fright. I was heading to O'Connor's for lunch. I would be delighted if you would join me. You look as if you could use some nourishment. What do you say, dear friend?"

"It's imposs ..."

"Now, now, David. Gather yourself, dear fellow. Let's chat about it over lunch. What do you say?"

The captain grasped the detective's arm and helped him along the sidewalk toward O'Connor's Tavern.

* * * * *

Except for the bartender and the two of them, the tavern was empty. The captain pushed his lunch plate away as he sipped on a cup of hot coffee. Cyra sat opposite him, still very much disquieted and doing more slurping than sipping at his coffee, lost somewhere in thought.

"Cornelius," Cyra finally blurted out. "I don't understand. I was following you."

"As you have said already. Why?"

"Please, enough of this. Don't change the subject. I was following you. You went around the corner. I followed you, but you ended up behind me. How is that possible?"

"I can't see how such a thing is possible. Unless you just imagined it all."

"I'm not imagining anything, Delightable."

"Then perhaps you only thought it was me. Perhaps you had mistaken someone else for me."

"No. That's just not ..."

"Then how else do you explain it, David?"

"I can't. I don't understand."

"I suggest that perhaps you were following me earlier but lost sight of me. You passed me up, and after rounding the corner, I came up behind you. Doesn't that seem more probable?"

"I suppose it is possible, I guess, but I don't remember losing sight of you."

"That's the only plausible explanation *I* can come up with."

"Yes, perhaps you're right. Perhaps I just lost momentary sight of you. But what about last ..."

"What's that?"

Cyra had almost carelessly tipped his hand. He couldn't very well let the captain know he had been spying on him last night, but he also felt it imperative

that the captain explain what he thought he saw last
night. He had to ask him about it, but not openly.

"I have a curious question for you, Cornelius."

"I'll answer if I'm able. Ask away."

"Can you tell me more about *riding the wind*?"

"*Riding the wind*? You want to know more about
that?"

"Yes, please, if you don't mind."

"I don't mind at all. It is a technique of
transporting one's physical body from one place to
another. It's quite simple to accomplish if you have the
correct training. It is not a technique that should be
abused, however. There are devastating consequences if
used incorrectly."

"I don't understand. What consequences?"

"Consequences of a ghastly nature — to the very
fabric of space-time."

"What do space and time have to do with it?"

"Not space *and* time, David. Space-time. The two
should not be considered different from one another, but
forever and irrevocably intertwined."

"What the devil are you talking about?"

"There's a young lad named Albert Einstein who
just a few years ago published his concept of space-time.
He's quite a remarkable young man. You'll hear a lot
more about him very soon."

"Albert who? Space-time? What the devil are you
saying?"

"Albert Einstein, David. Space-time. It is the
principle behind *riding the wind*."

"This makes no sense at all."

"It makes perfect sense if one desires to *ride the
wind*."

Cyra thought for a moment, and then decided to
abandon himself to the heart of the matter with some
minor twist of the truth.

"Look, Delightable. I was out walking last night,
and I ended up just outside your house. It was late, just

before eleven. I saw you smoking your pipe on the rooftop and then you disappeared. I was staring straight up at you, and poof, you vanished right before my eyes. Can you explain that?"

"You were at my home last night? Why didn't you let me know? I could have used the company."

"You're doing it again, Cornelius. You're trying to change the subject."

"Not at all, David. I was merely suggesting that next time you find yourself in my neighborhood, you should visit me."

"You're still doing it. How did you vanish from the rooftop?"

"David, it's quite simple. I needed to go back inside. It was cold out there. I had finished my smoke and wanted to go straight to bed."

Cyra was growing frustrated with the captain's ability to avoid a direct comprehensible response to his seemingly straightforward question.

"How did you vanish, Cornelius?"

"David, it should be plainly obvious to you by now."

"Dammit all, Delightable. How did you do it?"

"Now, David. There is no reason for such language. Calm yourself, man."

"I'm calm. Answer the question, please."

"How do *you* think I did it, David?"

"I think you *rode the wind*."

"There. Now, why was that made to be so difficult? You knew the answer before you even asked the question, didn't you?"

"But how?"

"I explained it already. It's a technique that I learned while on the island."

"You learned to dematerialize and rematerialize yourself while on the island. While on Minchon Island."

"It has nothing to do with my physical form, David. I don't dematerialize or rematerialize, you see. I simply move into and out of space-time, although we never used that terminology on the island. But you know, the vernacular changes with time."

"I'm not sure I understand at all what you just said."

The captain poured another cup of coffee from the pot on the table. He tried to spoon some sugar from the bowl but found it empty.

"Oh my, we seem to be out of sugar," he muttered. Then, noticing a sugar bowl on a nearby table, he reached out his hand and the bowl from the other table suddenly lifted off the table top and drifted over to the captain's hand.

Without a word, he set it upon the table and spooned some sugar into his cup.

"There now, that's better."

Cyra could only stare dumbly. His mouth moved absent any words. Finally he pointed to the sugar bowl.

"How...how ...?"

"How what, David?"

"H...how did you do that? I don't understand."

"Come, come, now. You sell yourself short. You are a most intuitive man, David. You know much that you deny yourself. Think, David, and use your great investigative intellect to give form to the path you wish to find."

"What path is that, Delightable?"

"Why, the path leading you out of the darkness, of course. Keep searching for it, David. It lies directly before you. Look hard and it shall be made manifest before your eyes."

"What the raging devil are you talking about now?"

"The path you seek, my friend. The path you seek."

"I have no idea what you're trying to tell me. You just levitated that sugar bowl. You *rode the wind* last night. And this...space-time, *riding the wind*, darkness, light, it's all gobbledygook to me, Cornelius. I think you are just trying to confuse me."

"Not at all, my dear fellow. I'm trying to enlighten you."

"You obviously already know that my repeated requests for a warrant have been quashed by Judge Harrison."

"I know of no such thing, David, but I'm not surprised at all. Your accusations are baseless. You know the truth, man. You try to deny it, but it lies within you already, deeper at times than others, perhaps. It's there, sleeping soundly for the moment. It needs only to be awakened."

"Now what are you handing me?"

"Nothing, I'm just encouraging you to wake up."

"Wake up to what?"

"To what you are really investigating."

"I'm investigating *you*, Delightable. What needs to be awakened regarding that?"

"Your true purpose, my good man."

"You're doing it once again. Trying to throw me off track with your clever babble and magic tricks."

The captain smiled. "David, my boy, do you really not see your true purpose?"

"Apparently not. So tell me, what is my true purpose? And how the hell did you move that sugar bowl?"

"It's plain enough to see if you look."

"I guess I'm blind. I don't see it."

"You're not *investigating* me, David. You're trying to find your own way through the darkness, your own true path. You are trying to learn from me how to discover that path."

"And just what is that path, Delightable?"

"That is for you to determine. I can only assist you in the search. I can point you in the right direction, but it is for you to make the discovery."

"Why is that?"

"If I tell you, you won't believe me. If you make the discovery for yourself, you'll know it is true. After you find it, you'll know it is right. It is sure to be a most exciting moment for you, that awakening."

"Why can't you just cut the bull and tell me?"

"I just told you why. You won't believe me."

"Look, Delightable, I'm not stupid. I saw what you did last night, and I'm not going to be quiet about it either."

"I wouldn't ask you to."

"I mean it. I'm going to tell everyone what I saw."

"Will it go into your report?"

"Absolutely. And the sugar bowl as well."

"I'd be careful about that, David."

"Are you threatening me?"

"Not at all, dear boy. I'm just saying that putting information like that into an official report could come back on you with disturbing results. Do you understand?"

Detective Cyra now understood what the captain was saying. Of course! Putting a statement in his official report that he saw an old man *ride the wind* or levitate a sugar bowl would be ludicrous. If he did that, it would be *he* who ended up in custody — and most likely in the nearby asylum for the insane. The captain was indeed right.

"You're right, of course, Cornelius, but why did you tell me? Why didn't you keep quiet and let me put it in my report? You would surely have won the whole battle right then and there. I'd most likely be locked away and unable to harm you. Why, Cornelius? Why did you do this?"

"I don't want to see you put away, David. I have no desire for that end whatsoever. Besides, dear man, there is no battle between us. The only battle you fight is against what you already know to be true within yourself."

"But why? Why are you being so kind to me?"

"You think I want to destroy you or see harm come to you, don't you?"

"Well, yes. I would do the same if I were in your position."

"That is one of the main differences between us, then. I don't ever want to see harm come to you, my friend."

"I'll ask again. Why?"

"Because, David, I understand your pain. I understand your needs. I understand your fears. Because I understand who you really are."

"And who might that be?"

"Just another brother trying to find his place in this world and too afraid to discover the truth. You are my friend, David. You might not understand that right now, but you are a part of me. I'm a part of you. We are one and the same. To allow something bad to happen to you is the same as if it happened to me."

"A lofty sentiment, Delightable, but untrue. There is another element to your purpose. I don't know what it is right now, but rest assured, I will get to the bottom of it soon enough. And when I do, you can also be assured, I will shout it out loudly enough for everyone to hear my words."

"When you discover your true purpose, David, you will not be able to do anything other than shout it out. The truth will be uncontainable. It will quite literally set you free."

"You, Delightable, like Ahab, are my white whale. I will pursue you to the ends of the earth and deep into the heart of hell if need be. I warn you. I will discover your little secret. Listen carefully, Captain. Soon enough, the shout you hear will be me exposing you."

"It warms my heart to hear you say that, David. Never give up, my boy. Tenacity and purpose are two of the real keys to success. I feel it in my bones, David. You are so close to your end goal. Don't let anything or anyone keep you from achieving it."

"Oh, Delightable, you *are* good. So clever. So wry. No one can ever tell me you're not a masterly, wise, and effective adversary. You're good at putting people off just enough to keep them wondering. But I assure you, sir,

I've seen it all before. I'm an excellent policeman. You might not believe me, but I am. The best con men that ever lived have tried to dupe me, but in the end it was they who wound up behind bars. The same will be true for you. Have no doubt about that, Delightable. I *will* find you out and I'll expose your little parlor tricks too. Levitating sugar bowls, indeed."

"And in so doing, David, I believe you will finally discover some wonderful truth about yourself. It will be a joyous day, I'm sure."

"Maybe, maybe not, but your little magic tricks will be exposed for what they are. And as for the warrior myth, I will end that charade as well."

"Then so be it, my friend. So be it."

Chapter 24

"Papa?" asked Wendy. "Did Detective Cyra leave the restaurant then?"

"Yes, Wendy. He left me there alone, but nestled warmly in a rich gladness."

"I see," she replied, continuing her notes.

"You, my child, are a true warrior in training. You do love it so, do you not? Your writing, that is."

"I *have* to write, Papa. That's all I know for sure."

"Someday I'm sure the world will take note of it."

"Papa?" Robert asked. "Did you study in the library every day?"

"You're referring to the island library?"

Robert nodded.

"Several hours every day were spent in study, Robert. There is no getting away from a student's responsibility to study. There is no shortcut to learning. But my learning was not confined to the books in the library. Wherever I went on the island I learned something new."

"When you learned to *ride the wind*, did you learn that easily?"

"Let me pick up from where we left off the other day."

Over the next month, Amog and Wigiwig took me — sometimes screaming mad from the sheer enormity of my lessons — through the shelves of the library they thought best for me to read and study.

The rush to plant the necessary knowledge into my tiny and inadequately prepared brain seemed at times to be a task too great even for them. But I labored long and hard over the following months to retain all they taught me. Although an arduous endeavor, it was with a glad and appreciative heart that I managed to get through it. Their patience and understanding were instrumental in my learning as fast as I did.

During all that time, we had heard no more from either Mata'pang or the spy. No other acts of sabotage occurred during this period either. It seemed that all animosity between the opposing factions was, at least for the time being, put to rest. All tempers calmed.

During this time also, Lelalu made the announcement of the day we were to be married. I need not tell you how utterly frazzled I was between getting myself prepared for our wedding ceremony and trying to cram years of gentle learning into only months in preparation for a war I felt certain was coming.

It should also go without saying that I slept as soundly as a downed log at night. I was exhausted by each day's end and could not carry on any meaningful conversation with Lelalu.

She knew this and did not press me about it. With my accelerated study under way, we did not find much time for lazing together under the shade of the trees near the spring. I pretty much galloped about from sunup to sundown. My duties as King's Captain also required me to make two trips per week out to the Forbidden Land in an effort to be certain that Mata'pang and his nation had not taken advantage of the lull in hostilities to secretly move an army towards us.

The days were grueling and the nights gone too fast. But with Lelalu being heavily occupied with preparations for the marriage day, and my being bombarded by Amog and Wigiwig with important learning, those months simply flew by, the time hardly noticed by me.

Before I knew it, the day of our marriage was upon us.

In the early morning hours, just before sunrise, Lelalu came to my hut and rousted me from my dreams.

"Come, my love. It is time to begin our preparations."

"What preparations?"

"For the ceremony. We must help to prepare the village for the midday meal."

"But I am no cook. It is our wedding. Why must we prepare the meals?"

She dragged me from the comfort of my bedding and made me dress.

"It is our obligation to prepare the village for the meal for our guests."

"I do not know how to prepare a meal for hundreds of people, Lelalu. This is very odd."

"Silly man," she chortled. "I did not say we must prepare the meal. I said we must help prepare the *village* for the meal."

I admit I still did not understand what she meant, being still fast asleep in my head.

I barely finished clothing myself before she dragged me from my hut and out into the center of the village. Once there, I was given a tub of water to wash my face. It was cold, and I was suddenly, unhappily, fully awake — though still utterly exhausted from both my studies and my march back from the Forbidden Land only five hours earlier.

Seeing me in such a tattered state, Lelalu hugged my neck and said, "I know you are beyond exhausted, Husband, but endure this morning and you will be refreshed by noon. I promise."

"If I survive until then." I smiled at her.

I was soon joined by my lieutenants, Adagi and Gamomo. I felt much better seeing them, for they looked as ragged and worn as I did. We took one look at each other and broke out in quiet laughter.

"I ask you, Adagi," I said, "do I look as terrible to you as you do to me?"

"I must, because it appears death lies wagging about in your eyes, Captain. Oh, wait! My mistake. That's only the look of a nearly married man, I see." He chuckled, as did Gamomo.

"Do not laugh so, Gamomo. I feel the way you look."

Another good laugh, and Lelalu approached from behind.

"The look of demise fills all your faces equally," she grinned. "So get to work. You will soon feel refreshed."

"Says the slave driver just before cracking the whip upon our backs," I jested.

Gamomo and Adagi laughed heartily until they saw the annoyed look in Lelalu's eyes.

"Sorry, Highness," said Adagi, who then grinned when Lelalu's own smile betrayed her.

Then she giggled. "But that I had a whip to launch you all into your duties. Now be off with you. Get some work done."

The three of us began setting up tables and benches in a line for all the guests.

"Thank you for your help, friends."

"Our captain goes to slaughter today," said Gamomo. "We could not just stand by and watch it happen. It is my hope that our assistance will hasten you unto your end." Gamomo then smiled that infectious grin of his.

We all started laughing as we continued our work.

"And you, Adagi. Do you find yourself in support of his position?"

"I do, Captain. For the quicker you are destroyed, the sooner I can go back to sleep."

Another round of laughter ensued, and soon enough we found ourselves refreshed, just as Lelalu had foreseen.

By ceremony time, the three of us had bathed in the spring and dressed thereafter as properly as we could, considering that we possessed no other clothing at the time.

We presented ourselves to Lelalu and took on sour expressions when she frowned at the sight of us.

"I have no other clothing, my dear. What can I do?"

"Go to your hut, Cornelius. A change of clothing is there for all three of you. A gift from the women of Minchon."

* * * * *

For the first time since arriving on the island as a tattered, shipwrecked wretch, I wore clothing similar to my Minchon brethren. It was good, I thought. Perhaps it was time to finish shedding all the vestiges of my formal life anyway. My bottom wrapping was of the same material as that of all the others. The design patterns were unique to me, as the other men's patterns were unique to them. My cloth was well adorned with diverse and colorful illustrations depicting the imported animals on the island and a many-masted ship with sails in full rise. English words, including One, brother, sister, and Captain, were embroidered along with their Minchon translations. The colors were bright and blithesome. It was a very festive garment, and I felt extremely honored.

My shoes had been replaced with thongs made from the indigenous plants and roots of the island, similar to those of all the other people of Minchon.

For my head alone, the womenfolk had prepared a ceremonial headdress made with the most aromatic flowers and plants on the island. It was more like a wreath that sat upon my head than a full hat, but it was grand in its design.

I found scented oils with the clothing and we each took turns rubbing as much of them as we could over our bodies. Then, of course, we each made fun of the others, smelling like women as we did.

When all was completed, we left the hut. I searched out Lelalu for her approval, but we were told she was sequestered in preparation for the ceremony set to begin within the hour. We were ordered not to soil our new clothing and to act more like adults, something we, in our newly refreshed state, hastened to ignore.

With a coldly delivered scolding from the elder women in the tribe, though, we were forced into capitulation and thereafter remained still, but never silent. Adagi, the wild child that he was naturally, and most similar to me, found it easy enough to pass the time making us laugh with his jests and chiding. One such example being:

"I weep this day for your passing, brother, but upon anticipation of your demise later this evening, rent apart as you shall be during the throes of passion with your new bride, I make this inquiry of you. Upon your death, might I take possession of your hut? It is much better than mine presently."

We howled as undisciplined children until a stern shaking finger from an elder woman quieted us once again. Light snickering continued, however, for some time after, being some form of latent last vestiges of youthful rebellion boiling off us and into forever, I would guess.

In that moment, still bursting with callow exuberance, I was not the King's Captain. I was but a young warrior student being brought into the first phases of manhood — with a wife to care for and to take responsibility for. At that moment, I allowed my wild youthful side its full head to do as it pleased, for upon completion of the ceremony, the man would rise up out of the burnt ashes of such puerile effrontery and take his new and rightful place among the other husbands of Minchon. No more would his adolescence be allowed to rise to the surface to be seen by anyone. After the ceremony, such wasteful, immature behavior would be gone, and in addition to his place as husband, he would also become provider and protector.

Upon later reflection, I believed the silliness of my thoughts to be true at the time. It was only after much growing that I understood the imperative to retain a child's presence within me. I had no idea whatsoever then that the child in me must necessarily remain to keep me well in balance. At that time, I still lacked much training in the art of maturing into manhood. I say *art* because growing up is much like the work of a sculptor.

Just as a finished sculpture already lies within a block of marble, waiting for the sculptor to reveal it, so it is with a man hidden within the youth of a boy. And as with the boy, the universe is much the same. All of it already exists and has existed forever. There is no discovery. There is only an uncovering, a revealing, if you will, of what already exists.

In the sculpting process, the clay or stone is systematically cut away, leaving the polished, finished product for all to gaze upon. For the piece to be successfully completed, however, the artist must draw out the personality of the person he or she sculpts, to make the sculpture seem almost alive and real.

So it is, then, with every person moving from youth into adulthood. It is important to carry forward all the critical parts of your life to keep you whole, complete, and moving forward on the path of your existence.

It is my belief that laughter and childlike wonder should always be a part of the finished person, for it seems to be that a child's exuberance keeps you interested in life. Lose that part of yourself through ignorance or will, and you necessarily lose your gift to move forward in any joy or wonder. A child's curiosity, living strongly within us, keeps us learning, searching, and reaching out into the unknown, to always discover, to be always excited, to be always amazed at something new.

I have to smile whenever I think back on all I did not know then. Learning what I needed to learn was like having a shade lifted from my eyes. The wonder of it all was sometimes more than I could bear with dry eyes. My heart swelled with joy with each new discovery I made.

An extraneous and gleeful shout from some children playing nearby brought me back to present thought, but only for a brief few seconds, for just as quickly, my mind settled back down upon the moments that were soon to follow. A marriage was to be accomplished: a joining of two people, two bodies, two hearts. And even more than that, an eternal partnership of spirits was about to be forged. To make it even better, it was to be a partnership with a perfect partner, someone like me, who reveled in discovery simply for the sake of discovery, a full and equal partner.

Hereafter, I would nevermore be alone, left to make discoveries without someone to share them with. I was about to embark on a lifelong journey with a traveling companion who had similar attitudes towards invention and learning, the same zest for life and friendship, the same youthful quest for happiness and completion.

Despite my frivolity on that day, I did not lose sight of the fact that Lelalu was about to put all her trust and hope into the likes of me. I was determined to never give her reason to regret her choice.

* * * * *

Nearing the appointed hour and facing the full force of the joining entelechy, I nervously took my place at the head of the procession and awaited the appearance of Lelalu. Adagi and Gamomo accepted their roles as best men and took up a supporting stance directly behind me.

Wigiwig, being on the elder council, would be standing immediately behind Amog, who would directly preside over the ceremony and actually create the joining.

The moment of Lelalu's approach, in all its simplistic beauty, was as stunning as any I have ever seen before or since.

Before describing the entourage's entrance in detail, I should first make note of the basic layout of the procession and ceremony stands relative to the village boundaries.

Imagine, if you will, a compass. Being a ship's captain and keenly related to such a favored device and its grand workings in finding my place among the chaos in the world, for more clarity I pick this instrument to set for you the points of arrival by those involved in the ceremony.

The platform for the joining ceremony was placed due south, and I stood directly opposite the platform on the north. The first of Lelalu's entourage were her parents, the king and queen. As I learned, there was often little regard for stuffy pomp and ceremony involved in official events on Minchon. There were certain rules of decorum, but they were simple and to the point. All knew quite well who the king and queen were; there was no need for an overabundance of pompous arrival dictums.

The royal family, dressed in their finest robes and headdresses, entered the circle from the east, walking slowly to symbolize the slow rise of the sun over the Minchon village, the coming of the light and restoration of the day, as it were. Chairs, lifting the anointed ones and carried by servants or such, were absent the affair. Instead, with plain dignity, the royal couple simply walked to their place of honor as drums pounded out a rhythmic cadence. Once they arrived at the throne, they climbed the steps and simply took their seats.

Next it was Amog and his wife, followed by the twelve members of the elder council, entering the circle from the west, symbolizing the setting of the sun, or where the rule of law, the King's word, the traditions and customs of Minchon are set down upon the people. They moved to the head of the joining platform, as it was called, and stood in silence. Once again, upon their approach, an appropriate cadence was drummed out, suitable for their position — the drumming of a heartbeat.

Then it was our turn to approach the circle. We approached from the north, which symbolized the position of the North Star. Although unseen from these latitudes, it remains a guiding point for the affairs of man that we might always know the way in which we are to go. We walked slowly and in rhythm to a single drum's cadence, in single file. We stopped short of the joining platform and turned to our left.

The flutes, as best as I can describe them, then sounded their greeting of the bride with a single high, fluttering, shrill note.

"The flutists are calling upon nature to bear witness to the coming event," Adagi whispered, offering the interpretation of the instruments.

After the flutes quieted, the drums began rolling with the sound of rising thunder toward a final clap.

"The sound of the drums alerts the higher spirits that a sacred joining is under way," Adagi explained. "It is also a warning to the darker spirits not to attempt any intrusion into the ceremony, for this has been ordained by the One."

The drums finally rolled to a single, full, hard beat and then fell silent.

Several musicians playing stringed instruments that looked like ancient lyres then plucked a soothing melody. I say lyres because I, having no talent for music or the knowledge to know the actual name for the instruments which make music, know not what the instruments were rightfully called. Nevertheless, they produced a very pleasing melody similar to that of a lyre. Hence, that is what I call them.

Soon the drums and flutes joined in and produced moving, harmonic melodies as Lelalu's entourage began its entry into the circle, also from the north.

When I saw Lelalu, her hair completely adorned with variously colored flowers, a lei of aromatic flowers, and dressed in the finest linen the Minchon people could produce, embroidered and shimmering with precious gems of various colors, and her face so glowing and beautiful, my heart almost seized within my chest.

Her dark eyes dazzled me to disbelief. Disbelief that this spectacular woman was walking toward me to become my wife. Wife to a lowly and humble ship's captain, the sole survivor of a night so harrowing that it was now purposely set to the back of my mind and nearly completely forgotten. Its memory was now replaced by the overwhelming joy of this wondrous moment. I dare say a man given more to emotions than I would have dropped to his knees and been caught up in it all, and wept from sheer joy…enough to swallow him whole.

I, instead, stood mesmerized to stillness as she approached to finally stand beside me, her glittering eyes staring at me, her smile causing me to choke, to almost cease breathing at all. Thoroughly struck dumb, I hardly dared to believe that this event could be true and happening.

Amog then stepped forward and with another lei of aromatic flowers loosely bound our hands together as he spoke. "From a time long ago, it has been destined that two people, once already bound together by desire before the One, should be sacredly and forever joined before the One. This is a time when a woman shall leave all that she has ever known to embark upon life's voyage with the man into whom she now places all her trust and devotion. It is a time when a man shall depart from the ways of a child to take unto him the duties and responsibilities of caring for the woman who has placed herself in his care.

"Take these words, therefore, seriously into your hearts and bind your will to serving each other with honor and distinction. Let not the evils of this world come between you. In all things, through this ceremony, you are now one with each other, and you are also one with the Great Law. Never take for granted all that has been given you this day, for this joining has been accorded you from the Source of all things.

"Lelalu, do you give yourself into the care and devotion of this man, Cornelius Alexander Delightable?"

"I do," she responded simply.

"Cornelius, do you give yourself into the care and devotion of this woman, Princess Lelalu?"

"I do," said I plainly as well.

"Then, by the law given to us by the One, you both, having surrendered your separate consciousness to be bound together in all things and manner, are hereby joined. Let your joining stand forever among the Singular Consciousness and let it be known across the universe that today Cornelius Alexander Delightable and Princess Lelalu are from now and until forever united together as man and wife."

We were then turned around to face the nation of Minchon, and Amog introduced us, saying, "Hear me now, People of Minchon. I present to you the united spirits of Cornelius and Lelalu, one with the other, as man and wife."

A shout went up from the crowd of Minchonians so great that it sent the birds in the surrounding trees scattering in every direction. Joyous hands were instantly upon both of us, coupled with shouts of congratulations.

I stood still, mesmerized by all the commotion surrounding me, but I no longer stood alone. I was, from that moment, to be forever counted among the married men of the world.

The captain rocked back and forth in his rocking chair, allowing those being entertained by his story a moment to catch their breath.

"Papa?" asked Suzanne. "How can any of this actually be real? How is it possible?"

"Mama struggles still, Papa," said Wendy.

"She does, my child, but soon she will see everything clearly enough."

"Mama," said Robert. "Just believe. You're making this far too difficult."

"Out of the mouths of babes." The captain smiled slyly.

"I'm trying, Robert, but there are great differences between children and adults."

"Then think like a child, Mama," offered Wendy.

The captain chortled. "Quick wit, that one."

"Indeed," agreed Suzanne. "Too quick, perhaps."

"Do you miss Lelalu, Papa?"

"Very much, Robert."

"What about great-grandmother? Do you miss her as well?"

"I do."

"Equally?"

"With equal longing for both, young man."

"How is that possible?"

"That remains yet a story for another time. It grows late. Time for bed."

The children rose up dutifully, kissed the captain, and departed the library, leaving a confused Suzanne still sitting on the sofa.

"And you, my child. What troubles you?"

"Every time I hear that story, Papa, you tell it exactly the same way, no changes, no embellishments. Exactly the same."

"That is the story, Suzanne. There is no other way to tell the story."

"Sooner or later you're going to have to tell the children the truth."

"The truth?"

"About Lelalu."

"What about Lelalu?"

"You're going to have to tell them that Lelalu is just a character in your story, Papa. You can't have them believing that she really existed."

"Dear me, my child. Is that what you have always believed? That she is only a character in a fanciful tale?"

"Of course, Papa. Please, let's not get into that again. It's late and I am very weary."

"You're the most obstinate person I have ever known, child."

"I'm a realist, Papa, with two children to raise. Good night. It's cold out tonight. Please don't go out for a walk. I'm afraid you'll catch your death out there on an evening like this."

"I won't. I'm going to bed soon. It has been a full day."

"I wish you hadn't spoken with that dastardly detective today."

"Actually, it was most enlightening."

"You never say anything derogatory about anyone, do you?"

"Perhaps, but only in jest. Why would I, child? What would it ever gain me if I did speak ill of someone? How would that ever benefit me?"

"You're an amazing old man, Papa. I'll say that for you."

"And you are a remarkable young woman, my dear. Someday you will learn just how remarkable you are."

Suzanne moved toward the door, opened it, and then stopped. She turned toward her grandfather. "I love you, Papa. You know that, don't you?"

"Of course I do, Suzanne. I love you also. Always remember that."

Suzanne nodded and left the room.

The captain smiled large. "I'm breaking through, boys. It won't be long now."

Chapter 25

The following night after dinner, the children dutifully helped their mother clean up the kitchen. Wendy was the first to finish her chores. She grabbed her pencil and notepad from the counter and made a beeline for the library.

"Papa?" asked Wendy, rushing in through the doorway.

The captain looked up from his map and smiled warmly. "Yes, child."

"I do believe it's time we continue the story."

"Do you, now?" The captain chuckled lightly.

"Yes, Papa, and I'm quite simply going to die if you don't tell me."

"My goodness, we can't have you dying over such a thing, can we?"

Wendy shook her head solemnly. Just then Robert scrambled in through the door and came to a stop next to his sister.

"Papa, are you going to continue your story now?"

"Apparently I must, Robert, if we wish to keep your sister alive."

Suzanne entered the room. "So it appears that story time is about to commence once again, I see."

"Yes, Mama," said Robert worriedly. "Apparently Wendy is going to die if we don't."

"What?" asked Suzanne.

"It seems our young scribe's existence depends solely on the continuation of my story," replied the captain with a wink.

Suzanne smiled. "I see."

"There's just one problem, though. And I don't want you to become overly alarmed, Wendy, but I don't remember where we left off last night. I hope you'll be all right," said the captain.

"Papa, I'm fine. Don't worry. You had just gotten married to Lelalu," replied Wendy after consulting her well-organized notes.

"Ahh, thank you, child. I recall now. Very well. Take your positions and I shall continue. Will you be joining us this evening, Suzanne?"

"I will, Papa."

"Glorious, child. I'm pleased."

With all settled comfortably in their customary places, the captain continued his tale.

Most men I know would awaken the morning after their joining in the warm embrace of their new wife and with the gentle cooing of her voice in their ears. My morning after, however, arrived quite contrarily sometime well before sunrise with a jolt of hollering, screaming, and thunderous racket.

Adagi stood outside my hut in the blackness of the early morning, pounding hard on the delicate wooden door. "Captain! Captain! Please respond! Captain, please!" he shouted urgently.

I threw a wrapping around my naked body and staggered to the door, sleep still fogging my brain. "Calm yourself, Adagi. I'm on my way," I shouted back.

Pulling the door open, I found my haggard First Lieutenant shuddering and perspiring profusely, his joining clothing and skin now blackened and smeared with soot and ash.

"Come, Captain. The spy has struck again, and we've suffered a great tragedy."

"What is it, Adagi? Speak slowly. And what has happened to you? You look a fright," I said, still somewhat sleepy-eyed, my brain trying to discover reason to shut the door and return to my badly needed slumber.

"The throne, Captain. The throne is burning and the guards are unconscious."

That startling news brought me fully awake in an instant.

"The royal throne is ablaze?"

"Yes, Captain. Come quickly."

Those words now spoken, he rushed away toward the center of the village and the torched throne.

I shut the door and began to dress quickly, trying not to awaken Lelalu, but of course it was to no avail. She turned from her side to her back and opened her eyes.

"You need to go, Husband."

"Yes, my loving wife, I know. Tragedy has once again befallen our fair village."

"It is the spy, my love. The spy has struck again," she replied matter-of-factly. "This time Mata'pang sends a challenge directly to the throne itself, and thus deep into the heart of the Minchon nation."

"Any challenge made is taken by me to be an offense against the Minchon nation, my love."

I finished dressing and dashed from my hut, forgetting to kiss my new wife or bid her at least a graceful goodbye. I ran to where the villagers were trying to put the blaze out, but it was to no good effect. The fire was hot, strong, and in full consumption of the wooden throne. It was beyond saving. All anyone could do was watch the blaze consume the throne to its terrible conclusion.

"The guards?" I asked. "Are they harmed beyond recovery?"

"No," answered Gamomo. "They are well, and now awake."

"Did they see their attacker?"

"No, it seems they were assaulted from behind."

"I suspect multiple attackers," I stated.

"Why is that?"

"None sounded an alarm, Gamomo. I must assume, then, that they were rendered unconscious at the same time, thus there were several attackers."

"Yes," said Adagi, "of course."

"Our problems have now been multiplied, gentlemen. We have a spy and several saboteurs. Like it or not, brothers, we are fully engaged in a battle, and it surely will only worsen before it gets any better."

"We are prepared, Captain."

"Nay, we are not prepared for such a physical affront; but by day's end we shall be."

Within several minutes the entire village had surrounded the burning throne, now merely a smoldering heap of unrecognizable charred wood. I had to face the awful truth within my own heart. A siege was now being calibrated by our enemy. An all-out attack was imminent. I had to act, and I had to calculate our response accurately in order to prevent a worse tragedy from befalling the good people of Minchon.

"Gather all the men of the nation," I commanded, "and have them dressed for battle and assembled in the center of the village within a half hour. I will address them all on the matter at that time."

Both my lieutenants bowed and rushed away. Seconds later, the king stood at my side.

"Great One," I immediately said, bowing deeply.

"Rise up, my captain. So it begins, I see."

"It does, sir," I replied, rising to stand tall. "This morning I intend to meet Mata'pang's challenge with my own. And there shall be no doubt as to my intent."

Before the king could respond, two guards with a man — hooded, gagged, and bound at the wrists — approached abruptly. They stopped and stood the man directly in front of me. The sight of him instantly sparked recognition.

"The spy, Captain. We caught him skulking about behind the village."

"Are you certain this is the spy?"

"Yes, Captain. By his own words he admits it."

"I shall hear those words for myself. Remove his hood and gag and let him speak. I would hear the truth spoken from his own mouth."

"You will not like what you are about see, Captain."

"I am already there. Do as I say."

One of the guards removed the gag from the man's mouth and lifted the hood from his head.

I admit my shock full out. I had no idea that such treachery could exist. The man stood quite still, his head bowed, his eyes pointed down toward the sand at his feet.

"Tainini! Why?" I asked.

He did not speak, but remained silent, his eyes unmoving from the sand at his feet.

"I will ask once more. Why?"

Tainini refused to respond.

I stepped forward until my face was only inches from his. "You hurt me, Tainini. I thought us brothers. You called me such. Was that also subterfuge?"

He raised his head and glared at me. "It was not subterfuge. Subterfuge requires that there be deception. There was no deception in my heart. I objected to you from the start. I only acted toward you as was required by your position in the boat. A position that should have been mine when Mata'pang was discharged."

"A simple boat position gave rise to your need to turn against the whole of your nation? Is that what you would have me believe?"

"A simple position to you perhaps, but a gloried position to me — and one stolen from me by you. I worked hard for three years to gain my position. Your position, exceeding mine, was gifted to you, given without merit or effort. You tore from me the honor of rising to my position. You dishonor us all on the boat. I have just cause to despise you, as we all do."

"All the crew, you say? Where are they now? Why are their faces not standing before me in disgust? Why do I not hear their words of hatred and grief in my ears? Nay, brother, I see them not. I see only you standing before me. I hear only your hateful words in my ears. Where are your brothers in this? Where is their hate? Where is their outrage? Where is their voice added to your cause? I see no one but you. I hear no objection other than yours. You strike a blow against me with your hurtful words, but are you not aware that the election was made not through my bidding, but by the village as a whole — while I was asleep in my hut and unaware of the election? You know this, Tainini.

"If my election was an affront to your honor, why did you fail to give it voice before now? And what of your rise after my departure? Are you not now in the position you have sought all along? Why, Tainini? Tell me. I do not understand."

"It was all done too late. What would you have done?" Tainini spat back at me. "Remove yourself from the position elected by the nation? No man would. You did nothing for that position. You captured it with charm and guile. You did not earn it ahead of me."

"You say I did not earn it, but I assure you, years on the ocean under my father's command, working my way up the difficult ranks to ship's captain, was not an easy journey. I possess command experience. Can you say as much?"

"Commanding a ship, Cornelius, is not the same as the honor of providing for the needs of the nation. I was proud of my work."

Tainini's words were truly spoken and I heard the pain in his voice; it reached my heart in a giant leap, and I immediately softened my attack. "Forgive me, Brother Tainini. It was wrong of me not to extol your excellent efforts on the boat. You are correct. The honor of providing for the nation is an esteemed one, but this jealousy and resentment directed toward me is unwarranted. I was new here and did not understand all that was normally required of a young Minchon man. You only had to give voice to your concerns and I would have sought to rectify them. Yet you said nothing. How was I to know of your dissatisfaction and hurt?"

I gave ample time for Tainini to respond, but he offered no words, just a saddened expression.

"May I assume it was you, Tainini, who destroyed an innocent tree?"

"It was I," he said, glaring at me.

"Born out of your resentment for me, you felt the need to destroy a tree which had no say who might lie beneath it and be shaded by its branches and leaves? You found it to be required by your sense of honor to strike out against a tree?"

"It was not the tree I struck out against."

"I know clearly enough your intent, friend and brother."

"Do not call me friend. Do not call me brother. I am neither. I do not deserve the titles."

"What you deserve is not the issue here. If we all received what we deserved, the world would be absent the plague of mankind."

"But I am a willful spy and a destroyer. Why do you show me mercy with kind words? You offer them, but I asked for none."

"Because I see you have been wronged, and I see also that the wrong was corrected too late. What I do judge against you, though, is your failure to give me opportunity to offer correction when it could have been done."

"Then I am judged."

"Are you also responsible for the destruction of the king's throne?"

"Not directly. I can only be judged for taking no action to prevent it. The acts were carried out by those who follow Mata'pang."

"By taking no action to prevent it, you are judged, in my mind, to have been as complicit in such action as if you struck the flint yourself."

"Then once again I am judged."

"For myself, this is a judgment to be corrected forthwith: I forgive your wrongs against me, brother. I am in no position to forgive your wrongs against the nation; however, I will speak on your behalf when the time comes."

"You are not in a position to speak for the nation, Captain," said the king finally, "but I am."

"Please, sir," I said, "I yield to you, Great One."

"Tainini," the king began, "the position in the boat was suggested by me personally. Your anger should thus have been directed toward me, not Cornelius. My reasons for placing him in that position are still justified in my mind, and I am not required to explain that reasoning to you. Your position had not changed. You would have had that same position if Mata'pang had remained. Your actions against Cornelius were, as he said, unwarranted, and should be suitably punished. Nevertheless, my captain has forgiven you. His gesture is a magnanimous one, and one which carries great weight with me. I am thus compelled by his action to forgive you also.

"I cannot, however, condone either your actions or your inaction to prevent destruction. Nor can I allow your actions and inaction to go unpunished. The penalty for such sabotage will be as follows. Because Cornelius has forgiven you, you will not lose your place in the boat. As penitence for your destructive action, however, you will plant a new tree upon the very spot where the one was destroyed, first digging up the root of the old by yourself.

"You will be fully responsible for its care and nourishment until it reaches the maturity of the tree you killed. This, I think, will demand years of attention on your part, and thus it will be a keen lesson for development of your personal responsibilities to yourself and to the nation. This duty will be added to you in addition to those on the boat.

"As for the throne, you did nothing to prevent its destruction. My captain finds you at equal fault with those who directly took part in the act — as much as if you had destroyed it yourself. I agree with his judgment. Therefore, in addition to your other duties, you will assist in the physical effort to restore the throne to its former condition. You will also stand before the nation and offer your apology for its destruction and for your deception. If you agree to these conditions and penalties, then nothing more will be required of you and you will retake your place among the Minchon Nation as a loved citizen.

"These are the judgments made against you. The decision to accept or reject them lies with you. Think carefully on this. If your decision is not to agree to the punishments as set down before you, then give voice to your objections — but know this clearly: if you do not agree, then the alternative is to be banished from the nation for all time. It has thus been put to you. What say you, Tainini?"

"I stand in awe, Great One. I am not worthy of such mercy. But as you have asked for my answer, I give it now voice. I accept your judgment and the punishments in full. I do not wish to be further separated from the nation. I wish to rejoin my brothers and sisters with restored honor."

"You shall be restored to the people. As for your honor, however, that can be achieved only with time and good intent. Your honor will be returned to you only after you have earned it.

"Tonight you shall stand before the nation and give voice to your regret and ask forgiveness of the nation. This matter is now closed, and with the concluding events of this evening, it shall never be spoken of again."

And so, a just trial had been undertaken and justice dispensed to everyone's satisfaction.

His binds were cut, and with his hands now free he approached me and extended his hand in the custom known to me. We shook hands and then hugged one another.

"I know that trust between us has been damaged," he stated. "I realize it may never be restored to the place it once was, but I ask you to consider it."

"There is nothing to consider, my brother. Trust is fully restored. From now on, though, if you have concerns with me, you must give them voice. Is that agreed?"

"You honor me, Cornelius. If I have argument, I will give it voice, but I suspect there will never be such a need."

"Let us hope, Tainini, for I value my friends highly and you are still counted among them."

Later that evening Tainini made his apology to the nation. It was well received, and in the days that followed he was treated no differently than he had been treated before. The Minchon people taught me more about the power of forgiveness that evening than I would ever learn anywhere else. It was a glorious lesson.

From that day, Tainini was known to be nothing other than a most honorable man. A few years before I left the island, he had risen through the ranks to earn the top place on the boat. He then excelled in Minchon Warrior training to further earn a place on the council of elders. I believe he still serves with great distinction and wisdom to this day.

"That was a great story, Papa," offered Robert.

"It was a wonderful story," parroted Wendy.

"Yes, it was magnificent. I recall it now," said Suzanne. "I remember how warm it made me feel when I was your age."

"What about Mata'pang, Papa?" asked Robert.

"That, my boy, is a story for another day. Time for bed and rest. Think on what you have heard this evening. The power of forgiveness is greatly understated, but its true power is even more misunderstood."

"What do you mean?" asked Robert.

"Forgiveness *given* cannot achieve all of its power, that which is necessary to transform the transgressor, through offer alone. It requires the spirit in which forgiveness is *received* by the transgressor to complete it."

"Forgiveness means nothing if it means nothing to the offender. Is that right?"

"Well stated, Robert. Indeed. Had Tainini not accepted responsibility for his transgressions and made honorable amends, the forgiveness would have had no lasting meaning or effect. Nothing would have changed. Forgiveness requires that it be both offered and accepted for it to have lasting effect. Do you both understand?"

The two children smiled knowingly and nodded. They turned toward the door, but Robert stopped, spun about on his heels, and stared at the captain.

"Papa," he said.

"Robert," mimicked the captain with a smile.

"The tree, Papa. What of the tree?"

"It stood proudly as of the day I left the island. I suspect it stands still."

Robert and Wendy both smiled, and then in a joyous dash, they departed the library, giggling as they went.

"Papa," said Suzanne, "I'm beginning to recall the value of your lessons. I see how they affect the children. It's wonderful to see their growth in these matters. I see their young minds ablaze with new knowledge and understanding every day. It's a wondrous sight. And I realize that whether the stories are true or not, they have great value. You're a most wonderful man, Papa. Please forgive me for resisting your efforts."

The captain stood and hugged Suzanne as she rose from the sofa. "My child, in this instance there is no need for the offer of forgiveness, or for the acceptance of such. I'm just delighted with the fact that you are beginning to recall your own lessons. You have endured much the past few years. After the tragic news from the battlefield, it was normal for you to withdraw inward to heal. I think now the healing is taking effect, and I believe your warrior training is once more taking its rightful place within your heart. Your healing will open doors for you that were closed while you were buried in your sorrow and woe. Hold fast to your restored hope, my dear. Soon you will see its reward."

Tears formed in Suzanne's eyes as she hugged her grandfather. "If there is any reward at all, Papa, it will be through your efforts that I might receive it."

"That is the reason for family, my dear."

Chapter 26

A mid-November chill that seemed colder than any ever remembered by the good citizens of San Francisco rose in the air. To be long outdoors on such a day seemed complete madness, especially to those saner folk who chose to hide from the blast of the whipping wind and biting raindrops coming in off the bay.

But there, in the very midst of it all, walking without a care in the world, Captain Delightable continued his afternoon walk as if it were a summer afternoon stroll along warmed and sunlit sidewalks.

His beaming smile shone into every face he saw safely protected behind the windows of warmed stores and restaurants — smiles that were returned by bewildered and concerned stares from those wondering if the old man had gone completely mad.

It wasn't that he was unprepared for such a day, for he was wrapped up tightly in his long woolen coat, a wool scarf hugging his neck and his captain's hat pressed tightly down upon his head. It was that he chose not to let the bluster of the day decide for him whether or not to take a walk. Filled with so much bubbling joy, he could not contain the energy of it without walking it off.

This is what made him unique in the eyes of all who had ever met him. He was a man who seemed quite content and willing to yield to his every joyful and pleasant thought, and a man who refused to give place in his mind to anything other than happy thoughts.

Joy simply defined the man.

On the other hand, skulking behind him, equally wrapped up but desperately unhappy, was Detective Cyra. As joy defined the captain, despair defined the detective. And as he followed Captain Delightable from a discreet distance, he grew darker in despair. He could not understand how a man could remain so happy for so long. No attempt to anger the captain seemed to work. It became clear that all his efforts to intimidate him had failed utterly.

The captain just took it all in stride, never missing an opportunity to treat him with joyful respect and courtesy. He realized that was what angered him most; try as he might, he could not get an angry rise out of Cornelius Alexander Delightable.

So here he was, the fool, as he had come to think of himself, following the captain down a blustery street, half frozen, to gain what? *What would the captain do today that would be different from any other day?* Maybe he was just hoping the captain would tire of such freezing conditions and disappear again. Yes. That was it. That was the reason he was following the captain once again. He wanted to see the captain *ride the wind* once more, if for no other reason than just to see him do it again. To know, finally, that he was not insane — to watch with certainty now, as the captain dematerialized before his eyes, unaided by the dark shadows of a moonlit night. He wished to see it clearly, in the full light of day.

The captain, however, seemed unwilling at present to comply with his wishes. No matter. He would follow him all day if necessary, and return later to the station frozen completely solid. Sooner or later, in this horrible chill, the captain would find it necessary to do something to rid himself of the freezing effects of this weather. And when he did, Cyra would be there to witness it.

And so it was a great shock to him when the captain finally stopped in his tracks, turned back toward him, and waved his hand, beckoning him.

Found out now, he yielded to the obvious. Begrudgingly, he approached the captain.

"Fine. It is no wonder you noticed me following you. There are no sane people out here to hide behind. Are you happy, Delightable?"

"I'm always delighted to see you, David. You should know that by now. But dear man, you look dreadful. You must be nearly frozen. What do you say to joining me for a nice hot cup of coffee at O'Connor's? Please say yes."

"Why not? It's better than being outside following you around and turning myself into an icicle."

* * * * *

Sipping on his fourth cup of hot coffee, Detective Cyra finally had some color back in his face.

"How do you do it, Cornelius? How do you walk about in such weather and not feel the effects of it?"

"I learned the technique …"

"No! Please don't tell me you learned how to ignore adverse effects of weather on Minchon Island."

"But David, to tell you anything else would be disingenuous."

"I can't take much more, Delightable. I'm forced to admit that you're too much for me. You're an insurmountable foe. You win. I surrender."

"David, you misunderstand. There is no contest between us. You're my friend. I enjoy your company. Is that so hard for you to accept?"

"I'm a policeman, Delightable. No one wants to befriend a policeman unless there is something to be gained by it."

"Well, you have me there, David. I do want something from you."

"Now we're getting somewhere. What is it you wish to gain by making a friend of me?"

"Your friendship. There, I admit it. I seek to gain your friendship, and perhaps your trust."

"Come on, Delightable. What is it truly?"

"That's it, David, the full of it. Well, almost. I also would like to see you happy and enjoying life. There, that's it, I think."

"Nothing else?"

"Not that I can think of at the moment. Except, well, maybe I'd wish for you to get your true wish, to realize your true dream."

"And dare I ask what that might be?"

"As I said before, only you can know that; but I have put much effort and long hours into thinking about you and your struggle."

"That's just lovely, Delightable. It warms my heart to hear that you care so much about my well-being. And although it is a full crock of nonsense, I'm glad my life occupies so much of your time. Your life occupies a great deal of mine as well."

"I'm grateful, David."

"Oh, I'm sure you are."

Chapter 27

With the spy now revealed, I could concentrate on tracking down the actual saboteurs. In investigating the scene, I noticed a particular footprint unlike any other. It would not be difficult to follow this footprint back to its source.

At the gathering of all the warriors, I asked each man present to remove his right sandal and place it in front of him for my inspection, without revealing my reason.

After viewing every sandal in the village, which took some time, seeing the great number of men in the village, I came to the happy conclusion that the saboteur with the special print was not among the villagers. This left no doubt in my mind that he was a part of Mata'pang's group of thugs, ruffians, and scallywags.

Leaving a few men behind to protect the village, I led the rest of the warriors, in full battle dress and armament, across the island toward the Forbidden Land.

Lelalu, King Gogui, Amog, and Wigiwig accompanied us as well. I pushed everyone hard to get there in the shortest time allowable. Thus, in just over an hour and a half, we arrived at our destination, albeit haggard and worn from the accelerated march. I immediately ordered the warriors to form a defensive perimeter about fifty yards outside the boundary markers.

Although exhausted, Wigiwig and I straightaway made the climb up to the Ledge of the Observer. A short while later, we were joined by Lelalu, King Gogui, Amog, and a few guards and servants.

From my vantage point I spotted a large tree in the distance, but well within the range of my archers.

"It pains me to sacrifice another innocent tree in this cause, but I see no other way to gain their attention," I said aloud.

"Then honor it with a quick death," said Wigiwig.

I ordered my archers to fix burning matter to the tips of their arrows, and then ordered them to set the tree ablaze. They fired as one, and within minutes the tree burned brightly even in the full light of the afternoon sun. Black billowing smoke also rose high into the air. It was a clear signal to all that something of great importance was taking place near the borderland.

It did not take long for those hidden within the Forbidden Land to take notice of my delivered message, and within a short time their army, dressed for battle, arrived at the border. Mata'pang, however, was nowhere to be found among them.

One large man among those gathered finally stepped forward, but remained on their side of the border. He looked to be a fierce warrior, and I don't mean that in the sense of a Minchon Warrior, but a man experienced in the deadly art of warfare.

He spread his arms wide and shouted something not discernible to my ears.

"I shall go down to meet him face-to-face, Great One. I would ask that you all remain here, safe on the high ground, in the event my words incite him to action."

"No, Captain. We shall all go down. Your king does not fear this man or his army."

"As you wish, sir."

And so we all went down to meet this large man face-to-face, though with the border between us.

Being the King's Captain, I stepped forward and announced myself to him.

"I am Cornelius, the King's Captain. To whom do I speak?"

"I am Gau'lo, the Chief Protector of the Sacred Nation of the Other. Why do you attack our land?"

"I am here to take custody of Mata'pang and those others who have attacked our village and destroyed our king's throne by fire on evening last."

"I know of no such attack. We live in peace."

"If you speak the truth, then there are others of your village who have acted in deception, and they deceive you still. We are here for them."

"You bring an army to seize a few?"

"We bring an army to demonstrate our seriousness in the matter. We wish no battle, but we *will* have those responsible or we shall know the reason why."

"You say it is our people who have done this harm to you, but how do I know you speak the truth? Could it not be some of your own who have done this thing?"

"No. One of those responsible left a distinctive footprint. I have inspected all the men of our village. I am certain he does not live amongst us. Therefore, he must be a man from your nation."

"The accusation you make is a serious one."

"This is a serious matter, Gau'lo, and one which I hope you intend to rectify with honor."

"So now you challenge my honor?"

"I do not. I only ask that you act with honor."

"Do you think me less than honorable?"

"I do not know you well enough to make that judgment yet. Tell me, if you will, where is Mata'pang? Why does he not show himself?"

"Mata'pang is not on the island at present."

"Not on the island! What does that mean?"

"He has gone to the other island where the rest of our clan reside."

On another island? I heard him say that plain enough, but I knew of only one other island which could be seen from the hilltop. It was perhaps a full league away, a long way to row a boat through such strong currents, but that is the only place I could think him to have gone.

"You speak of the island nearly a full league from here in a southeasterly direction?"

"The same."

"May I ask when he ventured to the island?"

"Two days ago."

"Then perhaps he had time to plan the attack and assign such to the others before leaving."

"Perhaps, but I am unaware of any plot against your nation. I speak for all here. We, Sons of the Other, have existed on this part of the island for a long time. We have existed in peace. We seek only peace, but you send arrows of fire against us today in a call to battle. We have no desire to do battle this day. However, we will not allow this to happen again without return of like manner."

"It is good you have said these things, for we also do not wish to battle. However, damage has been done to our village. We demand that those responsible be turned over to us for judgment and punishment."

"And what damage has been done?"

"The king's throne has been burned."

"That is a grievous thing, indeed."

"It is an act of war, but it is not war we seek. However, we shall not rest until there is an appropriate restitution made for the despicable act against our people and our nation."

"Mata'pang will return in three days' time. I ask you to wait that long for me to discover who is responsible for such a contemptible act, if in fact it is one of our people at all. Will you send your army away until then?"

"No. We shall remain in place during that time to demonstrate how serious we are about this matter."

"Then our army shall remain here as well, to respond in kind if you should send more flaming arrows into our land."

"Agreed, our armies shall remain in place. You have my word, however. There will be no further action taken against your land for three days plus a half. By noon of the fourth day, you will bring those responsible to us for judgment, or there will be more than flaming arrows shot against your people."

"You challenge boldly, King's Captain. But I wonder, are you prepared for what may follow if we don't send those to you?"

"You have three and a half days to ponder that question, Gau'lo. I seriously urge you to take the time necessary to discover the answer within yourself first."

With those words spoken, and not wishing to hear any more from him, I turned abruptly and walked away, leaving him to begin his deliberation on my words.

"Are you the one who snatches arrows out of the sky?" he called.

I stopped and turned. "I am," I responded, and then turned away once again.

He remained still as I returned to the king's side and stared back at him. I had the distinct feeling that my actions and words had left a solid impression on him. I felt confident he would not take my words lightly.

"Well stated, Captain. Well put," said the king.

"Many thanks, Great One. Time will tell, however, if a similar impact was made on Gau'lo."

"You feel it necessary to remain here?"

"Yes, Great One. I feel it imperative to remain here to maintain the pressure upon them to do the right thing. To leave now might remove from them the weight of such a decision. Sometimes it is the heaviness upon one's shoulders that makes the better impression."

"Very well, Captain. We shall remain. It is good to hear you speak with such wisdom."

"As ship's captain, Great One, it was my duty and responsibility to make the choices necessary to protect those under my command. As the King's Captain, I can do no less."

Lelalu remained quiet during all of this. She did, however, squeeze my arm from time to time, a sign of her pleased and supportive take on it all, I presumed.

After some delay, Gau'lo turned and walked away, leaving his army standing straight and tall on the line.

I took his tactic as one meant to set posture. It felt like a maneuver designed to determine the earnestness of my position and intent. I felt he was trying to ascertain if my words were brash bravado or the words of a man fully prepared to put them to the fire of certainty.

I believed also that my resolve was being tested as well. I wondered if he wanted to find some understanding as to whether or not I was truly prepared to go to battle and shed blood for my cause.

Secondarily, I think he was also testing the leadership of King Gogui. I hoped that wasn't true, for I knew well enough the position of the king and the honor of the man. He would do almost anything to prevent the shedding of blood, but once the order was given, there would be no ceasing until the objective was secured. I'm not sure Gau'lo was aware of that fact at that moment.

And I wasn't sure what Gau'lo intended either. This was as much a test for him as for me. What disturbed me most about all of this, however, was the simple fact that the man who had initiated this whole situation wasn't even present on the island, or at least that is what we had been led to believe.

This was disturbingly reminiscent of so many other scuffles and battles I had seen throughout my life. The instigators of the matter are rarely present when it comes time to bruise bones and shed blood. They incite others to violence and then sit back and watch the chaos they have created envelope the mad dogs of their passions, unwilling to dirty their own hands in the fight for their beliefs.

Over time, I had come to believe that those people — because of their cowardly inaction — were unworthy and undeserving of any good that might arise as a result of their incitement.

Now here was I, taking a bold stance that could, at any moment, with the wrong move, look, or ill-chosen word, bring a bloody battle into being.

I wondered something else: if the fighting should start, where would I find myself? As a general behind the action, shouting to my troops, encouraging them to summon the will to sacrifice their bodies for the cause while I sat behind in safety? Or would I leap into the midst of it all, directly into the path of harm, into the gut of the fray, as it were?

As I stared across the boundary and into the faces of the men staring back at me, I could not help but wonder what thoughts were going through their minds.

In my time alive, I have come to understand one thing for certain. It is one thing to shout out in anger or create a great and bold bluster in a spoken challenge; it is quite another to step forward and suffer the blows.

A heavy hand dropped onto my shoulder. I turned to see that it belonged to Wigiwig. He smiled at me. "Keep your spirit light, Cornelius. Do not let doubt creep in."

Under normal circumstances I would have inquired as to how a person could know my thoughts. But in this case I *knew* Wigiwig knew my thoughts as well as I did, for our spirits were as one.

I returned his smile with my own, although weaker. "I do not doubt our reasoning for this. I only question how I might react if this situation worsens into a physical confrontation."

"Calm yourself and go forward knowing that all men who have ever fought have faced the same question when reason turns to argument and argument then turns to blows. Let us hope the question raised today will not require an answer."

"Yes. Let us hope large for that."

* * * * *

First off, I must say that I know miracles do occur all the time. But I had only borne witness to a handful of them in my lifetime. Some would say I should be satisfied with what I had witnessed and give thanks for that, and they might be right. But the miracle which happened over the next three days would be more than anyone could ever hope to see. I still find it remarkable that I was not merely an observer of such a miracle, I was its unwitting instigator, the unknowing protagonist of it all.

I assure you I did not knowingly intend such an accomplishment, but it happened just the same.

Later that day, during our evening meal, I could not help but note that the Sons of the Other were not having a similar supper. Even from the distance separating our two people, I could almost see the starving eyes of the men staring back at me.

As I observed their supper preparations, I noted that it consisted mostly of fruit and breadfruit prepared in an almost cobbler fashion. What was more curious to me was that I did not see other staples such as fish or meat being served. In contrast, our meal consisted of nearly all the essential food groups, with the obvious exception of red meats, of course, and in plentiful amounts suitable to fill our bellies with leftover food in substantial amount.

As I keenly observed our rivals, I noted how they wishfully stared at us as we all but ignored our extra portions. They ate everything they prepared and looked longingly at us. In a flash, it all made sense to me. They lived on meager rations while we appeared to dine in abundance.

"Lelalu, I see an opportunity below that could prove fortuitous for all."

"What is that?"

"No time to talk about it. Come with me and I'll show you."

We rose from our finely woven mats and trotted down the hillside to the front lines of our encampment. Along the way I picked up an untouched platter of fish and gave Lelalu one of extra fruits and we walked to the boundary.

Two guards arose from their seats and stepped toward us, their spears now at the ready.

"Calm yourselves, friends. I bring no animosity with me, only extra food that has been prepared and would remain wasted and uneaten. I would not wish to waste such nourishment. Would you be so kind as to take it from us?" I asked.

"It is a ruse," said one of the guards. "It is poisoned."

"It is not poisoned," I retorted, taking a small piece of fish from the platter and placing it into my mouth.

I could plainly see the hunger in their eyes, but still they hesitated.

"Come forth, brother. There is little need to waste food when you perhaps have need of it. It appears obvious that you were rousted from your dwellings and came away unprepared for a long stay. We came prepared for several days. Come, eat. It is not much, but it might be of some help."

Their eyes were clearly fixed on the plate we held before them. The first guard took a step toward us, but he was restrained by the other.

"They would draw us near with this food to thrust at us with their weapons," said the restraining guard.

"They hold only a plate of food. I see no weapons."

"This offer of yours, it is not accompanied by malice or other deception?" said the cautious guard.

"Brother, we have eaten our fill and food yet remains. Can we not share with you on this evening?"

"To what end do you share? This offer will not change anything. We are prepared for any treachery on your part."

"Wonderful. Then eat in peace, knowing that you are prepared. We shall leave aggression asleep for ourselves as well."

I extended my arms outward and the first guard handed his spear to the cautious guard and stepped forward. He suspiciously took the platter from my hands and then lifted it to his nose, taking in the aroma of cooked fish and spices.

"It does smell delicious."

He backed up slowly to his former place and then, cradling the plate in one hand, he picked up a piece of fish with his other and stuffed it into his mouth. His eyes rolled in delight as the other guard then devoured a piece.

"Step forward, my brother," said Lelalu, "and take this platter of fresh fruits, please. It grows heavy for me."

The cautious guard laid down the spears and stepped forward to take the plate from Lelalu. He bowed reverently, recognizing her royal status, took the plate from her hands, and quickly stepped back alongside his partner. They stuffed slices of juicy mango into their mouths.

Seconds later, other warriors stepped up and snatched pieces of food from the plates. The food disappeared quickly, and then one of the new guards returned the empty platters to Lelalu with the same reverence.

"Brothers," said I, "bring others here. I will fetch other plates."

I signaled our warriors to lay down their weapons and bring the plates of uneaten food to where I stood.

Minutes later, a true miracle occurred before my eyes. Dozens of potential combatants were standing in front of each other, sharing food and light laughter.

A short time later, Gau'lo appeared. He barked orders and the men separated. He stepped forward and stared into my eyes.

"Why do you do this? What do you wish to gain?"

"I admit it, Gau'lo, there is reason for my generosity."

"Speak."

"I seek no war. I seek no violence with the Sons of the Other. I seek only justice for the wrong done to us. Is that cause enough?"

"If proven, then it shall be just cause. But as yet I have no proof it was men from our nation who have done what you say."

"I ask only that you make the inquiries and give me an accounting of what you discover. Do we have agreement?"

"You are a strange man. Your color is not the same as ours. You are not from the island."

"You're correct. I'm from the outside. I was shipwrecked on this island many, many months ago. I was a stranger to this island, but now I am a warrior student."

"A student? That is impossible. You command as a master."

"Gratitude, Gau'lo. But I would wish it not necessary to command an army. I would rather sit with brothers and share laughter."

"I also do not wish for violence, Cornelius, but it seems you have brought an army to our border well prepared for battle."

"Being *prepared* for battle should not be misconstrued as *intending* battle."

"I agree. Perhaps we should sit and talk further."

"I welcome that, brother."

"I shall consider it. We shall meet on the morrow at midday here. I shall give my answer then."

"On the morrow, then." I nodded.

He responded in like manner and then turned and walked away, leaving his men on the line to continue chatting with their rivals.

"He develops admiration and trust for you, my love," offered Lelalu.

"He is a cautious commander. He remains prepared nonetheless."

"As do you."

"It is the manner of command, my wife."

I set up a rotation of men on the line to reduce over-familiarity. Gau'lo did the same. We had established a modicum of trust, but neither trusted fully in the other. Such was the necessary mind-set of commanders, I felt.

Although both of us, I believed, wanted to embrace and be friends, neither of us could afford the luxury at that moment. To abandon our responsibilities as commanders would have been foolish and perhaps negligent. We both knew it. We both, I think, regretted such need.

Later that evening, after all the food was consumed, the armies pulled back to their original lines. We could not feed them all well, but our generosity aided sufficiently. Friendly shouts of jest shot back and forth for several more hours. I allowed it for a while, and then as the full of darkness fell upon us, I ordered such jesting to cease. I heard Gau'lo order the same.

Chapter 28

With the coming of night came also the uneasy need to listen for any incursion or aggressive movement along the line. I regretted that reasoning, but I held those thoughts inside my head. A commander cannot show any weakness, and I, as a former ship's captain, knew that all too well.

Once again on top of the hill later that night, surrounded by the king and his servants, I felt the need to be extra vigilant.

Too restless to sleep, I stood on the precipice overlooking the campfires of our purported rivals. Amog walked up beside me.

"You cannot sleep for worry," he said.

"Not so much worry as confusion."

"What confuses you?"

"These other people seem little different from us, and yet I agree with Amog, there is a chasm of history between us which makes us quite different. They do not seem to be a people prone to violent thoughts, and yet they take an angry Mata'pang into their ranks and give audience to his violent and vengeful ways.

"My mind asks a simple question: Why? And why do I feel so much anger toward Mata'pang? I am feeling a true hatred for the man even now. I know I should not feel such things toward another, especially for one so troubled, but his treachery burns inside me."

"It is only the last vestiges of youth burning their way out of your new being, like the boiling off of fat in a soup."

"It's more, Amog. I feel it deep within me. I *will* do battle with him. I'm sure of it now. And I will seek to do him great harm if I am able. And I would take his life right now if given opportunity. This troubles me. It troubles me greatly, for it sorely conflicts with what you have been trying to teach me.

"Still, knowing this does not quell the hatred I feel for the man. It grows steadily within me and even now I feel it seething within me. Great anger surges through me when I give him thought.

"I no longer fear the coming battle; in fact, I look forward to it. In that, then, I am resolved to attack Mata'pang before any other. It is my intention that he and I will face each other in mortal combat even before the battle takes root upon the island.

"As he steps onto the island, I shall charge full speed toward his landing skiff and plunge my spear into his black and rotting heart. I shall laugh in his face as the light of life grows dark in his eyes. I shall spit upon him in disdain and revel in joy knowing clearly, as he passes into whatever life follows this one, it was my spear that stopped the beating of his evil heart."

"Young one," Amog finally said with a gentle and understanding smile, "I see you are still possessed of a wayward and unruly spirit. I well know this unbridled nature, for I also was born with such a discourteous character. I strongly urge you, therefore, to heed my words so that you may be healed from your infirmity. I should encourage you to seek peaceful things so that they should find you as well; for if you continue on your present path in search of lesser things, know this: they also shall find you. And if these lesser things discover you unprotected — that is, without the knowledge and compassion to shield yourself — you shall surely find yourself in a black hole at depths you have not known before. Seek, therefore, companionship with the Light, for it shall raise you up on high so that your own light might be cast greatly outward into the darkness and be as a beacon of sanctuary for others.

"Seek not to know the Darkness, for it shall cast you down hard upon the stones and thorns, and crush the light from you."

I was confused by his initial words, and my heart grew heavier. These were not the words my ears had expected, and I think he saw the bewilderment in my eyes.

He paused for a moment, considering his next words carefully before he spoke. Then I saw sparkles form in his eyes just before he continued.

"Let me speak to you in other words and say to you this: seek always the ways of Light lest the Darkness find you and swallow you whole, cursed forever to dwell in the black belly of despair, hatred, and fear. Release your grip upon the Darkness, and rather reach your arms upward for the Light, that your spirit becomes the Light.

"Seek to glide upon the gentle breezes of affection and forgiveness, and avoid, if you are able, being tossed about by the darkened gales of loathing, rage, and dread.

"I believe, dear boy, that your weapon is loaded, not with powder, ball, and wadding, but with fear, angst, and vengeance. Know this: when fired, these things can strike with more damage than a lead ball. The ball will only break your flesh, but these shadowy things that possess you now, these things of Darkness, these wicked things of wicked intent that live in your heart, they have the power to break your soul.

"If these terrible things inside you are not summarily seized and harnessed, they will grow. If they are allowed to grow and they gain strength over you, I fear for you that your soul will surely become broken and shall fail you. And, dear student, know this most clearly: if your soul be broken and felled, it shall not rise again."

He placed the palm of his huge hand upon my forehead and then leaned over and kissed the back of his hand. It was a most high blessing that he offered me; the only one higher would be if his lips actually touched my forehead. Then, offering no other words, he turned and walked away from me.

I stood on that cliff staring out into the blackness of the early morning, my mind still cluttered with confused thoughts mixed with fury.

I understood the willful and evil intent of such thoughts, and if intent does create the paths upon which we walk, then mine was a malevolent and despicable path. I wanted to expunge such intent from my brain, but Mata'pang's face remained a strong vision before me, beckoning me further into the depths of Darkness.

I determined that if and when I should see the approach of Mata'pang on the water, I would not allow him to land upon this island and further infect this place with such wickedness, but I was only one man, one lowly and poorly equipped soul. *How was I to do battle with an overwhelming force such as his dreadful and infectious rage?*

Amog's words continued to twist their way through the coarse thicket that unfortunately shielded my brain, in search of harbor. I had heard the words clearly enough, and I had no wish to give my soul over to such detestation and apprehension, but I was also determined to protect my island and my people from the ravages of Mata'pang's rampaging spirit.

On my ship, as captain, I was duty-bound to protect the ship, cargo, and crew. I was honor-bound to protect what was right and just with any and all means available. But here, upon this island, this spit of sand and rock, despite my title of King's Captain, I was not a man of any power or influence.

I was but a student. I had no command of anything save myself. I was nothing but one man standing alone on a hill, trembling in the gloom of fear, feeling the gnaw of hatred aspiring to devour the last bits of goodness left stirring within me and urging me ever onward toward the Darkness.

From behind me I heard Lelalu's gentle voice. "Husband, you remain troubled, I see."

I continued staring out into the early morning's blackness as I answered. "Mata'pang will return soon, and I remain lost as to how to confront him without my wrath leading the way."

"Take ease, Husband. There is no need to worry. There will be no confrontation, Cornelius."

"Be not fooled by my consternation, Wife. There will surely be a confrontation when Mata'pang arrives. Be very certain of that."

As was her way, her hand found its way to the back of my neck, and as she rubbed lightly, she whispered into my ear. "Amog guides us, Cornelius. He has done so for many, many years. He is a powerful warrior. He has always protected us. He will continue to do so."

"But I am the King's Captain," I protested. "Such decision falls to me."

"You are the King's Captain, but Amog leads us in all things spiritual."

"My love," I replied, "the coming confrontation will not be a spiritual one, and Mata'pang possesses powerful weapons — his rage and his hate. And they both grow stronger, I fear."

"That power is weak compared to Amog's abilities."

"Perhaps so."

"And his soul is broken, Cornelius. He has few defenses left."

"That's what Amog just spoke of. He said that once a soul is broken and felled ..."

"It shall not rise again," Lelalu finished.

She then smiled. It was not a smile of joy, but one of gentle understanding; a smile, I felt, more given to a young child still steeped in childlike ignorance; it had more of a tolerant nature to it. "My husband, what am I to do with you?"

"I fear, Lelalu, that I am more trouble than I am worth to you."

"Not at all, dear one. It is still early in your training. Mata'pang's soul *is* broken, but he has not yet fallen. He may yet be saved."

My mind reeled in the presence of more hidden truths. I felt as though I were a castaway alone on a deserted island, or a stricken sailor adrift on a lonely sea. Everyone on the island seemed to live in a way I could not begin to grasp, let alone comprehend and act confidently upon.

Where I might look out onto the ocean in the coming morning and see an invading army seeking to conquer and kill — an army that needed only to be destroyed, not reasoned with — it might seem to everyone else to offer a long-sought-for opportunity for rescue, the safe retrieval of wayward children.

I finally turned and stared into Lelalu's inviting brown eyes. "Amog warned me about adopting the ways of the Darkness. I have heard that term said about the Sons of the Other. Yet I still don't understand who they are. I can only assume they must be of an evil design and intent. Wigiwig told me the island was once inhabited by two disagreeing factions. Was he referring to these two groups? Is that whose army stands before us now?"

I'm not sure you will want to hear of this, for it troubles me greatly to even speak of it this much."

"I most certainly want to hear about it, especially now. Please tell me."

Lelalu spotted a large, low rock. "Let us sit there and I will tell you a story."

We sat down upon the rock and I excitedly waited for her story to begin. For some time, though, she sat in silence. I surmised she was recollecting the account in her own mind and preparing its delivery. Then she looked at me directly and smiled.

"This tale is not a happy one, my love. In fact it is a story of true shame. It is an account the Minchon people do not often tell, for it is a description of one of the most painful moments in our history."

Being already intrigued, I shifted my position in anticipation of a wild and fantastic story.

"You have already heard of the difference between the One and the Other, have you not?"

"Yes," I replied. "Amog explained that to me the first day in the library."

"In the distant past, the Children of the One, or the Sons of Light — whichever you choose to call them — and the Sons of the Other were two souls both born of the same great Source. They were contentiously separated by a strong discordance of opinion.

"As more time passed, the Sons of the Other succeeded in giving themselves entirely over to the guile of the flesh and its entrapments. In so doing they destroyed their path back to the Light."

"Yes, Amog told me of this also. It has been labeled the Time of the Great Discord."

"Excellent, Cornelius. Yes, to make it worse, the Sons of the Other refused to accept their part in their own undoing — their unhappiness and despair. The Sons of Light, however, maintained their devotion and allegiance to the Source of All Things, the Singular Consciousness, thus retaining their unencumbered ability to move back and forth between the Singular Consciousness and the physical plane.

"In the great many years that followed while living upon Earth together, the two factions grew further apart until one faction, the Sons of Light, moved away to live in the land to the west."

"Is that now the Minchon Nation?"

"Yes, Husband, it is what finally evolved into the Minchon Nation."

"I understand."

"The other faction, the Sons of the Other, remained in the east, now known as the Forbidden Land. The ancient king, Gogui'alo, my great-great-

great-great grandfather, forbade anyone to ever cross the border again. My father still believes it holds a dastardly dark power over anyone who would venture there from the Land of the Light.

"As even more time passed, the island you see to the southeast, where Mata'pang has gone, arose out of the sea in a fiery birth. The Sons of the Other eventually moved to that island. The Forbidden Land, though, remained cursed and it is a great wonder to me now as to why they have come back to it, knowing its dark history."

"Perhaps," I interjected, "they found it safer here than where they were."

"It would seem so," she replied. "Anyway, as time continued its forced march, the Sons of the Other grew more and more jealous of the Sons of Light and their ability to communicate with the Source. Finally, the Sons of the Other sent a message that they wanted the Sons of Light to leave the island or face a great war. The Sons of Light, however, refused either to leave or to fight. As the time set for the confrontation approached, they instead chose to remove themselves from the disagreement altogether."

"But how? How was that possible? How could one escape the inevitability of the fight and continue living on the island? It makes no sense."

"I understand, Husband. I am trying to explain; but as I said, you might not yet be ready to hear it."

She reached out and took hold of my hand.

"The Sons of the Other gave a specific time and date when the Children of the One were to either leave the island or fight the war. Genatu, who was the High Priest then, was very wise and powerful, and extremely adept in the ways of the Minchon Warrior, more so than any warrior of the Sons of the Other clan.

"He suggested to King Gogui'alo an ingenious way to remain on the island and yet avoid the war. The king, eager to save his people and retain their home, quickly agreed.

"At the appointed hour on the appointed day, the Sons of Light gathered in the spot that was to be the battlefield and prepared themselves as directed by Genatu. They formed a square and knelt on the sand as Genatu began his prayerful chants.

"Everyone heard the thundering of the army of the Sons of the Other as it marched westward toward the battle zone, the large flat plain that we crossed on our way here.

"The deep rumble filled the air and the ground vibrated with each step of the advancing army of heavily armored warriors. Some noticed the strong glow coming from the east, the morning sunlight reflecting from the highly polished shields carried on the backs of the approaching army.

"The Sons of Light remained steadfast in their genuflections. Genatu continued in his prayerful chant. At the prescribed moment, all the people of the Sons of Light joined in the chanting. Their rhythmic sound grew stronger and stronger as the thunder of the approaching army also grew louder.

"A strong white glow slowly formed over the gathering of the Sons of Light as their mantra grew even louder, the glow growing in intensity commensurate with the volume of the chanting.

"It was reported and recorded by the lead brigade of the Sons of the Other that as they neared the valley of the expected battle, they heard the loud chanting rise to a crescendo and then there was a blinding flash of white light that stopped them momentarily in their tracks. Moments later, after their sight had returned, they resumed their march around the corner and onto the battlefield. It was then they discovered that their enemy had departed, leaving them victors of a battle never fought.

"It was a joyous moment for them, for they had defeated their hated enemy and the land was now theirs alone.

"In celebration of their great victory, they slaughtered many of their animals and prepared a great feast which lasted several days.

"Within a short time, however, they began to bicker among themselves regarding such things as which parcel of land would be controlled by whom and for what purpose.

"It seemed that their need for combat and bloodshed had not been satiated. Their need to hate caused them to eventually turn on each other. At first only small fights broke out between individuals, but soon they grew in both intensity and numbers. Combat began to include immediate families, and then gradually it came to include larger family groups, and then groups of like-minded individuals. The battles became more fierce and bloody. Atrocities committed on both sides grew ever more terrible in their nature and design.

"Not long afterward, their population began to decline drastically. Although alarmed over their dwindling numbers, they still found it impossible to rein in their atrocious nature and combative manners. It was only when they realized they were very near to killing off their entire race that there came a cessation in the hostilities on such destructive scale.

"Still, though, by way of their nature, hostilities only lightened in their ferocity. Only when they needed to survive more than they needed to make war did active battles cease; they finally came to understand there was strength in numbers and they needed the numbers to build their homes and irrigation systems and the other structures required for a community to exist.

"Disagreements and fights continued, but on a harmless basis. There was a seeming peace, but their souls remained broken.

"It was then that the Sons of Light made their historic return to the island. Today, most of us are born from the descendants of those returned Sons of Light.

"For the most part, we have healed the land; however, the blood living in the soil still cries out mournfully now and again. On occasion we can still hear their cries of anguish, fear, and loathing, although those voices are quieter today as a result of our continued healing of the land.

"Even now, when such cries are heard, we gather together to offer our healing chants, songs, and laughter. Such sounds have a soothing effect on the souls who fell in those long-ago battles, for upon hearing the sounds of joy, they know that although they may never rise again, they have not been abandoned and forgotten. We are with them. We hear them. We sing to them, and they are sent serenely back to sleep with the intent that they should dream of the peaceful moments they once enjoyed."

"Wait," I pleaded. "Where did the Sons of Light go at the moment the battle was to ensue?"

"This will be difficult for you to comprehend at present, my love. More so than understanding the story of our people. We don't know of days, months, or years, the way you do. To us, time is now. We live now. We eat now. We dance now. We exist now. There is no past or future for us. There is only now.

"This is the principle of *riding the wind* that Amog was in the process of teaching you before all of this began.

"Mankind has not yet learned this concept, but time is fluid. It is like a river. It flows in one direction, but we are not bound by its flow. We can go up the river and down the river if we choose to — and if we know how.

"It is in this manner that the Sons of Light escaped the battle."

"I'm not sure I understand."

"I know, my love. Try this instead. At a moment just before the Sons of the Other army rounded the bend and came onto the battlefield, the High Priest Genatu simply sent our people back up the river, so to speak, to a time before the great uprising. And there, for generations, we lived behind the time of the Sons of the Other."

"I think I understand," I said. "When Amog tried to describe *riding the wind* to me, he said it was as easy as sending yourself to a place either before or after a certain point in time and then allowing time to catch up or slip ahead. It seemed odd to me then, but it makes sense to me now — although I still have no idea how to make such a journey."

"You will, but it must be done delicately, or you might damage the fragile fabric of time that separates all events."

"So, why are you here at the same time as the Sons of the Other now?"

"Genatu set the pace a little quicker than normal time, thus allowing us to catch up with the current iteration."

"Are we still moving faster than the others?"

"No. We moved into the same time iteration just before your arrival. That is why the island was available for you to land upon."

"Then that is what you meant by saying that the island had now fully materialized?"

"Yes, Husband. Exactly."

"Then I was lucky to have arrived when I did."

"No. We knew you were on the way to us. We brought the island back for your sake."

"You understand that I'm taking all of this in without falling to my knees in wild shouts of insanity."

"You are doing very well with this information, Cornelius."

"Why me? That is my only question. Why me?"

"Destiny, Husband. It is your destiny."

"Why not others *like* me?"

"Only special warriors are attributed this grace. And you, my husband, are among the most high."

"And yet I sit here dumbstruck, as only a wide-eyed imbecile in these matters."

"In the years that follow, you shall become one of the greatest among us. You shall lead us forward into the eons to come."

"I hear you and I trust your words, Lelalu, but I feel so woefully inadequate to that task at present."

"The nation trusts in your future, Cornelius. And I, my husband, trust in you. Remember, you are the future hero of Minchon."

Chapter 29

It has been said, and wisely so, that chance favors the prepared mind. So it can be said for simple discovery as well. Over my lifetime I have come to understand that discoveries are made most often by two types of people: either the very studious or the foolishly lucky, but I suppose there are times when the two types might be combined in fortune.

I have been more often the lucky fool; however, my discoveries have been more by chance than through any scholarly pursuit. *Good* chance, mind you, but nonetheless chance.

As you might recall, just before my ship was torn apart in the great storm, I told you how the compass spun wildly. At that time, I had no idea how such a thing could be possible, but as I just said: chance oftentimes favors the lucky fool.

During the second day of our stay at the border of the Forbidden Land, I was sharpening a knife. It was a fine blade, made from the highest-quality steel I had ever seen. Just where it had come from originally, I couldn't say. It was given to me by Amog as a gift from him to the King's Captain. I know for certain at that time we had no source of raw materials on the island with which our forges could then produce such a quality of steel, but it rested in my hand just the same.

The blade held an edge exceedingly well, but spurred on by boredom while waiting for Mata'pang's arrival, I took to setting even a finer edge to it.

When I finished, I noticed a single tree growing out of a large crack in the rock some ten to twelve feet from where I sat.

In jest, mind you, or born out of yet more boredom, I decided to toss my knife at a particular point on that tree. I grabbed the knife by the blade, reared back my arm, and let it fly.

It started its flight straight and true, but as it neared the tree, it suddenly took a sharp left turn and slammed into the extremely large boulder which popped up out of the hillside and stuck, flat-bladed, against the rock.

I stood up immediately, and shaking my head in disbelief, walked to where the knife hung against the rock about five feet off the ground. I stared at it for several seconds, never before having seen a rock capture a knife!

I took hold of the handle and tried to pull the knife to me, but it held fast to the stone. I next tried two hands, but it continued secure to the stone. I then put a foot against the rock and pulled with great force. After much struggle the knife finally came loose and I tumbled backward onto my buttocks.

I had, quite by chance, discovered the cause of the wild compass gyrations. The entire massive stone seemed to be one huge magnet, or at least made of magnetic material giving it the same force as a magnet.

I, of course, made inquiries of Amog concerning the stone, and learned the huge rock was indeed known to produce highly charged magnetic effects capable of influencing compasses a long way out into the ocean.

Amog said that the magnetism was generated by what he called 'geothermal' activity deep within the island's core. I didn't immediately understand the concept, but he said the heavy metal contained in the stone combined with the activity below the island created something called a 'generated electromagnetic current' when the island was in the process of making its return to the material world. Of course, at that time the term *electromagnetism* had no meaning to me.

You must remember, this event occurred in 1800, well before man learned to harness such miracles as electricity and magnetism. I tell you plainly, I was astonished by the strength of the magnetic field created by this electromagnetic engine under the island, but I could see how it might affect a simple compass needle far out into the sea as it was materializing.

Later that day, I again allowed our abundance of food to be shared with our Other brethren. I, however, remained on the hill overlooking the gathering of the feasting brothers.

"You are gaining more wisdom every day, Captain," said the king, walking up behind me.

"Perhaps, Great One, but it seems to come slowly to me. You are referring to the gathering below, I presume?"

"I see your plan, and it is a good one."

"I do not wish a war between us and the Sons of the Other, sir. I believe the more the men see their enemy face-to-face, the easier it will become to make them friends. But am I wise to do that? This question haunts me more and more every minute."

"I cannot see how friends could come to slay one another. Do you?"

"But will they remember they are our friends when it comes time to finish this?"

Just then, I saw a parting of the Other forces. All voices quieted as well, and I saw Gau'lo, leading five bound men surrounded by other armed warriors, approach the boundary and stop.

"Our saboteurs, Great One."

I ran down the hillside and over to where the men now stood lined up. Gau'lo stood in front of them.

"Gau'lo. It is good to see you again. Are these the men responsible for the destruction of my king's throne?"

"These are the ones responsible for the action. I am told it was on Mata'pang's order that these men acted."

"Thank you, Gau'lo. You have shown yourself to be an honorable man."

"Do what you will with them. They have disgraced themselves and our nation. They are banished from our people forever."

"I would not have them banished for such an act. No one was injured. Only a wooden throne burned. But I would ask that they be required to help rebuild the throne before they are returned to your people."

"They are banished not for burning wood; they are banished for attacking a nation that has done us no harm. We do not seek a war with the Children of the One. We wish only to live in peace, as we have done for a long time."

"Surely this can be used to your advantage without banishment."

"You have moved an army to our border and threatened war. The destruction was a serious act to your king. Do you say now that it was not serious?"

"No, Gau'lo. The act was cowardly and unwarranted. It was seriously wrong. But lives were not lost. Only a *thing* was destroyed, a thing which can be rebuilt."

"Your guards were injured, were they not?"

"Yes, but only rendered unconscious. They are well now."

"You demanded that those responsible be brought to you for punishment. They are here. We give them to you for punishment. Do what you will with them. They have disgraced themselves. They have disgraced the honor of our nation. If honor can be restored, then it is upon their heads that this task must fall."

"Accepted, Gau'lo. We have only to take Mata'pang into custody and this matter is concluded. Do you feel hunger?"

"I could eat."

"Then come over and join us for our midday meal. Your army is welcome with you. We have plenty to share."

"You are a good man, King's Captain Cornelius Delightable. We will share a meal with you in peace."

As I said earlier, good fortune does show compassion to the foolishly lucky from time to time, but on that day we, the nation of Minchon, with the Sons of the Other, broke bread in peace and harmony and that was a fortune shared by everyone on the tiny island.

* * * * *

I have often heard it said that laughter is a cure for many illnesses. On the day we shared our meal with our supposed rivals, I learned just how powerful the cure was.

The two armies intermingled. Weapons were mixed together and heaped into a pile, forgotten and unguarded. Laughter abounded throughout the camp throughout the day.

Later, under the dying sun, many of us spoke earnestly about many things of more importance. As Gau'lo spoke, we learned that life beyond the boundary was a hard one. Trees bearing fruit were not bountiful here. Fishing on the eastern shores was not gainful due to the strong currents and eddies. It seemed that the fish preferred other shorelines around the island where it was easier to swim. In short, life was generally difficult in the nation of the Sons of the Other.

I inquired as to why they had not made themselves known to the Minchon people before.

"We did know you existed until recently," came Gau'lo's unexpected answer. "No one had ever ventured across the boundary. We were told that monsters of great destruction existed here."

"This, then, is the reason for so many weapons?" I asked.

"We were told the monsters could invade our world at any time. We keep prepared for the attack. Are there no monsters?"

"None at all."

"That is good to know."

"I find it odd how such legends are born and so easily accepted," I said. "I heard that the east was cursed."

"I think you're correct, Cornelius," said Gau'lo with a smile. "Life *is* hard here."

"I stand corrected, then, my friend. It would seem it is so after all. I do suspect, though, that all things will get better soon."

"What is your number?" asked King Gogui.

"We are few. Including our women and children, we number approximately one hundred."

"There are no more than that?" I asked, remembering the number I had witnessed during my incursion.

"There were many more a while ago, but they left with Mata'pang to prepare for war. We remained behind, not wishing to engage in such foolishness."

"Your people are welcome to join our nation, if they wish to do so," offered the king.

"Gratitude, Great One, but it is those still on the other island who trouble me most. They are wild and angry. They cast us out for not subscribing to their ways of war. That is why we are here struggling as we are."

"Of course," I said. "Now it all comes together for me."

"Explain, Cornelius," said the king.

"This is why we are here, Great One. This is why I feel what I feel deep inside me. It is not with Gau'lo's people that we are to battle. It is the true Sons of the Other who I feel are stabbing me in my soul. They will come, and when they find we have absorbed their people into our village, they will become enraged. They will bring war against us with the intent to do great injury to all of us."

"You are correct, Cornelius," responded Gau'lo. "This is why I hesitate to accept your kind offer. If we go with you, we might bring the seeds of destruction to your people."

"Mata'pang intends to do this anyway," I said, speaking out boldly.

"It is highly possible," said Gau'lo. "Mata'pang kept his anger mostly to himself, but you can see how he has infected some of us. The saboteurs I sent to you have never been known to be dishonorable before. They have always been men of peace, but it is the angry soul of Mata'pang that has turned them sour. Mata'pang asked to go to the island. I warned him of their evil and torrid ways, but he insisted on going over to them. It is very possible that he has incited them to attack you."

"What is their number?"

"Several hundred fierce warriors reside on the island, enough to make a terrible war here and win. They are full of hatred for the Children of the One. We never knew you were here, but knowing you are now will send shouts of war through their nation. They will gather and attack. I fear if they come and we do not choose to fight with them — as we will so choose — they will murder us all."

"Gau'lo," I said, "if you come stand with us, then our number will increase also. It will be a better defense for all of us."

"I have not the mind for issues of warfare that you possess, but it seems to be the best choice."

"Can you gather all your women and children and all your possessions and move them to our village at once, for safety?"

"We can do this quickly, for we possess very little."

"Then we should do so immediately, for Mata'pang leaves us little time to prepare."

"You have a keen military mind, King's Captain. You and Mata'pang are very much alike in this regard. You think strategy beyond the obvious."

A sudden realization filled my heart with fear and worry.

"Great One," I said, "what Gau'lo has just said troubles me deeply."

"Speak your mind," said the king.

"Sir, I believe that Mata'pang will think strategically. I believe he will not attack us here. He knows that we will enforce this area. I believe he will attack from the west, the other side of the island, the side we have left unprotected from incursion. We must gather up our army and march quickly to the other side and prepare our defenses there."

"Are you certain of this?" asked Amog.

"Yes. Mata'pang knows that I know he was seen here. He will believe I will position my army here to confront him as he comes across the boundary. He will send a light force against us through these gates, but it will be a ruse. He will attack with his great army from the other side — where the women and children are even at this moment woefully unprotected. If I were him, I would do the same. Capture the women and children and hold them hostage. He could achieve a quick and mighty victory without an arrow being launched."

"But to move an attacking army so far around the island? Is that possible?" asked Wigiwig. "Would not our sentries surely see them coming from the hills?"

"Not if they move under the cover of night. It is only three leagues away to the west side. That is only nine miles or so, a simple matter to row hard a few hours through the night for a dawn attack."

"Then we need to move our army now and prepare our defenses," said Wigiwig.

"Yes. We shall leave a small scout team here in case I'm wrong. But we need to begin moving everyone to the other side of the island. And I think I know the exact place where he will arrive. It is along the far western shores, a heavily wooded area where Lelalu and I have walked before. It would effectively mask the movement of his warriors until he wishes to attack."

"He is not due back for another day and a half. Will we have time to prepare our defenses by then?" asked Gau'lo.

"We have no choice. It must be enough time."

"Then we are with you," said Gau'lo.

"And your help is appreciated."

"I apologize, however."

"For what?"

"We are not warriors."

"But your men carry spears and bows."

"As I said, for the monsters thought to inhabit this land. To be honest, we would have dropped them and run away if you had attacked. Forgive me; it was but a deception only. We are peaceful people. We do not know how to make war."

I laughed loudly. Soon everyone else seated around me joined in. I then placed my hand on Gau'lo's shoulder. "You are quite the deceiver, Gau'lo. You had me well fooled."

"Our woeful trickery would not have lasted long once your army struck. We are outcasts because we do not subscribe to the philosophy of our brothers and sisters across the water. We do not believe in violence. In fact, you might call us banished cowards."

"I do not see cowards, Gau'lo," said Amog. "And never again label yourselves as such before me. I see instead a forthright and peaceful people. I see new brothers and sisters."

"And we are grateful for that. I regret our deception, King's Captain Cornelius, but it was only recently that I saw who you truly are."

"If honesty is the word of the day, Gau'lo, then let me be honest with you also. I was a merchant ship's captain. I have never fought anyone either."

Gau'lo's face fully expressed his shock and amazement. "You are, then, the greater deceiver, for I trembled hard for a long while after our first meeting. And while out of your sight, I was forced to empty my stomach for the fear of you and your army."

Everyone laughed heartily once again.

"Forgive my deceit also," I pleaded.

"It is done," Gau'lo responded with a grin.

Then I grew serious. "Tell me, my new friend, what of the saboteurs? What is it that they believe?"

"If you ask them, they will tell you that Mata'pang made you all out to be devils of sorts. They believed they were acting in the best interests of our people, of our nation. They are in deep regret over the incident, for they have misjudged your people as I did."

"Then they are forgiven their transgressions as well," said the king. "It is done and is now in the past. Captain, can they be unbound?"

"Of course, Great One." I looked to one of the guards. "You heard the king. Release the saboteurs and see that they are fed and made comfortable."

The guard bowed and rushed away.

"This is surely a day of miracles," said I.

"This is a day of great joy, Husband," added Lelalu.

I nodded.

Chapter 30

Returning to our side of the island was a quick affair.

Settling the newcomers into the village, I realized that although they had been a part of the race now surely paddling across the ocean to attack us, they were people very much like ourselves. Their greater faith was in peace and tranquility. This would almost certainly ease them in their transition to Minchon life, but it did not lay to rest the threat of Mata'pang and his people.

I felt that an attack by him and his followers was imminent. Thus, after leaving the women and children behind in the village with a squad of a few rear guards, the rest of us made a hasty march toward the western shoreline, reaching it just before sunset.

Upon our arrival, most were exhausted from the march. Many warriors lay down to rest, and there remained quiet and still. Others sparked fires and sat around, chatting amongst themselves.

My mind, however, could find neither peace nor rest, being filled to capacity with fearsome visions of the horrible battle I expected to begin near daybreak. Lelalu tried her usual soothing techniques on me by rubbing my forehead, but my mind would have no solace.

"Forgive me, my wife, but I cannot put these terrible visions out of my mind. I'm going to walk up to the peak of the ridge and see what there is to see.

"Only blackness, Cornelius. That is what you'll see."

"I realize it is night and my vision will be restricted; I'm not a complete fool."

"I wasn't referring to what your eyes will see out on the dark ocean, Husband. It is what your heart will see. Stay here and rest. You look exhausted."

"I may appear exhausted, but I cannot rest. Get some rest, my love. I go unwittingly in search of this darkness you speak of. I only pray it does not find me unprotected, as Amog has warned me."

I left her side, and alone walked a path to the top of the sharp ridge that overlooked the expected landing site. There I stared out over the black ocean, lit only by what light shone down from the full moon above.

"Tell me, sir," I said to the face above me, "how do you do it, staring down each night, dark or lighted, observing all the horror you see down here? How is that you keep yourself from weeping at the sheer terror of it all?"

I sat then still, my heart filled with a monstrous sorrow. How could I not have seen this thing coming? Why did I shout out to Mata'pang in such childish bravado? Why did I place a challenge so hastily before him?

As I continued questioning my motives while heaped in this great sorrow, anger soon replaced the despondency. I felt the change take place sharply within me.

There, sitting in the blackness of the night, feeling the darkness growing in my heart, I sharpened my spear point with a stone lifted from next to me, all the while cursing the approaching forces under my breath.

Suddenly that darkness took root, and, becoming stalwartly defiant, I shouted out a challenge for that army to step upon my island — all the time knowing that no one could possibly hear me, but caring very little if anyone did.

I then sent more cursing seaward toward the interlopers, vowing that their blood would surely stain the white sand of the island and mix with the blood of their ancestors. I promised them a swift and full defeat in defense of my home and my people.

Swearing then to whatever god would listen to my continued ranting, I promised to kill as many on the morrow as I possibly could. I felt suddenly inspired by my own hate and terror, and I thus grew more bold as I felt them coming closer toward their harrowing destiny.

During those night-filled hours, my hatred for those intruders grew steadily within me, and I seethed as a mighty storm brewed within my chest. I no longer feared the battle; I looked forward to it. I was determined to put my spear first through the heart of Mata'pang before any other. He and I would face each other in mortal combat even before the real battle took root upon the island.

Having only my belief that Mata'pang's forces would attack from the western shores, I unhesitatingly harbored a measured hope for an easy victory.

The western shoreline of the island was extremely difficult to negotiate, I reasoned silently, with its high, sheer lava walls and razor-like rocks. With the exception of a small point of land, which was flat from the sea inward, there was no other way to easily traverse toward us. This small point of flat land was very narrow and, being a bottleneck, could be defended rather simply. I believed if we could get to that area before Mata'pang's brigands, we might be able to trap them on the beach. There, we could completely destroy them one and all. My heart then took flight and soared with gladness.

The early morning, hinting at the rise of the sun, found me fully alert and now steely fortified by the hate surging through me.

It was in that moment I caught the slight silhouettes of canoes on the water.

I had been correct in my tactical thinking. Mata'pang was attacking where I thought he would. My hate now had company: joy and elation.

As the new sunrise climbed above the horizon and glistened across the ocean's surface, a new guest arrived: shock. In the new light, the size of the armada became apparent. There were hundreds of canoes coming at us.

From my position on the cliff overlooking the beach landing area, it was easy to start counting, though difficult to keep the count in my head.

I heard a shuffling sound behind me and turned to see Amog's approach.

"Greetings, Amog," I said. "See out there, the beast Mata'pang and his armada approach our shores."

Amog turned his eyes toward where I pointed, then raised a hand to his eyes against the glare off the ocean waters. He grinned as he did this, his white teeth sparkling brightly.

"Indeed, Cornelius, they do draw nearer. It seems you were correct. What more do you make of this?"

Standing tall and strong, yet still full of my hate and elation, I shook my fist boldly and announced my position on the matter with zestful intent and zeal of purpose. "We are well prepared for the coming battle, Amog. I shall not be a disappointment to anyone, for I shall dash out to meet Mata'pang's boat and slay him first. I shall stab at his heart, and I vow that he will be the first of his evil horde to perish in the coming battle."

Amog turned and stared deeply into my eyes. Then his mighty right hand dropped onto my right shoulder. I felt honored by his supporting touch. I felt his strength surge through me, blessing me with an even stronger desire to see this through, and even more fortitude than I had known before his arrival.

He opened his mouth to speak. My ears opened in preparation for his wise words. I anticipated that they would encourage me to be of great courage and strength during the coming war. I expected words which would instruct me to fight hard and destroy the enemy as much as I was able to. Aye, the confidence surged through me.

"Are you prepared for your task, King's Captain?"

"Yes," I replied boldly. "Calculating, in my head, they will be upon our shores within three hours, we will have sufficient time to prepare a just greeting for them. I have prepared my mind for the violence to come. And although I am plainly not a soldier, I have found the will toward violence in my heart. It is a desperate will, and also a frightful will because I have never felt these urgings before. This is all new to a young merchant ship's captain. It will be glorious, though."

"It will be a fierce battle, no doubt," Amog said. "When it is over, there will be much blood and torn limbs upon the ground. There will be the gnashing of teeth and screaming of painful words in the air. It will be a very frightening and terrible encounter. To be sure, I tremble at the thought of all the horror to come."

Then he turned and walked away, leaving me alone to consider what he had t said.

How easily are we able to deceive ourselves into thinking we are something more than we are when we are alone to fabricate that which we need at the moment to preserve ourselves.

It was then I was reminded of what an old monk once told me while we were anchored safely in the Port of Chennai. "It is a simple thing," he said, "to be a holy and righteous man in the absence of any temptation."

In the absence of a fight it was easy to see myself as a fierce soldier. Now, to look upon this invading armada of angry men, I shuddered at the thought of it.

How awful it is to discover yourself sorely lacking and realize the deception that has played so strongly in your heart and mind was your deception alone.

The vision of the actual fighting, all the blood and torn bodies, frightened me to instant paralysis.

I had earlier built a warrior in my mind's eye, but it was only in that eye that I was such. I had no idea how to use the spear I held in my hand. I suddenly had no idea how I was to command the forces put into my charge.

I knew nothing about the positioning of an army for battle. I well understood what a *flanking position* was, but I had no concept of how to employ it properly. I had also heard the term *rear guard action*, but I had no conception of what it meant on an actual battlefield, or how such a tactic would be used to defeat an enemy in the midst of a battle.

I was a babe in all of this, and the true fear of it abruptly overwhelmed me. I had felt brave and sure in making preparations for Mata'pang's expected arrival. I was confident in my own ability to stand and fight — right up to the moment of Amog's arrival.

But now his words haunted me. The reality of my naïveté struck me full force. I was scared, terribly afraid. What was to become of the King's Captain now that I had seen my true portrait?

Suddenly other horrible visions filled my head, and I could see them clearly in their brutal truth. When I dashed out to meet Mata'pang coming off his boat, would he find me a blithering fool and see clearly enough that I was no mighty soldier? Would he then slay me within seconds of our meeting and then step over my body without another thought for me? Could my command be terminated so quickly and inconsequentially?

Dear me, I thought, what by all the stars in the heavens was I doing here? What had I been thinking all along?

The slap of reality brought the truth of the matter to the front of my brain: I was no military commander. I was no longer even a ship's captain. I had no experience, no real power. I was nothing but a humble student, and a novice student at that.

Rather, and more importantly, I was but a silly bamboozler who had thought, for a few ridiculous moments in his foolish life, that he was something more.

Truth has a mighty way of pointing out all one's mistakes and self-deceptive practices with a staggering and terrible swiftness. It is a surety that shakes one into place and tosses all the folly into one's face with abrupt finality.

Immediately upon the arrival of truth into one's brain, the *fight-or-flight* reflex that all soldiers face at the moment a battle begins becomes painfully clear.

For me, it was an excruciating shudder of fact. I wanted to run. Run fast. Run far, and keep running. I felt, at that exact moment, I even possessed the ability to dash across the surface of the ocean without a concern of falling into it.

My heart beat from fright as it had never beat before. It seemed far more frightful than when I was cowering on the forecastle of my ship as it disintegrated before my eyes during that heinous storm.

The dread of this thing happening put me into a sudden and ruinous state of mind, and I felt it so come upon me.

I turned my fearful eyes and saw unmistakably, for the first time, the absolute dread and terror also in the eyes of the soldiers who had gathered around me. I thought it so much easier for them. They could show their fear openly and without hesitation, but I, as their commander, could not. And yet, I felt deeply certain, I was more frightened than they were by a magnitude several times greater.

Then, once again, an angry sensation swept over me. Only this time it had its sights on me. What arrogance! I screamed — within my own mind. *How arrogant can one truly become? Are there no limits to my conceit? How could I genuinely have convinced myself I would be capable of carrying off this ruse without the truth of it coming out?*

Now that actual lives lie in the balance, how am I going to pull off this battle? I was certain that Mata'pang was not Gau'lo. His anger was genuine and certain. His threats were real. His intent was to physically harm all if he could. Mata'pang was a fierce warrior, a seeker of blood and destruction. There would be no bluffing him.

When the time came to trade blows, he would be there to try and be first. Of that, in my mind, there was little doubt. If I were to meet him on the battlefield, it was certain that blood would be shed. The only question was whose blood would be shed first. I feared that the answer was simple enough. It would be mine.

My legs immediately began to quiver. Nausea struck my stomach. My head began to spin. My vision blurred. I was very near to passing out completely. If that happened, what would the Minchon people think of their future hero then, I wondered.

It was all I could do to stand on my trembling legs, which at that moment felt as if they were planted into the soil. And I was glad of it too, I don't mind admitting. For if they thought they could move at all, my legs most likely would have escaped this place in a crazy dash, taking me along with them, screaming loudly and rife with full-on terror.

And then, from some forgivingly gentle source completely unknown to me, a chuckle forced its way out of my mouth for no other apparent reason than the realization that I was blundering my way through this moment. I would be found out very soon, and the utterance was based on the folly of it all. I was, for all intents and purposes, laughing at my own foolishness.

One of the soldiers near to me on the right, however, heard it plainly enough. He turned his head, stared at me for several seconds, and then smiled.

I noted his gaze and nodded to him encouragingly, for reasons still unclear to me to this day.

I heard him then speak to another soldier standing next to the right of him, saying, "See the King's Captain. He laughs. What courage has he found? From where does it come? But if he finds the courage to face this armada, then I shall find it also."

"Yes," said the other soldier, "he stirs me to courage also. I have suddenly lost my fear. The king has obviously chosen his captain well, for he is a fierce-looking warrior, to be sure. I pity those who are about to attack us."

It struck me fully then and there. They had no idea how unsure and afraid I was, but there it was. The soldiers looked to me for their courage and surety. A sudden surge of self-confidence then shot through my body. I understood a simple truth: I cannot let these men down. Somehow, some way, I had to summon strength from deep within my being and not allow my fear to show. Whatever else might be churning inside me, only bravery and confidence must be expressed across my face and in my manner. Not for me, mind you, but for them, those soldiers who stood ready to charge into the fray on my command. I had to be strong for them.

I was instantly restored.

I was not, though, foolish enough to think myself actually worthy of such accolades. I had to find a way to stall the battle, if even for a little while longer. Lives of good and decent men depended on my ability to stave off a full physical assault if at all possible.

I feared that if such a battle began and they saw how pitiful a soldier I was, then all would be lost for them. It would be a slaughter of our people. I had to avoid a confrontation or watch many good people perish because of my bluster and false bravado.

I stared out at the approaching armada in deep consternation. Then, as if divinely ordained by an understanding deity, Lelalu moved up to my right side.

"I felt your fear rising, Husband."

"I have no doubt, Wife, for it flows through my veins with pounding resolve to tear me down. Look there, Lelalu. Hundreds of them. And they row with a frightening purpose. They seem an angry and willful lot."

"Your concern is unfounded, Husband. I have come to tell you this to calm you. There will be no battle today or any other day."

"Look at them," I pleaded. "Look at their numbers. And see how Mata'pang leads them. There will be death and destruction, I fear. And plenty of it for each to take some measure of it individually."

"I know it is frightening to look upon, Cornelius, but take heart. No violence will be accomplished."

"I hope and pray you're correct, Wife. Yet there he is, paddling toward us with his army of angry warriors. Hell-bent upon our destruction, it seems. I don't see how such a battle can be avoided."

Again Amog appeared, at my left shoulder. He signaled the nearby troops away with a flick of his hand. The three of us then stood alone.

"It is time," he said, "that we should tell the King's Captain of the reality that is to follow soon."

"What reality?" I asked, suddenly alarmed and fully confused.

"There will be no battle, Cornelius. This was meant only as a study for your learning."

"What?!"

"There will be no battle. No one on either side will be harmed."

"I don't understand, Amog! Do you not see the bitter-looking army sweeping nearly into our shore?"

"I see the invaders. They are clear to me."

"And yet you say there will be no battle?"

"True enough. There will be no battle."

"I realize I am only a student, I do not know much, but tell me, please, how are we to avoid battle this day? How are we to assuage the agony that lies within these hundreds of wounded souls looking for some retribution and conclusion to their pain? I look myself with want and desire in my heart to see this concluded without bloodshed, but I see only an unavoidable conflict."

"You see this because you are not yet trained in the Minchon ways. You lack the understanding necessary to retain joy and peace in your heart. It is a common thing, Cornelius. Do not be hard on yourself concerning this matter. You had to see for yourself what might have been. To allow this to conclude any other way would have been an injustice to you."

"Yet I stand here dumb anyway," I stated. "Fear wells in my heart as no time before. Not only a fear of battle, which I am totally untrained for, but fear to have it found out that I am no infantry commander, nor can I understand how I am to become the hero of Minchon."

"The *hero* arrives later, Cornelius, after your training is completed many years from now. You were a ship's captain. We knew this. You were never expected to be a battle commander. But in your acceptance of the charge given you, we saw the spirit of a true leader within you. In your excellent preparation we saw duty, honor, and the willingness to take responsibility. In your dealings with the people of the Forbidden Land we witnessed your courage, compassion, and wisdom. All things done and witnessed were necessary to bring you along with speed and purpose, Cornelius. Well done, lad. Well done.

"Now the next lesson will be a most wondrous joy to you. And it will demonstrate the true power of a fully trained and practiced Minchon Warrior."

Shock could not describe adequately what I felt deep within me. The point of the lesson, as the point of any spear, struck my heart instantly, deeply, and as surely and true.

It had all been done for my benefit, to accomplish in a short time what would have taken years if I had been born into this magnificent race and raised in its beautiful and gentle traditions.

Lelalu's hand clenched my arm, gaining my attention.

"Of course," I blurted out, great relief now evident in my voice. "How silly of me. Amog will remove the people from the battle as Genatu did before. I'm greatly relieved."

"No, Cornelius. I will not remove the people as Genatu did."

"You will not? Then how will there be no battle?"

"Remain here and observe what is to come," said Amog. "And when you speak of this magical tale in the years to come, and you will, for it is your destiny to be our storyteller, all who hear it will understand the majesty, glory, and love which lives in the heart of every true Minchon Warrior. Be well, young warrior. And keep vigilant forever."

Amog then turned away and strolled down to where Mata'pang was to land. Yes, I said strolled, as in walked leisurely toward the arriving angry armada, as if he were set to enjoy the surf, sand, and sun on a holiday.

From my hilltop I watched as the canoes came ashore and the fierce warriors charged at Amog. But I also witnessed the miracle before my eyes. None of the advancing warriors so much as lifted their weapons, let alone positioned themselves for an attack.

I could not hear what was said, if anything, but it appeared that Amog was speaking to them and they were listening.

After some time, Mata'pang then dropped to his knees, let his spear fall to the sand, and lifted his hands to his face, as if weeping uncontrollably. Soon enough, other warriors dropped their weapons also and collapsed onto their knees. Within seconds, all the warriors assumed the same position.

Then Amog stretched both his arms wide. As I watched what came next, I could hardly believe my eyes. I felt Lelalu grasp my right arm just above the elbow. She said nothing.

A white glow began to form around Amog. It grew brighter and brighter until it was so strong that Amog seemed to disappear into it. And then a second later he was gone, vanished into thin air. I looked hard and noticed that Mata'pang was gone also. Both, in one instant, had evaporated into thin air, and then the glow was gone also.

I watched as Wigiwig walked out onto the beach, stopping just before the horde of kneeling warriors. He also stretched his arms wide and appeared to speak some words.

When he made an upward motion with both arms, the marauders all stood as one and followed Wigiwig inland.

"What did I just see happen, my wife?" I asked as I began to wobble on my legs, now understanding why she had grasped my arm.

"Steady, my husband. The conflict is finished. All is well."

"But…Amog. Where did he and Mata'pang go? Dear me, what did I just witness?"

"True power, Cornelius. True love. True compassion. True caring. That is what you have witnessed. You saw the true ability of a Minchon Warrior. Was it not glorious?"

I heard her words. They were plain enough, but what I saw defied all reason and logic.

"They *rode the wind*," I uttered. "That's what I saw. They *rode the wind*."

"In a manner of speaking, Cornelius, but it was much, much more than that."

"Are they to return soon?"

"No. Amog has work to do with Mata'pang. They will be gone a long time. You shall see them on the island again, but it will not be soon."

"My training," I said, somewhat selfishly. "Who will train me now?"

"Wigiwig will assume the lead position, but it is the fullness of the nation's love for you that will train you, Cornelius. It is the nation...and I...that together will give you all you will ever need; we must prepare the future hero of Minchon for what will undoubtedly be your finest moment. Fear not, Husband. Your training will not suffer from Amog's departure, but his work with Mata'pang requires close support. That young man has much to learn, and Amog will guide him straight and true. Come, it is time we greet our new brothers and sisters. Even now the village is preparing a great celebration."

"Papa," asked Robert, "what did Amog say to Mata'pang?"

"That's between them, Robert. But let me ask you this: What words would you have chosen to speak to a heart so self-defeated, so hurt, so alone, so despondent?"

Robert thought a moment and then shook his head. "I don't know, Papa."

"Indeed, Robert. And at that very moment I could not imagine them either. But that was why Amog was the High Priest. His immense wisdom and experience gave him the words necessary to not only stop a war but also calm the raging of tortured souls and restore hope to a disquieted people so desperate for peace and harmony. Whatever the exact words, they were mighty ones, to be sure. Wouldn't you agree?"

Robert nodded his head.

Wendy stopped her note-taking long enough to look up at the captain and smile, adding: "They were magic words, Papa."

The captain chuckled. "Yes, Wendy. Whatever the words, they *were* magic."

Suzanne sat very still, her mind a thousand miles away, her eyes dancing about in her head as a new thought seared into her brain every second or two.

The captain smiled as he stared at his granddaughter, then turned to the children staring up at him, pressed his index finger to his lips, and remained very still and silent.

The words and images flowing through Suzanne's head seemed magical as well, for after a time a warm smile slowly formed on her lips and her eyes began to sparkle. Something wonderful was happening inside her.

Finally Suzanne returned to the present and turned her eyes toward her grandfather as if seeing him for the very first time. "It's all true, isn't it?" she asked softly.

"I have never lied to you, child."

"I mean all of it, Papa. Everything you've ever told me. It's all true."

Tears formed in Suzanne's eyes.

"As it is with all learning and all wisdom, it all depends on what you're truly willing to believe, Suzanne — what you're willing to allow to be manifested in your life."

"Mommy sees the magic now, Papa," offered Wendy.

"Perhaps she does," responded the captain.

"Papa," added Suzanne. "They weren't just stories. I mean all your stories, it all really happened to you. The shipwreck, the island, Lelalu, all of it."

"As I said, my child, it is for you to decide what is real and what is make-believe."

"Papa, I believe. I don't know why, but I choose to believe. Am I wrong?"

"You're never wrong to believe in something good, Suzanne. I'm just happy that your childhood lessons have returned to you. Perhaps you are now prepared for your next journey." The captain thought a moment and then grinned. "And perhaps it's time for another's long journey to end."

Chapter 31

Strolling down the sidewalk, Captain Delightable walked with a spring in his step. It was another glorious day to him.

He, of course, was heading straight for the park bench, knowing that it was nearing story time. Today he was early; he intended to sit alone and do some thinking before the expected crowd gathered.

That plan went awry when he noticed a solitary figure sitting on the bench, his elbows resting on his knees and his head cradled in his hands.

"David," the captain said gleefully, "how nice to see you. Am I disturbing you?"

Immediately upon hearing his name called out, the detective raised his head and stared at the captain.

"I don't know if I'm glad to see you or not."

"Considering you are well aware of the fact that this is where I come nearly every day to tell my stories, I'm guessing you came here expecting to see me, perhaps even hoping to meet me here."

"Maybe you're right, Cornelius. I really don't know anymore. But if you know that, then maybe you can explain why I'm here. I surely don't have a clue. Perhaps I'm a masochist and enjoy the punishment."

The captain chuckled as he sat down next to the distraught detective.

"I don't think that's why you're here, David, and I don't believe you think so either."

"Then tell me what you do think, Cornelius, because I've been sitting here for over an hour and not one good reason has entered my head. I give up. I surrender. You win. What am I doing here?"

"You've come for your answers, my friend."

"What answers are those?"

"The great answers. The answers to all your questions. The whats, the whys, the hows. All the questions that have burned within you all your life."

"That seems a tall order to accomplish, even for you."

The captain chuckled. "A simple task, my friend. A very simple task, for you already know the answer to every question you ask. They lie sleeping within you. You have only to rouse them from their slumber."

"You're speaking riddles again, old man. I don't need riddles. I need answers."

"And you shall have them."

"Then please tell me."

"I need you to find them inside yourself, David. I need you to search deep within your own heart, your own soul, and your own mind. That's where they lie, waiting for you to discover them again, to give them life once more. To give them renewed purpose."

"How, Cornelius? How do I discover that which you say I already know exists?"

"Go back in your life, David. Search backward to when you were very young. To a time when both your heart and your mind were open, fresh, and expecting every good thing to come your way. Search back to that moment when you knew for certain what you were and what you were to become. Find that one thing within you that identifies you most."

"Identifies me?"

"Yes, David, your true identity, my brother. Your true identity that lies within you now and always has. Search for it, David. Search your mind and heart for the reflection of your true self. It is beginning to rise within you."

"I have no idea what you're saying to me."

"You were once an angry young man. You felt the separation from the One. It hurt you to be apart from us.

Please, my brother. Search harder. You have been sorely missed. You are loved. And we want you back with us."

Cyra searched his mind for an answer, but it remained hidden, out of sight from his consciousness. He grew more frustrated and his eyes began to moisten. He felt his mind being torn apart.

Turning his damp eyes to meet the captain's, he saw the captain smiling warmly.

"Yes," said the captain. "Let it come forth. Open up to the truth of it all. See, David. See the truth within you. It begins its return, brother. The memories begin their rise through the darkness."

"You're trying to confuse me."

"That is only the darkness struggling within you speaking. It is in dreadful fear of its own demise, David. Show the darkness the light. There is no attempt to deceive, brother. You do not struggle alone with this. We are here for you. The One awaits your final return with a glad heart."

"My final return? To where? *From* where?"

"Search, David. You're almost there. You're almost home. Search, my brother. This is where you want to be, where you need to be. Where you're truly loved and missed. Push through it all, David. Cast the darkness aside and see the reality of what lies beneath."

"Who am I? Who do you think lies below the surface?"

"You know who you are. I cannot tell you, but you already know. Give it voice, dear brother, and see the darkness fade."

Detective Cyra's face began to glow with vision only he could see. "I am...I am ..."

"You're on the precipice, brother. Speak it aloud. Speak your true name. Bring life to it and see the truth for what it is."

"I am...I am...Mata'pang!"

The captain stretched out his hand and brought it gently down upon Mata'pang's forearm.

"Welcome back, brother. It's so good to see you once again."

"I was banished. You all banished me."

"Not banished, brother. You were taken away for your own good. Remember now Amog standing before you?"

"Yes!" Mata'pang said.

"You were taken away to heal your heart, to help you discover your path through the darkness and back into the light. Amog was there with you every step of the way."

"Yes!" Mata'pang said, the clear memory returning to his mind. "Yes. He worked with me constantly. He restored me. He guided me toward new purpose and intent."

"And you have done very well indeed, brother. You have done exceedingly well. All Minchon is proud of you and welcomes you back with love and openness."

Cyra then burst into tears and his head collapsed down upon his arms. He sobbed openly and unabashedly.

The captain remained silent for some time, allowing Mata'pang time to clear the emotion of his relief.

"Come with me," said the captain finally. "Someone wants to meet you again."

Without hesitation, Mata'pang rose and followed the captain, saying nothing.

They walked in silence, the captain allowing all the memories in their graced fullness to again take their rightful place within Mata'pang's heart.

Arriving at O'Connor's Wharfside Tavern, Mata'pang quickly noted several grinning patrons standing about as silent as mice.

The captain led Mata'pang to the closest patron.

"Do you recall my face?" asked the patron.

"Of course I do. Mr. Hotchkiss. How are you?"

"Just fine, thank you, but think again, brother. Who am I?"

Mata'pang scrunched his nose, trying to recall the man's face, but it was just beyond the border of clarity. He slowly shook his head.

Mr. Hotchkiss only smiled. "Think."

Then Mata'pang's eyes opened wide with recognition. "Gau'lo! You are Gau'lo!"

"Indeed. Welcome back, my good friend."

Mata'pang embraced Gau'lo, speaking his name several times, tears filling his eyes once more.

"Again, welcome home, brother," said Gau'lo. "You have been missed."

"Th-thank you," said Mata'pang, choking out his gratitude.

Another man stepped forward. "And I? Do you recall me?"

Mata'pang stared and then his face brightened. "Tony, the hardware store handyman. No!...Not Tony. You are Gamomo. You are Gamomo!"

"It is I, brother. Welcome home."

A third man then stepped in front of him. "And what about me?"

Mata'pang grinned. "Come on. Is this a joke? You're Buster, my partner, you scallywa...No! Of course not. You're...you're ..." Mata'pang fell silent and stared for several more seconds and then his face lit up brightly. "Tainini, my former boat mate! Is it you?"

"It is I, brother. Welcome home."

Mata'pang hugged Tainini tightly, tears flowing freely by now. "It is so very good to see you again."

"You too, brother. It has been such a long time."

"It has. Yes! It has been a very long time."

Mata'pang walked to each man and shook hands with a joyful smile, calling each by name and then giving each a great hug, speaking their respective names again as he did so.

"I remember you all," he cried, "some in Minchon, some of you in the Forbidden Land, some from the Other Island. I remember you all. I remember everything."

Everyone applauded loudly until the bartender finally walked around from the bar and stopped just short of him. "And what about me?"

"I know you also, Great One. You're Wigiwig!"

"Correct. Do I get a hug also?"

Mata'pang hugged Wigiwig tightly and continued weeping.

The tavern door opened and the judge walked in. All voices stopped instantly.

The judge walked over to where Mata'pang stood and smiled warmly at the sobbing man.

"You have successfully returned to the brotherhood, I see."

Mata'pang started to kneel, but the judge stopped him. "We do not do that here, Mata'pang."

"Amog, Great One, I did not understand before today."

"It was not intended that you would until you were ready. All of it before, Mata'pang, does not matter. It matters only that you have returned to your rightful place now."

"I don't recall yet all the time you spent with me. I don't yet recall all of your specific lessons, but thank you for all those years of helping me to find my way back home."

"It was all worth it, Mata'pang. It was all worth it."

"Cornelius," said Amog, "you have done well, very well indeed. You were correct about our brother here. Today, you are truly the hero of Minchon."

"Cornelius?" asked Mata'pang.

"Yes. It was Cornelius who believed you could be restored to us by bringing you to this time and place. All of this was his idea."

Mata'pang looked at Cornelius and tried to speak, but his mouth only quivered and could find no words. He simply stood, with a confused look on his face.

"Worry not about it now, brother," said the captain. "We have much time for all of that later. Now we celebrate the return of another son to Minchon."

Cheers went up in the room, and the celebration began in earnest. All faces glowed with warming smiles, all eyes glistened with joy.

After a few happy hours, the captain rapped his cup with a spoon and when all had quieted, he spoke.

"There is still much that needs to be done before our home is returned to us. I think we need to return to work and continue with our preparations. We shall play again very soon upon the sands of our island. Now Amog, Wigiwig, Mata'pang, and I must speak together seriously. May we do so?"

"You may, Cornelius," said Tainini.

"Then fare thee well, my brothers," said the captain.

Within minutes, all having said their goodbyes coupled with promises to get together again at the soonest opportunity, the tavern emptied, leaving Amog, Wigiwig, the captain, and Mata'pang alone.

"Cornelius," said Mata'pang, "I hear your words and I recall the faces. I remember the names also, but I do not recall the process by which I was sent here to this time and place. I still feel that I hang in the misty memory of something nearly forgotten. And what has become of the island that it needs to return? Can you explain it all to me?"

"Questions abound in you," said the captain. "I understand your need for the answers. You have been absent from the story for a while. Come to dinner tonight, and I will finish the story for your sake."

"I would be grateful for that. Far more questions than answers fill my head."

"By the time the story is completed, you will have all the answers you need."

* * * * *

That evening, with Amog and Wigiwig accompanying Mata'pang to the captain's home, they ate a hearty meal together in joy and gratefulness to be once more openly joined.

Suzanne, understanding all of it, welcomed Mata'pang into her home with hug and a kiss on his cheek, stunning him to silence.

"Welcome, brother," she said.

"I...I ..." stuttered Mata'pang.

"Say nothing, Mata'pang," she said softly. "Nothing needs to be said."

Then she hugged Amog and Wigiwig, greeting each by his correct name.

"He's waiting for you in the library," she said.

Wendy and Robert came up to the men.

"Welcome, brother," said Wendy, offering her hand. Mata'pang shook her tiny hand gently.

"Thank you, little sister," he said.

"There's more magic to come," said Wendy.

"Of that, child, I have no doubt."

"Welcome, brother," said Robert, offering his hand as well. Mata'pang shook his hand.

"Thank you, little brother."

"Come help me with dinner, children," said Suzanne. "You three, get on in there, He's waiting."

Mata'pang chuckled. Then they all walked down the hall toward the library.

* * * * *

With dinner completed and bountiful laughter filling the house, Amog turned to Suzanne. "Suzanne, my dear, that was a meal fit for a king."

"Thank you, A ...A...Amog."

Suzanne bit her lip in intense thought. "Sir," she started again. "I'm having trouble with all of this. Forgive me. I am not comfortable calling you Amog presently. I've always know you as Judge Harrison."

"Then call me Edwin, Suzanne."

"I'm not comfortable with that either. May I, at least for now, stay with Judge Harrison?"

Amog chuckled. "You may call me what you wish, child."

"Thank you, sir. Now, if you'll all retire to the library, I'll be in shortly with coffee and dessert. Children, I'll need your help."

* * * * *

"It was a wonderful day, Cornelius," said Judge Harrison, as Suzanne preferred. "I so recall the startled look on your face when I told you there would be no battle. What is the expression?…Oh, yes. I could have knocked you over with a feather."

"Indeed, Amog. It might have taken only a breath to do it. I was in total shock. And then to see you walk calmly out to the beach and stop the army in its tracks, well, all I can say is in that precise moment I understood, very clearly and for certain, exactly what I didn't know."

Everyone laughed.

"Papa," said Wendy. "Finish the story, please."

"It is finished, child. What else do you desire to know?"

"What happened after that? How long did you stay on the island? Things like that."

"Ah, well, the village had grown into a very fine nation practically in one instant. I spent another nine years there, living and learning all I could, with Lelalu by my side. Amog returned to the island some five years later, without Mata'pang, of course. It was during this period that I came up with the plan to rescue Mata'pang. We lived in harmony all that time until it was time for me to come here. That's about it."

"Wait! I have a question."

"Certainly, Robert. Ask your question."

"It's for Mata'pang."

"Ah," said Mata'pang. "Ask away."

"On the morning you and your army came ashore on Minchon Island, Amog met you on the beach and spoke some words to you. Can you remember what he said?"

"Robert," said the captain. "We spoke of this, did we not?"

"Yes, Papa, but is it not the duty of every warrior student to ask questions?"

Amog was the first to laugh out loud. "There it is: the question of a true warrior. The wish to know all. You sound very much like your great-grandfather, Robert."

"I'm sorry, Robert," said Mata'pang. "I cannot yet recall them exactly, but I do remember being shouted at, for they were screamed at me in silence."

"What does that mean?" asked Robert.

"It means that my heart heard them loudly."

"They were whispered to you, old friend," corrected Amog.

"No. They were deafening, as a roar."

"You only received them that way. I assure you, they were only whispered."

"Whatever the volume, the message got through. I recall that now. And for that I am eternally grateful."

"Amog," asked Robert, "can you recall them?"

"I recall them exactly, young student warrior, but you do not need to hear them. In fact, young one, let us hope there will never be a need to hear such words spoken. Do you understand?"

"Yes. They're words needed only to bring one back onto the correct path."

"Well put, lad," said Wigiwig. "You'll make an excellent warrior one day. There is no doubt of that."

"Indeed," agreed Mata'pang. "I only hope your path is an easier one for you than mine was for me."

"There will be some stumbles along the way, no doubt, but he comes from excellent stock," said Wigiwig. "He'll do well."

"Finish the story, Papa," begged Wendy. "I need to hear all of it."

"It's late, darling. Let's finish this another day."

"But Papa, something wonderful is about to happen. You might forget."

The captain smiled.

"She is gifted, this one," said Wigiwig. "A true warrior already."

"Perhaps too gifted," said the captain. "I promise, child, I shall finish it tomorrow. We will make time."

"Okay, Papa."

"Time to leave," said Amog. "We'll have many other days to continue this relationship. This is not the end, only the beginning."

Amog turned to Suzanne. "It was delightful, my dear. You look so much like your great-grandmother it's almost like seeing her."

"You even have Lelalu's smile," said Wigiwig.

Robert opened his mouth to speak but was cut off by the captain.

"Yes, Robert, Princess Lelalu was your great-grandmother. And yes, she went ahead to prepare the island for our return, but that's a story for another time. All right?"

Robert only smiled and nodded.

"Let us be off, then," announced Wigiwig.

"I'll walk you to the door," offered Suzanne.

"Good night, Cornelius."

"Good night, Mata'pang. Let's share lunch tomorrow."

"I look forward to it."

All said good night to each other one final time and Suzanne closed the door.

"What an incredible day!"

"It's not over, Mommy. Something wonderful is about to happen."

"You're just a ball of sunshine, aren't you?" said Suzanne.

They had all started back toward the library when the doorbell rang.

"Oh dear," said Suzanne as she turned toward the front door. "One of them must have left something behind. I'll get it."

"Children," said the captain, "come into the library and close the door." They did so as Suzanne answered the front door.

She spoke as she opened it. "What have we forgotten, gentlemen?"

Her eyes first focused on the dark form standing before her in the dim front porch light, and then they went completely blank.

"Hello, my love," said Jonathan, her husband.

* * * * *

In grand fashion, joyous tears were spilled by everyone, and when all had calmed down, Jonathan tried to explain. "From the perspective of the world," he began, "I suffered through a long sleep when a bullet struck my head in a glancing blow, rendering me unconscious. On the way to the aid station, they apparently confused my identification papers with those of another chap who didn't make it and had no family to miss him. I have lain in a coma for the past three years under his name. When I came to, I remembered exactly who I was, and after convincing the doctors that I wasn't out of my mind, they sent me home. I got here as fast as I could."

"Daddy," said Wendy, "you said 'from the perspective of the world.' What does that mean?"

"It means, my precious daughter, that while my body was lying in that hospital, I was really somewhere far away, going through an intense training. Do you understand?"

"Of course I do, Daddy."

"Where were you, father?" asked Robert.

"That is a story for another time, son."

"I understand," replied Robert with a knowing smile.

"Yes," said the captain. "Of course you do."

"My, how you both have grown," said Jonathan, studying his children. "I'm so impressed." Then he turned toward the captain. "Grandfather, how can I ever thank you for what you've done for my family?"

"Jonathan, my boy, they're my family too. What else could I do?"

"Tomorrow," said Suzanne. "Let's finish this discussion tomorrow. I need rest. This certainly has been a day of days. Besides, I need to get reacquainted with my husband," she added with a beaming smile.

"It has been such a long journey home, I'm in desperate need of some comfort right now," responded Jonathan.

"Papa, can you put the children to bed? I need to comfort my husband."

The captain smiled. "Certainly, child."

"What does she mean, Papa?" asked Wendy.

"It means it's time for us to retire, young writing warrior," said the captain. "Now off to bed with you."

The children hugged their mother and father and, of course, the captain and then scooted from the room.

"Welcome, back, Son."

"Thank you, Grandfather. It's good to be home."

The captain kissed his granddaughter on the forehead. "Now take it easy on him, dear. He's been in a hospital for the last three years."

"Stop that, old man, and go to bed."

The captain chuckled and then started out the library door.

"Papa!" said Suzanne.

The captain stopped and turned just as Suzanne rushed to him and hugged him tightly.

"I love you. I hope you know that."

The captain giggled. "I know it very well, child."

"One hundred fifty years old?" she asked.

"And counting," he replied with a sly smile. "Good night."

He left the room and walked down the hallway, checked in on the children, and then skipped toward his own room, turning a corner and stopping to look at the hasp and lock on the attic door.

"I'll be. She did put a lock on the door. Imagine that."

He walked into his room and lay down on his bed, fully clothed. He laid his right arm across his eyes and sighed. "What a glorious day."

* * * * *

The gentle rolling back and forth is what awakened him. He opened his eyes and looked about. "What is this?" Captain Delightable uttered. "Dear me! Where am I?"

He arose to a sitting position and looked about the room. He recognized the surroundings. He was on a ship. More correctly, he was in his captain's quarters. The gentle rolling he had felt was the ship passing over the swells of an easy sea.

Grabbing a mirror on the near table, he gazed into it to see his thirty-year-old face staring back at him. "Oh my," he muttered.

Feeling rejuvenated, he began dressing when a knock on his door startled him.

"Enter," he said.

It was Randall Jenkins, his first mate.

"Good morning, Captain. Feeling better, I see."

"Yes, yes. Much better, although somewhat confused. What happened to me?"

"You've been down ten days, sir. The doctor said it was some form of food poisoning."

"Indeed? Well, it certainly gave me fits."

Mister Jenkins filled in the captain on the status of the ship and her crew over the last ten days while the captain laid infirmed. He then left him to finish preparing himself to return to duty.

Later that morning, Captain Delightable ventured walked out the door and up the steps and out onto the mid deck. In front of him lay a calm ocean, but there were bright, blood-red skies above.

"Welcome, Captain," said the first mate from the aftcastle.

"Thank you, Mr. Jenkins. Bright red, those skies, no?" he looked back up at his first mate.

"Aye, sir. Red they are. Ah, Captain, I don't want to quash your return to the deck, but you might want to have a look aft, sir. I think we're about to have a run-in with some trouble. I'm glad you're back with us. I think we'll need you."

He moved to the larboard rail, stared out behind them toward the west, and saw the black, threatening skies moving quickly toward them. It looked to be a hellish storm approaching. It all came back to him.

"Oh dear," he said knowingly. "Here we go again."

Epilogue

It was all true, of course, and what my great-grandfather dreamed during his illness on the ship was simply the heralding of the magical life he was eventually destined to live.

In order to preserve the island for their eventual return, the Minchon people moved the island into the time stream and along it to the modern day. I hear it made its glorious arrival right on schedule. My great-grandmother, Lelalu, was already there to greet it warmly.

After my daddy came home, on the twelfth of December 1920, it was like living my own magical story. To all of our delight, our young family was reunited and would remain so for many, many years to come.

Our lives in San Francisco were incredible years spent together and filled with wonder and excitement beyond measure, with much friendship, laughter, and joyous times.

When it was time for each of us to gather up our lives and return to Minchon Island, whence each of us, in our own way, had come eons ago, it was "Uncle" Amog who chose to lead the way.

He left for the island on April 20, 1968. It was a glorious transition, with smiles and warm hugs and a quiet, gentle departure. "Uncle" Wigiwig followed soon after, on June 10. His journey began elegantly with a final peace-filled exhalation. I was there to see him off also. It was a joyous event for all.

My other "uncles," Tainini, Gau'lo, Gamomo, and Mata'pang, each followed separately, in his own way, just after Wigiwig and in the same gentle manner.

My father, Jonathan Delightable, moved to the island on August 8, 1969. He said he was going ahead to finish preparing the way for the rest of us. He left us peacefully in his sleep on a beautiful warm evening, a gorgeous smile upon his lips.

My mother, Suzanne, followed him on January 5, 1970. She gracefully departed in her sleep as well. It seemed a wonderful and serene exit.

My great-grandfather, Captain Cornelius Alexander Delightable, departed for the island on his 200th birthday, March 30, 1970. His last words to Robert and I were to take our time, there was no need to rush.

My brother, Robert, graduated top of his class from UCLA medical school in 1935. He joined the United States Marine Corps as a doctor in March 1941. In 1942, during the days of World War II in the Pacific, he left for his warrior training in somewhat similar fashion as my father for three years somewhere in the Solomon Islands.

Upon his return, he spent the rest of his incredible life helping others to recover from their illnesses, or assisted them on their own journeys with kindly spoken words, peace-filled eyes, and his sweet, understanding smile.

He joyfully departed for the island on September 24, 2001, at a ripe ninety years of age. His warrior wife, Regina, joined him seven years later. His two children, Becky and Adam, grew up appropriately schooled in the ways of the Minchon Warrior. At the time of this writing, they are still living magnificent warrior lives.

I, myself, have lived an incredible life as well. I published my first book in 1933, when I was twenty-one. Throughout my lifetime I have written over 100 books, including this one. The others were mostly guides for the warrior spirit living in all of us; guideposts for discovery as we walk our paths through life. The books were well received and I lived a good and easy life.

I married a wonderful man named Thomas. We had two children of our own, Emily and Jonah.

With the inspiring help of my immediate family and of course my wonderful "uncles," the children grew up masterfully wise to the ways of the warrior. They are doing quite well, thank you.

Thomas, a well-schooled warrior himself, went ahead of me to the island one year ago.

Now, coming up to my 100th birthday, I have decided I have spent long enough here in this life and have done all that I can do. I will depart very soon for the island as well. I'm excited to see my family once again. I need only prepare this book for publication and then I will be on my way.

Dear Reader,

I am Emily.

My mother, Wendy, gave me wonderful gifts: her life, her guidance, her love, her support, and a deep desire to write.

She left for the island on July 26, 2012. She was 100 years old. She left me with a kiss on my cheek and a pat on my hand, telling me she would be waiting with the rest of the family on the island for me.

It was a stunning departure.

Before she left, she gave me the ability to see the island during her glorious exit. I share it with you now as best I can describe it.

It was a warm, sunny afternoon when my mother's small skiff drifted in toward the shore and settled gently against the white sandy beach of Minchon Island. As she stepped out onto the sand, her young face was bright and smiling happily.

From out of the bushes lining the shoreline walked her rejuvenated family to greet her. Joining them were, of course, my great-uncles Amog, Wigiwig, Tainini, Gau'lo, and Gamomo.

Then, from the bushes, appeared my great-great-grandfather, Captain Cornelius Alexander Delightable. His young, fresh face glistened in the sunlight as he and his beautiful wife, Lelalu, strolled to greet my mother. My great-uncle Mata'pang walked with them and they shared a secret laugh amongst themselves on the way down to greet her. They all met amid warm embraces and tender kisses.

I watched her walk away with my whole family back toward the village. Along the way, the captain whispered something into my mother's ear that stopped her in her tracks.

My heart warmed as I watched her turn toward me, smile, wave, blow me a kiss, and mouth the words that she loved me.

It was magical.

The End

About the Author

Val Edward Simone was born in Seattle, Washington, and has been writing since 1980.

Val has published adult-themed action/adventure novels; historical fiction; western novels; short stories; a collection of thoughts, musings, and observations; a collection of children's short stories; and several children's picture books. He continues to work on many other novels and short stories.

He is also a strong advocate of early childhood reading and continues to work with schools, local libraries, and directly with children through parent-assisted workshops, helping children to discover their own creativity through reading, writing, and drawing.

Val currently lives and works in Colorado.

His websites:
www.ekidslandpublishing.com
www.morningsidepublishing.com
www.morningsidepublishing.com/TwinHorse.html

Connect with Val Online:
Twitter: @valsimone
facebook: val.simone1@facebook.com
Linkedin: Val Edward Simone

Other Books by Val Edward Simone

Morningside Publishing, LLC

Novels
Blood Trackers: One Crazy Love Story
Blood Trackers 2: Revenge of an Angel
About Things I Lost Long Ago . . . scribblings from a foolish heart
The Wondrous Life of a Long-Ago Man
Comes the Devil to Crooked Creek
Captain Delightable's Magical Tales of a Minchon Warrior
A Minute of Forever
The Firestone . . . Is Mankind Ready?

Short Stories
Manifest Destiny
The Secret Life of Goner Andling
Love Bytes
Dragons Within
The Problem with Dragons
The Unfortunate Dragon

Ekidsland Publishing, LLC

Children's Picture Books:
Felix
The Gingerbread Pony
The Littlest Bell
Mean Muley McGrudge
Otto and Kevin
Proton Gator
Sammy Sparrow Spy
The Fairy Collection

Short Stories
Through the Waterfall
Fairy Forgotten
Emily's Wish
Kaylee's Secret
The Wizard of Sebastianville

Children's Coloring Book:
Proton Gator & Friends Coloring Book